Matthew Ryan Davies is a freelance copywriter and editor, mostly for the healthcare sector. He ghostwrites non-fiction books, edits university textbooks for medical and nursing students, and writes scripts for educational videos and documentaries. In 2019 and 2020 he worked with the Royal Commission into Victoria's Mental Health System to deliver its interim and final reports.

Matthew is also the author of the young adult novel *This Thing of Darkness*, which was highly commended in the Victorian Premier's Literary Awards. He lives in Melbourne with his wife and two grown children.

To find out more about Matthew and his work visit www.matthewryandavies.com.

Matthew Ryan Davies

THINGS
WE
BURY

MACMILLAN

Pan Macmillan Australia

Pan Macmillan acknowledges the Traditional Custodians of country throughout Australia and their connections to lands, waters and communities. We pay our respect to Elders past and present and extend that respect to all Aboriginal and Torres Strait Islander peoples today. We honour more than sixty thousand years of storytelling, art and culture.

First published 2022 in Macmillan by Pan Macmillan Australia Pty Ltd
1 Market Street, Sydney, New South Wales, Australia, 2000

 A catalogue record for this book is available from the National Library of Australia

Typeset in 12/16 pt Bembo by Post Pre-press Group

Printed by IVE

 The paper in this book is FSC® certified. FSC® promotes environmentally responsible, socially beneficial and economically viable management of the world's forests.

What you can't say owns you.
What you hide controls you.

—Anonymous

THURSDAY

1

Stephen Harding always told his kids to not let obstacles get in the way of achieving what they wanted. 'If you hit a wall,' he'd say, 'don't let it stop you. Work out how to climb it, go through it or get around it.' The irony of this was not lost on Josh, Stephen's youngest, given that his dad had, just two days ago, accidentally driven his Jaguar F-Type nose-first into a wall, and it had most definitely stopped him.

''Scuse me?'

Josh turned his gaze from the train window, streaked with rain, to where a woman—white, mid-twenties—stood in the aisle. She held the hand of a young boy in a *Frozen II* t-shirt, faded and food-stained.

'Can we sit here?'

Josh nodded, pulling the bill of his cap further down his forehead to hide his face.

The woman directed the boy onto the seat opposite, the one

closest to the window, and he shuffled in, clutching a white-haired doll in a grubby fairy dress.

Josh had chosen a seat away from other passengers when he'd boarded in Melbourne. But now there was this woman and her child. Would she recognise him? She looked like the kind of person who might watch *Relationship Rescue*—skinny, with dark roots seeping into blonde hair tied at the back, the tail of a dragon tattoo creeping its way around her neck.

Josh shifted in his seat and the woman glanced up, catching him observing her. She gave him a smile, not at all hesitant; still, he diverted his eyes to the window. The rain had eased, but there were storms ahead—there always were in Pent.

The train screeched to an abrupt stop, thrusting him forwards. At this rate, he'd be late. It didn't matter—Dad would still be in a coma in an hour's time. And it would only be Jac waiting for him at the station.

He looked again at the woman, but she was busy trying to negotiate a pink straw from a bottle of chocolate milk into the boy's reluctant mouth. Josh's posture eased and he looked again through the window—wheatfields, cattle sheds and disused silos whizzed past like a tracking shot in a film.

He'd recorded an episode of *Common Law* on a train once, but the view through the window had been superimposed in post-production to resemble a brighter day. 'TV is aspirational,' the director had said. What she meant, though, is that it is fake—artful deception. *Common Law* was history, but the sting persisted: those ten years it had taken to build his career and family after leaving Pent and the one Twitter post it had taken to blow it all up.

The train jolted back into motion, scraping along the track, as if resisting that last stretch of the journey. Josh sensed something touching his feet and he looked down to see the boy's doll on the floor between the seats. It must have fallen when the train jerked forwards. He picked it up and handed it to the boy. 'Here you go, mate.'

The woman smiled at him. 'Ta.'

Then a new look passed over her face, a look first of recognition and then of horror. 'Oh my god, you're . . . *him.*' The horror quickly turned to anger, her eyes narrowing, jaw clenching. 'Get away from me, you . . . you . . . *dog!*'

She flung her hand out, hurling chocolate milk over his head and chest. The shock of it, the cold of the milk, made his breath hitch.

The woman shouldered her calico bag, hoisted the boy onto her hip and marched down the aisle to find another seat.

Josh looked down. Chocolate milk soaked into the crotch of his jeans, the pink straw clinging to his sodden t-shirt.

He closed his eyes and exhaled.

Welcome to Pent.

2

Jac Harding glanced from side to side, through the windows of the car, but it was hopeless—she was severely off course.

For the past two hours she'd followed the M31 north from Melbourne Airport but had veered off at Violet Town for food. Ma used to tell her that she was too impulsive. But she always had a good reason. Like a freshly baked beef-and-mushroom pie.

Then she decided to avoid the highway and take the back roads to Pent, just for a change of scenery. But that didn't work out either. So, sitting on the roadside under a sky-scraping gum, a ketchup-stained paper bag screwed up on the passenger seat, she gave up and typed 'Pent Train Station' into Google Maps.

She glanced around while the app calibrated. On the side of the road, about thirty metres ahead, an animal lay dead, contorted in a heap. She'd seen lots of roadkill on the way up—two wombats, a koala and a kangaroo with its small arms outstretched. She'd forgotten how brutal country drives could be. This one looked like a fox.

When the phone started giving her directions, she tossed it onto the passenger seat and pulled the rented Toyota back onto the road, the tyres spinning slightly on the gravel shoulder. It was only four-thirty, but the sun was already making a lazy descent towards the fields to the west, burnishing the trees with gold.

As she approached the mangled beast on the roadside, she couldn't help but glance over. But then she wished she hadn't. It was no wild animal; it was a dog. A spitz or maybe an elkhound. She held her breath as she passed, imagining a child somewhere crying. That's why she'd never owned a pet. What if it ran away? Or got hit by a semitrailer, like this fella? The only way to protect herself was to avoid that trap altogether.

By the time she arrived at the train station twenty minutes later, the sun had faded almost completely, dyeing the town grey. The car park looked full, so she pulled the hatchback into a parking space fifty metres from the station entrance. She got out and made her way to the station proper, walking alongside a row of blossoming wattles that separated the car park and the tracks.

Out of the car, it was colder than she'd expected. Damp, wintry air lingered, even though they'd hit spring.

The station, an imposing colonial-style building, looked mostly deserted these days. The gates to the toilets were padlocked, the door to the old stationmaster's quarters boarded. Across the street, a cafe sold takeaway coffees to commuters through a folding window. That was new.

She took the underpass, emerging on the station's central platform. On one side, a single track stretched towards the city; the track on the opposite side ran all the way to Albury.

The outbound platform was quiet—it was often hours between trains—with only a handful of people waiting on the city-bound platform. She angled her eyes up to the board; Josh's train was due in six minutes. The signs had been modernised—digital now—but other than that, the station looked the same as always.

Behind her, an approaching train scraped along the tracks as it pulled into the platform. A moment later, the doors whooshed open and office workers and students piled out. She spotted a face she recognised and, at first, anxiety twitched in her stomach, but then she raised her hand. 'Amy!'

Amy turned, her expression bending from confusion to awareness. 'Jac!'

They met in the centre of the platform, forcing passengers to step around them.

'How are you?' Amy asked, kissing her on the cheek.

This was a much different Amy from the last time they'd caught up, nine or ten years ago. This was grown-up Amy. Heels-and-tailored-jacket Amy.

Amy's eyes swept Jac's body. 'I hardly recognised you. You grew your hair out.'

Jac felt for the tresses at the back of her neck. 'Yeah.' It was long enough to tie in a stubby ponytail now. Longer hair gives you more options for bridal styles, apparently. She was trying it out. Seeing how it went.

'Heard about your dad,' Amy said. 'I'm sorry. How's he going?'

'He's in an induced coma.'

Amy's mouth opened, then closed.

'It's okay, though. The signs are good. It's just until the swelling goes down. He's got swelling. On the brain.' She used her thumb to turn the ring on her finger. It was her new nervous habit, but it was better than biting her nails.

Amy turned her face north, and Jac followed her line of sight.

'Ironic, isn't it?' Amy said. 'They put in the overpass to make it *safer* for cars.'

Three or four hundred metres up the line, the track ascended from the ballast, curved east through the trees, then disappeared from view.

She watched Amy's face from the side. A tendril of brunette hair had fallen from its tie and caught between Amy's lips, wet from the saliva in her mouth.

Amy turned back. 'You coming or going?'

'I'm here to pick up Josh.'

Like all small towns, Pent bred two kinds of people: the ones who were born to stay and the ones who broke out at the first opportunity. Amy was a stayer.

'How's Josh doing?'

Jac gazed along the track towards the city; his train was silently snaking its way into Pent. 'Okay. I think.'

'That's some shitstorm he's got himself into.'

That was Jac's cue to say something in her brother's defence—something about innocent until proven guilty—but she didn't want to get into a debate on the platform. Amy had been a social justice warrior in high school, cartwheeling from the plight of one marginalised group to the next, so Jac already knew which side Amy would land on. And besides, she'd had too many of these futile conversations with work colleagues and friends, when she was in fact as sketchy on the truth about what happened on that TV show as anyone. (She might have pretended she wasn't related to Josh, since he'd switched to Ma's maiden name for 'professional reasons', but everyone knew they were siblings.)

'What are you doing catching the train?' Jac asked.

Amy hitched her bag further up her shoulder. 'Work. I teach in Wangaratta now. Trying to reduce my carbon footprint and all that. You still with the police? In Sydney?'

She nodded. 'Fraud.'

Amy's eyes widened.

Jac didn't want to kill the illusion. Truth was, she examined documents, made notes, maintained databases and filed stuff. It was her fourth job with the police in nine years. As soon as she started feeling hemmed in, as soon as co-workers started inviting her to their birthday parties, it was time to move on. Starting over kept life interesting. At least, that's what she said in job interviews—*I want to extend myself.*

'It keeps me busy,' she told Amy.

The brakes squealed as the train approached the platform.

'Hey, a bunch of us from work are going to the Cherry Tree tonight,' Amy said. 'Celebrate the start of holidays. You should pop by.'

'That a new place?'

'Used to be the Anchor?'

Jac nodded; she'd known the Anchor well once.

'I wanted to go to the wine bar in the square,' Amy explained, 'but I was outvoted.'

Pent had a wine bar now?

'I'm visiting Dad, and then I should probably . . .'

Amy gave her a tight smile. 'Yeah, 'course. Spend time with your family.'

The train came to a halt and the doors swished open.

'Okay,' Amy said, 'I'm gonna . . .' She hooked a thumb towards the car park.

'No worries. Good to see you.'

'Yeah, you too.'

She watched Amy disappear down the ramp between the platforms. Seeing her, it was as if something Jac had misplaced had been returned to her, but now it was gone again.

People spilled from the train around her, Josh among them.

He was only identifiable by his shuffling walk and the fact that he gave her an almost imperceptible nod. Dad and Josh cast the same shadow—packed down, with outward-curving chests and chicken legs. Now, they also had matching bellies. Josh wore a scraggly, months-old beard and his eyes were red-rimmed, as if he'd been crying or hadn't slept. And his t-shirt was saturated, like a bottle of drink had exploded in his face.

'What happened to you?' she asked once he was within earshot. They didn't kiss—the Hardings never did that—but she was close enough to smell nervous sweat radiating off him.

'A woman on the train.' He turned to look at the closing doors as if worried she might still be after him. 'People throwing things at me is my new fan mail.'

She twitched her nose. 'You smell like . . .'

'Sunshine and roses? Are you saying I smell like sunshine and roses?'

'I wish, but no. Baby vomit.'

He nodded approvingly. 'I like the innocence of that. Can we get out of here, please?'

She squeezed her eyebrows together. 'We should probably visit Dad first.'

'I meant leave the station,' he said, deadpan.

'Oh.'

'I need to change before Ma sees me.'

She sighed. 'I know what you mean.'

3

D ane Harding launched through the front door, moving this way and that, struggling to hold everything at once. He juggled the eggs, bacon, teabags, sliced bread and Ice Magic, none of which were for him, closing the door with the tip of his leather boot. The vacuum-packed bacon slid from the hood of the egg carton, but he righted it before it could plummet to the floor.

In the kitchen, Ma stood over the twin tubs of the stainless-steel sink, her back to him, peeling potatoes. She twisted her neck halfway around, glancing briefly, but then returned to her work. 'What took you so long? It's been five o'clock for twenty minutes.'

He unloaded the groceries onto the stone benchtop, where diced celery and carrot mingled on a chopping board. 'Work,' he said. 'Plus, I forgot the teabags, so I had to go back.'

The kitchen was gleaming, the benchtop reflecting dull light from the towering windows that concertinaed to a covered-in deck at the back of the house. 'Tidy as you go,' Ma always said. 'Clean up one mess before you start another.'

'Did you get the chocolate sauce for Josh?' she asked.

'Yeah, 'course.' He snatched a carrot cube from the board and crunched it between his teeth. 'Remind me again why I need to be here?'

Ma turned to him; her face was fresh with make-up and she'd fixed her hair into an elegant pile on top of her head. She was a sight—still striking, even in her sixties, even standing over a sinkful of potato peel in her butcher's apron. 'To greet your brother and sister, obviously. Your obligation as the oldest. Everything under control at work?'

'Of course, Ma, yes.' The kitchen brimmed with the sweet smell of fried onion, and his stomach grumbled. He snatched another piece of carrot.

'Because if you need help . . .'

'I can handle it,' he said as lightly as he could.

Ma pushed stray strands of blonde out of her eyes with her wrist and picked up another potato, turning it over, deciding where to begin. 'There's no shame in asking for help this time. That's all I'm saying.'

He parked his hip against the island bar, crossed his arms, then uncrossed them. 'I'm fine.' He forced a smile. 'It'd take more than a few days to undo forty years of Dad's work.'

She raised her eyebrows. *If anyone can, you can,* she seemed to say. 'Did you see him today?'

'I'll go tonight with the others.'

She ran her hands under the tap, flicked the excess water off and dried them on the front of her apron. 'Visiting hours finish at eight. Pass me that thingy, would you?'

He handed her the pale pink colander, and she lowered it into the sink. 'Where are the boys?' he asked.

She cupped her hands, scooping cloudy potatoes into the colander, and opened the tap again. 'Ngaire picked them up early. Said something about . . . Oh, I can't remember.'

'She picked them up?' He tossed an arc of celery into his mouth, trying to work out why she would've collected the twins early. What day was it? Thursday. What happened on Thursdays? Did they have soccer practice?

'Amazing, I know. An afternoon to myself,' Ma said with sarcastic flair. 'Now I'm stuck in the kitchen.' She gave the colander a shake and shut off the tap.

'You don't have to go to any trouble, Ma.'

She made a clucking sound with her tongue, turning to face him. 'Your brother needs a home-cooked meal.'

He went to grab another piece of carrot, but she slapped his hand away. 'I didn't have lunch,' he complained.

'Dane . . .'

'No time!'

Ma sighed. 'There's leftover spaghetti in the fridge. Heat that up.'

He opened the fridge and scanned for the pasta. It sat alone on the top shelf in a small white bowl covered in cling wrap, red sauce smearing the sides. Otherwise, the shelves were almost bare. No wonder she'd asked him to shop.

He decided he wasn't hungry anymore and began grabbing the cold-store groceries he'd bought—the eggs and packaged bacon—and loading them into the fridge. He held up the Ice Magic. 'Where do you want this?'

'Pantry. Leave the bread out.' Ma rested the paring knife on the board. 'Dane, I haven't told your brother and sister.' She took a fortifying breath. 'About your father. Have you?'

'That he's in hospital?' No, that was ridiculous. Of course she'd told them that. Jac and Josh needed a good reason to make a trip to Pent.

'About the . . . circumstances?'

Dane paused inside the pantry door, the box of teabags tight in his hand. 'No, I haven't.' He found a space beside the cornflour, slid the teabags onto the shelf and closed the pantry.

'Josh is fragile right now.'

Josh. He sighed inwardly.

Ma turned to him, her lips trembling, a sudden desperation clogging her eyes. 'You tell them. I can't.'

It was strange seeing Ma like this—a stitch loose in the seam that kept her self-assurance firmly intact—and it stilled him.

Gently, he nodded.

Ma's face relaxed and she rotated back to the pot. 'Is Ngaire bringing the twins back for dinner?'

He shook his head. 'I'll go home and get them. She's got book club.'

He heard Ma sigh, whether she actually did or not.

Out the front, a car pulled into the driveway, followed by the crunch of a handbrake. 'They're here,' Dane said.

He weaved his way across the blond floorboards through the lounge room to the large front window. Ma followed, loosening her apron and casting it over the easy chair, then ran her fingers through her hair.

He peered out the window. Josh was hauling a duffel bag from the back seat of a compact Toyota. In the driver's seat, Jac looked confused, as if trying to work out a complicated equation.

Josh had grown a messy beard and had the beginnings of a pot belly, narrowing their ten-year age difference. He wore a cap and baggy trackpants. Things were worse than he'd realised.

Ma rushed to the window. 'Does he look okay?' she asked, the words catching in her throat.

A few moments later Josh sang out from the open doorway. 'Hello?'

Dane and Ma hustled to the centre of the room so Josh wouldn't know they'd been watching him through the window.

Josh furrowed his brow. 'What's with you two?' He lifted off his cap and flung it and his duffel onto the three-seater.

'Nothing. Hello, darling.' Ma embraced Josh, tight and long, as if he'd just been discovered after a night lost in the wilderness. Dad's crash must have had her on edge because she rarely hugged any of them.

'You alright, Ma?'

'Mm-hmm.'

Josh was the shortest of the Harding men, but he still had to lean well over so Ma could wrap her arms around his neck. He pointed his chin to the side as if he needed the extra space to breathe.

When she finally let go, Dane shook his brother's hand, but their eye contact was fleeting. 'Josh.'

'Where's Jacinta?' Ma asked.

'Trying to work out something with the car. How's Dad?'

She didn't answer, so he swivelled his head to Dane.

'No change,' he said.

Watching Josh, the way his breathing had heavied and the sheen of his skin flattened, Dane felt a stab of guilt. He should have called more. Maybe gone to visit him. It was only two and a half hours in the car. But he was so busy . . .

Josh nudged a patterned cushion from the corner of the three-seater, bright against the light-grey fabric, and sat himself down.

'I'm making your favourite for dinner,' Ma said.

Josh surveyed the room. 'Awesome. Haven't had a roast in ages.'

'No,' she said. Her shoulders drooped. 'Shepherd's pie.'

'That was my favourite when I was, like, twelve, Ma.'

She blinked. 'Oh, well, I can—'

Josh held up a hand. 'Shepherd's pie is fine.' He cast an eye at Dane. 'Early finish for you?'

Ma straightened. 'I thought it would be nice for us to be together for a bit.' Her eyes moved from Dane to Josh and back again, but neither reacted. 'Spend some time.'

'That's new.' Josh extended a finger towards a large, framed print that had appeared over the fireplace about six months before.

'That's me.' Ma turned to the print—a photo of herself stylised in cartoony oranges, yellows and blues from a long-ago album cover.

'Wow. Psychedelic.'

Ma snickered. 'It was the eighties, darling, not the sixties.'

Josh gave an approving nod. 'Cool.'

Ma curved her lips—a small smile tinged with melancholy—but then seemed to snap herself out of it. She shooed him with a flap of her hands. 'Go get changed, then we can have a drink.'

Josh's eyes darted to his outfit. His trackpants were worn at the knees and the hem of his t-shirt was frayed. 'I'm twenty-eight, Ma. I think I can decide what to wear.'

'Okay, darling,' she said in a way that stated it was not at all okay. 'How is my adorable little granddaughter? Haven't seen any pictures for a while.'

'Crawling everywhere, or so I'm told. Not walking yet.'

'Well, of course not; she's only eight months old. And Jordan? How is she?'

'Next subject.'

The front door slammed and Jac appeared in the entranceway holding a small, light-blue suitcase in one hand and a single black car key in the other. There was something different about her. Maybe it was her clothes—a loose, delicate top and figure-hugging pants that tapered at the ankles. Too feminine maybe. And was she wearing make-up?

'Hello, darling,' Ma said, hugging her. 'Good trip?'

'Fine. Hey, Dane.'

'Hey, Jac.'

Ma's cat, a ginger named Harry, rubbed against Jac's calf and she nudged it away with her foot. She lifted her case a little higher. 'Where should I put my stuff?'

Ma gestured to the corner of the room. 'Just leave it there. I've set you up in your father's study.'

'How *is* Dad?'

'The same.'

Jac planted the case on the floor and set the key on top. 'What do the doctors think?'

Ma looked at Dane, imploring him to say something, but he looked away. Why was all the hard stuff his responsibility?

'Why are you two being weird?' Josh asked.

'We're not being *weird*,' Ma said, sounding very weird. 'You've grown your hair, Jacinta,' she said. 'It looks nice. Prettier.'

Jac touched the back of her hair. 'I'm still deciding if I like it.'

'Oh my god!' Ma suddenly shrieked, sending Harry scampering from the room. She pointed at Jac, her hand trembling. 'What's that?'

'Oh.' Jac reddened, splaying the fingers of her left hand in front of her. 'I got engaged.'

Ma looked to Dane, then to Josh: *Did either of you know about this?* They both shrugged. Ma's eyes searched the room, blinking, settling on Jac's ring finger, staring at the gold band as if it were some kind of cyst or hideous lesion. 'But you can't be,' she said. 'You're not even seeing anyone!'

Jac let her hand drop. 'Well, clearly I am, Ma. And people usually say congratulations when you tell them you're engaged.' She spoke with what sounded to Dane like a deliberate composure, as much as it must have taxed her to.

Ma waved her hands in the air like she was swatting away
flies. 'Of course, darling. Sorry. I'm just so . . .'

Dane, too, searched for the word on Ma's lips. *Happy? Shocked?
Relieved?* All three, no doubt.

Ma gave Jac an awkward kiss on the cheek. 'Congratulations,
darling.'

Dane and Josh followed suit.

Dane's eyes lingered on his sister. Jac was engaged? She didn't
seem the type to want to settle down with another person.
She was too used to her independence, too set in her ways. She
seemed to treat the people in her life like visitors to a museum—
you can come in, maybe stay a while, but we close at five.

'What's his name? What's he do?' Ma asked, pausing to catch
her breath.

'His name's Gillon. *Gil.* He's a management consultant. That's
how we met; he was consulting for the police.'

'He lives in Sydney too?'

'Yeah.'

'How long have you been together?' Dane asked.

'A few months,' she said, glancing down.

Ma inhaled, readying to speak, but then seemed to edit herself.
'That's wonderful, darling. When will we meet him? Not at the
wedding, I hope!' she said with a kind of hysterical laugh.

Jac bunched her lips, delaying the answer. 'No wedding,' she
said finally at a muted volume. 'Well, not a big one. Registry
office, probably.'

Ma stiffened. 'I see.'

Poor Ma. Dane's own wedding had been so long ago and
Josh's was a last-minute shotgun job. And now the situation with
Dad. She needed something to look forward to.

Jac closed her eyes. 'Can we talk about this later?' she said.
'I could murder a beer.'

'Yes, of course.' Ma turned to Dane. 'In the bar fridge. I've got a bottle of chardonnay already open, too.'

On the way to the bar—housed in a nook between the dining room and formal lounge—his phone rang in his front pocket. Leigh, the other project manager from work.

'You know the restaurant job on the highway?' Leigh said. 'We're supposed to be starting tomorrow but Joel Hutchison's causing a stink.'

Behind the counter of the small corner bar, Dane pulled open the fridge door. 'Didn't his own report give it the all clear?'

'Well . . . it said the site had *potential* for instability. He recommended we do another test—drill deeper to be sure.'

'And we didn't?' He grabbed two stubbies of lager and set them on the bench.

'The geotech complied. It was just a recommendation. Stephen said to go ahead.'

'So, what's Joel's problem?'

'That we didn't follow his recommendation, I guess.'

Dane blew out a stream of air and looked at the ceiling as if the answer might be there. 'Just organise the other test.' That was the right thing to do.

Leigh hesitated. 'The guys are booked to start. And, mate, the cost overrun.'

Dane leaned against the dining room wall, staring at a centrepiece of dried flowers on the table, dead, not the least bit decorative. 'It sounds like you've made up your mind, Leigh.'

'You're the boss right now. I thought you should know. But Stephen *did* authorise it. Just saying.'

Dane flipped the tops of the beers and binned the caps. His gut told him to delay, but his gut had been wrong before.

Leigh spoke again as Dane carried the bottles, the necks

pressed between the fingers of one hand, back to the lounge room. 'Stephen was pretty clear about what he wanted.'

Dane exhaled. 'Okay. Fine.'

He rang off and handed the beers to Jac and Josh.

'What's wrong?' Ma asked.

'You look like you're about to vomit,' Josh added.

'Nothing. Just . . . work.'

'You must be the boss man now that Dad's laid up, right?' Josh said.

'Yup.'

Josh gave him a worried look.

'What?'

'Nothing. I mean, it's just that *last* time Dad left you in charge . . .'

Dane's jaw clenched. 'God, that was *years* ago. Man, why can't everybody just— At least no one's taking *legal* action against me.'

Josh reared back. 'It's not a legal thing.' He shook his head. 'Fuck's sake.'

He didn't want to start off this way, especially with Dad in hospital. He gave Josh—not a smile as such (that would have been too much of a character break), but more of a conciliatory bending of the lips that he hoped his brother would interpret as a well-meaning olive branch.

'Let's sort out the plan for tonight,' Jac said. 'We should visit Dad *before* dinner, then we won't have to rush to get there before they shut up shop.'

Josh gave him a barely detectable nod of acknowledgement and Dane turned his mind back to work. He should look at Joel's soil report, see for himself what it said. 'I have to take care of something at work.'

'You mean go in?' Jac asked.

Did he need to go in? Was there anything he could do from home? No. He'd left his laptop at the office. Maybe Leigh could email the report and he could read it on his phone? No, he didn't want to bother him. Or alert him. 'Yeah, I have to pop in.'

'Okay,' Jac said. 'Meet us at the hospital? About six-thirty?'

'And pick up some bubbles on the way back, Dane,' Ma said. 'We need to celebrate Jacinta's news. Oh, Jacinta, do you have a photo of him?'

Jac pulled out her phone.

'Shit, the twins!' Dane checked the clock on his screen, trying to remember what time Ngaire had to leave. 'I need to pick up Marcus and Dylan.'

'I've got a car,' Jac said. 'Where are they?' She passed her phone to Ma. 'This is us a couple of weeks ago.'

Ma's eyes widened. 'Lovely.' She passed the phone back.

'Where are they?' Jac asked again, handing the phone to Josh. 'What time do they need to be picked up?'

He looked at the ceiling again. 'Home. Quarter to six.'

'That's in, like, fifteen minutes,' Josh said, his eyes skimming the screen. 'Jeez, Jac, how *old* is he?'

She snatched the phone back, a blur of white hair flitting past Dane's eyes. She pocketed her phone. 'So, what about the boys?'

He couldn't think.

'Dane,' Ma said, with a pitch of admonishment in her voice, 'don't you need to tell your brother and sister something before you go to the hospital?'

Dane looked at Jac, then at Josh. Both stared back expectantly, as though waiting for the punchline of a joke.

'What is it?' Jac said, drawing her eyebrows in.

'It can wait,' he said. 'Meet me in the foyer. We'll go up together.' He'd tell them before they went in.

'You go to work,' Josh said. 'We'll pick up the boys and drop them off here. They can stay with Ma while we're at the hospital.' Josh raised his eyebrows at Ma to get her approval.

'Yeah, I'd like to see them,' Jac said. 'What are they now? Three?'

'Five,' Dane said, drawing out the word for emphasis. 'They've started school.'

'Oh, yeah.' Jac bit her bottom lip.

His mind shifted back to the office. He had a plan. Good planning was how he would get through this period at work while Dad was away. Planning would save him from making any million-dollar mistakes this time.

4

Jac was lost again. She'd taken the long way around from the car park, following the signs to emergency, passing a loading dock and two rank-smelling dumpsters before finally spotting the glow of the main entrance. Josh didn't seem to mind, trailing her without a word. Passing through the sliding glass doors, she scanned the foyer, which wasn't big compared with city hospitals, but there was no sign of Dane. Her stomach rumbled. It was six-thirty and a metal shutter sealed off the coffee shop that abutted the lobby. Damn. She could use a snack right now.

The foyer was empty of people except for an older woman sitting at a computer at one end of a reception desk made for two.

'Let's have a seat,' Jac said, pointing to a long, upholstered bench next to the florist. Then she changed her mind. 'Actually, you go ahead. I'll be back in a sec.'

She'd only been to the hospital in Wangaratta once before, when Dane was knocked out playing football. But that was in high school. Pent had a hospital too, but it was mostly for geriatrics and maternity care. No emergency department and certainly no ICU, which was what Dad needed. Living in the country, it was lucky her parents had such a good hospital less than half an hour away.

She passed the florist and, in a small alcove, found what she was looking for—the bright lights of a vending machine. Did she feel like sweet or savoury? She wasn't much of a sweet-snack person, but if she got chips Josh would no doubt demolish half the packet.

She swiped her credit card and punched the numbers for a Snickers, watching the coil of wire twist until a bar dropped. Tearing the wrapper open, she began eating immediately, leaning against the soft hum of the machine. She could really use a coffee too.

A woman holding the hand of a small child peered into the alcove but then moved on. Must have been looking for the toilet. That would be her one day, Jac thought—holding a child's hand and leading them through the world. One day soon. She was thirty-six; Gil could be her last chance.

She scoffed the last of her chocolate bar and returned to the foyer, where Dane was chatting to Josh.

'Where'd you get to?' Josh asked.

'Had to go to the loo.' She didn't want to be judged for not sharing.

'Sure you did.' Josh licked his thumb and wiped something from the corner of her mouth, like Dad used to do when they were kids.

She rubbed the wet spot with the back of her hand while Josh erupted into laughter. 'Don't be gross.' She lifted her arm and wiped the spot again with the cuff of her denim shirt. She'd changed out of that flimsy top from earlier into something more substantial.

Meanwhile, Dane shifted his weight from one leg to the other and then back again, with the face of someone who'd just stepped off a jerky amusement park ride.

'You okay, Dane?' she asked. 'Worked out the problem at the office?'

'Yeah, yeah. 'Course I did.'

She raised her hands in conciliation: *Just asking.*

'Anyway, before we go up,' he began, 'I just need to . . .' He looked at the sliding doors; an elderly couple was entering, clutching onto each other. It had started to drizzle outside. 'The police think—well, they sort of know . . .'

The moment stretched out as Dane looked to Josh, then back to her, glimmers of emotion passing across his face.

'Know what?' she prompted.

Josh stiffened. 'Spill, Dane.'

Dane spoke in a low voice, as if not wanting to startle the old people, who were now shuffling past them. 'Dad's crash wasn't an accident.'

Jac was suddenly confused and she spoke louder than necessary. 'Not an accident?' *A car crashes into the pylon of a bridge and it's not an accident?* 'Did someone deliberately run him off the road?'

'He was trying to kill himself,' Dane said.

The air suddenly rushed from her body, like someone had punched her in the stomach.

'What do you mean?' Josh asked.

Dane drew in a breath. He clasped his hands together below his waist, straightening his arms like he was about to swing a golf club. 'Apparently there were no skid marks. If it wasn't for the airbags, he'd be dead.'

Jac blinked rapidly. 'But that can't be right,' she heard herself saying. 'He wouldn't try to kill himself. Why would he try to kill himself?'

Dane's eyes brimmed with tears. 'Depression, I guess.'

'*Depression?*' she repeated, the word sounding horrible and foreign. Nothing to do with Dad.

'There was a witness, too, someone walking nearby at the time. He said Dad looked kind of . . . determined. He sped up, aimed right for—'

'Bull,' she said. Dane had it wrong. 'Who's this *witness*? Probably a stoner. Druggies hang out around there. Marshall Road, wasn't it?'

'Jac,' Josh said. 'It sounds pretty—'

'Oh, how would you know, Josh? When was the last time you visited him? A year ago? I want to speak to this *witness* and this *police officer*,' she spat. 'This is bullshit. I know people. I'll get my own expert.'

'Okay, Jac,' Dane said, his voice soft. He looked at his phone. 'Maybe we should get up there. Ma's made dinner and there's—'

'Of course. Let's not disappoint *Ma*,' she said, with too much emphasis in her voice. She'd turned shrill, verging on hysterical. She was not a shrill person. She hated shrill people. She was cool-headed. Logical. She didn't overreact to things. But she believed in justice. And these things being said about Dad were not true and she wouldn't stand for it.

'Let's wait until he wakes up,' Josh said, his voice, by contrast, calm. 'Sort it out then.'

She exhaled. Yes, she would sort it out then. Thank God she'd come back when she did. Who knew how far this story would go otherwise?

★

The carpet-squared halls on level three were empty except for the lady delivering tea and coffee from a cart, clanging cups and saucers together. Jac could also hear the muted mechanical beeps of monitoring machines and a nurse coaxing someone to put their pants back on.

Her heart was still pumping hard after what Dane had said about the crash. Maybe the road was wet? Or Dad had been drinking? No, they would have tested his BAC. Perhaps he'd fallen asleep? Yes! That's why there were no skid marks.

She tugged at Dane's shirtsleeve. 'He probably fell asleep,' she whispered.

His eyes darted from left to right. 'Not now, Jac, okay?'

What else did he know that he wasn't telling her?

They passed a nurses' station, where a lone man in a hospital-issue shirt tapped at a keyboard. Off the hallway, doors opened into mostly four-bed wards, few with any empty beds. Indefinable food smells hung in the air and her stomach rumbled again. The chocolate bar had barely touched the sides.

'High dependency unit,' Dane said, pointing straight ahead.

The HDU was quite a large room, but all she could see was Dad—lying there, so pasty, so still—with tubes coming out of his arms. The bed next to him was vacant.

Tears trembled in her eyes. He looked so helpless, and the white of the sheets and the walls made the room look cold. Only three vases of flowers perched on a high shelf near the small, suspended TV gave any colour.

She approached the bed.

'He's in an induced coma,' Dane said, as if they didn't already know.

Dad's breathing was quiet, his eyes closed, and he wore a washed-out green hospital gown. Couldn't Ma have brought in a set of his own pyjamas? A white gauze-type dressing covered his left eye and a violent purple bruise smudged the other side of his face.

'He's fractured the bones around his eye,' Dane said. 'Apparently he involuntarily punched himself in the face when the airbags deployed.'

She pictured Dad punching himself, like a punishment, and felt something heavy settle in her stomach.

He looked thinner, although his face was puffy and pale, like an unbaked pavlova. His hair was whiter. When was the last time she'd seen him? Christmas. Nine months ago. She'd been no better than Josh when it came to visiting home.

She wiped her cheek. 'Hi, Dad. It's Jac.' She took his hand. It was warm. At least there was some sign of life.

'Hi, Dad,' Josh called out from near the window, where he'd helped himself to the one chair in the room.

White whiskers covered Dad's jawline, chin and neck. For some reason, she found this the most disturbing thing of all. He was always so careful with his appearance. He would hate to look like this. For people to see him so scruffy and unkempt. So out of control. Maybe she should ask one of the boys to give him a shave. Or at least bring a set of clippers to him so he would look somewhat more like her father.

She kissed the crown of his head, which was strange, because they never kissed each other, but she wasn't sure what else to do. 'It's Jac,' she said again, louder this time, as if coma equalled deaf. She lowered her voice. 'Josh is here. And Dane.'

A machine by the bedside beeped gently and she watched the rise and fall of his chest under the heavy white sheet.

The tall set of wheelie drawers next to the bed was bare on top. Usually when you visited people in hospital, you'd find magazines, a jug of water, the person's reading glasses, maybe a bag of lollies. But there was nothing here because he couldn't make use of any of those things. All he could do was lie there.

'What exactly are his injuries?' Josh asked Dane.

'Too much pressure in the brain. Something to do with trapped fluid.'

It was bizarre talking openly about a person while they were lying right there. If they were asleep, you'd speak quietly, but this was just *weird*. Could he hear? He *looked* asleep. As if he could wake at any moment.

'What's going on, Dad?' she asked, squeezing his hand, hoping he would wake up and answer her. But then she remembered that he was in an *induced* coma. They probably needed to pump him with an arousal drug to get him out of it.

'They're pretty optimistic,' Dane said.

'So, he'll make a full recovery?' Josh asked. 'Back to normal?'

'They'll know more when they wake him up.'

Jac kept stroking the back of his hand. That hand she'd held so many times as a little girl.

'When will that be?' Josh asked.

Dane shrugged. 'Maybe a couple more days.'

She stared at Dad's face, wondering what was going on inside his head. Was he having thoughts? Did he know what was happening? Was it a jumble of worry in there?

'Hey, Dad,' Dane began. 'The Panthers made the finals. Maybe they'll make the granny, and by the time you get out we can go to the game together, eh?'

A silence descended on the room, heavy, like a winter blanket.

Dane continued, 'Things are going well at the office, so don't worry. But we're all looking forward to you coming back. Everyone says hi, by the way. Gayle and Leigh. Jan and Olivia. They all miss you.' Dane scratched his head, ran his hand across day-old stubble, then kept talking. 'The apartments are selling well. I'll ask Leigh how many now and let you know when I come in tomorrow.'

Then, having run out of things to say apparently, he looked to Jac and Josh to keep the energy up. Josh cowered in his corner. Jac studied her ring, wondering if she should mention her engagement. No, better that everything wait until he woke up.

Entering the lift to head back to the foyer, Jac's mind lingered on the image of Dad lying there, abandoned, his body battered from the accident. *Accident.* Was that what it was? Physical injuries she could deal with; they could be seen, diagnosed and fixed. It was the invisible wounds—the mental kinks—that wouldn't be so easy.

She knew all about that.

She watched the floor numbers descend—two, one, ground. 'Let's go out for a bit,' she said. 'That place that used to be the Anchor.' Amy would be there, and she could avoid going home to Ma for a bit longer.

Dane scrunched his lips in contemplation. 'I have to get the twins.'

'Can't they stay over at Ma's? She said she's looking after them tomorrow anyway.'

Dane glanced at his phone. 'But what about dinner?'

Jac felt momentum build, but to what, she didn't know. 'We won't stay long. Couple of drinks. We can drop your car at home. Josh?'

Josh shrugged. 'What the hell.'

Dane, too, conceded with a nod.

A few drinks, good company—might take the edge off, ease the pain.

The lift doors opened and she walked into the bright light of the foyer.

5

Dane took his first long sip of tap beer at the Cherry Tree, allowing himself a moment to enjoy it. He closed his eyes, but the tension that lived inside his body wouldn't fall away. Neil Diamond was too loud, coming at him from every direction, and the lights from the dancefloor bounced off the mirror ball and into every corner of his brain.

Reading the soil report for the restaurant had done nothing to put his mind at ease. Even though it passed muster, the strongly worded recommendation that further tests be carried out knotted his stomach. Why hadn't Dad ordered the second test? If the foundations began to fracture after a year, they would have to pull the whole thing down and start again. He'd done what Dad wanted and kept the project moving, but when he woke up would he even acknowledge that?

'What was Dad depressed about?' asked Josh from the other side of the mock timber table. 'Is it work?'

Dane realised he was being spoken to and flipped his attention back to the present. 'Business is good,' he said, much louder than his normal speaking voice. 'Sweet Home Alabama' blared from the speakers now. 'Everything's fine.'

Dane surveyed the room. When the place had been the Anchor, all through his high school years, it was a rite of passage to mosey up to the bar and confidently order a drink as soon as you hit eighteen. Pent had another bar in those days, called Vegas, but it appealed to a much older crowd—thirty- and forty-year-olds trying to recapture their youth. He wondered if that was how high schoolers saw him now: an old man—a dad—with his hair gone, clinging to his younger years.

A 'wine bar' had also cropped up in the past year. But it was too pretentious—the kind of place where people went to drink overpriced Californian gewürztraminer, eat tapas and take selfies for Instagram.

'Has Ma done something?' Jac said from beside him.

At Josh's insistence, they'd found a table in a dark corner, and Josh had sat himself in the spot that faced the wall, his back to the dancefloor. He yanked on his cap's visor, pulling it down to his eyebrows, while Jac's eyes darted anxiously around the room. They looked like a couple of fugitives—him hiding from the world and her playing lookout.

'It's not Ma,' Dane answered. 'Ngaire reckons sometimes—'

'Ngaire knows?' Jac leaned forwards. 'No one tells *us*, but *Ngaire* knows?'

'She's my wife!'

'We're his kids! Why didn't you call me?'

'Ma didn't want me saying anything.'

'I can understand her not telling Josh, but . . .'

Josh tilted his head to one side. 'Oh, great. So now I need to be protected from everything?'

'Yeah, maybe,' Dane said. 'Are you seeing someone?'

'Christ, Dane. Jordan just kicked me out.'

'I meant a counsellor,' he said.

Josh sniffed, then rubbed his nose. 'Not anymore.'

Dane was conscious of how he must have sounded—like a father scolding his teenage son—but Josh needed to hear it. 'Don't you think you should?'

'No, Dane, I don't. I'm fine.'

'But with what's happened with Dad . . .'

'I just can't believe it,' Jac said. 'Do you really think he would do this to himself?'

Josh swirled the dregs of his beer around the base of his glass. 'Lots of people are in pain, Jac. In all sorts of ways.'

Jac looked away.

'He's alive,' Josh said. 'When he wakes up, we'll find out what's going on.'

'But what if he tries again?' said Dane.

Josh and Jac exchanged an apprehensive look.

'He won't,' Josh said. 'We'll get him help. We'll . . . pay more attention.'

For the past two days, an uneasiness—a mix of guilt, confusion, shame and anger—had bored its way through Dane's insides. He was the one who saw the most of Dad, outside of Ma. He worked with him every day. Why hadn't he spotted the signs? Maybe he was too caught up in his own shit to notice anything out of the ordinary. He wondered if his siblings blamed him for not realising something was wrong.

'Amy!' Jac said out of nowhere, calling out to a tall girl with long brown hair as she passed.

'You came,' Amy said.

Jac's eyes flitted across the table and then back to the woman.

'Just wanted to get out of the house for a bit. You remember my brothers?'

'Hi, Amy,' Dane and Josh choloused. Dane recognised her from around the traps but hadn't seen her in years. Even under the bulk of her ripped denim jacket, he could see she had an athletic body.

'I'm heading outside for a smoke,' Amy said. 'Do you want to . . .?' She gestured towards the door.

'Sure.' Jac pushed out her chair. 'Back in a minute.'

The music changed to something slower and the girls who'd been dancing, five or six of them, left the floor.

He'd been to a lot of bars lately, all over the High Country, always on his own. He and Ngaire didn't eat out much together. It was too hard with the kids. They'd tried a new steak restaurant called the Brown Cow last month, but they'd spent the whole night talking about the twins and were in bed by nine. For them, nightlife was a relic of the past.

With Jac gone, he arched over the table to Josh. 'What do you think about Jac's news? I mean, of the whole *thing*.'

Josh leaned back, his hand over the rim of his beer glass, twisting it left and right. 'Maybe he's the closest thing she's found to Dad.'

Jac and Dad were close, but Dane had never understood psychological theories about how parents' relationships with their children affected who they chose as a partner.

'Do you really believe all that stuff? Ngaire's nothing like Ma. Do you think Jordan is?'

'Jac's a special case.' Josh circled his glass in only one direction now. It was empty, and he was getting restless. 'Maybe she wants kids,' he said. 'Maybe she's running away from something. Like Ma did.'

Dane scratched his forehead. 'What are you talking about?'

'Bro, I live two hundred kays away and I know more about what's going on than you. Her music career was going to shit so she took the easy way out and married Dad.'

That didn't make sense, Dane thought. Ma *had* been successful. She'd made a huge sacrifice to get married and raise a family. 'Meaning?'

'Dane, it's lucky you know something about construction because—'

'Why would you say that?'

'About construction?'

'Stop fucking around.'

Josh gave a small smile to show he was toying with his brother. 'She was in the spotlight and then she wasn't. The amazing Blaise Vanderbilt disappeared. That can be hard to deal with. Believe me, I know. She got married and had a family so she wouldn't have to think about it. Now she's raising *your* kids.'

'She's not *raising*— I'm not talking to you about this.'

'Then don't bring it up.'

Dane took a long sip of his beer. But he couldn't let it go. 'Relationships expert now, are you? Yours isn't looking too good.'

Josh gazed into his empty glass, dodging eye contact.

He'd taken it too far. 'Have you spoken to her?'

Josh's mouth drooped at the sides. 'It's complicated.'

'How complicated can it—'

His brother jerked his head up. 'Should we go back to talking about Ma raising your kids?'

Dane squeezed his lips together to avoid saying anything else. He didn't know Josh anymore, not that he ever did.

The music picked up again and a small group of women marched back to the dance space, making whooping sounds and holding their glasses high, even though a sign barred drinks on the dancefloor.

Josh's posture loosened, and he let his elbows rest on the edge of the table. 'How's working with Dad? Still treating you like his apprentice?'

Dane shook his head. 'No.' Even to his own ears he sounded unconvincing. 'He likes things done a certain way, that's all. You know how he is. He's been doing this a long time.'

'And no one could do it better than *his* way.'

Dane agreed but couldn't say it. Not when Dad was lying in a hospital bed.

Josh held up his empty glass. 'Another round?'

'Yeah.'

Josh didn't move, looking at him expectantly. 'I'm unemployed!'

Dane came back from the bar with two more beers in hand and a packet of chips between his teeth. He'd lost count of drinks, but they'd brought Jac's car after leaving his at home, so he didn't have to worry about driving.

He placed the drinks down and yanked the packet from his mouth, dropping it on the table.

Josh peered at the bag. 'Salt and vinegar?' he said with a tinge of disgust.

'And people say you're hard to live with.'

'Who says that?' Josh tore open the bag and shoved a hand in.

Dane didn't respond, snatching the packet out of Josh's hand before he could finish the lot. 'Jac's been gone a while.'

'Maybe she got a better offer,' Josh said with a smirk.

'Don't be crude.'

Josh shrugged, sipping his beer.

'Do you think she's . . . that she might be . . .?'

Josh waited for him to finish, enjoying his discomfort. 'Gay? Is that the word you're groping for? Bi?'

'Do you?'

'Who would know? I don't even think she knows. She plays it close to her chest.'

'What about you?' Dane asked.

'I'm definitely straight. Straight as a dart.'

'No, I mean, what are you going to do?'

'About what?'

He raised his eyebrows. 'About *you*?'

Josh pulled away from a sip of beer. 'I just need some time. And a job.'

Josh's words were starting to run together.

'A job's not going to fix things, Josh. It might make it worse. Being back in that environment? All those temptations?'

As Josh hid behind another long sip of beer, guilt stabbed at Dane's chest. 'I'm sorry,' he said. 'I don't mean to sound all superior. I should have been checking in with you more.'

'It's fine.' Josh's eyes panned to the bar.

It wasn't fine. He'd shirked his responsibilities too. 'Can I tell you what I think?'

'Can I stop you?'

Dane took a breath, redacting what he'd been going to say. 'Maybe you should try and patch things up with Jordan? Go back to her with your tail between your legs. If you can get things sorted out there, the other things'll work out.'

Josh shrugged the subject away, as if getting his family back together wasn't the most important thing.

'For Christ's sake, Josh. Get your priorities straight!'

Josh squared his shoulders. 'Priorities? You mean *your* priorities.' He reclaimed the chip packet, clawed out another handful but held them in his palm. 'Some of us aspire to more than being a dad and having an okay job that pays the bills. Your problem is you've been locked inside that mindset—that *world*—for so long that you've lost who you are, if you ever knew. You've decided that this is it and you're happy with that. One day you might end up running the company, but you'll still have to go home to—' Josh shook his head of something. 'Maybe you'll live through your kids—their footy wins, good grades at school—but as for yourself, what are you ever going to have of your own? Because one day the kids will be done with you, you'll retire, and what will you have to look back on? A few structures around town that were built on the back of *Dad's* company?'

The words slammed into Dane's chest and he took a swig of beer to wash them away. He placed his glass back on the table and pivoted in his chair, slinging one arm over the back. If Josh was looking for a reaction, he wasn't going to get one. He should tell Josh about his plans, but his brother didn't deserve to know now. 'All I'm saying is, you act as if you don't have any responsibilities. You can't run around being a player forever, because one day you're going to wake up, your youth will be gone and you'll realise you're alone.'

Josh looked at him strangely, as though trying to solve a puzzle, but then chose another route. 'That's how I wake up every morning.'

'Can we have a serious conversation for once?'

The muscles around Josh's mouth tightened. 'Here's the difference between us: if you do something dodgy or embarrassing, a few people find out and it's forgotten in a week. You don't understand anything about me or my life or what I want or how much I hate that Dot can't—that I can't . . .' He waved his hand aggressively, as if beating off an annoying insect, and directed his eyes to the dancefloor.

'One: that's not true. Stuff sticks to you here like you wouldn't believe. And two: my life's no less important because I'm not in the public eye.'

'That's not what I meant.'

'I've got things I want to do too. Stuff beyond *Dad's company*.'

Josh exhaled, running a hand over his beard, his face, his hair. 'I think we need another drink.'

Dane took a breath. 'I think you're right.'

6

Jac watched Amy draw on her third cigarette in fifteen minutes, blowing smoke into the night air.

She stood on the deserted footpath, a few metres up from the Cherry Tree entrance, admiring the view. Amy stood on an angle—leaning with one shoulder pressed to the brick wall—her denim jacket puckered at the chest.

'Stop looking at me like that.'

Jac's breath caught. *Like what?*

'I know what you're thinking: it's the 2020s—why am I still smoking?'

She shook her head. 'I wasn't.'

'I only took it up again three years ago.' Amy peered at the glowing tip. 'I don't know how I'd get through the day without them.'

Jac wondered what could have been so bad. They'd already covered the basics—Amy taught high-school maths at an elite boys' school now, she lived alone in her grandmother's former house, wasn't seeing anyone, and her dad was doing okay (he still lived in the same flat in Pent). Her older brother lived with his wife and kids in Singapore. Jac hadn't revealed that much. She'd talked about her work but didn't go into details. She didn't tell Amy about her four years in the missing persons unit, which she'd left because it became too depressing. Because there was something about all that searching and never finding that she couldn't deal with. She didn't say she'd moved to the dog unit, which was okay, but that fraud suited her much better. She got to nail the bad guys and then move on to the next case. There was an end point. She didn't think about it at night, and no one's mental health was at stake. Least of all hers.

'I'm getting married,' Jac said, apropos of nothing.

Amy exhaled more smoke, this time towards the street. 'I was wondering when you were going to tell me.' She jutted her chin in the direction of Jac's ring finger. 'What's her name?'

'*His*. Gil.'

Amy raised an eyebrow. 'He must be one out of the box.'

'He is.' Jac swallowed. 'He knows about . . . everything.'

'*Everything*? Really?'

'Well . . . the fundamentals.'

Amy exhaled dense, woolly smoke. 'And he's okay with that?'

Jac nodded.

'Are *you* okay with that?'

'Of course.'

Amy's lips parted, like she was about to say something, but closed again.

'What?' Jac said.

'Nothing.'

'No, really, what?'

Why was she was pushing so hard?

'You do realise that marriage is a team sport?'

'Yes.'

'You hate team sports.'

Jac rubbed her nose. 'I'm . . . adaptable.'

'Okay,' Amy said in the most condescending way possible.

'How can you—'

'I said *okay.*' She held her hands up in mock surrender. 'I'm not judging.'

'It sounds a lot like you are.'

Amy pressed the end of her cigarette into the brick wall, bending the filter into a small V shape and tossing it into a nearby bin. 'At least your parents will be happy.' She plucked the cigarette packet from the inside of her jacket.

'I'm not doing it for them.' Jac's eyes travelled along the street towards the square and the office of Harding Construction. The town was quiet. In the time they'd been standing there, maybe six cars had gone by—all four-wheel drives or utes.

Across the road, beyond the lofty fir trees, the lake sprawled. She couldn't see it, but she knew it well—heavy and inky black at night. That was one of the things she remembered most about growing up in Pent—how dark the nights were. Funny how the 24/7 radiance of a big city like Sydney can be so exposing in some ways but allow you to live so anonymously in others. Pent didn't let you get away with that. The only way to hide was to leave.

'Dad tried to kill himself,' she said suddenly. 'I don't know if you heard.'

Amy looked momentarily confused. She was probably trying to work out the connection between Jac getting married and her father trying to kill himself, since that might have been the logical thread of the conversation.

Amy touched Jac's arm and it pulsed through her. 'Are you okay?' Amy didn't seem as shocked as she'd expected.

Jac nodded, but she was far from okay. Nothing made sense. The world had tilted or something. Did Dad really attempt suicide? It was so drastic, so final. How could he be that unhappy?

'Is the business in trouble? I heard about that apartment project he's doing. It's sparked a lot of debate in the *Gazette*.'

'No, nothing like that,' Jac said with a confidence she had no right to. What did she know about what was really going on with her father?

Amy took another drag of her cigarette and blew the smoke away. 'Depression is such an invisible disease. Still. You'd think after all this time, all the exposure it's had . . .'

Depression. That word again. She was about to object to Amy using it to describe her father, but what would be the point? She didn't know him.

Josh was right. She needed to stop thinking this way. Dad had sent out a cry for help and, thankfully, there was still time to answer it.

A rowdy group of three women and two men, all dressed like they'd come straight from the office, spewed out of the bar's front door. They must have been in their twenties. Jac had never experienced Pent in her twenties. She'd spent the year straight after high school here, pulling beers in a bar in the next town, sleeping in, getting her heart broken and avoiding Ma's questions about what she was going to do with her life, until it got to be too much and she'd left.

Amy lifted her hand to scratch the back of her head and the front of her jacket opened. Already, it was getting too much again.

'Blaise must be happy about your news. How *is* your mother?'

Jac shivered against the chill. 'Same.'

Amy knew what that meant.

'Hey, Jac and Jill,' Amy said. 'Sweet.'

'It's *Gil*.'

'Like a fish?'

Amy laughed and Jac joined in. Not because what Amy said was funny, but because Amy thought it was funny. She was playful like that. Her jokes were always bad. What had Amy said to her on the first night they'd met at Tink's? *Do you have any raisins? No? How about a date?*

Amy butted out her cigarette. 'I'd better get back to my drunk workmates.'

'Don't you drink?' Jac asked.

'Not a lot now. The occasional whisky, when I'm in the mood. That's usually when I'm alone in my house at night. Is that bad?'

'No.' Sad, though, she thought. It sounded familiar.

They stood looking at each other. Jac didn't want to say goodbye. There was only one other person in Pent she felt this relaxed with, and he was in a coma.

'I wonder what kind of shape my brothers are in,' she said. 'They may well have killed each other.'

Amy nodded, but didn't smile. 'It was good to see you, Jac. Good luck with everything.' She hesitated a second and then made for the door.

'I'm getting married for the right reasons,' she said to Amy's back.

Amy did a half-turn back and smiled properly now. 'Right. We'll see.'

She would.

When Jac re-entered the bar, Dane and Josh were alone on the dancefloor, side by side, drunk, swaying back and forth, singing along to the Eagles' 'Desperado'.

Jac stayed where she was, enjoying this rare moment of brotherly . . . something. It wasn't love, she was sure of that, but a kind of shared bond brought on by alcohol, being back in their home town together and the grief turning to joy that came from knowing their father could have died but he'd survived.

'Desperado'. Her dad loved that song. It reminded her of a family trip they'd taken in the nineties. She'd forgotten where to. All she could remember was Dad singing along to an Eagles CD in the front seat while she watched on from the back. He'd seemed so affected by it. Dane had his ears muffled with headphones and Josh was colouring in, rocking his head back and forth. Ma was humming. She had a great voice but never sang properly after giving up her career.

Jac mouthed along to the words: *These things that are pleasin' you can hurt you somehow . . .*

In some ways, it felt as if Dad was already gone. Knowing he'd tried to kill himself would change how people saw him. And in Pent, that would follow him everywhere. *There goes Stephen Harding. He's the one who tried to kill himself.*

She inched towards the dancefloor. Josh was smiling through his singing. He caught sight of her and his smile widened. It lingered loose on his lips and he gave her a roguish wink.

Dane's eyes were closed, concentrating on the lyrics. He was lost in the feeling. Or maybe he was swimming in a long-ago memory too.

She elbowed her way between them, and Dane's eyes snapped open. His face lit up and he gave her a hard kiss on the forehead, his hand gripping the back of her head so she wouldn't reel back. She joined in, their voices getting louder as the song progressed. They knew all the words . . . *Your prison is walking through this world all alone.*

They had that in common. They would always have their childhoods in common.

They swayed together, green and red lights bouncing off the mirror ball and off their faces. They sang with feeling, as if there was no one else there. The unnamed fear that permeated everything she did was absent now.

The boys loved Dad too, in their own ways. They must have been feeling the strain just as much as her.

They roared through the final verse, swinging from side to side. The bar's other patrons had at some point emerged from the blurry sidelines of her world and now sang along to that haunting piano.

You better let somebody love you, before it's too late.

7

Josh hadn't anticipated the gutter, or that the footpath outside the Cherry Tree would be pulled out from under him like that. He felt himself going down.

'I've got ya,' Dane said, grasping him by the elbow. Josh slung one arm over Dane's shoulders. With the other hand he undid the top button on his jeans, which had been digging into his stomach all night.

He glanced down and registered that he was standing on the road. Wasn't he just on the footpath?

Jac had left half an hour before, driving her hire car back to the house. Home was a good two kays from the pub, but that didn't matter. 'We'll walk! It'll be fine!' He'd done it so many times in high school.

A cold gust swept through the tall trees that bordered the lake, and he wondered what the time was. Not that time mattered anymore. Time was irrelevant when you didn't have anything to get up for in the mornings.

He broke away from Dane. Patting his back pockets, he found his phone and held it up to his face. The background photo illuminated to life. Dot, in her highchair, her doughy face smeared with custard, smiled back at him. Something crumbled inside and he'd forgotten who he wanted to call. No, the time. He was checking the time.

It was 12.26.

'It's cold,' he said. 'Should we call Jac?'

Dane shook his head. 'Home's closer than you think.'

With 'Wonderwall' radiating from inside the Cherry Tree, they started towards the house. The streets were empty. Nothing had changed in a decade.

'Never realised how much I missed that old music,' Josh said.

'Good music never goes out of style.'

'*Baby*,' he sang, humming the tune to 'Wonderwall'.

It wasn't just the tunes, he thought; it was a feeling that warmed you right through to your bones. Maybe it had something to do with a different time in his life.

They approached the square, passing Pent's most pretentious landmark plonked in the middle. To the uninitiated it looked like a confusing spiral of concrete painted red on the outer surface and off-white on the inside. It was supposed to be a swirling section of apple peel, representing Pent's history as a fruit-growing region.

'Let's get in *The Peel*!' Josh said.

'No,' Dane whined. 'My pants. I just had them dry-cleaned.'

Josh grabbed him by the wrist. 'Come on!'

They stumbled across the concrete path, then over a thin strip of grass, narrow gum trees soaring overhead. Coach lamps boxed *The Peel* in like soldiers guarding their king.

Reaching the edge of Pent's monument to pomology (he'd learned that word in school when they'd built the thing),

Josh paused, staring. *The Peel* looked the same, elevated on a knee-high pedestal about four metres wide and three deep, but it somehow felt unfamiliar now, as if he had no claim over it anymore.

They had to duck as they climbed inside and sat, Dane brushing dust off the surface with his hand before lowering his bum into the curving base.

In high school, *The Peel* had been the exclusive domain of Year 12s—senior students had a standing reservation at night and on weekends. The NO CLIMBING sign had been defaced so many times that the council stopped replacing it. He would come with his mates and they'd drink and smoke inside, because that's what the Year 12s before them had done. He wondered if that still happened.

'Have you got any weed?' he asked Dane.

'Yeah.' Dane reached into his trouser pocket.

His heart gave a jolt. His brother had weed?

Dane pulled his hand from his pocket and made a show of opening it slowly, revealing a five-dollar note and a register receipt. 'Aw, sorry,' he said, overacting. 'Must have left it in my other pants.'

'Ha! You mean your school pants?'

Dane looked outwards, across the square. 'I never smoked weed in high school.' He turned back. 'Did you?'

Josh made an exaggerated pfft sound. 'Is that a serious question?'

Dane shook his head in mock disappointment. 'You were such a delinquent.'

You don't know the half of it.

'Some things change, some stay the same,' Josh said, turning the words over in his head. 'That's in a song, isn't it?'

Dane began humming a familiar tune.

Josh rested his head on the curved concrete behind him and tried to remember what it felt like to be eighteen. It wasn't that long ago. He thought he knew everything then. He thought he'd just turn up in the big city, grab all the success he deserved, and everything would be alright. But there was always something on his tail, something chasing him that he couldn't shake. If only he could rewind to this spot, in *The Peel*, ten years ago.

'It smells like piss in here,' Dane said, interrupting his thoughts.

Josh made the mistake of taking a whiff for confirmation. 'This place has gone to the dogs since I left.' He trailed his fingers along the bumpy surface above him. It was cragged there but smoother where he sat, where bums had been rubbing against it for fifteen years.

'This isn't much bigger than my flat,' he told Dane.

Dane huffed a laugh. 'Where is this flat exactly?'

'In a suburb you've never heard of.'

'You're renting?'

He shook his head. 'You can't rent when you don't have a job. It's my agent's.'

'Nice of him.'

'*Her.* It's only temporary.'

'You'll get past this.'

That wasn't what Josh had meant. He'd meant that Kelsey had made it clear that he wasn't to think of it as a long-term solution.

'Your agent must have faith in you if she's letting you use her place.'

That was true. If Kelsey really believed he had no future, she wouldn't bother trying to help him, right?

Dane drew his knees close to his chest, wrapping his arms around them. 'What do you *do* with yourself every day?'

Josh searched his mind for a way to put a positive spin on it. 'Let's just say no one's ever got better value out of Netflix. And I'm single-handedly keeping Uber Eats afloat.'

Okay, so he didn't succeed. It sounded grim.

'So how do you—?'

'We've been having fun, Dano,' Josh cut in. He didn't want to think about stuff he didn't want to think about. 'Let's not— Let's just . . .'

'Okay.'

But, damn it, now it was in his head. The hangover of that Twitter explosion. Waking in the darkness most mornings, still dressed, on the couch, with takeaway containers and empty bottles cluttering the floor. Sometimes he'd take himself off to bed. But mostly he'd just stay there, roll over, cram a cushion under his head and go back to sleep.

When the sun came up, he'd pop two Panadol, eat toast with peanut butter and go back to his room. The more daylight hours he spent in bed, the fewer reminders there were of all the other places he should have been if he was to resemble a functioning human being—the gym, the supermarket, home. But leaving the flat invited too many stares and comments behind hands cupped over mouths. Nobody wanted selfies with him anymore.

But it wouldn't last forever. People would work out that that woman, Tabeetha, was lying. People would see that she was only doing it to create a sparkle around herself. Then everything would go back to normal.

'I'm gonna open my own bar,' Dane said.

'I'll be there.'

'I'm serious.'

'So am I!' Josh sniffed. 'That's a hard gig, bro. Believe me—I've worked in my fair share of them.'

'I've done my research.'

'It's gotta be different. Unique.'

'I know. I've got it all worked out. *Regional* is going to be my point of difference. Everything local—the food, the alcohol, even the music. Live bands from around here, and when there's no band playing, Aussie music only.'

'What, no Scotch whisky?'

'No Johnnie Walker, no French champagne, no Peroni. Aussie brands. Exclusively.'

'Do we even make whisky?'

'There's distilleries here. And gin. And vodka. I've looked into it.'

'Told Dad yet?'

Dane turned away.

'Can I be there when you do?'

'Definitely not.'

All this talk of bars and he suddenly craved a smoke. 'Have you got any weed?' he asked. Had he already asked that?

Dane stood, ducking his head so he wouldn't bump it. 'Time to go.' He brushed off his pants.

They started down Stanley Street, past Jac's old horseriding club, but Dane pointed towards Baker. 'Let's go this way.'

'But Stanley's quicker.'

'Come on.'

Streetlights shone off Dane's bald head, creating a kind of glow around him. Josh looked at the moon hanging over the trees that surrounded the lake only about two hundred metres south of where they stood. The moon was almost full, with just one darkened corner—a cookie with an edge crumbled away.

They walked for another four or five metres before he realised why they'd taken this route. 'It's the mall, isn't it?'

'Come *on*.' Dane beckoned him with frenzied waves of his hand.

'I bet you never shop there either, do you? Is Ngaire allowed to shop there?'

'Of course!'

'How long's it been? Four years? Five?'

'Let's go,' Dane said in an agitated way, as if they were late for something.

Lakeside Mall was the reason no one trusted Dane to run Dad's company. Josh couldn't remember the details, but he knew Harding Construction had partnered with a developer to build what was to be Pent's first real shopping complex. Contracts had been signed, celebratory drinks consumed by the truckload, and Dad had left on a well-earned holiday to Broome with Ma. While he was away, the developer contacted Dane asking for a costing document or something. Dane accessed Dad's files and emailed what he thought was the right version. It wasn't.

The developer cancelled the contract. Dad cut his holiday short and tried to smooth things over, but the trust was gone. The developer partnered with another construction company and this version of Lakeside Mall was the result.

'Fine,' Josh said. 'We'll take the *long* way.'

They turned off Baker and continued down Winchester, passing the primary school, and stopped when they reached their old house. They stood out the front, hands resting on the picket fence. The current owners had painted the weatherboard in shades of grey and white.

He'd only been seven when they'd moved out. He remembered his bedroom—a shrine to the Power Rangers and the X-Men cartoon—and the kitchen area, with its beechwood cabinetry and shiny steel benchtops. The backyard had an enclosed trampoline and a shed where Dad would spend hours, reportedly toiling away at small carpentry projects, though Josh never saw any evidence of it.

'I had some good times in that house,' Dane said, a wistful smile curling his lips.

'Isn't that where you got Ngaire pregnant?'

'No.' Dane shook his head, disappointed in something. 'You're not very good at maths, are you?'

'Don't need maths in showbiz.'

Dane went quiet.

'So, who *did* you fuck in that house?'

'No one. Got a blow job from Zoe Hilderman. Ngaire was my first real girlfriend, though.'

'Your first fuck. That explains everything.'

Dane unhooked his hands from the pickets and turned to him. 'Why have you all got it in for her?'

He shrugged. 'We haven't. I just— Do you think you would have married her if she hadn't got pregnant?'

For a millisecond, Dane hesitated. 'I stepped up.'

'Noble.'

Dane started back along the street.

Ngaire lost that first baby and couldn't fall pregnant again. It took another ten years to produce the twins, and then only with the help of IVF. Given her trouble, there'd been a lot of quiet talk about whether she'd been pregnant that first time. None of this was ever said in front of Dane, of course.

'That's exactly what you did when Jordan got pregnant,' Dane said when Josh had caught up with him. 'You stepped up.'

'What is it with unplanned pregnancies in this family?' Josh mused. 'Us Harding men must have super strong jizz.'

He hadn't referred to himself as a Harding in a long time. It sounded weird. Joshua Harding was a child. He was Josh Vanderbilt now, although the brand was tarnished.

'Not me,' Dane said. 'Don't tell me you've got issues because you think you were an accident?'

Josh tripped on uneven pavement but corrected himself without falling over. 'I wasn't thinking that, but thanks for bringing it up. I'll make a note for my counsellor.'

'Thought you'd stopped going.'

'I have.' He put his arm over Dane's shoulders. 'You used to be better at spotting jokes, bro.'

'Yeah.' Dane ducked out of Josh's hold and bound him in a headlock. He yanked Josh's cap off his head and rubbed his hair with his knuckles.

'Get off me!' Josh cried from the inside of Dane's elbow, his face squished against his brother's soft belly.

Dane released his grip.

Josh straightened, then bent down to retrieve his cap from the road. It had been too long since he'd been with Dane like this. Maybe since primary school.

He gave Dane a shove. Dane shoved him back harder than he'd expected, and he stumbled onto the road, his feet crunching on broken plastic scattered across the bitumen. He looked up, his heart screeching to a halt. 'Dane?'

'What?'

Dane went to shove him again, but he held up his hands in surrender.

'This is where he did it,' Josh said quietly.

Dane lifted his head.

The bridge Dad crashed into loomed over them. It was a new bridge over the train line, built to replace a level crossing. Scuff marks streaked the white-grey pylons that held the bridge overhead. On the road, small shards from the headlights and blinkers glistened in the moonlight.

Josh kicked at a small pile of plastic that had gathered in the gutter, sending it skittering across the road. 'This is all so fucked.'

Dane stretched an arm across Josh's shoulders, and they stared at the bridge.

He imagined the scene. Dad angling his prized Jaguar towards the pylon and flooring it. His determined, maybe slightly frightened, face. Josh shut down the image.

The police were right. There were no skid marks on the road. And it wasn't even that close to a bend, so no one could say he'd misjudged the turn.

'What if he dies?' Josh asked.

Dane squeezed Josh's shoulders. 'He's not going to die. Not from this.'

Josh's eyes began to burn. If Dad died, they'd never get the chance to iron out the deep creases in their relationship. 'Will he get help, do you reckon?'

'I hope so, little brother.' Dane took his arm back. 'Let's go.'

8

Jac lay on the fold-out in Dad's study turning her engagement ring. She was on top of the covers, still dressed, although she'd kicked off her Converse. Her jacket smelled of cigarette smoke, but she didn't want to take it off just yet.

She tipped her head to the side, looking at Dad's heavy wooden desk. What was going through his head right now? Did people in comas have thoughts? If he could sense what was going on around him, he'd know that people were talking about his suicide attempt. He'd hate that. She shouldn't have talked about the crash when they were in the hospital room with him.

Did he do it? she wondered for the hundred and fiftieth time. What could be so bad? There must have been something. There must be an answer.

She swivelled off the bed and crossed the hall to the kitchen for food. The bulb over the stove cast a buttery glow through the room, enough light for her to find the Special K in the pantry.

Back in the study, she rolled the castors of Dad's high-backed leather chair across the rug, away from the desk. She sat, placing her cereal bowl on the sparse desktop—only a leather-bound cup for pens, an unopened phone bill and a paperweight that she'd made in primary school. It was supposed to be an ashtray, not that Dad ever smoked, but it was the easiest thing to make in pottery class. She'd applied a jade-green glaze—his favourite colour—and the teacher had it fired in a kiln somewhere. It was ugly, but it meant something that he'd kept it on his desk all these years.

Sometimes, when she was a girl, she would play in his study when he wasn't there. But that was at the old house on Winchester Street, before she moved out, before they upgraded to something befitting Dad's status in Pent. She would sit at his desk, click open a ballpoint pen and jot down made-up tasks: *Buy paper, Order post-it notes (in all colours), Call clients, Build houses.*

She would pick up the phone, pretending she was his PA. 'Stephen Harding's office, Gayle speaking,' she would say. 'I'm sorry, he's in a *very* important meeting right now. Can I take a message?'

The study had always been a dark room, even in the daytime, with only two small, TV-shaped windows perched high on the wall. Outside was a sideway and next door's garage, so no view to speak of anyway.

The decor didn't help with the light situation. One wall was a built-in floor-to-ceiling bookcase made from dark timber with a small ladder connected to a rail at one end. But it was just for show; she couldn't imagine Dad climbing that flimsy thing to fetch a book from the top shelf, which wasn't that high anyway. The walls were painted a heavy green, and a Persian-style rug in deep red covered most of the floor.

She scanned the bookshelves. Dad wasn't an avid reader, but he'd never thrown out a book to her knowledge. Some had been passed down from her granddad—a set of bound encyclopedias that Grandpa had probably bought by mail order, a thick dictionary and a huge Bible bound in marbled black leather. Books about golf filled one section and novels another—spy thrillers mostly, some with faded covers, others that looked pristine, as if they'd never been opened. Dad's previous study had good natural light, not like this one, and many of those older books had suffered because of it.

She stood to get a better look at the books, which were arranged by category—fiction, reference, biographies—and in descending order of height. Then there were paperbacks with dramatic titles: *Dare to be Great!*, *Unleashing the Real You* and *Everyday Confidence*. She spotted one called *Unf*ck Yourself*. She slid that one off the shelf and leaned her backside against the desktop. The cover was yellow, and it had a subtitle: *Get Out of Your Head and Into Your Life*. She flicked through the pages, catching the odd chapter name: 'I am wired to win', 'I embrace the uncertainty', 'I expect nothing and accept everything'.

Why would Dad be reading these books? She returned it to its place among the other self-help stuff.

An image of Dad's car slamming into the bridge slipped into her head like a coin dropping into a slot—the moment of impact, in slow motion: the rev of the engine, the thunderous crunch of metal, glass showering the road. What was he thinking in that moment? Was he scared? Calm? Maybe he was relieved that all of life's struggles would soon be over.

The cat wandered in, likely looking for Dad. He sniffed around, pressed his head into the hard corner of the desk, then pounced, impossibly lightly, onto the fold-out. He pawed the quilt a few times, did a turn or two, then plopped down.

She spun the chair right way around again and sat, finishing off the last spoonful of Special K, which had turned to grey mush at the bottom of the bowl.

She reached for the dangling brass knob on the top right drawer, swaying on a decision, then yanked it open, not sure what she was looking for; maybe a glimpse into his life.

The drawer had small, in-built compartments where he stored all his essential stationery items—a stapler, sticky notes, paperclips, a couple of USBs. Everything had a place.

She tried the left-hand drawer. A calculator, a metal ruler, a tube of hand sanitiser, a spiral-bound address book. On top of the address book sat a small stack of index cards held together with a thick red elastic band, the kind the post office used to use. The top one had a quote scrawled in Dad's precise hand with a thin black marker: *You wouldn't worry so much about what others think of you if you realised how seldom they do.* He'd attributed it to Eleanor Roosevelt.

She picked up the cards and rolled off the elastic band, flicking to the second one: *Believe you can and you're halfway there.*

The third: *You were born to be real, not to be perfect.*

The fourth: *It's not who you are that holds you back, it's who you think you're not.*

There were more, but she'd seen enough. She left that last one on top and stretched the elastic band back around them, returning them to the drawer.

Dad said things like this to her sometimes. Six months ago, when she was about to join the fraud unit, they'd spoken on the phone.

'You're changing jobs *again*?' he'd said. 'I can't keep up with all these moves.'

'It's time. I've been with the dogs long enough.'

'Well, you should do what makes you happy, I guess. But remember that happiness is a direction, not a place.'

Something in his tone made her miss him more. 'Why don't you come to Sydney this weekend?' she'd suggested.

'That's a place.'

Ha-ha. 'We could go to a show. Or just drink beers in a seedy pub somewhere. There's so many to choose from here. You could break out that new shirt I sent you. Have you worn it yet?'

'It's a bit big on me.'

'Is it? You should have said something.'

'I would have if you'd given it to me in person.'

It had been too long since she'd visited, but he didn't usually ride her about it. The silence felt endless while she invented an excuse, but Dad gave her a reprieve. 'Anyway, your mother's helping out with the Pent Fair this weekend.'

I wasn't inviting her. 'Perfect. She'll be out, and you'll have nothing to do.'

'I was looking forward to the quiet.'

'Come on . . .'

'Things are complicated at work. I was planning on cracking a shiraz and catching up on some of my shows that your mother hates, falling asleep on the couch . . .'

'All weekend? Aren't you golfing?'

'Not this week—I've got a dicky shoulder. Why don't you come here?'

'It's fine, Dad. We'll do it another time.'

In the study, she closed the left-hand drawer and slid open the slim centre one. She found a box of tablets and read Dad's name printed on the label stuck across the face. It contained a drug called citalopram. She slid her phone out of her pocket and brought up Google. Citalopram was an antidepressant. She looked at the box again—it was dated only a month ago.

Under the box, she found a wad of A4 pages, maybe a dozen, secured with a single staple in the top-left corner. She flicked through them—printouts of emails and letters, some unsigned, all typed, addressed to Dad or versions of 'CEO of Harding

Construction'. They were all to do with the apartment development Amy had mentioned—the one on the site of St Augustine's
Church. All were angry.

You will rot in hell for pulling down our church . . .

*There's nothing more disgraceful than a lapsed Catholic. Shame on
you, Stephen!*

God sees all. You will get what's coming to you . . .

Jac laid the stack on the desk. Had Dad reported these to the
police? Some of them constituted genuine threats.

Wait. No skid marks. Had someone tampered with his car?
She would find out. That would be tomorrow's task. First, she'd
have to ascertain where the car was. Probably some local tow
yard in Pent. Had the local cops even considered sending it off
for forensic analysis? Or had they already made up their minds
that it was a suicide attempt?

She changed into her flannelette pyjamas, shunted the cat
off the bed and got under the covers. The sheets were freshly
laundered but cold. She missed her electric blanket, she missed
her own bed, and she missed her own little flat.

She'd told Gil she wasn't prepared to give up her apartment
when she moved in with him. They could rent it out, he'd said,
but she liked the idea of leaving it as it was so she could go there
whenever she wanted. But that didn't make sense financially. Gil
was right—they'd have to make a decision about it soon.

She'd liked Gil from the moment they'd met. One nippy
Tuesday night towards the end of his project with the police,
the whole team assembled at a raucous city bar for drinks. She
didn't usually go to after-work gatherings, but they'd struck
up an easy friendship and he'd persuaded her to join them. By
eleven-thirty, the rest of the team had dispersed—to other bars,
home to their partners, into the back seats of Ubers with each
other. All Jac and Gil had eaten was a bowl of wedges and a plate

of barbecued chicken ribs from the bar menu, so they found a twenty-four-hour pancake place nearby and feasted on potato pancakes with sour cream, bacon and chives. He'd talked about growing up in a smallish town on the New South Wales coast and she'd given him a heavily edited version of her childhood in Pent. He spoke of his hope to retire by sixty, and she told him that she would prefer not to work at all if she didn't have to. Before they knew it, it was 2 am.

Afterwards, he'd suggested they do it again sometime, and she'd agreed.

The next time, they'd gone to a Turkish place not far from his apartment. Over gozleme and a bottle of pinot noir, she'd asked him if he'd ever consider getting married again.

'I didn't think I would, but now I'm not so sure. I thought I'd be fine on my own, but I miss the companionship. I guess you get used to a certain comfortable way of living. I'm not kidding myself, though. At my age? I don't expect I'll ever fall madly in love again.' He smiled. 'Well, I might, but I don't like my chances of whoever I fall in love with feeling the same way about me.'

'I fall madly in love at least once a year,' she'd said. 'Most of the time the lucky person doesn't even know it.' She wasn't sure why she'd said that. She'd never admitted that to anyone. She shouldn't have had those last two glasses of wine.

He must have sensed her discomfort so changed the subject. 'Do you want kids?'

'Yeah. It would be nice to . . .'

'Nest?'

'Settle.'

'I hope you mean *settle down* and not *settle for less*?'

She smiled. Three weeks later they were engaged.

FRIDAY

9

Jac found Ma at the kitchen table, picking at a piece of toast with red jam. A cup of something, scarcely touched, sat at her elbow. The burnt, nutty smell of freshly roasted coffee infused the air.

'Morning, Ma.'

'Good morning, darling. Would you like some coffee?'

Ma pushed her chair back, but Jac held a hand up to stop her. 'It's fine. I can do it.' She'd spoken too sharply and gave a tight smile in lieu of an apology.

'You know how to use the pods?'

The remains of the twins' breakfast sat in the sink—two bowls with Weet-Bix dregs crusting at the edges.

'They're too strong for me,' she said, flicking the lever down on the electric kettle. 'Instant's fine.'

Ma looked as if she were about to say something—probably about the vulgarity of instant coffee—but held her tongue.

At eight forty-five, sitting up in bed, Jac had phoned the Pent police station and found out Dad's car was in fact in a local impound yard and they had no intention of doing anything with it for the time being. There was no need to, they reasoned, because Stephen had not been 'fatally injured'. They would wait until he regained consciousness to question him.

In the backyard, Marcus was counting, eyes covered with a hand, while Dylan darted about searching for a hiding spot.

Jac found one of Dad's mugs—*My doctor said I needed more iron, so I went golfing*—then the coffee tin, and levered it open with a teaspoon.

'Did you have a good time last night?' Ma asked. 'The twins enjoyed the shepherd's pie.'

Jac willed her facial muscles to be still. This was the kind of passive aggression she'd endured for those nineteen years in her mother's care. She preferred, if she had the choice, blatant aggression. 'Yeah. We had a good talk.' She spooned coffee granules into her cup and thumped the lid of the tin closed with the heel of her hand. 'How did you sleep?'

'Me? Oh, fine.'

Jac filled the cup with steaming water and brought it to the table. 'What are you doing today? Hospital?'

'At some point,' Ma said, her eyes roving to the backyard. 'When those two head home. Are you going in?'

Jac wrapped her hands around the cup to warm them. 'Of course. Who knows what time Josh will surface, or what state he'll be in.'

Ma rested her elbows on the table, interlacing her fingers as in prayer. 'Did he *say* anything last night? About the . . . allegations?'

'Not to me. He might've said something to Dane. They stayed on after I left. Is that park still there on Leveson?'

Ma nodded, her eyes unfocused.

'I might take the twins for a play. Curb some of that energy.'

'That would be lovely. Thank you.'

Jac leaned back into the chair, extending her arms to reach the mug. 'They're my nephews and I hardly know them.'

'Well, that's—'

She held out a hand. 'I know it's my fault. I want to change that.'

'Does that mean you might . . .?'

'Don't read anything into it, Ma.'

Ma tilted forwards. 'It would be nice if you . . . you know— for your father, too.'

She would visit more; she'd decided that during last night's fitful sleep. Her mind had flashed from image to horrible image of Dad hurtling his Jag into that overpass—not that she'd ever seen the overpass up close, but the film sprung to life regardless. The questions, too, would not stop. How could she have not seen he was in pain? Why had no one else noticed?

She took another sip of coffee, then rested the cup on the tabletop. 'Ma, Dad had the accident *days* ago,' she said. 'Why didn't anybody tell me about the . . . circumstances?'

Ma glanced at the half-slice of toast in front of her, then nudged the plate to one side. 'We thought it was the kind of thing that's better said in person, that's all.'

'Did you know he was taking medication for depression?'

Her mother swept non-existent toast crumbs into her hand and brushed them onto her plate. 'He didn't like to talk about it. It was just another thing to him—like the heart medication he was on. He said it was helping and that I shouldn't worry.'

'So, you didn't?'

'Well. You know Dad.'

They would have to step things up when Dad came out of hospital—get him more help. They would cajole him into counselling, reassess his medication, compel him to take time off work—hide his car keys, if necessary. Then she remembered he no longer had a car. Should they get the old one fixed? It was probably a write-off anyway. She, for one, never wanted to see it again.

Jac sipped her coffee and another thought from the night disentangled itself. 'And why isn't he wearing his own pyjamas? He'd want his own pyjamas.'

'There's plenty of clean sets in his dresser.' Ma's voice hardened. 'Choose one.'

'Good. I will.'

Jac took another mouthful of coffee. It *was* rather rank. She'd have to buy a better brand if she was staying a while.

'So, when are we going to meet Gilbert?'

'*Gillon.* Soon. When Dad's better.'

Saying Gil's name reminded her that she had another life outside of this house, but it seemed so far away, so separate from her family and Pent.

'Jacinta, I don't understand why you didn't tell us about this. We're your family.'

She avoided Ma's gaze, looking outside. 'I know.' She'd been planning to visit for Father's Day—which was only a week away—and to bring Gil with her. Like Ma said, some things are best handled in person. She'd kept previous partners away from her family because she didn't want to scare them off. Or maybe it was because meeting the parents felt like too big a leap forwards, making it much harder to back out.

'The registry office is so cold and impersonal,' Ma said. 'Don't you want to be surrounded by family and friends?'

What family? What friends? She could only think of about five people who she would really want there.

Ma waved a hand. 'I'm not sure why I'm bothering. You always do what you want anyway.'

Josh appeared in the doorway dressed in pyjama bottoms and a faded Iron Maiden t-shirt, probably only manufactured last year. Had he ever even heard an Iron Maiden song?

'Man,' he said. 'Those kids can make some noise.'

With his bed hair, swollen eyes and mangy beard, he looked like a bear emerging from hibernation.

'Would've thought you'd be used to that by now,' Ma said.

He ignored the comment, resting a hip against the benchtop and knuckling sleep out of his eyes. 'One of them came into my room looking for the other one.'

'We're used to empty rooms in this house,' Ma said. 'Sit down, darling, I'll make your breakfast.'

Ma reached into her lap and her hands emerged holding the cat, bundling him up by the belly. Jac hadn't realised he was there.

'We're taking the boys to the park,' Jac told Josh. 'You and me.'

'I just got up!' He peered into her coffee cup and turned up his nose. 'Where are the pods?'

'On the benchtop,' Ma said. 'I'll do it.'

Jac wondered if this was how things worked in Josh's world. He asked for stuff and people brought it. No wonder he wasn't coping living on his own.

'It's fine,' he said, rummaging through the container of bulging coffee capsules and reading labels. 'I need to do a load of washing, by the way.'

'Just put it in the laundry basket,' Ma said. 'I'll wash it with everything else.' She opened the fridge door.

His eyes flashed to Jac. He was worried about Ma seeing the chocolate milk stains.

She couldn't believe she, too, was going to rescue him. 'You make his breakfast, Ma,' she said. 'I'll put the washing on.'

Josh gave her a grateful smile, then said, 'Is that what you're wearing? To a park?'

She looked down to remind herself what she'd pulled from her bag—denim capri pants and a stiff white shirt she'd picked up on sale at Zara. It wasn't her. Not the old her, at least. It was the new Jac—the one who was soon to be married. The person she had convinced herself she wanted to be.

10

Josh adjusted his sunglasses and leaned back into the park bench, watching as Marcus and Dylan played on the swings. A hoodie covered his head.

'You look like the Unabomber,' Jac said.

'I don't know who that is.'

'He blew up shit all over America for twenty years. Got caught in the nineties.'

Josh nodded. 'Good. Hopefully people will keep their distance.'

Next to the swings, a girl played on her own, making her way across the multicoloured two-level plastic structure of tunnels, climbing apparatus and rope bridge, soft rubber matting stretching out under her. A plaque said the playground was opened by the local mayor two years before and he wondered if Dad had anything to do with it.

'This park's about ten times better than when we were young,' he said to Jac. 'The equipment was a lawsuit waiting to happen.'

'There was nothing here when I was a kid,' she said. 'Just an empty block with a sign saying "park".'

The sun was so damned bright, even though the air was cool. His sunglasses weren't blocking the glare. He was used to dark spaces now, to living in a closed-in city where the buildings were high and the streets narrow. His eyes had become accustomed to hard edges and grey shadows. Not this. This was so open and exposed.

Marcus and Dylan swung their legs, challenging each other to go higher. *Those boys don't know how lucky they are*, he thought—*growing up as twins, getting to experience everything together.* They would always have someone to play with. Someone to fight with. Because even the fights were a good part of growing up as brothers.

'Remember that swing set we had in the backyard at Winchester Street?' he asked Jac.

'Sure. Dane and I played on it for hours.' Jac let out a small laugh. 'Hard to believe Dane and I were that close once. Guess we had no choice, especially on family holidays. You were either not born or a baby. Ma and Dad wanted to do literally nothing but sit by a pool all day. At night, they'd go to a bar. So we had to entertain ourselves.'

He pictured eight-year-old Jac and ten-year-old Dane playing together and something brightened inside him. 'What did you two get up to?'

'On holidays?'

He nodded.

'I don't know. Swam, knocked on people's hotel room doors and ran away. Pressed all the buttons in the lift. Usual stuff.'

'Sounds fun.'

Jac angled her head, letting the sun warm her face. 'I suppose it was.'

'I hardly remember any family holidays. I guess Ma and Dad left us at home once you two were old enough to look after me. I thought it was pretty good at the time—home alone without parents. But when you're six or seven and nobody . . .' He shook his head. 'It wasn't like you two wanted to hang out with me.'

'You had your magic tricks.'

'Yeah. Shame I couldn't make anyone *appear.*'

They stopped talking and watched the boys. Dylan was winning. How blissful it would be to be five years old!

On the way to the park that morning they had walked past his old primary school, where the twins went now. The last time he'd been inside was on the night of his graduation. He remembered the shirt he'd worn—it was dark blue and had little stars on it. All the parents were there, gathered around large round tables eating a spit-roast dinner. After the main course, the school captain got up and gave a speech about how he would always carry the memories of Pent Primary, and Poppy Anderson sang a Beyoncé song. Josh and four other kids performed a skit. They'd played the roles of some of their teachers, and his impersonation of their PE teacher, Mr Blakely, got more than a few laughs. But when he looked at his parents' table, Ma wasn't in her seat and Dad was busy chatting to Lachie's dad, who was sitting next to him.

Later, when he asked them about it, Dad said the skit was 'great' and Ma said she was watching from the back. But he didn't believe them. As they were leaving—Dad with a red wine stain on his shirt and Ma carrying her stilettos—Ellie Webber's mum caught him by the shoulder. 'You're a natural, Joshua,' she'd said. He had to admit, the praise from Ellie's mum and the rousing applause at the end of the skit was intoxicating, like a thrill ride at a country fair. He'd been living to recreate that feeling ever since.

'How's your head?' Jac asked now. 'After last night.'

'Fine. I'm used to it.'

'Sleep okay in your old bed?'

He couldn't remember the moment he'd climbed into bed. He'd been at the overpass with Dane and then somehow back at the house trying to be quiet. He woke in fright during the night, his phone pressed against his face. 'I had a dream that Harry was trying to kill me.'

Jac pulled at the collar of her woollen shawl; it must have been itchy. 'That's why I hate cats. So unpredictable,' she said with a straight face.

'It was scary!'

The image had mired in his brain—Harry's angry, menacing face, saliva dripping from his pointy canines, trying to bite into his face and neck. It was so random and upsetting that he couldn't fall back to sleep afterwards. He wondered what it meant.

'Reckon there's a cafe around here?' Jac asked, looking around.

Josh raised his eyebrows. 'You literally *just* had breakfast.'

'That was, like, an hour ago.'

He looked at her. 'And you're already hungry?'

She shrugged. 'Never fully satisfied, I guess.'

A guy passed the bench leading a greyhound, his eyes dwelling on Josh a few seconds too long. He was used to this—people seeing him in the street and realising they knew him from somewhere. Once, sitting across from a guy on a tram, the man leaned over to him and asked if he'd attended some high school that he'd never heard of. He'd said no and the guy said that was strange, because he looked so familiar. 'I'm on TV,' Josh told him. '*Common Law*?' 'Oh,' the guy said. 'Never watched it.' Nowadays, he'd mutter something like, 'Sorry, I don't think we know each other,' and move on. That had become his go-to reply over the past three months.

One of the boys cried out and the image was gone. When he looked over, Dylan was facedown on the rubbery ground, his legs flopped to one side.

'What happened?' Josh called, running the nine- or ten-metre distance between them.

Marcus had stepped off his swing and now stood over his brother. 'He fell off.'

'I can see that.' He rested his hand on Dylan's shoulder blades. 'Dylan? Are you okay?'

Jac appeared behind them. 'What happened?'

'Dylan fell,' Marcus repeated, as if everyone was going mad.

'How?' Jac asked.

'He tried to do a flip off the end like Jackson.'

'Who's Jackson?'

'A kid in our year.'

Dylan hadn't moved, still crying into the glittery rubber.

'Look at me, buddy,' Josh said. 'Are you bleeding? Have you still got all your teeth?'

Marcus giggled, but Dylan kept crying.

'He did this last time, too,' Marcus said calmly. He didn't seem concerned that his brother was bawling his eyes out.

Dylan still didn't move, so Josh placed his hands over Dylan's biceps and squeezed like a vice, lifting him to standing. He was light, but limp. He turned Dylan around and tried to get a look at his face, but Dylan let it flop to his chest as if trying to hide.

He tilted Dylan's chin upwards to inspect him for damage. His face was red, and a small graze blossomed on his nose, but he was otherwise unscathed.

'Does it hurt?' Marcus asked. Josh detected a hint of hope in his voice.

Dylan nodded, the tears still flowing.

Josh pulled Dylan close, allowing the boy to rest his chin on his shoulder. He wrapped his arms around the boy. Being like this, their chests pressed together, he felt Dylan's sweetness and innocence seep into him and he didn't want to let go.

He glanced up and Jac was staring at him, a blank look on her face.

'What?'

'You.' She smiled.

'*What?*'

'Nothing.'

He pushed Dylan away so he was at arm's length. He'd stopped crying but his face was blotchy. 'Okay now?'

Dylan nodded, snuggling in for another hug. His hair smelled soapy fresh and his little body was warm. He was a skinny kid, and under the weight of Josh's arms, his skeleton felt brittle, like an eggshell.

'Josh, you've got snot on you,' Marcus said, pointing to the shoulder of his uncle's t-shirt. He laughed.

'Okay, you two,' Josh said, flicking the snot in Marcus's direction. 'Do you want to play more or go home?'

'More! More!' Marcus said, jumping up and down.

'Dylan?'

The boy nodded, and off they went.

'Five more minutes!' he called after them.

Jac still had that weird look on her face when they sat back on the park bench.

'What?' he repeated.

The boys were already scaling a mini climbing wall, Dylan's injuries forgotten.

'Nothing. I've just never seen this side of you.'

'What *side*?'

'The daddy side. I guess I've never thought of you like that.'

'I *am* a dad.'

'I know, but . . .' She let the sentence go. 'I don't know if I could do what you just did. I'd freak out.'

'Or tell them to quit their whining and get on with it.'

'Or that,' Jac conceded, fiddling with the fringe of her shawl. 'Gil has a kid.'

'Really?'

'Well, not a kid. He's twenty-four. Jacob.'

'Was he married before?'

She nodded. 'Clarissa. Olympic-level bitch. Only lasted five minutes.'

'Jac, the evil stepmother,' he said, to try it out.

Jac twisted the ring on her finger.

On the play equipment, Marcus had reached the top of the wall and was staring, hands on his hips, at Dylan, who was only three-quarters of the way up.

'Speaking of evil women . . .' Jac began.

He wondered how long it would take for someone to quiz him about what had happened on the set of *Relationship Rescue*.

'What was her name? Tabitha?'

'Tabeeeetha,' he corrected. 'Nothing happened. She came on to me. I rejected her. I told you all this at the time.'

'I know, and I believed you. *Believe* you. But why do you think she . . .?'

'Why do any of them?'

'*Any* of them? How many have there been?'

'No, I mean . . .'

Jac sighed, looking across the park as two women strolled by with takeaway coffees.

'Why didn't you defend yourself? Come out fighting?'

He shrugged. 'Didn't want to fuel the fire, keep the story alive.'

'Yeah, but if you're innocent . . .'

'If?'

'You know what I mean. And it's not going away.'

'I know that.' He looked at her. 'If this is a pep talk, could you fast forward to the peppy part?'

'Come on,' she said, bumping him with her shoulder. 'Talk to me. I'm your sister.'

'Well, you should know—I'm interviewing other people for that position.'

'Ha!'

'And you're so open with me.'

She exhaled. 'So what are you going to do? About work?'

'What *can* I do? I've been chopped off at the knees.'

'You're giving up?'

'Taking a breather. No one's going to book me at the moment anyway.'

Jac considered him. 'Couldn't you . . . No, I guess you don't have any other talents. You don't even have your looks anymore.' She said it in a purposely flat way.

He smiled at her droll humour. The boys were on the swings again, competing to see who could lean back the furthest without tipping off. And right off the back of having fallen off not three minutes before. What it must be like to be fearless.

'Maybe you're right about lying low,' she said. 'Concentrate on one thing at a time.'

'You mean Jordan.'

She nodded.

'I have to get my career sorted first. I'm useless to her without it.'

'I'm sure she doesn't feel that way. She probably—'

'Well, I'm useless to *me* without it. And if I've got nothing, I've got nothing to give. I need something to give.'

'There's more to you than your career. Find another one.'

'What? Real estate? Banking? Everywhere I go, people will know who I am. It's a noose.'

'Mate, you tied the knot.'

'*It's not my fault!*' How many times did he have to repeat himself?

When he turned to her, she was shaking her head at him. 'I don't understand how you couldn't see . . . I mean, a show like that? People don't go on there to fix their marriages. They want their faces on TV. They're all egomaniacs.'

'The fans are worse. Like the chocolate-milk thrower on the train.'

'She didn't douse you in milk because of trumped-up drama on the show.'

He watched two girls, older than the twins, climbing a rope wall. Their mum stood at the bottom, her arms poised to catch them in case they fell.

'What ever happened to that ski jumper you dated?' Josh asked. 'Neil?'

'Noel.'

'Did he ever hit the big time?'

'We lost touch.'

'I liked him.'

Jac stayed quiet.

'Why'd you break up? Did he have ugly toenails? Smell a bit too much like dirty lake water?'

'He wanted to paint the kitchen yellow.'

He frowned at her. 'What a psychopath. You're lucky you got out.'

'Right? Who paints *any* room yellow?'

Josh shook his head. 'It's a real puzzle why you've been single so long.'

Jac turned to him. 'It's better to cut things off at the pass. Before you sink too deep.'

He looked across the large expanse of grass to the greying sky beyond. 'That's fear creeping in.'

'Well, we haven't had the best templates. I mean, Dad and Ma? Dane and Witch Woman?'

'It's the women who are the problem. And you're more like Ma than you think.' He faced her. 'Icebergs.'

She looked at him, appearing more flattered than offended. She probably thought he meant that she had hidden depths—that there was more going on underneath the surface than people expected.

'I meant cold,' he clarified.

'Wow. Thanks. Do you think it's salvageable with Jordan?'

He didn't hesitate. 'Yes.'

Jordan never called him, and when *he* called *her*, her responses were one word, maybe two on a good day. She was unenthused about making arrangements for him to see Dot, let alone anything to do with their future together. She didn't know he was in Pent but probably should. It wasn't the pain of her absence so much as the clinging to hope that was killing him. 'Yes,' he repeated.

'At least you've got a place to crash. I have to decide where we're going to live after we're married,' Jac said. 'Gil's place or mine.'

'Where does he live?'

'Darlinghurst. It's more central than mine. And bigger.'

'So what's the problem?'

'I can't leave mine empty. It doesn't make sense. Financially.'

'You won't sell it, though?'

She shook her head. 'We'll rent it out.'

Then he saw the problem. She wanted a foot in both camps. He knew how that felt and where it got him. 'Sometimes you just have to choose.'

She didn't like the sound of that, shaking her head. 'But I don't want to.'

The answer was obvious to him. 'Keep it as an Airbnb,' he said. 'Then you can leave it furnished and take it back if you need to.'

'But there's upkeep, admin, the cleaning.'

'Pay a cleaner!'

She lifted one shoulder. 'Maybe.' Then she looked at her phone. 'Can you take the boys back? I'm going to see Dad.'

'I'll come.'

'I want to go on my own.'

He understood. 'Okay.'

Jac took off and he watched the boys a while longer. Marcus was hanging precariously by one arm from the monkey bars while Dylan looked on, unfazed, from below. Josh wondered if Dad ever brought the twins to the park when they stayed over on weekends. Maybe he was a better granddad than dad.

Dad had never taken him anywhere as a kid. That was Ma's job. Even then, she'd drop him off at swimming or taekwondo and return when the class was over, never staying to watch.

Josh was determined not to do this to another generation of Hardings. He would be a better parent than his had been.

11

Dane inhaled deeply through his nose, letting the air seep down into his stomach, and popped another two aspirins from the blister pack, watching them spill across the keyboard of his laptop. He'd had a good time last night, so it was worth it, but if he could just shift the headache from splitting his skull open, he could get on with his day—finishing the quote for the Ferguson extension, approving invoices for Jan, updating the budget on the Catoggio new-build.

The office was quiet. Gayle had stepped out for an hour but left the radio burbling at reception. Jan was at her desk—it was the end of the week, so she probably had the pays to do—but he wasn't sure where Leigh was. Olivia was downstairs in the sales office.

He picked up the tablets and dropped them in his mouth, took a generous gulp of water, and placed the glass back on his desk. He really shouldn't go hard like that anymore. His stomach had lost the tolerance for it, like an old engine that can no longer hold oil, and his body didn't bounce back like it used to. Maybe if he wasn't so grossly out of shape he'd recover quicker.

He closed his eyes and leaned against the slanting back of the chair, feeling the thumps of last night's music pulsating in his temples. When he'd landed back at Ma's with Josh lagging behind, he figured he'd crash in his old room. Not that it resembled his teenage bedroom anymore. The month after he'd moved out, Ma had converted it into a craft room (although he'd not seen one item of craft produced out of it). When the twins came along, she'd bought two single beds, pasted a football decal across one wall and started referring to it as 'the twins' room'. Josh's room, on the other hand, was untouched.

Upstairs, he'd said goodnight to Josh and stumbled down the hallway to his old room, bouncing his fingertips off the walls for balance. But inside, under the soft blush of a nightlight, he'd found the boys asleep in their matching beds, Dylan with the covers pulled up to his chin and Marcus spread like a starfish, one foot dangling from the mattress. He'd stared at their sleeping faces a minute then traipsed back down the stairs.

He'd texted Ngaire then collapsed onto the couch, which turned out to be a mistake. It wasn't designed for sleeping, especially for a man of his size. He should've just gone home.

He'd woken at six-thirty, sandy-eyed and his tongue feeling like it had grown fur, and walked home under a steely sky to take a long shower. He'd eased himself onto the bed next to Ngaire for just a minute then woke to find her standing over him.

'Dane, I'm going.'

'Already?'

'It's almost nine.'

He'd bounded out of bed, got dressed and hitched a ride with Ngaire because he was probably still over the limit.

'Remind me again what we've got on this weekend,' he'd said as Ngaire edged her SUV out of their driveway.

'Tomorrow: Auskick. Tomorrow night we've got the Weismans for dinner, so if you could cut the grass? Sunday—'

'Can you take the boys to Auskick?'

She checked the rear-view mirror. 'I've got my writing group.'

'Isn't that in the afternoon?'

She flicked the indicator to turn left. 'It's my submission we're workshopping. I need to prepare.'

He didn't know enough about how these things worked to argue.

'Sunday: soccer,' she went on. 'They're playing at home, so you won't have to leave too early.'

You. Have to.

He tried to remember how it used to be—before they'd dived headfirst into the credit pool, before the kids, before life got so damn busy. But when he thought about it, he realised they hadn't changed that much at all. He'd always let her take the lead on organising their lives on the home front. They made a good team that way, her picking up the slack for his shortcomings.

What he did miss was the way she used to look at him—like he was the last chip in the bag, all smothered in sauce.

Ngaire pulled over on the highway side of the square. 'I'll just drop you here.'

He unbuckled his seatbelt and she reached her hand across the centre console, finding a place on his thigh. He looked at her face, and for a moment it all came back—her pulling him into the bedroom on a random Sunday afternoon and impromptu getaways to places with sand and surf in summer or crackling open fireplaces in winter.

He felt a scratching on his leg and realised she was removing something brown and powdery from his pants with her nail. 'When did you eat chocolate?'

Now, in the office, the morning sun pierced the windows at sharp angles. He lowered the shade. Normally he loved the way the sun streamed into the space near his desk each day, as if the world was born again, but it was too intense for this particular morning.

With the shade closed, he looked across the square, beyond the gums and *The Peel* to slivers of the lake between the large fir trees that bordered the main road. The square and the lake were Pent's best assets. If only there weren't so many trees in the way, it would be perfect.

Dane tapped the keyboard, bringing his laptop back to life. He *had* to work, but his head was full and fuzzy, crammed with shaved polyester like a stuffed animal. He toggled out of the spreadsheet and brought up Google, typing 'induced coma'. One website described it as a state of temporary hibernation that allowed time for the brain to recuperate. Another said it was a method doctors used to minimise brain swelling and inflammation after an injury. What he really wanted to know was how long Dad might be under.

The answers were vague but indicated it could be anywhere from a few days up to a few weeks. Induced comas longer than a month were, apparently, rare.

He flicked over to his emails, finding one from Adam Sergeant—the local real estate agent with whom he'd had a quiet word about locating a site for his bar.

Hey Dane!
Hearing whispers that the Commonwealth Bank are vacating their building on Main Street. I know you like the old ones, and this one's

*a beauty! No pics yet, but soon as we can get inside, you'll be the first
to know.*
   Cheers,
   Ad

Leigh approached Dane's desk, spinning a pair of sunglasses by
the arm. 'Whoa.' He play-acted pulling up short. 'You look like
shit.'

Leigh was unshaven and wore a high-vis vest over his
union-branded windcheater. He must've come from a worksite
somewhere.

'Thank you.'

'We all have our coping tactics, I guess. But you gotta know
your limits. Where's Gayle?'

Dane was in no mood to bite back. 'Said she'd be here mid-
morning. What do you need?'

'Nothing—just got a question about . . .' He glanced across
the room to Dad's empty office. 'I'll wait till she gets in.'

'Can't I help?'

'Probably not. Any word on Stephen?'

'No change.'

Leigh probed his mouth with his tongue, as if he might have
food stuck between his teeth. 'How long do they reckon now?'

That, of course, was the million-dollar question. No one at
the office talked about the particulars surrounding the crash. At
least not in his presence. Everybody probably knew his father
had tried to kill himself, but no one acknowledged it. It was
hard to keep something like that on the down low in a town like
Pent, where somebody's brother-in-law was a cop or somebody's
best mate was an ambo.

'Depends on his progress,' Dane said. 'For now, they say it's
safer to keep him in the coma.'

Leigh responded with a slow nod, considering something. 'So, we've got a few days? I mean, we've still got some time to get all our ducks in a row before he comes back?'

'I guess. Do we have wayward ducks?'

''Course not.' He made a dismissive noise.

'Did construction start on the restaurant this morning?' Dane asked.

'Right on schedule.'

'Good,' he said, trying to inject confidence into his voice.

'Joel will be pissed off,' Leigh said. He widened his stance, anchoring his hands on his hips. 'But you had to make the tough call.'

You had to make the tough call. Leigh hadn't seemed worried on the phone last night.

'You did the right thing, Dane. The sooner it's finished, the sooner we all get paid.'

The sooner *you* get your commission.

Leigh's nose twitched. 'Do you think you should be here right now?'

'Yeah. I'm fine. Really.'

''Cos you look a bit dusty.'

A woman's voice called out: 'Hello? Anybody here?'

Dane and Leigh's heads both turned, peering through a plate-glass wall to the reception area.

'Fuck the fuck off,' Leigh said. 'What's *she* doing here?'

Local historical society president Katherine Warren stood at the reception desk, craning her head, looking for bodies.

'Your project, no doubt,' Dane said. His stomach contracted. 'Has something happened?'

'Not since she was here two days ago.'

In the reception area, Katherine—dressed head to toe in khaki, her greying hair loose in a bulbous bun on the top of her head—held out the current issue of the *Pent Gazette* at head height.

'What's this?' she demanded.

Dane recognised the front page, the headline screaming, CHURCH DENIED NATIONAL TRUST STATUS, with REJECTED stamped across a photo of St Augustine's. His heart, too, had sunk a little when he'd read it.

'Good morning, Katherine,' Dane said. 'You didn't know about the National Trust decision?'

'Of course I knew,' she snapped. 'But it says here—and I quote from your father—*Now we can go ahead and build these apartments as planned.*'

Leigh crossed his arms over his chest. 'So?'

'So . . . you can't build yet. I've got another application in with council to stop you, and a petition with two hundred and twenty-one signatures.'

Dane did a quick mental calculation. With a population of around fifteen thousand, that was only one and half per cent of the townspeople.

'You'll have to take that up with council,' Leigh told her. 'They're the ones issuing the permits.'

She turned to Dane, probably hoping to find a more sympathetic ear. 'Look, I'm sorry about your father's . . . troubles . . . but the town doesn't want this development. We don't want to see more of our historical landmarks obliterated in the name of so-called progress.'

In principle, he agreed, but he couldn't voice that opinion to Katherine Warren, a woman who lived and died for her causes, like preserving the 1930s art deco maternal and child health centre and refusing to get out of the way when the arborists stepped in to fell a copse of hundred-year-old trees on the Lakeside Mall site.

Leigh stepped forwards. 'Tell that to the thirty-three buyers who have already paid deposits. We're seventy per cent sold, lady,' he said, too smugly for Dane's liking.

Dane held up his hand to stop Leigh from continuing. 'I'm sorry, Katherine, but as Leigh said, this is a council process. If all the paperwork's approved, there's nothing to stop us from going ahead with construction. Whatever issues you have, you'll need to take them up with council.'

She folded the newspaper in two, jammed it under her arm and stormed out.

'And stop hassling our staff at the sales office!' Leigh called out after her.

'Leigh . . .'

'See what fun you can have while Stephen's away?'

Dane exhaled and turned back towards his desk.

12

Jac joined the queue, four deep, at the counter of the hospital's cafeteria. Maybe they'd wake Dad today, she thought. Maybe hearing her voice, he'd become strong enough. She had to let him know that he didn't have to worry about anything anymore.

She stepped forwards one place in the queue and slid her phone from her jeans pocket: 10.46. No messages, no missed calls. Situation normal. She turned the ringer off and switched it to vibrate in case someone phoned while she was with Dad. At quarter to eleven, Gil would probably be in his home office, dressed in a shirt and pants even if he didn't have any client meetings scheduled. If it was the weekend, she might walk up behind him, wrap her arms around his chest and kiss the smoothness of his cleanly shaven face. He would hug her hands, maybe lean back for a peck on the lips, and they would talk about plans for the day. A walk on the beach? Brunch somewhere?

Suddenly she was hungry again.

Fresh muffins on a low pedestal caught her attention. Savoury would be better. Healthier. But the ones with the cream cheese frosting and the little candy carrot on top looked so good.

Sometimes you just have to choose.

It was amazing that she could eat anything at all, considering the sick feeling that had persisted in her gut ever since Dane had told her about the real circumstances of Dad's crash.

The space ahead of her cleared and she ordered tea; the server, a guy in rimless glasses, wrote 'Jack' on a paper cup. The bean grinder hummed and the steamer hissed as she took her place among the huddle of people waiting for hot drinks.

She'd have to speak with Dane, too—he'd need to rearrange things at the office so Dad could take a step back if that's what he wanted. He didn't need any more stress in his life. Maybe they could go on a family holiday . . . God, what was she thinking?

She eyed the muffins on the counter again. It was simply too hard to choose. So she'd do what she always did when she couldn't decide—she'd go without.

Man, how long does it take to fill a paper cup with boiling water and drop in a teabag?

She would make such a bad mother. She had no patience. And having to deal with incidents like the one at the park with Dylan? She lacked compassion, too.

'Jack?'

She collected her cup from a girl with chipped blue nail polish and a dusting of chocolate powder on her nose.

She would love her kids, though; she knew that for sure. But was that enough?

On the third floor, the corridor was livelier than the previous night. Staff leaned over the nurses' station, chatting, and old people wandered the halls in dressing-gowns and slippers, the smell of scented cleaning products in the air.

Through the glass doors of the high dependency unit, she saw a woman sitting by Dad's bedside. Strange. She'd thought only family could visit patients in the HDU. Maybe it was a social worker or the hospital chaplain. Did they still have those? They were probably called something PC and non-denominational these days, like *pastoral supporters* or *spiritual advocates*.

As she elbowed the door open, she could see it was Gayle, Dad's long-time PA. She was clutching Dad's hand.

Sensing her there, Gayle looked up, then slipped her hand into her lap. 'Oh, Jac. Hello.' Gayle's face flushed red as if she'd been caught stealing something.

'Hi, Gayle.'

She rolled her lips together as if she'd just applied lipstick. 'I was just seeing how your dad is.' She stood, knocking the chair with the back of her legs. 'I'd better be going.' She pressed a flat palm against the sides of her blonde bob. 'Leave you to it.'

Gayle was the same age as Dad, in her mid-sixties, and was dressed for work in a white skirt that was both flattering and professional, and a short, bolero-style jacket in a dusky pink. She gripped the strap of her handbag as if someone might swoop past and snatch it.

Dad looked the same as the night before—lifeless except for the slow movement of the sheet up and down at chest height. Damn it! She'd forgotten to bring pyjamas.

'You don't have to go,' Jac said, edging towards the bed, although she'd prefer if she did. Gayle had a long history with the Hardings; she understood the family dynamics. She might have questions Jac wasn't inclined to answer.

'No, it's fine,' Gayle said. 'I have to get back to the office anyway.'

'I'm sure there's no rush. The boss isn't there.'

Gayle smiled, and the wrinkles around her eyes and mouth came alive.

Jac looked at Dad more closely. His cheeks appeared more sunken, his body disappearing further into the bed. The bruising on the left side of his face was changing colour, ripening to a yellowish-brown.

'He looks peaceful,' Gayle said. 'Funny. I was just thinking last week that he really needed to take a break, but this wasn't what I had in mind.' She gave an uneasy smile.

'Any update this morning?' Jac asked.

'The nurse was around before, but I didn't speak with her. I was planning on calling your mother later.'

Gayle gave Dad one last look before turning to leave.

'Has he been working particularly hard lately?' Jac asked.

Gayle's eyes twinkled. 'You know your dad. He always works hard.'

'Is the apartment project okay?'

Gayle blinked, surprised. 'Yes. It's going well.' Her brow furrowed.

'I found some pretty angry letters at home.'

'Oh, those.' Gayle seemed to relax. 'They're harmless. Just people with nothing better to do than complain.'

'Some threatened his life.'

'I wouldn't . . .' Gayle bit her lip. 'I don't think Stephen took them too seriously.'

She thinks I mean the letters affected him emotionally, Jac thought.

'Your father was . . . Well, there have been some . . . disappointments, but . . .' Her voice trailed off.

'Disappointments?'

'Not with work. With community stuff. That damn overpass, for one.'

The only overpass she knew of was at the site of Dad's crash. 'What about it?'

'You didn't know?'

She shook her head.

Gayle looked at Dad, as if seeking his permission to continue. 'He was against it. He wanted them to go under the road, not over. But it would've been expensive and no one was listening. They were all just grateful that the old level crossing was going. I'd hate to think he chose that spot because . . .' Gayle shook her head. 'Stephen thought council gave in too easily and that they valued their relationship with city politicians more than the people of Pent.'

That must have been a while ago, Jac thought, because the overpass was finished.

'Are you well?' Gayle said, clearly looking to change the subject. 'You look well.'

She was suddenly aware of what she was wearing—a kind of poncho in zigzagging wool that had been scratching at her neck all morning. It was new, but ridiculous, really. She looked as if she'd just wandered off the set of *Dances with Wolves*.

'I am. All things considered.'

Gayle gave another smile, this one more sympathetic. 'Of course. I'm sure your being here will do wonders for him.' Gayle rounded the end of the bed and touched Jac's arm. 'I'll see you later.'

'Thanks for coming.'

As she walked out, Jac got a whiff of her perfume. It was sweet. Better suited to a younger woman, but nice anyway. Growing up, Jac had always thought Gayle was so glamorous, with her big blonde Dolly Parton hair, low necklines and thigh-hugging skirts. And she got to spend all that time with Dad!

Jac tried sipping her tea but it was too hot. She flipped the cap and set the cup on the bedside table, leaving the teabag sagging in the lid. She sat in the still-warm chair that Gayle had vacated but was too far away from the bed. She stood, pulled it closer, and sat again, taking her father's hand in hers, the way Gayle had.

She ran her thumb along the back of his hand. It was strange touching him this way, intimate, and not something she would have done if he were conscious.

She once thought they had an invisible line to each other. That each knew the other like no one else could. But now she saw that it wasn't true, and that sat heavy in all parts of her.

'What's going on, Dad?' she heard herself saying aloud. She squeezed his hand gently, willing him to answer. But nothing happened. He didn't move. The fluid kept dripping through the long thin tube that entered him at the wrist and the quiet beep-beep-beep of the heart monitor continued to sound.

She pictured the crash: him driving, determined, towards the concrete pylon. She hated that her mind went there, but it did.

Her mobile vibrated in her pocket, dislodging the image. It was Gil. She didn't want to talk in front of Dad—it felt rude—so she rejected the call. But now, with the phone in her hand, she brought up Google and searched 'symptoms of depression'; she had to help the family prepare for when Dad came home.

She clicked on the first link and it took her to a series of bullet points. Under the heading 'Behaviour', it listed: *not going out anymore, not getting things done at work/school, withdrawing from close family and friends, relying on alcohol and sedatives, not doing activities they usually enjoy, unable to concentrate.* None of that sounded like Dad. He was outgoing, didn't drink to excess and must have been able to focus considering everything he was achieving at work. Under another heading, 'Physical', she read: *tired all the time, sick and rundown, headaches and muscle pains, sleep problems, loss or change of appetite, significant weight loss or gain.* Again, none of that seemed to apply. He hadn't mentioned difficulties sleeping, feeling ill or pains. It *did* look like he'd lost weight since she'd last seen him, but wasn't that a good thing?

She sat there half an hour more, drinking her tea and watching him. There was something inhuman about his breathing—it was too perfect, each exhalation the same length, none of the normal nasally irregularities. A nurse poked her head in at one point, gave Jac a smile, but then left again.

Dad would be hating this. He didn't want to be alive and now he would wake up in a world where everyone knew something about him that he hadn't wanted them to. Could he handle that?

And if he couldn't, would he try again?

13

At lunchtime, Dane stood at the counter of the Circle Cafe eyeing the glass case overflowing with pre-made sandwiches and focaccias. He flinched at all the noises: the clang of cutlery, the hiss of the milk steamer, the ding of the cash register; but it was the smells—the fresh-ground coffee, the heated pastry and the melted cheese—that made his stomach sway. But he had to eat.

To his right, a woman, maybe twenty, also took in the contents of the glass cabinet. Her hair was the colour of beach sand and she wore a long, loose dress with thin straps, one of which had fallen off the shoulder closest to him. Her deep, permanent tan suggested she travelled regularly or was a local of someplace else—somewhere sticky and warm. She glanced at him, the slightest polite smile touching her lips. He sucked in his stomach and ran a self-conscious hand over his bald head, but she'd already turned away.

When he was her age, the looks from girls lingered much longer and the smiles were playful. But now he was invisible to women that young, and maybe even to women his own age. He imagined how he must look to them. When he was training for footy three nights a week his body was hard and moved from football fields to pubs to parties with an agility he could no longer imagine. He could eat anything back then, and lots of it, and his physique only got better—bigger in all the right places and narrower around the waist. Now his body had that slipped, spongy quality of so many men past their prime.

He ordered a sausage roll—maybe greasy food was the answer to his upset stomach—and bought a can of Coke.

Back at the office, he re-wrapped the remaining half of the sausage roll in the grease-stained paper bag and shoved it to the side of his desk.

How much longer should he stay? Bed might be the best place for him. Man, when did he get so old? He could go home. He *should* go home. No one would be there to disturb him. Ngaire was at the library and the twins were at Ma's.

First, he needed the bathroom.

On his way down the hall, Jan called him into her office, halting when she saw his face. 'You okay?'

'Fine.' He didn't like the impatience in his voice. 'Thank you. What's up?'

She extended her chin, motioning to a small mass of invoices on the corner of her desk next to a glamour photo of her teenage granddaughters. 'You haven't signed these.' She'd beaten cancer a few years before and, ever since, had kept her hair short, only an inch or two all over, but still dyed it the colour of gingerbread.

He grabbed the stack of invoices and flicked through. They were all for Leigh's jobs—the restaurant out on the highway, the church project and the community hall refit. 'Sorry. I hadn't seen them.'

She removed her eyeglasses and rubbed the lenses with the sleeve of her stretchy white top. 'Well, I can't process them without a signature. And with Stephen away . . .'

'Sure. I'll have a look. Why didn't Leigh give them to me first?'

Jan shrugged. 'Ask him.'

He delayed his bathroom break and approached Leigh's desk, but the laptop was closed and Leigh's phone gone.

14

Josh was in the easy chair, flicking through an old photo album, when his phone rang, reminding him he still needed to call Jordan. Jac was back from the hospital, lying on the couch beside him, one knee propped up in a triangle, her eyes closed. The twins were upstairs watching TV.

Josh placed the cup on the side table—his coffee was cold now anyway—and grabbed his phone. A filtered photo of his agent's face stared back at him. It had been a while, but whenever her name appeared on his screen it ignited a spark of hope. Maybe there'd be another season of *Relationship Rescue*? Maybe she was calling about a new project? He'd always wanted to have his own late-night variety show. Interviews with other famous people, live music, a stand-up comedian or two. He let himself have these thoughts. Or maybe it was a form of self-torture—the kind of self-destructive behaviour that other washed-up TV stars accomplished with drugs, alcohol and sex with strangers.

'Hey, Kelsey.'

'Hey, Josh. Did you see it?'

He paused. 'Do I want to?'

'Why didn't you tell me you were heading home?'

He tried to work out the connection between coming home and what 'it' might be, but his mind drew a blank. 'Sorry, I didn't think anything urgent would come up over the next, say, six months. How'd you find out I was here?'

'Online, of course.' She said it the way Kelsey said everything—with a kind of distant air, as if she was carrying on another conversation on the side. 'There's a video doing the rounds,' she continued. 'You in a crappy-looking bar singing country songs with drunk locals.'

Someone had filmed him last night at the Cherry Tree singing 'Desperado'. He shouldn't have gone out.

'That was my brother and sister. Why does anyone care?'

'Because you're a famous fuck-up. Who doesn't care about that?'

No one could accuse Kelsey of mincing her words. She had a knack for cutting through the bullshit no matter who she was speaking to—clients, TV executives, children.

'So, what's the angle?' he asked. '*Josh hams it up while his dad lies in a hospital bed*?'

'Your dad's in hospital?'

'Yeah. Car crash.'

'Oh, sorry, but, no: *Josh parties while Tabeetha picks up the pieces.*'

He tipped his head back into the padded crown of the armchair. 'I'm not even allowed to have a drink now.' It had been three months and still they couldn't leave him alone.

'Looks like you'd had more than one, Vanderbilt.'

He squeezed the phone. 'Fucking vultures! What should we do?'

'Let's *not* say you're in town visiting your dying father.'

'He's not dying.'

She continued as if she hadn't heard him. 'That won't go over well. We can get some talk going about the fat comments.'

'What fat comments?'

'Didn't I mention that? They're having a go at your ballooning weight, too. I'll get some people to tweet about fat-shaming, blah, blah, blah. Two days, it'll be over.'

'For them, maybe,' he said under his breath.

'What's that?'

'Nothing.'

'How are you doing, anyway?'

'Fantastic—never better,' he said in a falsely animated way, given the world was rubbing salt into the already festering wound that was his life.

'Good to hear. Gotta fly. Talk soon. Mwah!'

'Oh, wait, Kelsey—'

Too late.

'So, I googled you,' Jac said, once his phone was back on the table beside him. Her phone, meanwhile, was in her hand, and she was squinting at the screen.

'Is nothing private?'

'It's the internet.'

'I mean in this house.'

She gave him an *as if* look and pressed the screen. Tinny music began to play from her phone's speakers. The Eagles.

'Hmph,' she said. Harry leaped onto her lap, but she shooed him away.

'What?'

'My hair *does* look good a bit longer.' She tapped the screen again and flicked her finger upwards. 'Big brother is everywhere. How do you spell Tabeetha?'

'You're not.'

'I am. I want to get another look at this chick.' She typed something into her phone. 'Hmm, hot.' She arched an eyebrow. 'In a fake-tan, collagen-lipped sort of way.' She pressed the screen again with her forefinger. 'She went on *The Midday Panel*?'

'Don't, Jac.'

Tabeetha's voice vibrated through the speakers.

'He came into my room and closed the door. He was in his underwear.'

'Bathers,' he corrected.

'He asked me to take off my clothes.'

'I told her to get changed for the—'

Jac waved her free hand at him. 'Shh! I want to hear what she says.'

He raised his arms, giving up.

'He told me that I was the most beautiful woman he'd ever seen, and that after the show was finished, he'd make sure I got a job in the media.'

He expelled a loud breath.

'But you had to sleep with him first?' the oldest of the all-female panel asked.

'She's nodding,' Jac said for his benefit. 'Tabeetha's nodding.'

'I love my husband. We were having problems, sure—that's why we were on the show—but Josh Vanderbilt took advantage of my vulnerability.'

He hated the way she used his full name like that, just in case someone might mistake who she meant.

'She's a piece of work,' Jac said, tossing the phone onto the couch.

He'd liked Tabeetha. He sensed something in her that he'd recognised in himself. A burden, maybe. 'She's alright,' he told Jac. 'She's just— I don't know. Desperate for . . . something.'

'*Des-perado*,' Jac sang.

'I'm glad this is all a joke to you.'

Jac gave him a one-shoulder shrug. 'If you don't laugh, you'll cry.' She stood. 'I'm going to the kitchen. You want anything?'

'A good disguise and a getaway car?'

'I was thinking more along the lines of a beverage.'

He shook his head. 'I'm going to my room.'

Josh's bedroom was exactly the way he'd left it when he drove out of Pent ten years ago, except now it was tidy. His dumb-bells sat paired in the corner next to the blanket box where he stored all his magic paraphernalia. As a teenager, when he wasn't playing PlayStation, he was practising card tricks. He liked the idea of dazzling people; it appealed to the performer in him. He became known for it at parties. No audience was ever too old to appreciate some sleight of hand with a deck of garden-variety playing cards.

On a floating shelf above the large oak desk that he only ever used for gaming, *Star Wars* bobble heads and Pez dispensers stood in formation. On the walls, classic movie posters—*Scarface*, *Full Metal Jacket* and *Platoon*—hung in large black frames picked up from the two-dollar shop.

He'd wanted to be an actor. That's what he'd told people he was going to do when he finished school. Not that he joined the Drama Club or took part in any school plays. He couldn't sing, and the productions were always musicals. And if he couldn't get a lead role, why bother? Instead, he sat in his room and watched films. He studied the greats—Brando, De Niro and Pacino—and pictured his future: red carpets, premieres, trips to Cannes, the Oscars. It was all possible as he lay in his bed at night staring at that same brushed-silver light shade hanging from the ceiling.

Kelsey was his second agent. His first was a hack called Simon Fincher who tried to feel his arse one night after a meeting.

He wouldn't have minded the arse-grabbing so much if there had been good work opportunities to go along with it, but without that, why hang around?

Kelsey was hungry, like him, and she didn't smother him with platitudes.

'You're an instrument,' she'd said from behind a desk piled high with scripts. 'That's all. Don't take things personally. I'm only going to put you forward for parts you actually have a shot at getting, not the ones you really want. You'll thank me.'

Kelsey organised two auditions in the first three weeks after he signed with her. He landed his first on-air role as Brock, a handyman in a long-running soap. He was only on set for two days, but it was a start. Soon he landed another minor role on a made-for-TV movie called *Trapped* that required him to stand shirtless on a beach in the middle of winter (although it was supposed to be summer) in the role of a surf lifesaver who becomes stranded in a remote cave with three other people. Next were roles in two pilots that didn't get picked up, but then he'd nabbed his first lead, as a private detective in a courtroom drama. *Common Law* was built around the high-flying practice of ball-breaking lawyer Tess Heywood, and he played Jase McKay, her right-hand man who did all the field work to help in her cases.

The first season of *Common Law* was a success ratings-wise, and the show was nominated for a couple of Logies—one for outstanding drama series and another for popular new female talent for Emalie Flood, who played Tess. The on-screen legal cases were intelligent and complex, but viewers tuned in every week for the sizzling sexual tension between Tess and Jase. Will they or won't they? Six years after leaving Pent, he'd finally hit the big time.

But then, in the week after they began shooting season two, Emalie was in car accident. She didn't die, but being paralysed from the neck down destroyed her bit by bit. In some ways that was worse. Production shut down, and eight weeks after her accident, Emalie overdosed on painkillers.

Josh didn't work for six months. The loss of the show and what happened to Emalie almost crushed him. He didn't have the energy to get out of bed, and the days, coated in black, loomed long. He remembered having to talk himself into small tasks to get through. *Just get up*, he'd say. Then, *Just make some toast*. Then, *Just get in the shower.* If he'd tried to face the whole day at once, he would never have left his bedroom.

Kelsey lined up some opportunities, but his auditions were crap. The energy was forced, and that came across on camera. He'd lost his fever for it and no one wanted to book him. He couldn't blame them. He turned up at auditions edgy, jittery, not having slept and trying to cover the fact with uppers. Even when things were going well, his paralysing self-doubt stymied him; in the bad times, it levelled him like a demolished house.

Kelsey suggested he take a break from acting, pitching him the hosting gig on *Relationship Rescue*. She sold it to him as three months in an island paradise, and all he had to do was wear a suit and read an autocue. It *did* sound good. He didn't have to think about his character's *motivation* or learn lines or have TV commentators pick apart his dramatic performance. It would be like a holiday: plenty of sun, great scenery, meals cooked every night. Lots of colour for Instagram (not to mention the opportunities to post shirtless photos—he would be on a beach day after day, after all).

But all that sunshine, all those beautiful people, all that freedom. The holiday feeling had gone to his head, making him tipsy, carefree and open to anything.

And he had never been strong-willed enough to turn down an irresistible opportunity.

15

It was late afternoon when Leigh finally returned to the office, parking himself at his desk. Dane approached him, holding out the pile of invoices. 'What are these?'

Something passed over Leigh's face. He dropped his sandwich half onto a white paper bag. 'Invoices.'

'You gave them to Jan unsigned.'

He swallowed. 'Sorry. With Stephen not being here, I didn't know what to . . .' He plucked the papers from Dane's hands and thumbed through, finding what he was looking for. The company name Solid Rock caught Dane's eye before Leigh placed it face down on his desk. 'I've just got to double-check something with this one. The rest are fine.' He handed the pages back.

They really needed to move to an online invoicing system.

Then another thought occurred. 'What's this other application for St Aug's that Katherine was talking about?'

Leigh shook his head, as though he didn't understand the question.

Dane leaned against the four-drawer filing cabinet next to Leigh's desk. 'So, nothing that could hold us up?'

'Don't worry—it's under control.' Leigh turned back to his sandwich.

'When are we expecting the building permit?'

Leigh exhaled. 'Any day. We were just waiting on geotech.' He took a large bite. 'Stephen put me in charge of it.'

Two years ago, the Catholic Church stopped running Sunday Mass at St Augustine's and the priest, Father Gibbons, left Pent after dodging questions about his private life. Decades-old stories of child sexual abuse began to surface and the unpopular church became even less popular. It seemed pointless to carry on.

Last year, Harding Construction purchased the site, taking out its biggest-ever bank loan, and submitted plans to council to demolish both buildings—the church itself and the presbytery—to erect a six-storey, forty-eight-unit apartment complex, Pent's first low-rise apartment block. It was quite a milestone, for the council and for Harding, but also a gamble—Harding Construction were builders and renovators, not property developers. The *Gazette* had chronicled every petition, every defacing of the church walls with spray-painted messages of hate, and every plea from former parishioners to re-establish the site as a religious space.

'So that's it?' Dane said. 'We're right to go ahead?'

'We will be.' Leigh rubbed his hands together, as if removing dirt. 'It's under control, Dane. Stop worrying.'

Dane's stomach churned, and he didn't know if it was the hangover or something else. He needed to stay out of it. It wasn't his project, and Dad would be back in the office soon. Still, responsibility tugged at him.

'We should've had our weekly catch-up this morning,' Dane said.

'Without Stephen?'

'It's important we're on the same page with our projects.'

Leigh squared his shoulders. 'Mine are under control.'

Getting combative with Leigh was never going to work; it'd only get his back up. 'No doubt. But with Dad not around, we might need to step in for each other.'

'Okay, sure. Monday then?'

'Yeah.'

Without Dad there, Dane had the perfect opportunity to prove that he could manage the business. There might not be enough time to make any big impact, but he would show Dad how well he could keep all the balls in the air. He still had an opportunity to reclaim Dad's respect before leaving the company for good. His own future in business awaited.

Dane arrived at Ma's to pick up the boys at ten to six. He'd crossed off five of the seven items on his to-do list at the office and felt lighter for it.

At the house, Josh, Jac and Ma were in the lounge room, an empty wine bottle and four stubbies of beer queued along the coffee table. The air was thick and warm, as if someone had been smoking, and a sharp pong of white wine twitched his nose. Maybe some had splashed onto the rug.

'Dano!' Josh yelled over the velvety hum of Dean Martin coming from Ma's hidden speakers. His brother only called him Dano when he was hammered.

'You all look very happy,' he said.

'Join us!' said Ma. Glossy-eyed, she raised her glass in his direction, wine sloshing up the sides.

He glanced at his phone. 'Can't tonight.' He'd told Ngaire he'd be home by six. 'Where are the twins?'

Josh picked up a chip packet, looked inside, scowled, and then scrunched it into a ball, lobbing it towards a second empty packet that lay crumpled and abandoned on the floor.

Jac slurred her words. 'Sit and have a drink with us. It's fun!' She'd been wearing lipstick but it had faded, gathering in the corners.

He frowned at her. 'You're not making the compelling case you think you are, Jac. Anyway, I can't. I have to get the boys home and go back to the office.'

'Ngaire's car in the shop, is it?' she asked.

'What?'

'Couldn't she pick them up?'

'She's got— She's making dinner. It's fine. Are they upstairs?'

Josh propped his feet on a footstool. 'Last I saw them they were playing chicken in the traffic out front.' His eyes had that glazed quality of someone not only drunk but baked as well.

'Good one, Josh,' he said in his best dopey voice. 'What's going on here? You're all plastered, and you don't even know where the kids are.'

'Oh, relax, Dane,' Jac said. 'We know where they are. They're in the neighbours' pool.'

'*What?*'

'Kidding! They're upstairs watching TV.' She pointed to him. 'Your face!'

Their frivolity made the veins in his temples twitch. What would it be like to have only yourself to worry about? His envy quickly spilled over into anger. 'It's fine for you lot to sit around drinking all day. Some of us have to work!'

Ma went to say something—probably to come his defence—but Jac interrupted.

'Not Ngaire, apparently,' she murmured.

'Would you get off her case?'

'Well, fuck, Dane. Every time I speak to Ma she's got to run because she has to collect the kids from school or take them to a playdate or wipe their arses. What does Ngaire *do* all day?'

'She's writing.'

'Writing? Writing what?'

'A book.'

'A book?'

Dane scanned the room. 'Is there an echo in here?'

'What kind of book?'

'A biography. Memoir, I think they call it now.'

'Oh, Jesus, if that's not the most self-indulgent thing.'

He blew out a stream of air. 'I'm not discussing this with you while you're smashed.'

'I've had *one* drink. Maybe three.' She pressed the back of her hand to her mouth but failed to conceal a giggle.

He shook his head. There was no use arguing with them. He had to get the kids home. 'I've had a long day, alright?'

'What's going on in there?' Ma asked. 'Is it the church project?'

'I don't get why people want to keep that church anyway,' Jac said. 'Wasn't it just a front for a paedophile ring?'

'That's all been blown out of proportion,' Ma said. 'There's no proof. Plus, you have to remember that people got married there, had funerals, baptised their children. It holds a lot of good memories.'

'Try telling that to the little boys those bastard priests diddled with,' Josh said.

'Oh, Joshua!' Ma turned to Dane, her spiel forgotten. 'Are you staying for dinner? We've got shepherd's pie! Still.'

'No, Ma. We talked about this.'

'Did you visit your father today?'

'I didn't get time.'

'Dane . . .'

'You try running a business on your own sometime.'

'She does,' Josh said. 'It's called a childcare centre.'

'Fuck off, Josh!'

'I'm sensing some hostility from you,' Josh said.

The annoyance Dane felt was because Josh was right. But this was the last day; the kids would stay home with Ngaire in the second week of the school holidays.

'Anyway,' said Jac, 'they say they're bringing Dad out of it soon. Tomorrow, probably.'

'Out of the coma?'

'Uh-huh.'

'For real?'

Jac nodded.

Something lifted inside him. 'Well, that's great news.' This was step one. Soon Dad would be out of the hospital, getting stronger each day, and then he'd come back to work. 'Why didn't you say anything?'

'Why do you think we're celebrating?' Jac held up her glass. 'It's worth celebrating, right?'

'Yeah.' He let out a long breath. 'It's worth celebrating.'

After the boys were in bed and the dishwasher stacked, Dane joined Ngaire in their formal lounge at the front of the house, flames hissing softly from the wood heater lodged in the cavity where the real fireplace used to be. He'd loved that fireplace, and had restored it himself, but Ngaire hated the smell and said it was dangerous for the boys.

Dane set his stubby on the coffee table, using a copy of *That's Life!* magazine as a coaster, mulling over his plans.

On the way home from Ma's, he'd driven along Main Street, pulling his Ranger in to the kerb across the road from the bank, the twins twitching in the back seat. The location was ideal for foot traffic and—Adam Sergeant was right—the building itself had Edwardian charm: a two-storey, narrow red-brick construction with a band of concrete rendering wrapped around the middle, the words STATE SAVINGS BANK 1927 imprinted into the stucco. It would make a perfect spot for his bar.

'Ngaire?' he said now.

'Hmm?' she said without looking up, engrossed in her phone. She was already in her pyjamas, white crescent moons on a pink background. The ribbed soles of her ugg boots, parked on the coffee table, rose like a stop sign between them.

Dane sipped his beer. The relief over the prospect of Dad coming out of the coma had reignited—no, hastened—his need to plan his future. But he'd made a promise to Ngaire.

'Was it on our second or third go at IVF that I had that *really bad* constipation?' she asked, swiping her index finger up and down her screen, over and over.

'Ah . . . I don't know.'

'I shared it with the group,' she said, intensifying her flicking. 'But do you think I can find the damn post?'

'Yeah, annoying. Anyway—'

'This is *so* frustrating.' She relinquished the phone to the seat cushion beside her. 'I knew I should've kept a journal.' She wound an index finger, nail chewed to the quick, through the handle of a steaming cup of green tea and lifted it to her lips, blowing air across the surface.

He took another sip of his beer, a longer one this time, weighing his words. In the corner of the room, the fire crackled and popped, throwing off sparks that collided with the heavy glass door.

'Anyway,' he said, 'so I know we agreed that you could have

two years off, but I really want to open the bar *next* year. Maybe in Feb or March. Dad will be back on board by then. And there's this site—'

'You don't know that.' Ngaire set the mug back on the table.

'The doctors said they'd be bringing him out of the coma tomorrow, so that's a good sign, right? He'll need a few months to recover properly, I guess, so I'll wait till the end of the year, then I'll tell him I'm leaving. That'll give him time to find someone else.'

'No.' Ngaire picked up her phone again; she was done with the conversation.

'No?'

She sighed, closing her eyes as if steeling herself for something. 'We had a deal. And it's only been twelve months. I can't finish the book, have it edited *and* find a publisher by the end of the year.'

Dane had anticipated this. 'Can't you finish the writing part and then do the other stuff around work?'

'No.'

'You said there'd be a lot of waiting when it's with the editor and after you send it to publishers?'

Ngaire wouldn't meet his eyes. She knew as well as him that he couldn't take the time he needed to set up the bar— fit-out, establishing relationships with suppliers, hiring staff, marketing—while Ngaire wasn't working. Three bouts of IVF had drained them financially, and in every other way possible.

'Maybe we could both work part-time while I'm setting things up?' Dane suggested.

She looked up from her phone. 'We had an agreement.' She delivered the words slowly, as if to ensure there was no room for misunderstanding. 'I've planned it all out based on a two-year timeline.'

He hated to go back on his word, but there was much more at stake now. 'I don't think I could stand being there once this St Augustine's project goes ahead.'

Images of the project's trajectory flashed through his mind: the demolition of that beautiful church, the underground car park excavation, cement spewing from a long line of cement mixers, steel beams stretching into the sky, Dad and Leigh endlessly high-fiving each other.

'Sorry, Dane,' Ngaire said, just as a loud crack burst from the wood heater. 'You made a commitment.'

16

After dinner, her head slightly hazy from three beers (or was it four?), Jac backed the Toyota out of the driveway and sped down Schofield Street.

She slowed as she passed the lake and the square. Everything looked better than she expected. Maybe it was the night concealing the ugliness she remembered. Maybe it was the beer.

The gum trees in the square twinkled with fairy lights and, even in the dark, the shopfronts seemed bolder, more confident. The ones that had remained for years seemed to assert their right to stay and the newer ones had a youthful energy about them that felt at odds with the Pent she knew.

She'd been back many times since moving away, of course—she'd seen the childcare centres and aged care places pop up on sites that were once vacant, and the town limits slowly swell further into the farming land that divided Pent from Wangaratta—but the tone had altered over the past few years, too. Unlike many country towns its size, Pent had taken a step forwards. It still had the intimacy of somewhere small and protected, but at the same time there was a sense that a discerning guard stood at the town limits, allowing only the best parts of the outside world in. She was sure that Dad, in some way, had had a hand in this.

She coasted past the community swimming pool and skate park and wound up outside Pent High. She came to a stop on the shoulder alongside a red Australia Post mailbox but kept the engine running.

The school's grounds had improved—more attention given to the landscaping—and they'd added shelter in the area where kids waited for the bus in the afternoons. Other than that, it looked the same—enough to cause a twist in her gut. The school buildings themselves seemed scarred with emotion. The taunting, the relentless slurs. The gibes for dressing like one of the Beastie Boys and wearing her hair swooped up like David Beckham.

Those kids had stamped out her will to be in any way different. Sometimes, alone in bed at night, she could still taste the bitterness of that time in her mouth, thinking of how much it would hurt to feel that way again.

Gravel crunched under the tyres as she edged back onto the road and continued south. She directed the Toyota around this corner and that, through the darkened back streets of Pent, until she found herself outside Amy's Californian bungalow.

Amy answered the door in black leggings shrink-wrapped around her thighs and a light-grey hoodie unzipped halfway down her front, revealing a nicely filled sports bra.

'Hello,' Amy said, surprise in her voice.

They stood in the doorway for a second.

'Come in.' Amy stepped aside and Jac crossed over the threshold.

Amy pointed down the hallway. 'You know the way.'

Jac took in the framed sepia photographs of long-dead relatives lining the hall, passing a formal sitting room where time stood still. It had a chunky, art deco two-seater and two matching armchairs with wide armrests that curved like waves falling to the polished floorboards. They took up most of the tiny room but looked majestic in an olde-worlde way. The place resembled a gentlemen's cigar club.

She smelled food—fried onions, she thought—as she headed towards the open-plan kitchen/dining/lounge that Amy's grandmother had added to the back.

When her grandmother died, Amy inherited the house and all the old furniture. Amy had always loved the house, probably because she'd spent so much time there as a kid.

The kitchen had been updated, she noticed. The new layout was more suited to a modern lifestyle, with spacious cabinets and an island bar. But the cabinetry was, stylistically, in sync with the rest of the house; the cupboard doors had a heritage profile rather than the flat look that dominated so many kitchens now.

An oven dish with the remains of a meal sat on the stovetop, and Jac wondered what Amy had eaten for dinner. Whatever it was, it had filled the house with an intoxicating aroma.

'You want tea? I was about to have one.' Amy's hair was tied in a ponytail, loose tendrils falling around her face. She gestured to a backless stool at the island bench.

Jac didn't feel like drinking tea and screwed up her nose at Amy's offer.

'Would you prefer something alcoholic?' Amy asked. 'A Manhattan?'

She weighed up her combined alcohol intake for the evening. She'd only had three beers. And she'd eaten a meal of last night's shepherd's pie, so that would have soaked up most of the alcohol. She felt fine. Maybe a little breezy and more carefree than usual, but fine. Home wasn't far down the road. 'Okay. Thanks. Have you got any—'

'No cherries. Sorry.'

Jac shrugged and wandered over to the lounge area. The furniture had slimmer lines but still suited the aesthetic of the house. Knoll armchairs with short, dark timber legs skirted a large Marrakesh shag rug that spanned the hardwood floors.

From a heavy, antique bureau, she picked up a framed photo of Amy and a woman Jac didn't recognise. Amy didn't have any sisters. Past girlfriend maybe? Current girlfriend? No, she'd said she was single. Something tugged at her gut.

Behind her, Jac heard the clink of ice cubes tumbling into glasses. She returned the photo to the bureau, angling it back into position. 'How come you never left Pent?' she asked.

If Amy was put out by the question, she didn't show it. 'Diving right in, are we?'

'I've been driving around a bit tonight.'

Amy must have caught something in her speech, because she said, 'Are you sure another drink's a good idea?'

'I'm okay.'

Amy carried two small glasses across the room to a drinks cart with mirrored shelves, the top one steepled with two genie-shaped bottles of rust-coloured liquor. One, Jac knew, contained sherry. Amy's grandmother used to love sherry and would often share one with her granddaughter when Amy was a kid.

Next to the decanters stood an old-fashioned ice bucket and soda siphon. Jac watched in silence as Amy removed a globed stopper, poured an inch of whisky into the two glasses and topped them with sweet vermouth and drops of bitters.

'So?' she prompted, still waiting for an answer to her question.

Amy handed her a glass. 'I like it, I guess.'

'Really?'

'Yeah. It's small, I know, and it's even smaller-minded sometimes, and it can be suffocating, but it's home and I can't imagine
living anywhere else. Plus, I like being close to Dad.'

Jac scanned the bookshelves. They were built-in, heavy,
and reminded her of the study where she was sleeping. Amy's
shelves, though, were lighter on books, dotted instead with
ornaments and photos in thick frames. Black-and-whites of
more ancestors and a couple of her parents—together, then
alone—at various ages. One of her brother and his family.
A hulking Bible covered in what looked to be dark red leather
sat open on a timber stand. Amy was not at all religious. An
heirloom, no doubt.

They clinked glasses, and Jac took her first sip, feeling the
alcohol warm her throat as it went down.

Then, buoyed by the beer she'd consumed earlier, she asked,
'So, you're not seeing anyone?' She already knew the answer
from their conversation outside the Cherry Tree the night
before, but she hoped Amy would reveal more.

Amy opened her mouth, but at first no sound emerged. 'Not
at the moment.' She swirled her glass, the ice tinkling. 'But it's
been a very long moment.'

Jac gestured to the photo on the bureau. 'Who's that?'

'That's Penny.'

Jac expected her to continue, but she didn't.

'Got anything to eat?' she asked.

'Sure,' Amy said, like she was surprised or embarrassed by her
lack of hospitality. She placed her glass on a lacquered timber
side table and made for the kitchen. 'I baked some sugar-free
cookies this morning.'

'I don't have much of a sweet tooth.'

Amy turned and gave her a droll look. 'They're *sugar-free*.'

She shook her head no.

Amy opened a corner pantry. 'Biscuits and cheese?'

Jac grimaced.

'Pasta bake?' She said it like a joke.

'Yeah, okay.'

Amy closed the pantry. 'Didn't you eat dinner?'

'Yeah, but that was, like, an hour ago.'

She watched from the far side of the island bar as Amy considered what was left in the baking dish on the stovetop. Amy rested a spatula halfway along and raised her eyebrows for approval.

Jac made a move-it-along gesture with her hand until she'd moved another five centimetres. 'Don't worry about heating it up,' she said. 'It'll still be warm enough.'

Amy transferred the pasta onto a plate, her tongue catching between her teeth, and dug out a fork from a drawer. 'You're weird.'

'I like to eat.'

'I can see that.'

Jac pulled her phone from her back pocket and placed it on the bench. 'I'm going to wash my hands.'

In the guest bathroom off the hallway, with its tessellated tiles in warm creams and burgundy, she turned on the hot tap and took off her rings, placing them on a small glass shelf above the pedestal basin. She considered her reflection in the round, bevelled mirror. What was she doing here? She felt like she'd snuck behind enemy lines in a stolen uniform.

No, she told herself, she was there for a friendly chat and a break from her family. That's all. It was fine.

She pumped soap from a ceramic dispenser and lathered her hands under the warm water. The bedroom had an ensuite, so this bathroom, she figured, was for guests; there was nothing of Amy's visible. No cabinet to snoop in or perfume to smell.

By the time she returned to the kitchen, Amy had collected her glass from the lounge area and was leaning against the stove. 'You alright?' she asked.

''Course.'

Back on her stool, Jac took her first bite. The pasta was good, maybe a little heavy-handed on the pepper for her liking, but still delicious. They sat in silence, Amy watching her eat.

'Is Gil a good cook?'

'Yep,' she said through a mouthful of pasta.

'Just as well.'

Jac pointed to the plate with her fork. 'This is tasty. You made this?'

Amy nodded. 'How is it being back?'

'You already asked me that.'

'A whole day's gone by since then.'

Had it only been a day? It seemed longer. 'It feels like home, but it also feels like . . . I don't know.' She shoved another forkful of food into her mouth so she wouldn't have to complete the thought.

'Like you don't belong?'

She nodded.

'I know I've never gone anywhere,' Amy said, 'but belonging is a decision. I don't care if it's a book club or your job or whatever. You belong if you say you do.'

Jac licked red sauce from the corners of her mouth. 'Nothing's changed really. I felt hemmed in as a teenager and it kind of feels the same now.'

'And when you're home in the city? How do you feel there?'

She loaded more food into her mouth because she didn't want to admit that she felt exactly the same way in Sydney. Maybe Pent wasn't the problem.

'It's a wonder you're not the size of a house if you eat every time you don't want to face something.'

She pretended she didn't catch the subtext in Amy's comment. She wasn't there to discuss Gil or Ma or her dad's suicide attempt. 'Fast metabolism. I hardly do any exercise.'

Amy drew in a breath as if to say something but held back.

Rather than meet Amy's eyes, Jac scanned a row of matching powder blue canisters along the benchtop near the stove. They descended in size and were labelled *Flour*, *Sugar* and *Coffee*. Everything about Amy's place felt warm and homey.

'Are you out?' Jac asked. 'At school?'

Amy ran her tongue over her teeth. 'I don't broadcast it. But I don't hide it either. I've never wilfully deceived anyone.'

Jac wondered if that was a dig at her.

'The world today is so . . .' Amy began. 'Everyone, women *and* men, seems to be struggling with themselves—who they are, who they should be, how they should act, the public persona and the private—more than ever.'

Jac kept eating, settling in to the rhythm of Amy's voice. Amy used to be so passionate about *everything*—the human genome, oil spills, the Iraq War, veganism—and it was nice to see Pent hadn't squeezed all the life out of her.

'I read a study,' Amy went on, 'that found women are at their most confident at age— Actually, you tell me. What age do you think?'

Jac wiped her mouth with the back of her hand, thinking about when women might finally get past all their insecurities and start feeling comfortable in their own skin. For her, it felt impossibly far away. 'Sixty-five?'

'Try nine.'

Jac raised her eyebrows.

'Isn't that sad? After that, we start to worry too much about what other people think of us. We're not free to express ourselves for fear of being judged. Bit like the way you won't dance in front of anybody.'

'That's because I have no rhythm.'

'So? It only matters that you feel it.'

Jac shrugged, not agreeing but not wanting to get into a big thing about it.

Amy drained the last of her drink, crunching into a piece of ice. 'How is it spending time with your brothers?' she asked. 'You were quite a trio on the dancefloor last night.'

Jac swallowed the last mouthful of pasta and placed the fork in a slant across the plate. 'Dane's . . . the same. Still doing what he's told.'

'Blaise?' Amy said with a smile in her voice.

Jac smirked back. 'Ngaire. And, yes, I do see a pattern. Josh is struggling, but he won't talk about it. It's so unfair what's happened to him.'

Amy scoffed. 'Him? What about that woman?'

'People just assume he did it.'

'Didn't he?'

'I don't know. I wasn't there. But no one seems to care about the truth. It's as if it's irrelevant. The accusation is enough. Tried and convicted. People get an idea about you and it sticks.'

Amy stared at her then, silent, as though waiting for something.

Jac continued, if only to fill the void. 'It's not how it's supposed to be. Whatever happened to innocent until proven guilty?'

'I'm not sure he could ever prove his innocence.'

'Like that woman could ever prove his guilt.' She picked up the fork again and scraped up the last remnants, then pushed the plate to the side. 'Thanks.'

Amy acknowledged this with a nod but wasn't finished with her sermon. 'It's not a man-bashing thing, Jac. The same thing would happen to *anyone* in *any* workplace. If a student accused me of something inappropriate, I'd be gone. Stand down first, investigate later. Not that an investigation would make any difference; I'd be tarnished forever. Who would hire me?'

'Don't you think that's wrong?'

'What's the alternative? They couldn't exactly let me keep teaching. The parents, the board—there'd be an uproar. It's not a courtroom. It's the real world.'

'Yeah, well, it sucks. And Josh is left hung out to dry.'

'Maybe this'll be a wake-up call for him.'

'Amy . . .'

'Maybe he'll think about his wife and child next time. Although I imagine it's his career he's more worried about.'

'Amy!'

'Most men probably don't even realise what they're doing,' she said. 'They know there's a gender pay gap, they know sexual harassment and violence against women is wrong, but they just can't see the link between their own behaviour as individuals and those bigger gender issues.'

'I'm sure that's— Let's change the subject, shall we?'

'Fine.' Amy took the plate and left it by the sink. 'When's the big day?'

Pasta churned in her stomach. 'I think I liked the last subject better.'

'Second thoughts?'

'No, not really.'

Amy gave her a penetrating look.

Jac downed the last of her whisky, the ice cubes cooling her lips. She would have liked another, but she still had to drive home. She needed something to shore her up for this conversation.

'It's not Gil,' she said. 'He's wonderful. But with Dad in hospital, and being so . . . unstable. It doesn't feel like the right time.'

'Maybe it's the perfect time. For the family, at least. Something to look forward to.'

Jac angled her head to the side. 'I don't know.' She rotated her glass on the benchtop, smearing condensation.

Amy pointed at a pair of plank chairs in tan leather in the lounge area. They could have been brand-new or fifty years old; in the lamplight it was impossible to tell.

Jac collected her empty glass from the benchtop and lowered herself into the one furthest away. 'You've changed your tune since last night,' she said.

'About?'

'About me getting married.'

'If it's what you want.'

'It is.'

She hadn't made the decision to marry Gil lightly. She knew she'd be giving up one thing to get another. And it wasn't like she was swindling him; they didn't have any secrets between them. Well, maybe *little* ones. But didn't every couple?

Amy crossed one long leg over the other. 'You don't have to decide anything right now. Your dad will come out of it—'

'Tomorrow, maybe. They're bringing him round.'

'Great, so your dad will come out of it, you'll get him some help and then you can go back to your veiled life.'

'My life isn't *veiled*,' she protested.

Once, during one of her many moments of vulnerability, she'd asked Gil why he'd persisted with her. 'All those walls up?' he'd said. 'I knew they must have been protecting something pretty special.' She knew right then that she would disappoint him.

'Do you have any friends where you live?' Amy asked now. 'Close friends?'

'I've got . . .' She squirmed in her chair, although it was surprisingly comfortable. 'There are people.'

'So, no.'

She didn't respond. Of course she had friends. People she caught up with for dinner from time to time and people she followed on social media.

'There's nothing wrong with keeping a low profile,' Amy said. 'But you don't need to shut yourself away. Isolation isn't good for anyone. Take a lesson from your dad.'

Jac had already grown tired of everyone prematurely diagnosing Dad. 'He's not isolated. That wasn't— *isn't* the problem.' Not that she actually knew.

'You don't have to be alone to be lonely.'

Jac held up her glass, shaking the small lumps of ice that remained intact. 'You don't run a very good bar here.'

What was she doing? She usually made a point of not getting drunk around people she was attracted to.

Amy bowed her head in assent. 'A thousand apologies.' She heaved herself out of her chair and took both glasses to the cart.

Jac got up and followed. As Amy bent over the cart, instinct took over. She reached out and placed both palms flat on Amy's back. She could feel her bra under the hoodie.

Amy turned and their faces were only centimetres apart. Jac could smell the whisky on Amy's breath and something inside her thrummed. She leaned in, but Amy ducked away.

'Sorry,' Jac said.

Amy blew out a puff of air. 'I'm not the one you should be apologising to.'

Jac's mobile vibrated on the countertop. She craned her head to see Josh's photo on the screen. Probably good timing, really. At least she didn't have to look Amy in the eye.

She crossed the room and swiped right. 'Hello?'

'Where are you?'

She risked a glance at Amy, who was facing the cart. 'Out. Why?'

'You need to meet us at the hospital,' he said in a voice he was fighting to keep steady. 'Dad's dead.'

SATURDAY

17

Josh's legs shuddered, his head pounded, and he thought he might pass out. His heart was on the verge of ignition. After a three-month hiatus from running, it was like his body had lost all memory of physical exercise.

He pushed his way around the lake, one burning foot in front of the other. He'd been a runner in high school, but now he was twenty kilos heavier and his breathing was laboured. The icy air burned his nose as he inhaled and blew out in short, sharp bursts.

He'd woken early, the sky colourless outside, but he knew he wouldn't be able to go back to sleep. He turned over a few times, moved his head to a different position on the pillow, even tried ditching the pillow and sleeping on his stomach. His mind wouldn't stop; it replayed the same images over and over. Dad driving at that wall. The smash of the car, the crack of his head against the steering wheel, then it flopping backwards, lifeless.

Josh pictured him alone under the bridge, smoke billowing from the bonnet, blood seeping from a gash above his eye. Dead. This was not how it happened, of course, but it didn't stop his brain from imagining it that way.

Now it was seven. The sun was up, but the sky had a dull greyness that made it feel colder than it was. He hadn't packed running clothes as such, but a pair of sneakers, trackpants and a hoodie did the trick. He'd lowered the brim of a Boston Celtics cap over his eyes and took off into the gloomy morning. Caps, beanies, sunglasses—he owned a lot of these things. Items that helped to shield him whenever he left the house.

He picked up speed as he passed the old bandstand and the car park where he used to bring girls when he first got his licence. Up ahead, he could see the old rowing clubhouse. It had been converted into a cafe. Yellow light glowed from inside, where two young guys placed small vases of flowers in the middle of each table. They'd retained the rowing theme, a bright red boat suspended from the ceiling and crisscrossed oars adorning the walls. The outdoor tables were empty, the tops shimmering with dew.

He'd clocked the changes in Pent over the years since he'd left—some, like the youth-focused street art, with a kind of humouring dismissal; others, like the addition of a state-of-the-art gym, with genuine curiosity—but it was the arancini and cannoli bars, the trained baristas and the annual wine and cheese festival that signalled bigger changes. You think you know all there is to know about a place, but then you discover depths you didn't realise existed. Transformation is possible.

He jogged around the second bend, again picturing the scene under the bridge. Dad was dead. He would never see him again. It didn't seem possible that he couldn't just pick up the phone and call him, no matter how stilted the conversation might be.

He rarely felt the inclination, but now it was the only thing he wanted to do, and it made him feel wobbly inside. But what would he say? Sorry for letting their relationship fizzle and die? Sorry for behaving like a spoiled brat?

A pair of wood ducks glided across the silvery surface of the lake, three babies trailing behind. But Josh faced forwards, not able to watch what became of them. Would they flit off in different directions? Or stick together, in a line, facing the future as a family?

The last time he'd spoken with Dad was the day he moved into Kelsey's flat. The pilot light on the gas hot-water service had snuffed out, and relighting it was an exercise in patience that he couldn't mobilise. The sun had bleached all colour from the instructions on the inside panel, the print on the sticker crinkled to an indecipherable blur. YouTube tutorials on the subject didn't make sense.

'And you're turning the knob to "Pilot"?' Dad had asked down the phone.

'For the third time, it's a picture of a spark and, yes, I *can* follow simple instructions.'

'Doesn't sound like it. Are you sure you're holding the button down long enough?'

'Yes, Dad! Thirty seconds.'

'Maybe the gas is disconnected or shut off at the meter?'

Jesus. 'I said that, like, ten minutes ago!'

'Alright. A bit of gratitude wouldn't go astray.'

'Forget it. I'll work it out myself.'

He was about to end the call when Dad spoke again, taking one last chance to disparage him. 'City living's made you soft.'

'Maybe no one ever took the time to teach me these things.'

'Like you would have stood still for five minutes to learn without that bored look that never left your face. At least Dane listens. He knows how to thread a whipper snipper and replace a spark plug.'

Vital life skills. 'I'm sorry I wasted your time.' He hung up and called a plumber.

It was another version of the same conversation they'd been having since Josh hit puberty, each blaming the other for the fractured state of their relationship. Now it would never be resolved.

He jogged on, his thighs on fire. Break through the pain barrier, he thought, then he'd hit his stride. When he finished, he'd drop to the footpath for some push-ups and a couple of rounds of stomach crunches. Then, back at the house, he'd dust off his dumbbells.

This was what he used to do: when times were tough, when life was taking a big shit on him, he'd run. It was his go-to brain cleanser, his anger-buster. But for the past three months he couldn't even do that. The outside world was too overwhelming. This felt like a reversion.

As he heaved himself forwards, his mind turned to Jac. She'd been a mess at the hospital the night before. They'd had to drag her out of there in the end. When they got back to the house, she'd gone to her room to call Gil but then hadn't come out for a while. When she did, her eyes were blotchy and red. Dane had stayed and they'd had a few drinks. Josh had raised the question of what next, but Dane and Jac had shut it down.

He couldn't run anymore and slowed to a walk, even though it was only three-point-eight kilometres around the lake. In high school he would run it three times in a row without breaking a sweat. Now he was struggling to get around once. He should have brought his phone so he could listen to music. That would have helped take his mind off the pain in his calves and thighs.

He decided that breaking up the pace might help. He switched to high-intensity intervals—better for fat-burning. Short, hard bursts of work followed by brief breaks. The breaks were probably longer than they should have been and the hard bursts not so hard, but he kept at it.

During one of the slow sections, a woman approached from the other direction, running slowly, dressed head to toe in black lycra. Her body was tight and lean and a blonde ponytail jutted out from the back of her Nike cap. He made eye contact as they neared each other and he gave her a neighbourly nod; he didn't want to draw attention to himself with anything more. As she sailed past him, he drew in a deep breath of air through his nose, hoping to catch a whiff of her. She smelled like freshly laundered clothes and it was the most comforting smell he could imagine.

People didn't approach him as much as they used to—they probably didn't recognise him now his appearance had altered. Although that didn't stop him being hyperconscious of every person whose eyes lingered too long or who held a phone in his direction, even though they were probably only taking selfies or a pic of the streetscape behind him.

Once, at the height of *Relationship Rescue*'s success, when the show was smashing it every night in the ratings, fans would stop for a selfie and ask about the contestants. What were they like in real life? Were they still together? Was that fight between Dakota and Ava real or just for the cameras?

It was annoying. But it wasn't. He missed that now—now that he was overweight, jobless and potentially about to drop dead from a heart attack beside Pent's famed lake.

His body started to overheat and so he used that as an excuse to slow down. Didn't want to overdo it on the first day. All Ma needed now was for her son to have some kind of seizure. He unzipped his hoodie.

He could smell his sweat, ammonic and rancid. God knew what was seeping out from his pores—three months of beer, takeaway curries and two-minute noodle spice.

He'd nearly finished one lap when his knees began to ache. It wasn't worth starting another. He imagined taking one of those tests to determine your biological age and finding that he'd already reached forty, even though he was only twenty-eight.

Then an idea struck him. Maybe he could turn his fight back to fitness into a reality show? *Josh Vanderbilt: The Road Back*. No, that sounded like he was stuck out in the wilderness. Or maybe it *would* be a good idea to embrace his predicament? Maybe people would respond to that? *Josh Vanderbilt: Fighting Back*. No, he wasn't a boxer. *Josh Vanderbilt: Reinvented*. No. *Reignited*.

Maybe.

Revamped. Not bad. He liked the sound of *Vanderbilt* and Re*vamped* mashed together.

Or maybe *Remade*. Any one of those would probably work. He'd mention it to Kelsey when they spoke next. They could work up a proposal and pitch it to a few networks.

Wait. Why the hell was he thinking about this now? His dad had just died, for fuck's sake.

He slowed to a walk. It was busier at the lake now, though it was only thirty minutes since he'd arrived. Across the other side, which was only about fifty metres away, the cafe's first customers were arriving. He stopped at a park bench and reached out a hand to steady himself while he stretched. Given how out of shape he was, he'd be sore the next day if he didn't.

He thought again about the reality TV idea. He couldn't help it. Maybe he could start working on a proposal of his own before talking to Kelsey about it? It would be good to have some more fleshed-out ideas first. He'd been front and centre on two hit shows that had ended before their time. That had to count for something. He could do it again.

His breathing returned to normal. He'd achieved more in the hour he'd been out of bed than he had in three months. And it had only just gone seven.

He looked up. A few rays of sunshine were trying to peek through the clouds.

18

Jac and Ma sat at the kitchen table in their nightwear, too exhausted even to shower. They clutched coffee cups, although the steam had long dissipated. The blinds were still down; the day was trying to leak through the edges but they wouldn't let it.

'We'll have to start calling people,' Ma said.

Jac stared into the black of her cup. 'Why don't you post something on Facebook?'

'*Facebook?*'

'People do that.'

'No, I don't think so.'

Last night, after spending half an hour hunched over Dad's dead body, they'd come home to a cold house. Jac hid in the bathroom, where she'd sat on the edge of the freestanding tub, the stench from the hospital clinging to her clothes, watching her tears pool on the gunmetal-grey tiles. After twenty minutes of that she'd called Gil. He said he'd come to Pent as soon as he could. Probably Tuesday. Definitely before the funeral.

She'd needed to be alone then. Her brothers had coaxed her out of her room for a drink, but when Josh wanted to talk about burial versus cremation, she'd gone to bed. Speaking about Dad's death meant it was real. Undeniable. So she'd lain there, crying, listening to the sound of rainwater dripping through the down-pipes. On one level, she was fully aware of it, but a part of her still believed it hadn't happened. That Dad was still in a coma and that he would recover and come home. Maybe there was a small pulse somewhere in his body that still beat?

'Josh,' Ma said now, a lilt of surprise in her voice.

Josh had shown up silently in the kitchen while Jac's mind had been AWOL.

'I didn't know you were up,' Ma said. 'Have you been out?'

The exercise gear should have been her first clue.

'Went for a run around the lake.'

'Oh.' Confusion contorted her face, as if she didn't quite understand what he was saying. 'Good.'

Josh grabbed a small glass coffee cup from the counter, set it under the spout and launched the machine. He opened the fridge, grabbed the milk and gave it a shake. 'We need milk. I'll do a shop.'

He splashed milk into his cup and left the carton on the counter.

'Don't take Edmundson,' Ma told him. 'They're doing road-works. And avoid Parker. They're putting in those extra-wide speed humps on the corner of Dundee. It's a nightmare. Honestly,' she said, more to herself than to her children, 'I don't know why people have to go and change everything all the time.'

'Okay.'

'I rang Gil,' Jac announced. 'He's coming for the funeral.'

Ma glanced at Josh. 'Have you called Jordan?'

'Not yet. But I will.'

Josh sipped his coffee.

'Can you still pay bills at the post office?' Ma asked out of nowhere.

'Yeah, I suppose so,' Josh answered.

'There's one on his desk.'

'Don't worry about that now, Ma.'

'It might be overdue.'

'I'll take care of it.'

Ma pitched her head to one side and exhaled. 'Thank you, darling, but I'll have to learn.'

'Don't worry,' he repeated. 'You want food? I can make eggs?'

She shook her head.

'Jac?'

Jac's thoughts were elsewhere—at the hospital, the night before. 'How did this happen?' There was accusation in her voice. 'I mean, we were told that he was *out of the woods*, that it was just a *matter of time* until they woke him up. They were going to bring him out of it! How do you go from *that* to . . . *dead*?'

The doctor had stood there, hands clasped behind his back, talking dispassionately about the possibility of a broken piece of bone rupturing a blood vessel in Dad's brain, and she'd pictured a small shard cutting through nerve tissue.

'I guess they can never predict it for sure,' Josh said. 'Things go wrong.'

'*Things go wrong*? He was in a hospital, for crying out loud.'

Josh didn't respond, instead taking another sip of his coffee.

'We should request a post-mortem,' Jac said.

The hospital had offered an autopsy the previous night—something they did for all unexpected deaths, the doctor said, but it was clear from his tone that he thought it was pointless, and the family had agreed. She should contact them before it was too late.

'What's that going to achieve?' Josh asked.

Jac's eyes widened. 'Make them accountable.' Wasn't that obvious? 'Prove that he died from something they could have prevented.'

'It won't bring him back, Jac.'

Jac turned to him. 'No, but it might stop it happening to the next person,' she said, voice raised. She glared at the table, muttering under her breath, 'Incompetent fucks.'

She was burning with anger. Why? Why, why, why? That question wouldn't leave her alone.

19

Dane gripped the banister, descending the stairs from his bedroom to the kitchen. The twins sat shoulder to shoulder at the table behind broken domes of soft-boiled eggs in sky-blue cups. Ngaire stood at the kitchen counter—a mess of envelopes, school notices and store receipts—bent over her iPad.

'Morning, everyone,' he said.

The boys looked up from their plates. 'Morning, Daddy,' they said together. They wore matching football jerseys and their hair was still messy from bed.

Ngaire straightened. 'You're not going into work, are you?'

He usually wore tracksuits on the weekend, or his gardening pants to mow the lawn, but this morning he was in khakis and a long-sleeved polo.

'Yep.'

'But it's the weekend.' She lowered her voice so as not to alert the twins. 'And your father.'

He, too, kept his voice low. 'I have to start calling people to let them know. I'd rather do it from the office.'

'*Okay*. But . . .'

He knew what she was going to say—about all the things he had to do. Cut the grass, take the boys to Auskick. *Have to, have to, have to.*

Ngaire caught his eye and motioned to the twins with her head. *You have to tell them.*

He pulled out a chair and sat. Marcus was most of the way through his egg, with only one piece of buttered toast soldier to go. Dylan had barely started his.

'Boys . . . Pa's . . .' He squinted at Ngaire, who widened her eyes for him to continue. How did you explain to five-year-olds the concept of forever?

'You know Pa's been in hospital, right?' Dane said.

Marcus nodded.

'Well, it turns out he was sicker than we thought.'

Marcus continued eating his egg and Dylan took a sip of apple juice.

'Boys, can you look at me, please?'

They looked up.

'Pa died last night.'

Dylan's face changed, becoming inquisitive. 'How do you know he's dead, Daddy?'

'The doctor told me.'

Marcus returned the last piece of his toast to his plate and brushed crumbs from his fingers. 'But now he won't be able to come to our game tomorrow.'

'No, mate. He won't be able to come. But we'll all be there.'

'Josh too?'

'I hope so.'

He hadn't taken the boys to see Dad in hospital. He didn't

think he'd be there that long and he didn't want the boys to see him like that. Maybe he should have taken them. Or maybe it was better that their memories of him would be all about soccer games and sleeping over on weekends. One day he would have to tell them the truth about the way their grandfather died, but that was a long way off.

Dylan pinched a length of toast between two fingers and held it over his egg. 'We won't be able to see Pa ever again, will we, Daddy?'

'No, Dylan. We won't.'

The realisation of this, that he would never see Dad again, punched him in the stomach and tears pricked his eyes. He scraped his chair backwards and climbed the stairs to the bedroom.

He sat on the bed, staring at the doors that led to the ensuite and walk-in robe. His eyes stung, pressure swelled in his head and all strength left his limbs. Dad wouldn't be at the soccer game tomorrow. He wouldn't be in the office on Monday. He wouldn't be anywhere on any day ever again. It would just be him now. The only Harding man left in Pent. He would have to look after Ma, he would have to look after the family business and he would have to go on without the anchor of his dad.

The weight of it all suddenly felt suffocating and his airways constricted. He bent over and buried his head in his hands.

'Are you okay?' Ngaire asked from the doorway.

He shook his head and she lowered herself onto the doona beside him. She wrapped an arm around his shoulders and eased his forehead onto hers. He inhaled the smell of coffee from her breath and they stayed like that for a minute.

'You be alright today?'

'Yeah.'

She broke away. 'What time are you heading into work?'

'Soon. I have to keep things going for Dad.'

'But today?'

'What else am I going to do?'

He sensed a list coming.

'Don't forget I've got my writers' group this afternoon.'

'Hmm.'

'I guess I could ask Zach's dad to take the boys to Auskick,' she said to herself. 'Can you get wine on the way home? The Weismans like pinot, but I've—'

'Cancel it, would you?'

'Dinner? I've already bought the seafood.'

'For Christ's sake, Ngaire, my dad just died!'

She didn't speak for a moment and he couldn't bear to look at her. Then she said, 'I guess I could freeze it.'

Dane was surprised to find Leigh, in gym gear and a cap, unlocking the office door when he arrived twenty minutes later.

'What's up?' Dane said.

Leigh's body jolted, his head whipping towards Dane. 'Holy fuck! You scared the crap out of me.' A flush crept up his face.

'What are you doing?' Dane asked.

'Nothing. Just leaving actually.'

Oh, he was *locking* the door.

'You don't have the girls this weekend?'

'Nuh.'

Leigh's wife had divorced him a year ago and moved their daughters to Shepparton. He'd kept the family home in Pent, but buying her out had stung him financially.

'Can you stay for a sec?'

Leigh checked his phone. 'Sure. What are you doing here?'

'Let's go inside.'

He led Leigh to the conference room, which felt unnecessarily formal, but their normal desks seemed somehow not respectful enough for the news he had to break. The office had a strange energy. Even though Dad had been away for almost a week, his absence now was different.

Seated in the conference room, Leigh looked as though he had eaten something rotten, placing his phone and keys on the table. 'What's going on, Dane?'

'Dad died.'

Leigh blinked. 'What?'

'Last night.'

Leigh slumped forwards, leaning on his elbows, then looked back at him, maybe hoping that he'd got it wrong or misheard.

Dane sucked in a breath. How many more times would he have to deliver this news before it felt real?

'Jesus.' Leigh got up and stood for an uncertain second before clapping his hand on Dane's shoulder. 'That was unexpected, wasn't it?' He removed his hand.

Dane nodded. 'We were told he was going to be fine. Well, physically, at least. And then last night, I s'pose he . . .'

Leigh reached for the table, wrapping his hand around the edge. 'How's Blaise?'

Dane shook his head. 'In shock, I guess. Like all of us.'

Ma's demeanour the previous night had been an odd mix of stoic silence and manic organisation. While he, Josh and Jac sat around drowning their grief in a bottle of merlot, Ma set about cleaning the house. 'People will be coming over,' she'd said in a state bordering on panic. They'd appealed to her to join them, but she kept saying things like, 'What else am I going to do? Sit around thinking about it? Crying about it?' *Yes!* But there was no use in arguing, so they'd let her be.

Josh, meanwhile, was silent, burying his emotions in his drink, and Jac just seemed annoyed. Angry, even.

'Man, I can't believe it,' Leigh said. His eyes flitted to his phone. 'What are we going to do?'

He meant with the business. It was a fair enough question, if slightly premature, but this possibility had been on his own mind since he'd found out the car accident wasn't actually an accident.

'We'll keep going,' he said. 'That's what Dad would have wanted.'

'I'm with you all the way,' Leigh said. 'I just can't believe it,' he repeated, wrapping his arms around his chest like he was hugging himself. 'Let me know if you need anything. Really.'

'Maybe we could start with an update on all the projects you're managing?'

Leigh hesitated. 'Now?' He shot another glance at his phone and car keys on the table, suddenly eager to be somewhere else. 'I mean, sure. If that's what you want.' Another pause. 'Don't you want to be with your family today?'

'Rather be busy right now,' he told Leigh. 'I'll feel a lot better if I know things are under control here.'

Leigh rubbed his nose. 'I understand. Let me check on a few things and I'll come back to you with an update. Give me twenty?'

Back at his desk, Dane called Gayle to break the news, but she already knew. Her ex-sister-in-law worked at the hospital. Then he called the other staff. Jan was at the supermarket and Olivia didn't pick up. He didn't leave a message.

The office was quiet without the usual noise of Gayle's radio, the printer churning out pages and people talking on phones. And it was cold without the heater on; he was glad he'd grabbed a fleecy windcheater from the stack in his walk-in robe.

He checked his emails, his eyes moving to the one from Adam, the real estate agent. He hadn't replied yet, and now the timing wasn't right. He couldn't abandon Dad's business, not now; they were committed to the St Augustine's development, which had two or three years of work to go.

Twenty-five minutes passed before Leigh approached Dane's desk with his notebook and a pen. 'Should we just do it here?'

'Sure.'

Leigh grabbed his chair and rolled it closer to Dane's. 'How'd the calls go?'

Dane tapped his pen on the desktop. 'Couldn't get on to Liv.'

'I can't believe it,' Leigh said again. 'It's just so . . .'

'I know. Bring me up to speed, would you?'

Leigh talked for the next ten minutes about his various projects—the community hall refit, the kindergarten extension, the new kitchen and bar area at the bowls club and the highway restaurant.

'And St Aug's?'

'Nothing new.'

Something about his off-handedness made Dane's muscles twitch. Dad had been on edge about it too, overseeing the finest details of marketing, poring over schematic drawings, taking long meetings with council. It wasn't only the dollar value but the milestone of building Pent's first apartment block. That prestige was important to Dad, and now it was Dane's responsibility to uphold it.

'Maybe I should meet with council about it,' Dane suggested.

Leigh's head jerked up. 'What for?'

'I don't know. Just to confirm everything's okay.'

'It's under control,' Leigh said, giving each word equal weight. 'Don't worry.'

But he did have to worry. He had to shoulder all the worry now, and something about Leigh's tone troubled him. 'I'm sure you have. But just the same, I should probably make an appearance,' he said.

'The permit's practically issued. Do you ever make an appearance when they're rubber-stamping permits for your new rumpus rooms or pergolas?'

Dane bristled but let it go. 'No.'

'So what's the difference?'

'The scale, for one. Plus, it's probably time I got to know the players a bit better.'

Leigh gave a small smile as if he were humouring Dane. 'If we were at the start of the process, I'd agree with you. But this is all about the paperwork now. There's nothing left to discuss. Let's wait for the next one, okay?'

He nodded. It wasn't worth arguing over today. 'How many sold now?'

'Still only thirty-three. Well, thirty-three buyers have put down their two-grand deposit,' Leigh clarified.

'But that's refundable, right?'

'Or it goes towards the first instalment.'

'Which is due . . .?'

'Monday week. They'll come into the sales office, pay the first instalment and sign the paperwork. But we need at least thirty-eight sold—eighty per cent—before we can start, otherwise we won't get the capital to begin construction.'

'Got it.'

Dane nodded and Leigh stood to leave.

'Oh, Leigh?'

The other man hesitated.

'I know you've got a bit on,' Dane said, 'but I might need you to look after a few of my projects as well, if that's okay.'

'You taking some time off?' He struggled to keep the hopeful inflection out of his voice.

'No, but— I'll give you the Catoggio file for starters. And maybe the Caluzzi extension.'

'No probs. Whatever you need. But we'll have to get someone else in, you know that, right?'

He did. Without Dad's support, and with Leigh having to work on St Augustine's almost full-time, they'd need another project manager. Would Dane move into Dad's office? He would have to learn the business side of things. Or maybe they could hire a general manager? Too many decisions too soon. He couldn't think about that now.

Leigh disappeared through the foyer, the glass door making a muted thud as it closed behind him.

Dane's eyes cut to Dad's empty chair. They lingered there a moment before he got up and walked to Dad's office. The door had been left open for the past few days, but it still had a faint scent of him.

The room felt empty now, like a display home staged with furniture that no one ever used, and when you opened the wardrobes, they were bare.

Dane ran his finger along the expansive desk, the same one from which Dad had run the company for twenty years. The laptop was positioned at the edge, which was unusual. Dad liked things a certain way, and he always left it in the middle of the desk. Had somebody been using it? Maybe the cleaners had moved it.

He walked around the perimeter of the desk, wheeled the chair along the midnight-blue carpet squares and sat.

Dad's smell was imbued in the leather, and grooves had worn in the arms from his elbows. On the desk sat a photo with Ma taken maybe five years before at a local function. They weren't smiling as such, but their faces were relaxed. Content.

When had Dad stopped being happy? Was he ever really happy? He seemed to be. He got pleasure out of golf and his role at the council. Winning a new contract at work also buoyed his mood, and the company was doing better than ever. What did he have to be unhappy about? Sure, he would get down from time to time, but that was just him. Dane knew to leave him alone, and the next day he'd be back to normal. Maybe he should have asked more questions. Perhaps Dad had been teetering on the edge of a cliff for years.

Sitting in Dad's throne for the first time filled him with a strange unease, his body stiffening. It felt intrusive or opportunistic, as if he were trying to step into his father's shoes while his body was still warm.

Dad, he realised, had never properly involved him in business planning or talked to him about his vision for the future. He'd never taken him to one side and talked strategy or sent him on any management courses. He'd never even invited him to a meeting with their accountant or lawyer. Technically, Dane was a director of the company, but that was only on paper. Ma was too. It was all for tax reasons wound up in a family trust or something—financial arrangements he didn't fully understand. He supposed Dad had thought this day was so far off that he didn't need to involve him. Plus, Dane never expressed any real interest in learning the business because his job always felt temporary.

Returning to his own desk and laptop, Dane opened his inbox and scrolled down until he found the email from Adam Sergeant.

He ticked the message and clicked delete.

20

Jac parked the Toyota on Bolton Street under the shade of a jacaranda choked with shin-high weeds at the base. She cut the engine. Her eyes burned after a sleepless night and her stomach felt not sick so much, but unsettled, as if she were nervous about something. A constant pressure pushed at the insides of her skull like there were too many thoughts, too much emotion to fit inside.

She squeezed the steering wheel until her knuckles turned white and tears stung her eyes. It was true. It happened. She took in a breath, willing the banging in her heart to subside.

The police would have to examine the car now, she thought. Now that Dad could no longer be interviewed. She would drop into the police station that afternoon.

She loosened her grip on the wheel, noticing that she wasn't wearing her rings. She must've left them on the bedside table last night. It was still a novelty, wearing an engagement ring, but she wasn't usually *that* forgetful.

She stepped from the car, locked the doors with the remote and walked three-quarters of the way along a shared driveway to unit number two, where a jade plant in a glazed pot and a fat cherub statuette guarded the front door.

She'd found Gayle's address in Ma's floral telephone book. It was a neat villa unit in a block of three—probably built in the eighties, judging by the caramel-coloured brickwork and arched opening for the roller door.

Jac pressed the doorbell. Gayle had downsized after her kids left for university and her husband left for a Pilates instructor. Stan hadn't been a wealthy man, narrowly making ends meet as the owner of a key-cutting-cum-shoe-repair place that didn't seem like a viable business even in the 2000s. And half of nothing didn't go far. Why a younger woman would be interested in him eluded her. He was handsome enough, but what else could he offer? His only contribution to Gayle's life seemed to be eating her food, spending her money and belittling her in front of strangers.

Footsteps shuffled down the hallway towards the front door and Gayle's face peered out from the thin, curtainless window that abutted the entrance. She opened the flyscreen dressed in a quilted dressing-gown buttoned to the top and slippers, which explained the shuffling footsteps. Without speaking, she seized Jac by the shoulders and pulled her into an embrace. It was a frantic kind of hug, as if she hadn't held anyone in a long time. 'I'm so sorry, Jac.'

Jac wasn't surprised Gayle knew—the bush telegraph flowed well in Pent.

'Me too.'

Gayle released her grip and dabbed her reddened eyes with a tissue. 'Come in.'

Gayle stepped to the side, and Jac passed through the doorway.

Inside was warm and white. The timber flooring was bleached light grey, the walls pale. Even the artwork was all muted tones: ships coasting past watercolour sunsets; bamboo huts rising up a mountainside; elephants frolicking under a peach sky.

As Gayle led her through a compact entranceway into a combined dining and lounge room, Jac's phone vibrated in her pocket with a message. She ignored it.

Gayle gathered a mess of papers from the coffee table and cleared away a smudged wineglass in a hasty attempt to tidy the place.

None of the furnishings looked more than a year or two old. It felt like a fresh start.

'I love your unit,' she said.

'IKEA and Kmart,' Gayle confessed with a faint smile. 'It's amazing what you can do with a few cushions and a bright throw rug.'

It was odd seeing Gayle without make-up. Her face seemed to have aged in the two days since Jac saw her at the hospital, although her hair was so thick and so straight that she couldn't imagine it ever looking anything but flawless.

Gayle suddenly stopped her fussing and stood before Jac, like she was unsure of what to do. She took Jac's hand in a tight grip, and began to cry. 'I truly can't believe it,' she said.

Jac squeezed back. 'I know.' And her tears started to come too.

'I'll make tea.'

Jac tilted her head back, steadying herself with a long exhalation. She couldn't remember the last time she'd cried in front of another person before the previous night. Had she ever? Not anytime as an adult that she could recall.

While Gayle had her back turned preparing the tea, Jac checked her phone, finding a message from Amy.

Hope you're doing OK. Get in touch if you need to talk. xx

Almost immediately, her phone flashed with a second message. *BTW you left your rings in my bathroom.*

Jac texted Amy back: *I'm OK. I'll swing by this afternoon.*

Reply: *Won't be home. Will leave in an envelope behind the screen door.*

After she'd received Josh's call the night before, Amy had offered to drive her to the hospital, but she'd declined. She didn't cry at Amy's and she didn't cry for the whole shaky drive to Wangaratta. It wasn't real then. It wasn't until she saw Dad that it hit her.

In the kitchen, Gayle turned. She was holding a silver tray with tea things. 'If you're here for answers, Jac, I'm afraid I don't have any.'

Something deflated inside her. Of course that's the reason she was there. All night the questions had swirled around her head as she burned with silent rage, knowing the only way to extinguish it was to find out the answer to that question—why.

Jac watched Gayle pour tea from a plain white pot, nudging a plate of shortbreads across the table with her other hand. 'Milk?'

She shook her head.

It was warm for September and Gayle's courtyard was dotted with bright annuals in glazed pots. A wattle tree, bursting with yellow blossom, hung over the fence from next door, shedding its foliage into a pedestal birdbath.

'Do you mind if I ask what the cause of death was?' Gayle said without diverting her eyes from the spout. 'I couldn't get any details.'

Jac bit into a biscuit. 'A brain haemorrhage.'

Gayle closed her eyes and compressed her lips as if trying to ward off physical pain. She passed over a dainty yellow cup without a saucer. 'I just can't *believe* it,' she said again. 'Less than a week ago he was fine. At least, I *thought* he was fine. I couldn't have been more wrong.'

'You know about the not-so-accidental accident?'

Gayle nodded.

They didn't speak for a moment, then Jac asked, 'Was he— I mean, did he ever . . .?'

Gayle shook her head. 'He got in moods sometimes. Not angry moods; kind of down moods. But I never thought . . .' Gayle let out a breath. 'I've been thinking about it nonstop since I heard. Looking back, wondering if I missed the signs. I think about the morning before the crash, but there was nothing. He was a bit frustrated after a meeting with Leigh, but that was normal.' She shook her head. 'This church project . . . he was so invested in it.'

'What's going to happen with it now?'

'Dane will manage it, with Leigh's help. Half the town wants the damn thing gone and the other half are up in arms. It's a no-win.'

Dad must have felt that rising tide of adversity from the town, she thought. She made a mental note to get Dane's take on it.

'I keep replaying my conversations with him over and over,' Gayle went on, 'trying to find some clue, wishing I'd asked if he was okay.' She exhaled again. 'But he *was* okay. He was good, actually. But maybe I wasn't looking hard enough. I don't know.'

Jac knew what she meant. She, too, had been replaying their last conversations in a loop, searching for any indication that something was wrong.

'It's funny, the things you reflect on,' Gayle said. 'You know, for all his success, I don't think he ever truly felt proud of himself. It was like his successes were a surprise or a relief rather than a true achievement. He never gave himself enough credit.'

Jac processed this in silence. She thought back to the self-help books lining his bookshelves and the index cards inscribed with affirmations. *I'm on the path to being someone I'm equally terrified by and obsessed with. My true self.*

'I found these little cards in his desk at home,' she said. 'They had inspirational quotes. He had a lot of motivational books, too.'

Gayle nodded. 'He was always looking for answers.'

'What were the questions?'

Gayle rested her teacup on the glass tabletop. 'The big ones, I guess. The meaning of life, why he was here.'

It's not who you are that holds you back, it's who you think you're not.

Gayle continued. 'Now I think about it, he'd been spending more and more time on his own. He'd disappear during the day for hours. I don't know where he went. People would tell me they'd seen him sitting in his car at the lake just staring across the water. I honestly didn't think anything of it. In fact, I thought it was probably good that he got away from the office and had some quiet time alone. I realise now that those quiet times probably weren't very reviving.'

She pictured Dad sitting at the lake in that Jaguar he loved so much, just . . . staring. She wished she could visit him there now. To ask what was wrong. To turn back time and reverse what had happened.

She hadn't noticed a little white dog lying in a padded basket near the back door until it got up stiffly, sluggishly, to change positions. She was glad Gayle had company.

'What did you mean at the hospital when you mentioned disappointments with the council?'

Gayle reached for a shortbread but then changed her mind. 'There was some bad business going on there,' she said. 'I never got the full story.'

'You mean there was there a technical glitch somewhere in the Pent grapevine?' she joked.

Gayle smiled. 'Apparently. A modern-day tragedy.' Her smile fell away. 'It was something to do with the election of the new mayor. I think Stephen wanted to nominate, but something stopped him. He didn't talk about it. I'm not exactly sure what went on behind closed doors.'

'Who *would* know?'

Gayle considered this for a moment. 'Maybe Damian?'

'Davenport?'

The other woman nodded. 'He works at the council. They played golf every week.'

Jac sipped her tea, watching a bird land on the cap of the paling fence briefly then fly away.

'How's your mother coping?' Gayle asked, then said, 'Sorry, that's probably a stupid question.'

Jac shrugged. 'She hasn't said much.'

'Maybe you two will become a bit closer now?'

The thought of herself and Ma being close, of sharing things, not bumping heads. It seemed unnatural. 'I don't know.' And then she asked, 'Did you two ever . . .? I mean, you and Dad?'

Gayle's eyes crinkled around the edges as if she was fighting to hold in a smile. 'I wanted to.' She let out a rueful sigh. 'God, I've never admitted that to anyone, probably not even myself. But he was far too good a man for that. He worshipped your mother.'

It's amazing, Jac thought, *that you can be so close to someone and yet see things so differently.*

'If only he had told someone how he was feeling,' she said.

Gayle rested her chin on a closed fist. 'Who would he tell? He certainly wouldn't have spoken to his friends at the golf club about it, or anyone at the council. He wouldn't have wanted to seem weak or out of control. He didn't have many, or maybe *any*, real friends, come to think of it. And I'm sure I don't need to tell you that your mother's not the most compassionate listener.' Gayle shook her head, chastising herself. 'Sorry, that sounds like I blame her for this. I don't. Stephen must have been more troubled than any of us realised. He hid it well, but I can't shake the feeling that I should've seen the signs.'

If only . . . It took up so much space in her brain she wondered how she would ever think about anything else. 'Me too.'

'Strange thing was, he seemed great at the start of the week. I remember thinking that he must have had a good weekend, because on Monday he was content. Relaxed, even. Better than I'd seen him in ages. I meant to ask him about it, but work was busy and'—she shrugged—'you know how it is. And then on Tuesday night . . .' She shook her head.

Jac sipped her tea. 'How do you think you'll go working for Dane?'

Gayle rested her hand on the table. 'Oh, fine. Dane's easy, if a little anxious. He'll be okay. I was planning on retiring at the end of the year; I'd spoken to Stephen about it. But not now. I couldn't do that to Dane.'

'He'll deal with it.'

'I'm sure he could, but just the same, he'll have enough change to cope with without me adding to the mix. Hawaii can wait.' She tried to summon a smile but failed.

As she said goodbye at the front door, Gayle touched Jac's forearm like at the hospital. 'Jac?' A sheen of tears varnished her eyes. 'You were his favourite. Did you know that?'

Jac's bottom lip quivered. She did know that, although he'd never said it in so many words. It was in the way he always took her side in an argument, the way he'd put up with her petulant teenage moods, and the way he seemed to worry about her the most of all his kids. 'Yeah. I knew.'

But whose favourite would she be now?

As she turned to leave, Gayle gripped her shoulder. 'He loved everything about you, Jac. *Everything.*'

She nodded her understanding. Dad had heard all the things she did not say.

Jac went home via the police station, where they agreed to have the car checked over. At Ma's, the house was quiet. In the study, she found a box sitting on Dad's desk, *Jacinta* scrawled across it in Ma's writing. The red lettering advertising the removal company had faded and a thin sheet of dust from years sitting uncovered in the garage coated the top.

She tore off the thick brown packing tape and peered inside, flecks of dust floating to the floor. She recognised its contents instantly as the things she'd left behind when she'd moved out—bits and pieces of random stationery, her Year 12 school diary, some books, photos in an unsealed manila envelope and odd pieces of clothing. She was surprised at how much of herself she'd abandoned.

She cringed at a hat she used to wear all the time in her teens: a stone-coloured fedora with a dark-brown band. She'd bought it because she'd seen a photo of David Bowie wearing something similar. But now, picturing herself in it all those years ago, heat rushed to her cheeks. The thing was ridiculous—on her, at least. No wonder she was the object of ridicule.

Her eyes fixed on a blue flannelette shirt with the sleeves cut off. That it was still in one piece defied belief, considering how often she'd worn it. Wash, wear, wash, wear. Unfolding it now transported her to another time, and another person. The eighteen-year-old Jac; the Jac who, on the outside, didn't take any shit, but was constantly trembling on the inside.

She peeled off her pale green jumper and dragged the shirt over her head without undoing the buttons, just like she used to. The musty smell of history embedded in the fabric wafted up her nose, making it tickle.

She was wearing this shirt the first time she kissed a woman. It was in the coolroom at Tink's. Her name was Mackie and she was at least ten years Jac's senior. Mackie's lips were dry and her breath blasted cigarette smoke. At first, Jac did nothing; she might have even kissed her back a bit, but then she pulled away, feigning outrage.

'What did you do that for?' she'd asked.

Mackie grinned. 'Didn't you like it?'

'No! I'm not . . .'

She shoved Mackie aside and ran out the back door, past the rubbish bins and two smoking kitchen hands, to hide behind her Lancer. She'd lied to Mackie; she did like it.

It was strange, that time in her life, because at Tink's women only liked women. It wasn't that simple for her. And why did she have to decide? It was so fuzzy in her eighteen-year-old brain.

She'd loved that shirt but it reminded her of when she'd been most uncomfortable in her own skin. At times, she'd even hated who she was, and what she felt inside. And that hurt had radiated out all around her.

Dad knew, and sometimes over the years he would try, delicately, to draw it out of her. 'Are you happy?' he would ask over the phone. 'I'm fine,' she would say back, graciously, letting him know that she appreciated his concern but that she didn't want to discuss it.

She yanked the shirt back over her head. Picking at the scabs of her past wasn't going to help anything. She forced the shirt to the bottom of the box and closed the lid.

Lying on the fold-out, she could almost believe that Dad would come through the front door at any minute and that the last few days would dissolve into a bad dream. Only yesterday she was holding his hand in hospital.

Who else could she speak with? Who else could unjumble what was going on with him? Gayle had suggested Damian Davenport.

She rolled off the bed and opened the left-hand desk drawer, remembering the spiral-bound address book.

It wasn't an address book, she discovered when she peeled back the plastic-coated cover, but a notebook. Three or four loose sheets slipped from the lined pages to the desktop—printouts of articles from the *Pent Gazette* about St Augustine's Church. There was one about it ceasing services and the priest leaving town, another about a poll asking readers what to do with the site. On the pages of the notebook itself, Dad had pasted clippings, more recent and also from the *Gazette*—the property sale to Harding Construction, community outrage, artists' impressions of the planned apartment block, pushback from the local historical society. There were pages of them, filling the first third of the notebook. Some articles, too long for one page, crinkled where they were glued to the paper underneath and then folded over to fit.

The last two-thirds of the exercise book were empty, except for the last page, which contained a list of four names, in Dad's handwriting, all with dollar amounts after them:

Wayne Harper	*$25,000*
Mike Vincent	*$35,000*
Peter Harman	*$30,000*
Damian Davenport	*$20,000*
TOTAL	**$110,000**

The only name she recognised was Damian's. So who were these other guys? And what did the money mean? Was Dad in financial trouble?

She pulled out her phone to snap a photo of the list. Dane might be able to shed some light.

She opened the book so it was flat on the desktop and lined up her shot, but an envelope on the desk was in the frame, so she pushed it to one side before taking her picture.

Then she had a thought. She snatched up the envelope and tore it open. It was a phone bill, with large red letters emblazoned across the page. OVERDUE: FINAL NOTICE.

What did this mean? That Dad hadn't paid the bill . . . or that he *couldn't* pay the bill?

Maybe Dad was in more trouble than any of them realised.

SUNDAY

21

Dane found Josh in the garage, sitting on a worn leather couch at the far end, staring at rows of large plastic tubs stacked high on metal shelves. Each tub was methodically labelled with printed A4 pages sticky-taped to the front—*Christmas decorations, Electrical, Garden, Files: 2000–2010, Files: 2010–2020, Tax.*

'Hey, Josh.'

Josh turned and Dane got a good look at his brother. Under the flicker of the fluorescent tube, his face was ashy and drawn. Dane tried to intuit what Josh might be thinking. 'Ma said you were going through some of your old stuff.'

'She asked me to.'

Next to Josh's couch, three moving boxes with his name scrawled on the top sat unopened on a wide strip of carpet that had once covered the bedroom floors. He wondered what could be in them, considering Josh's teenage bedroom was still intact. 'Doesn't look like you got that far.'

'Didn't know where to start.'

Dane sat on the matching two-seater opposite.

'Ma's on a cleaning spree,' Josh said. 'Should have seen her yesterday—rearranging the linen press, the pantry, God knows what else. A cleaning cyclone.'

A continuation of her behaviour from the night Dad died.

Josh kept talking. 'Some of her friends came by, like, an hour ago, so the garage was the safest place.' Josh's expression changed—he'd remembered something. 'Ma's got some food for you to take home. We won't eat it all.'

'Who's it from?'

'Friends, neighbours. Ma reckons she's never met half the people in the street, but they've obviously heard the news.'

Dane gazed at the shelves and an image of Dad lying in a cold steel locker blew into his mind. *Stop it. Just stop it.* He looked around, trying to refocus, his eyes settling on his old exercise bench upended in the corner. He sucked in a breath, drawing in the faint smell of petrol fumes and fertiliser, and wondered what Dad would ponder when he sat out here staring at the rows of tools suspended on the walls and the boxes of nails, screws and cleaves, all in neatly labelled cubby holes.

'How was soccer?' Josh asked.

'Okay. They lost. Not that there's an official score.'

'Sorry we didn't come.'

Dane waved a hand in dismissal. 'I get it. It's fine.'

It was hard enough for Josh to go out in public at any time, let alone when everyone would be on him offering their condolences. That's why Dane had watched the game from his car.

'You okay?' Dane asked.

'I think so.' Josh nodded, but Dane wasn't sure which of them he was trying to convince.

Neither spoke for a moment.

'You?' Josh asked—to crack the silence, it seemed.

'I guess. Haven't wrapped my head around it yet.'

'No one expected it.'

'And that's the kicker. You think they're going to be okay and then all of a sudden . . .'

Josh picked at a frayed piece of fabric on the inside edge of the couch. 'I had some good times on this couch, when it was in the lounge room and no one else was home . . . Lizzie Meyer, Jessica Edrees, Lena Koutoufides . . .'

Dane pressed his palms to his knees and heaved himself off the squelching leather. He opened the fridge—another piece of furniture that had started in the house and finished in the garage after an upgrade. Everything rejected ended up here.

'Want a beer?' he asked.

'Sure.'

Dane spoke into the white light radiating from the fridge. 'Dad's only got that low-carb crap out here.'

'That'll do.'

Dane twisted the top off one, tossed the cap into an old ashtray and handed it over.

Josh angled the bottle, pointing the lip at Dane. 'Cheers.'

Dane, too, held his stubby aloft, then lowered himself back onto the couch, allowing the silence to press in. He sipped his beer. The taste was surprisingly not awful.

'Went for a run yesterday morning,' Josh said.

'Good work. How was it?'

'Almost killed me.'

Dane touched his stomach. 'I need to get back into exercise. It's finding the time.'

'Time's not my problem.'

Josh took a mouthful of beer, as if underlining the real issue.

'I wonder what Dad used to *do* out here,' he said. 'It's so clean. None of the tools look like they've been touched in years.'

'Just sat probably,' Dane said. 'With a beer. Like we're doing now.'

'On his own?'

'Grandpa Vanderbilt did the same thing,' Dane said. 'You wouldn't remember. He'd sit in his big tin shed in the backyard drinking VB, smoking Winnie Blues and staring at his veggie patch in the quiet—as far away as possible from Grandma.'

'They didn't like each other much, did they? Grandma and Grandpa.'

'Can't remember one saying something to the other that wasn't cutting.'

'That explains a thing or two about Ma. And I always thought *we* were the problem.'

Dane narrowed his eyes at Josh. 'She loves us. She just doesn't know how to— She loves us.'

Dane stretched his neck from side to side, as if working out a crick. Then he thought about their family, the Hardings and the Vanderbilts, and the straight lines pencilled from one generation to the next. 'All families have their own . . . stuff,' he said. 'They're like secret societies.'

Sometimes Dane wondered what gene pool he'd swum out of, not seeing either of his parents in his own personality. Then he thought of something he'd said to Dylan a couple of days before.

'Why are you smiling?' Josh asked.

Was he? 'I was just thinking about how you believe you're nothing like your parents, or you don't wanna be, but then . . .' He clicked his tongue. 'I caught myself saying, "Because I said so" to Dylan the other day. Remember when Ma used to say that all the time?'

'Hated it.'

Dane took a long chug of his beer. He had so many questions for Josh. He wanted to ask about Dot and how it felt to miss her, about being someone who everybody knew, and about what really happened with that reality show contestant. But he didn't ask any of it because he didn't want the stillness of the garage to turn into the Cherry Tree on Josh's first night in town.

'I wanted to be a talent agent,' Dane said instead. 'Did I ever tell you that?'

'You?'

'Sports management.'

'Thought you wanted to be an AFL star?'

Dane shook his head. 'Wasn't good enough.'

Josh glided his hand through the air like a plane and then crashed it into the arm of the couch with appropriate sound effects. 'And the legend dies.'

Dane turned away, looking around again at the Harding memories that no longer belonged in the house, thinking of a time in his life when the most complicated decision he had to make was whether to handball or take a shot at goal, or which top to wear to a party.

'What happened?' Josh asked.

Dane studied the label on his stubby. 'I got into the course. I was all set to move to Melbourne. Then Ngaire got pregnant. We decided to get married, so I had to get a job.'

'So you went to work for Dad?'

'It was only supposed to be temporary.' He shook his head. 'I didn't even like construction.'

'Who would?'

'Yeah,' he said to himself. 'Who would?'

He'd been trying to leave for years but something always kept him there—loyalty partly, finances mostly. First, when he got engaged, he had to save for a house, then there was the mortgage, then multiple rounds of IVF, then the twins came, now Ngaire's two-year 'sabbatical'. There was never a right time to take a financial leap of faith.

Josh leaned over, resting an elbow on his knee. 'Dane, you know you can sell it if you want. I mean, I don't want to speak for Jac and Ma, but I'm sure they don't want to own a construction company either.'

Dane kept peeling at the label until it ripped. 'I couldn't do that to Dad. It was his life's work.'

'Yeah, *his* life.'

He jerked his head up. 'I'm not you, Josh. I can't just walk away.'

Josh let the slur go through to the keeper. 'Who would care?'

He exhaled. 'It's not that bad,' he said, like his take on the low-carb beer. Maybe it would surprise him? 'The construction business is as good as any.'

'No it's not. It's boring.'

Dane lifted one shoulder then lowered it. He didn't mind boredom. He wasn't expecting to go to work and be thrilled by it every day; no job was like that. It was just that he wasn't contributing to anything truly worthwhile. He wanted to bring people together; that's why he wanted to open a bar.

Josh spoke again. 'Maybe you could keep the business but change it to suit you. Concentrate on big jobs, like those apartments. Or just do small, private stuff. Whatever.'

Dane closed his eyes. He couldn't think about it now.

'*Or* . . . this could be the break you need. Go open your pub. Think about yourself for once.'

'That's just it, Josh—I can't,' he said, his voice brimming with frustration. 'There is no *myself* anymore. I've got a wife, kids. And I owe it to Dad.'

Josh shook his head. 'You and I are so different.' He let out a strange laugh. 'Maybe that's why you've still got a marriage.'

Dane didn't want to discuss those things—not the business, not his marriage, not his future—because none of it was panning out as he'd imagined. So they sat again in the quiet, Dane looking at a row of paint tins, all lined up in height order, as if they'd just been brought home from the hardware shop and never opened. 'I wish he'd talked to someone,' he said.

'It's not that easy,' Josh answered. 'And in a place like Pent? There's no anonymity, and that would stop a lot of guys.'

'I guess.'

'That's another tick in the city column—people leave you alone. Usually.'

Dane sensed the gap between him and Josh widen and, again, he felt the need to close it. 'No, man, that's what's *good* about Pent. Your neighbour's sick, you make them food and buy their groceries. Some old dear needs her house painted and everyone pitches in. At least, that's how it used to be.'

'And now?'

'It happens. But, I don't know, the feeling's changed. People are busy, obsessed with the day-to-day, worried about themselves first and foremost. It's like these massive speed humps they're building. You know—on the corner of Parker and Dundee?'

Josh shook his head.

'They're at the start of the intersection, so people in wheelchairs and electric scooters can cross the road easier. Anyway, they'll only benefit a few, but they're a good thing, right? Because they're for vulnerable people.'

Josh shrugged. It was clear he wasn't following.

'But everyone's whingeing—the traffic hold-ups, the congestion, the *inconvenience*. Not a thought for those who'll benefit. It pisses me off.'

'Same thing would happen in the city. Worse. People would be ringing up the radio, posting stuff on social media.'

'That's the city. It shouldn't happen here.'

Dane loved that Pent was changing—becoming a modern place where young people wanted to live—but there was a trade-off. Some parts of city life, of city thinking, should stay in the city.

Josh lifted his feet, resting them on a box edge. 'Did Dad ever talk about me?'

'Sure.'

'What did he say?'

Dane sipped his beer. It was almost finished. 'I don't know. That he'd seen you on TV or at an awards show or something. He loved Jordan and Dot. He was proud of you.'

'Liar.'

'He was!'

'He never told me.'

'You're not Robinson Crusoe there, mate.'

One of Dad's sayings.

'Maybe he wasn't proud of either of us. Bet he told Jac.'

'I doubt it. He wasn't like that. Doesn't mean he didn't feel it.'

'Did you feel it?' Josh asked. 'From him?'

Dane picked at the last of the bottle label. 'Not always.'

He thought about what Josh had said about the business. Maybe he *could* scale it back; he didn't want to have to manage people like Leigh anyway. Keep it small—only jobs he could take care of himself. He could close the office and work from home, like they did during COVID. He could set up a proper study—Ngaire on one side of the desk and him on the other. They'd both be there every day when the kids got home from school.

Maybe that could work. Maybe there was a compromise somewhere in all this that he could live with.

'So what were you going to call it?' Josh asked.

'What?'

'The pub.'

'Oh. Doesn't matter.'

'Tell me.'

Dane leaned forwards. 'I hadn't actually decided yet, but something to do with the boys. *Twins. Two Blond Boys* maybe. Or *Marlan's*.'

'Marlin's? Sounds like a fish-and-chip shop.'

'L-*A*-N. The first half of Marcus's name and the second half of Dylan's.'

Josh nodded. 'Cool.'

'But it's not going to happen now. Not for a while, at least.'

He held up his empty bottle to Josh and Josh nodded. Maybe the low-carb beer wasn't as good as the real thing, but he had to think of the long game.

22

Josh sat at the table rotating his empty coffee mug with one hand, the crumbly remains of supermarket apple pie and vanilla ice cream smearing the bowl in front of him. Between the four of them, they'd polished off the whole pie for dessert. They'd cut it in eight. Ma had reluctantly finished her eighth, Dane had eaten his in about three mouthfuls, Jac had gone for seconds (even though she was always saying that she didn't really like desserts) and he ate the rest. There was no point letting it go to waste. And those frozen pies were always light on filling anyway.

After Ma's friends had left at around two, they had made an unspoken decision, the four of them, to spend a quiet afternoon at home, although it turned out not to be so quiet. The phone rang repeatedly, and when the phone wasn't ringing, it was the doorbell with flower deliveries. Two people brought food. Jac went for a walk around the lake and Ma sat in the lounge staring at the image of her younger self above the fireplace. Josh himself hardly moved from the upstairs couch, watching Netflix with Dane and resting his aching legs.

Now, Jac nudged her bowl aside. 'We should talk about the funeral.' She looked at Ma. 'Did he ever mention a funeral home or any other preferences?'

'Tyler's Funerals. They're the best.' Ma began to stack the bowls and Dane stood to help. 'Your father played golf with Anthony Tyler.'

Dane cleared Josh's bowl. 'Wouldn't he want to be cremated?'

'Yes, he did,' Ma said, looking surprised by her own certainty.

'We should ask the funeral people over,' Jac said, tossing her paper napkin, scrunched into a ball, onto the table.

'I'll call,' Josh said.

Jac and Dane both looked at him oddly. Ma was in the kitchen rinsing dinnerware under the tap.

'What? I don't have anything else to do.'

Suddenly, pain skewered his chest and he drew in a sharp breath through his teeth. He'd eaten too much. Or maybe it was yesterday's run. Too hard, too soon. No, it was probably indigestion. Ma was serving him big plates of food and he was eating everything.

The pain disappeared as fast as it had arrived.

Ma came back to the table, drying her hands on a tea towel. 'We'll have the wake here.'

'Ma,' Dane began, 'there'll be so many people. Where will we—'

'He would have wanted it here.'

Josh wondered how she could've known that, but Jac did the asking for him.

'Would he?' she questioned. 'There must be a place in town that could—'

'No. Here,' Ma said with finality.

'Okay,' Jac said. She raised her eyebrows at Dane. 'Do you know any good caterers?'

'Look in the local paper,' Ma said. 'Wait.' She held up a finger. 'I think the cafe in the square does it. Actually'—she rested her finger on her chin—'Awatif from yoga used someone for her fiftieth. *That* was at home.'

Dane tapped the tabletop repeatedly—tap-tap, tap-tap, like a dripping faucet. 'We'll have to write some stuff down for the funeral people,' he said. 'For the eulogy.'

Ma grabbed a notepad and pen from beside the home phone and placed them in front of Jac, who opened to a fresh page and started dictating for everyone's benefit.

'Stephen Giles Harding was born on—'

'We should talk about his service to the community,' Dane interrupted.

'Okay,' Jac said. 'We'll get to that.'

'And about his golf. He loved golf.'

'Yep.'

'Then there's his work. He built up a—'

Jac ripped a page from the pad and handed it to Dane. 'Why don't you make a list?' She overplayed a smile. 'In silence. And we'll get to it all later. Let's just do the basics for now. Ma, have you got another pen?'

Jac kept writing, but this time without the narration. She looked up after a moment. 'Was James Street his first house or the one on Baldwin?' she asked Ma.

Ma shrugged, handing a spare pen to Dane.

'Does it matter what street he lived on?' Josh asked.

'Of course. This is his eulogy—a record of his life.'

'Don't we want to tell stories?' Josh asked. 'Like, share memories? They can publish his life story in the newspaper.'

'I don't think they do that anymore.'

'In Pent they do,' Ma said. 'The *Gazette* will do a story. No question. Well, they *should*.'

Josh tried to pin down a memory but images whipped past him in a blur, like cards being shuffled in a casino.

Dane looked up. 'I've a good story. Once, when I was at footy . . . I think we were playing Greenview at home.' Dane looked at the ceiling. He tapped the table with the pen. 'No, it was against Fish Creek. Anyway. It was the third quarter—no, the fourth . . .'

'You were playing footy,' Jac said. 'We get it. What happened?'

'I was coming to that. It was the fourth quarter and we were down by . . . um, let's call it three points. I think it was about three points.'

Jac mock-snored and Dane gave her a look.

'It was right on the siren and I'd taken a speccy about forty metres out. I pulled up my socks, flicked some blades of grass in the air to check the wind conditions and began my walk towards the goal, slow at first then—'

'Dane!'

Josh got up and headed for the ceramic jar at the end of the bench while Dane described, in microscopic detail, his run up to goal. Josh lifted the suction lid on the jar. Party mix, caramel buds, freckles. He gave the jar a shake. No black cats.

'Anyway,' Dane continued, 'it sailed across the top of the right-hand post. I thought it was a goal, but the ump didn't agree. He put up one finger, but before he could reach for the flag, Dad had grabbed both and was swinging them like a crazy man above his head.'

Jac had pretended to fall asleep and Dane gave her a shove with his hand.

She opened her eyes theatrically, as though startled. 'Sorry,

Dane. I hung in there for as long as I could. And in case you're interested, I gave up right around the time you first mentioned football.'

'Seriously?'

'I gave up right around the time you first mentioned football,' she repeated, this time in a more serious voice.

Dane looked to the sky for strength.

'Mate,' Josh said, 'that story's not really about Dad.' He took two milk bottles and tossed them in his mouth.

'Dad was there.'

'So were a hundred other people, probably.'

He replaced the lid and wound his way around the bench back to the table.

'I've got one,' Jac said. 'Remember that time when Dad took us snorkelling at Moonlit Bay and we—'

'I know what you're going to say,' Dane said. 'It was Jacksons Cove.'

'No,' Jac insisted. 'It was Moonlit Bay. I distinctly remember—'

'It was Jacksons Cove,' Ma said flatly. She stood at the breakfast bar dunking a teabag into a delicate-looking cup. 'The time when he fell off the pier?'

'Yeah. Wasn't that Moonlit Bay?'

'No.'

'Thank you, Ma,' Dane said.

Ma picked up her tea. 'I'll find Awatif's number.' She walked out.

'It was Moonlit Bay,' Jac said, her voice losing its edge. She glanced at Josh.

'Don't look at me. I was probably in a pram then.'

'What about the time he bought that cheap sunshade tent thingy from the Reject Shop and it collapsed as soon as the first gust of wind hit it? That was *definitely* at Moonlit Bay.'

'Yeah, that time it was,' Dane said. 'He was never very good at constructing things like that, which was weird considering he was a builder.'

'*That* was the problem,' Jac said. 'He thought he knew everything and wouldn't read instructions.'

'No self-respecting man does,' Dane said.

'Gil does.'

Josh again racked his brain for a story of his own, something worthy of a funeral speech, but he came up blank. All his memories of Dad felt like fleeting exchanges. Talks at the dinner table, questions about school and grades, pressure to join a sporting team to 'build character' and his father's insistence that he get a part-time job as soon as he turned fifteen. Most of his memories were observations—watching Dad come and go, talking with *other* people. Very few involved him actually conversing with Dad. By the time Josh was acting, Dad was probably sick of cheering from the sidelines. Dane's footy and Jac's horse shows had been enough. Or maybe he just wasn't interested.

The pain returned to his chest and he gave it a little rub.

'What's wrong?' Jac asked.

'Nothing. A bit of indigestion.'

'We should have fruitcake at the wake,' Jac said. 'Lots of fruitcake.'

'It's not Christmas, Jac,' Josh said. 'No one likes fruitcake, anyway.'

'Dad did.'

He wanted to point out that Dad wouldn't be there to eat it, so it would be a waste, but he didn't. He kept rubbing his chest.

'Old people like fruitcake,' Dane said.

The pain knifed him again and he clutched his chest with both hands. Was he having a heart attack? Was that what was happening? At twenty-eight?

'Josh, your face looks . . .' Dane began. 'I'll get you some water.'

Jac slid her chair back and came around beside him while he rubbed hard circles over his rib cage.

'What's going on? Is it worse? Are you getting shooting pains down your arm?'

He shook his head. 'Just give me a sec.' He tried to take in deep breaths, to quell whatever angry reaction his body was having.

Dane handed him the glass of water. He took a few sips and gave it back.

'How do you feel now?' Dane asked.

The pain had subsided to a dull ache but wasn't altogether gone. And his whole body was pulsating now, like after sex. It was as if every tiny capillary was throbbing. 'It's okay, I think.'

'Are you sure?' Jac said. 'Should I call an ambulance?'

'It's okay now,' he repeated.

'Maybe it was a panic attack?' Dane offered. 'The stress of the funeral and everything?'

Jac cupped her chin in her hand, then, when it started to shake, took it away. 'You better go get checked out,' she said. 'Want me to drive you to the hospital?'

'No, no. I'm better now.' But whatever it was, it couldn't have been good. Stabbing pains in the chest weren't nothing.

'We should go,' Jac insisted. 'Ma couldn't stand to lose her husband *and* her favourite child in the same week,' she said light-heartedly.

He closed his eyes, tried again to concentrate on his breathing. 'I think I'll just go to the local doctor. I'll see if I can get in tomorrow.'

'Let's go to Dr Sampson,' Jac said. 'I'll take you.'

'Is he still alive?'

'Yep, and he prescribed Dad tablets, which proves he knew about his depression. He's going to get a piece of my mind.'

'Jac, calm down.' Josh held up his hand. 'You can't go around blaming everyone.'

'I'm not *blaming* anyone—well, not *everyone*. Don't you want to know what happened?'

'No. I mean, I *do*, but . . .' Josh's face felt heavy, as though there was a weight pulling at his chin. 'His pain was too much. That's what happened.'

'What pain? What *caused* this pain?'

'I don't know. We'll probably *never* know.'

'But—'

'I'll go to the doctor's on my own.'

He rubbed his chest again, wondering what was going on inside. Maybe drifting into the next world while he slept that night would be the best outcome for everyone.

Josh relocated to the lounge to get away from all the talk about family holidays and how involved Dad was in Dane's life.

The room was lit by a flickering candle and Ma was on the couch with her teacup cradled in her palm. The scent from the candle sweetened the air—a flower of some kind—and Harry was curled up in a tight ball next to her. It was only then he realised that she hadn't come back to the kitchen. Maybe it was getting too much for her as well.

'Finished already?' she asked.

'No, I just needed to . . .' He sat in the easy chair. 'Dane and Jac know more about him than I do.'

Ma nodded, sitting with her thoughts a moment. 'We had a good life together, you know, your father and me. You get to know someone pretty well over forty-odd years. You can sense when . . .' She trailed off. 'But then you get so used to them that the way they . . . it becomes normal—the ups and the downs—and you don't . . .' She shook her head of something. 'I had lots of boyfriends before I met your father. I could have had my pick.' She smiled. 'But I picked him. He didn't care that I was famous; I don't think he'd even *heard* of The Ripleys.' She held up a finger. '"Mr Wrong"—that was the song we had out at the time. Life was one party after another. But then it was nice to get away from it all sometimes. It can be suffocating, you know?' She looked up. 'Of course you know. You're the only one who knows.' She took a sip of tea then rested the cup on her thigh. 'So I followed him back to Pent—that was the deal, no negotiation. It was like stepping out of a buzzing nightclub into a quiet street at midnight.' She smiled, remembering. 'But it was my choice. I chose to walk away, to give it all up for him.'

Josh was only half-listening because he'd heard it all before. What she wasn't mentioning, he noted, was that The Ripleys (named after Sigourney Weaver's character in *Alien*) were on a downward spiral by then. Dennis, the band's manager and chief songwriter, was crippled with 'second album' anxiety and never happy with anything he wrote. So instead he wrote nothing at all. He preferred to spend his nights getting high, waiting for inspiration that never came. None of this was a secret—it was all on Wikipedia.

'I understand what's it like, Josh. Your life.' Her voice seemed to take on a clarity that wasn't there before. 'There's so much going on, people throwing themselves at you. Things get . . . blurry.'

He registered a pause in her monologue and looked up. 'What?'

She gave him one of those looks where her eyebrows joined up in the middle, as if she was deciding something. 'Nothing. Never mind.'

He hated when she tried to compare his fame to hers, as if
the world hadn't moved on since the early eighties. The worst
that could've happened in her day was that the paps would camp
out in the neighbour's bushes snapping long-lensed photos, or
a sensationalised story would run in *Woman's Day* alongside
the latest Princess Diana wedding gossip. Now, people sifted
through your digital life as if they were panning for gold—every
interview, every social media post, every photo—looking for
a glint of a time when you might have slipped up, for that one
occasion when you said something sexist or racist that, ten years
later, sounded ten times worse. She couldn't possibly understand
what it was like for him. But he didn't say that because he didn't
want to sever the one connection they had left.

'Have you spoken with Jordan?' Ma asked.

'I texted her.'

'And?'

'It's only been a few hours. She's probably busy.'

Ma took another sip of her tea. 'She's good for you, you know.'

'But I'm not so great for her. Apparently.'

Her face seemed to shrink, pleading. 'Joshua, don't give up.
Your father raised you never to give up.'

'Did he? Was that his big life lesson? I guess by the time I
came along he'd discovered that parenting was overrated.'

'Of course he didn't! He took you to . . . your stuff, and he
was always very proud of you.'

'He never said.'

She didn't respond, eyes cast into the mug, sipping her tea to
avoid the truth.

'No one in this house ever used the word love, Ma.'

She raised her eyebrows dramatically. 'Oh, now I've heard
everything.'

'We didn't.'

'Don't be ridiculous.' She didn't look at him. 'It's only a word. Just because we never told you, it doesn't mean we didn't . . .' She couldn't even say it now.

'It's a good word, Ma,' he said. 'People like to hear it.'

Something in Ma changed, a hardening of her posture, and she stamped her cup onto the coffee table. 'You think he wasn't a good father? You think he didn't hug you enough or spend enough time praising you? He taught you to be independent. Resilient. He taught you to make your own way in this . . . this apathetic world we live in. That's what's got you where you are in your career, and that's what will get you back out there again. You learned to be strong. That's a gift! You learned to rally against all the shit things the world throws at you—all the *crap*. That's what Dad gave you, so stop whining and start counting your goddamn blessings!'

Ma could have slapped him across the cheek; it would have felt the same. He touched the side of his face as if she had, and stood. There was a modicum of truth there, and it stung.

'I'm going for a walk,' he said.

MONDAY

23

Everyone was already at the office when Dane arrived, huddled around the high part of Gayle's desk that shielded the mess from visitors. Jan was crying, Gayle rubbing her back. Leigh rested his elbow on the uppermost section of the desk and Olivia, the part-time communications/marketing person, stood nearby in a plain black dress with a thin belt around her waist looking shell-shocked.

He could guess what they were thinking, and what they were feeling. The rope that had hitched Harding Construction to the dock had severed and they were all, the five of them, floating out to sea.

Gayle's eyes pegged him and she pulled away from Jan and wrapped her arms around him instead. She didn't need to say anything. They'd spoken on the weekend and she'd offered her condolences. She stepped back and Jan took her place, mewling into his shoulder. 'I'm so sorry,' she managed to get out between sobs.

'Thanks, Jan. It's okay.'

'He was such a wonderful man. Just so . . . so . . . *wonderful.*'

'Thank you.' He broke away.

Olivia, who only worked on Mondays and Thursdays, mainly in the St Augustine's sales office, touched him on the shoulder and squeezed, offering her sympathies. Leigh gave him a compassionate smile.

'Thank you all for being here,' he said.

He'd spent Sunday night rehearsing what he'd say to the staff. He hadn't planned on making his speech now, but here they all were, so the time felt like it demanded it.

The words he'd practised were more comforting than inspirational, more practical than motivational. He searched his brain for the first line, but it eluded him. 'Um . . .' If he could only remember the jumping-off point, the rest would flow. 'Um . . . Dad loved you all and deeply appreciated your support, not just for the company, but for him personally.' His mind scrambled to catch up. 'Being the family business that we are, he considered you all family and he . . . and he . . .' He lost his train of thought and stopped speaking. He couldn't remember what else he'd planned to say.

Gayle gave his hand an encouraging squeeze.

'Thank you all for being here,' he said again, 'but please feel free to go home if you like. Nothing urgent needs doing that can't wait until tomorrow.' He didn't actually know if that was true. Maybe Jan had invoices to pay or orders to settle. Maybe Olivia had meetings set up. But he had to exude confidence and give the impression of being on top of these things.

'I'd like to stay,' Gayle said.

'Me too,' Jan said.

Olivia and Leigh nodded their agreement.

So it was unanimous. Were they doing it to support him or were they worried the ship would go down with all on board? Maybe they really did have pressing work to do.

They all drifted off to their desks.

For the next thirty minutes he stared at a spreadsheet on his laptop, trying to find a way to shave six thousand dollars from a quote. He thought that $198,000 sounded better than $204,000—but did $198,000 sound too contrived? He wasn't selling cars.

He was still trying to decide when Olivia presented herself at his desk. She stood with one leg crossed over the other and her hands clasped at her waist like she was about to be photographed at a film premiere. 'Dane?' She tucked black hair behind an ear. 'Sorry to have to bring this up, but I think it's important.'

Olivia was the daughter of one of Dad's council people. She was still at uni—marketing and communications—and wanted to work in PR. She'd been with the company part-time since the start of the year, but her path and Dane's rarely crossed. She reported to Dad and worked mostly on the St Augustine's development. Dane nodded for her to continue.

'I think we should issue a press release, or at least draft a letter to all clients, to explain what's happened.'

Explain what's happened? He nodded slowly, his mind already constructing what the letter might say. *Stephen Harding died unexpectedly on Friday* . . . Or: *Following a car accident last Tuesday* . . . No, they couldn't say it was an accident when it wasn't. *After sustaining life-threatening injuries in a road* . . . something, something . . . *Stephen succumbed to his injuries* . . .

'We should do it soon, before clients start hearing it through other people,' Olivia said.

'Yep. Good call. Can you get started on something?'

She nodded. 'What do you want to say about . . . the circumstances?'

And there it was. *The circumstances.* He'd avoided the topic with clients up until now, hoping that the subject would never have to be broached in one-on-one conversation.

'Nothing too specific,' he told Olivia. 'Have a go at something, then we can talk.'

'Okay.' She fidgeted with the thin silver clasp on her belt. 'We should also include a statement about the future. We don't want clients to worry about their projects. We need to give them confidence that things will go on as normal. Well, not *as normal*, but you know what I mean.'

'Yes. Yes, we should.'

Dane Harding, Stephen's son and a long-time leader in the firm . . .

Stephen's second-in-charge, Dane Harding, will be taking over as CEO and managing director . . .

As of Friday . . .

Immediately . . .

'Dane?'

'Sorry. What?'

'What should I write about that? About the future?'

'Um . . .' It was his first big decision holding the reins at Harding Construction and it felt unreasonably heavy. Was it always going to be like this? *Every* decision? Who was he kidding with Josh's idea to scale back the business? They were committed to the St Augustine's construction. He couldn't scale back anything until that was complete.

He looked at Olivia, who was trying, unsuccessfully, to keep her face neutral. She twisted her lips, then pressed them together.

'Just say we'll be transitioning into a new structure over the coming weeks and that we look forward to the continued support of our clients through this difficult time and so on and so forth.'

'Okay.' Olivia looked through the window and then back at him. 'So, just for my own knowledge, will there be any *immediate* changes?'

She was worried about her job.

'No, Olivia. We've got a lot of work ahead of us with St Aug's. We'll all be fine.'

She exhaled, then gave a small smile. 'Okay. Good.' She pointed vaguely towards her desk. 'I'll get on to that letter.'

At lunchtime, when everyone was out, Dane stepped behind Dad's desk and sat in his chair. He could see the whole office— the reception, the six empty workstations in two rows, flowers in vases on every flat surface, and the doors that led to the kitchen and the bathrooms. That floorspace he'd occupied every work day for the past twenty years now seemed bigger than it ever had. All the blinds were open and he had the impression of the office stretching out over the square, beyond the lake and across the whole town of Pent. His father's legacy was so much bigger than what sat between these four walls. It was in the refurbished tennis club, the council chambers, the Stone's Bakery refit and the Jenkinsons' second-storey addition.

The weight of it all bore down on him; he could almost feel it pressing down on his shoulders. But he couldn't let himself be overwhelmed by the task ahead. Instead, he would focus on smaller things—the day-to-day tasks. If he did those successfully, the business would run smoothly. Then he could start looking at the bigger picture.

He looked at the workstations. He could manage a few staff. He glanced at Jan's glass-walled office. He'd get his head around the finances, too.

These small steps were like the rungs of a ladder he would climb to get where he knew he could go.

In the afternoon, and back at his own desk, Dane got stuck into the business's finances. He'd set a time to catch up with Jan the next day and would make an appointment with their accountant for the following week. He'd found the financial statements from the previous year on Dad's hard drive—balance sheet, profit-and-loss statements, summary reports—all prepared by Sam Donovan.

Leigh approached from behind. 'Why don't you go home, mate? We've got everything covered here.' He leaned on the empty desk opposite, picking up a stray paperclip.

'I'd rather be here,' Dane said. What he didn't say was that he wanted to be useful; he wanted to keep the business secure for Dad. It didn't matter that, at this particular moment, he felt like he was in a darkened room, his arms reaching out blindly for something to hold on to.

Leigh fashioned the paperclip into a straight line. There was something in the way Leigh looked at him, a crease forming between his eyebrows, that irked Dane. It was the kind of crease that let you know he was sceptical. Whether he was sceptical of Dane wanting to stay at the office or his ability to run Harding Construction in general, he didn't know.

'Did we get the building permit for St Aug's?' Dane asked.

'Came through this morning.'

'That's pretty momentous, yeah?'

Leigh nodded. 'In other circumstances we might be popping champagne, but it doesn't feel right, you know?'

Dane nodded, letting the silence speak for him.

Leigh continued. 'We got deposits for another two, by the way.'

Dane did a quick mental calculation—only three more until they reached their eighty per cent target. That was a relief. Maybe he should just let Leigh run with it and not interfere. He glanced at Dad's office, imposing with its glass walls, oversized desk and expanse of unused floorspace, and wondered again if he should move in there. It would be symbolic more than anything. It would send an unequivocal message that he was in charge now.

Maybe after the funeral.

24

Josh sat in a hard, armless chair, back against the clinic wall, staring at a gigantic ocean, a lone island poking out from the never-ending blue. Next to that picture was another island shot, this one a close-up with palm trees draped over golden sand, turquoise water lapping at the shore. Paradise had never looked so depressing, he thought, surrounded by sick, gloomy people, tattered magazines with the crosswords already done, and the buzz of daytime television assaulting his ears. Maybe he should go home. He hadn't had any more pains since the previous night. Maybe it *was* just heartburn?

Dr Sampson's rooms hadn't changed since he was a kid, although the reception desk had been updated to a taller one, clad in fake oak and with a perspex screen erected during the COVID pandemic, no doubt. The previous receptionist must have retired. Or died. She was nice, called him 'Master Harding'.

Across from him, an elderly woman of about eighty and her husband, who looked about ninety, stared blankly at a mounted television that was airing a talk show. The panellists were discussing the latest celebrity scandal—a sportsperson he didn't recognise. Judging by the content of the tweets superimposed on the screen, it had something to do with racist comments.

Two seats up from the elderly couple, a young girl swung her legs back and forth under her chair. She gazed around the room, a bored expression spoiling her face, as her grandma tried to make conversation.

He wondered what Dot was doing and how Ma would fit into her life. She'd only seen his daughter a couple of times—once as a newborn and another time when she was in Melbourne to see a musical with a friend.

He glanced at the coffee table in the middle of the room; it was barely visible under a blanket of women's magazines. Tabeetha's sullen face poked out from beneath a couple of more recent issues. *Christ.* He scanned the room, lowering the bill of his cap, then slipped the magazine out from under an old issue of *OK!* with Taylor Swift on the cover and a headline trumpeting: PREGNANT! He touched the magazine with a trembling hand, taking in the quote slapped across the top of Tabeetha's photo: 'HE RUINED MY LIFE'.

Right back at ya, sister.

He debated whether or not to pick it up. He'd done his best to avoid all media over the past few months, particularly social media. It was full of celebrities crafting an image of their perfect lives in a world he was no longer part of. It was fake anyway. Hell, he'd played that game himself—posting selfies at parties, dinners, premieres, festivals and with fans he met on the street. It was exhausting sometimes, even when you were in everybody's good books.

Everyone wanted a selfie. Everyone was *such a big fan*. But all they wanted was an image for their own social media feeds for the exact same reason he wanted them. The only time he showed up on social media now was in blurry photos taken from a distance by people wanting to photograph the car wreck that was his current life. And waistline.

The healthiest thing he'd done in the past couple of months was to shut the door on that cancerous form of self-abuse. Now he stuck to American basketball games and YouTubers who talked about American basketball.

A door next to the reception desk opened and an old guy wobbled out. Dr Sampson was behind him. 'You'll go and pick up that script now, Vin?'

'Yes, yes,' the man said, and he shuffled out the door.

'Joshua?'

Josh tore his eyes away from Tabeetha's pout and stood, extending a hand to Dr Sampson.

'I was sorry to hear about your dad, Joshua,' Dr Sampson said, ushering him into the same small office he remembered. 'He was a remarkable man.'

'Thank you.' Josh sat in the chair next to the doctor's desk.

The room was smaller than he remembered. It still had the white-sheeted examination table set up along one wall, anatomical charts pinned to a corkboard and shiny silver column scales standing like a naughty child in the corner.

'How's your mother?'

'She's doing okay,' he said. She wasn't huddled in a ball sobbing all day or anything—not that the face you presented on the outside necessarily reflected what was going on beneath the surface.

'And the rest of your family?'

'Fine.'

Josh couldn't make a guess at how old Dr Sampson would be. He'd always looked old, with his white hair, reddish cheeks and narrow waist. He wore neckties, too; Josh remembered that.

'So, what can I do for you today?'

'I've been having chest pains.'

'Just since your dad passed or before that?'

'No, only once. Last night.'

'Can you describe the pain?' Sampson asked.

'I guess my heart was beating, like, fast. Racing.'

Sampson nodded. 'Shortness of breath?'

'Yes.'

'Did you feel overwhelmed—worried you were losing yourself or had to escape?'

Josh smiled. 'Er . . . always.'

In Sampson's world, humour was in short supply. 'Sounds like a panic attack. They often come on suddenly and can pass just as quick—within a few minutes usually. We can do an ECG to be sure, but I don't think it's necessary.'

A panic attack. No tests needed. That didn't sound too bad.

'Okay,' Josh said.

'Would you say you feel anxious most of the time?'

He conceded this with a nod. He had an uneasy feeling in his stomach that never let up. He had it now. 'I've got a prescription for anxiety tablets. Diazepam?'

'I see. Have you been taking those?'

'Not much.'

'Well, you should only take them when you really need them.'

They sat in silence while Sampson made notes on his computer. He wondered about the last time Dad would've been in this office.

'Dr Sampson?'

'Hmm?' he said, without looking up from his screen.

'Do you think we could have stopped it? Talked him out of it, maybe?'

He turned now. 'Your father?'

Josh nodded.

Sampson ran his fingers through his hair. 'Maybe. But possibly only this one time. For some people, it'd be like trying to talk them out of having a heart attack. It simply wouldn't work.' He turned back to his screen. 'He was depressed, Joshua. And I suspect you are too.'

It wasn't a surprise about Dad, knowing what most people knew about depression now. His moods were so erratic when Josh was a kid—up one day and down the next for no apparent reason. But no one called it depression then. It was just Dad. Overworked. Moody.

Josh's own diagnosis shouldn't have come as a surprise either, what with the torrent of disasters in his life and his natural tendency to absorb rather than deflect setbacks. Still, it felt as if he'd failed some kind of test. 'So, what can I do?'

'Counselling, medication. We usually find a combination of the two works best. Antidepressants don't work the same for everyone, and there can be side effects. It's trial and error, mostly.'

'Okay.'

At least the diagnosis explained why he felt so shitty all the time. It was chemical. It was not, like he'd thought, because he carried a spare tyre around his waist and had to stand by and watch as his career and family imploded. He had felt like this, in one way or another, for years. Maybe it was both—biological and his flailing life.

'There are a lot of people in your shoes,' Sampson said. He hit a button on the keyboard and the printer began to whirr. He turned back to Josh. 'When I was your age, young people took drugs in the hope of discovering all the weird things in the world. Now, it seems, people take them to find the normal.'

Sampson slipped the page from the printer and signed it. He handed it over. 'I heard what happened on the TV show.'

Josh nodded.

'Have you thought about counselling?'

'I tried it, but . . .'

'You're grieving, Joshua, and I'd say you have been for a while.'

'But Dad only died a few days ago.'

'We grieve for many different reasons, and you've already suffered two big losses—your family and your career. Has anyone talked to you about unresolved grief?'

He shook his head.

'It's exactly what it sounds like, and it's cumulative. It can affect all areas of your health.' Sampson handed him the script. 'I'm glad you came. Half of men with symptoms just like yours don't.'

He wouldn't have either, if not for the chest pains, if not for Jac's insistence.

'Give it a month,' Sampson said. 'You're not going to notice any change right away.'

He held up the script. 'Can I take these with the other stuff?'

'Should be fine. I'm starting you on a low dose. Are you staying in Pent long?'

He shrugged. Today's decisions seemed hard enough. He didn't have the headspace to consider anything beyond the funeral.

'Well, go and see your local GP if the side effects get too much. But the basics are always good: eat well, exercise and get good rest. It's not ground-breaking advice, but it helps.' Sampson leaned into the back of his chair. 'As soon as you start taking control of your life, you'll begin to feel better.'

On his way out, as his first act of taking control, he snatched up the issue of *Take5* with Tabeetha on the cover, folded it once, and wedged it under his armpit.

25

Jac drove along Main Street scanning for a parking space through the spotted windscreen. She passed the Harding Construction office, at the rear of the square, without finding a park, so decided to drive around; she was ten minutes early for her coffee with Dane anyway.

On the wide footpaths that bordered the street, people walked their dogs, kids biked and women wheeled prams as if everything was normal. The town—this town that Dad had dedicated his life to improving—should have been quiet, in mourning. It was insulting the way people carried on with their lives—shopping, eating pastries from paper bags and talking on phones—as though the universe had not altered irrevocably.

She turned the corner at Edmundson, just along from the roadworks, and waited for a pair of girls in black jeans and Doc Martens to cross at a set of flashing pedestrian lights. They laughed as they walked and Jac wondered if they were really happy.

Dad probably spent most of his life pretending to be happy when, inside, there was nothing but dark clouds and desolation. That must've been exhausting.

As she passed the bowling club, she searched her mind for any signs from her childhood that things weren't okay. He used to go on fishing trips on his own and never came home with much. He said he didn't care; it was about the experience of sitting on the water. It occurred to her now that he never talked much about fishing and he didn't have any fishing buddies. Did he really go fishing? If he wasn't fishing, where did he go?

She drifted past the dental surgery where she'd had six teeth extracted in early high school, and the pharmacy where she'd done work experience in Year 10. Everything felt familiar but somehow different. Cafes set up tables on the footpath and previously blank walls were painted with luminous murals of children's faces and local war heroes. There was 'street furniture', for God's sake.

She passed the street where Amy had lived with her dad and brother. She could still visualise Amy's bedroom—pictures of Pink and the Dixie Chicks (as they were called back then) cut from magazines adorned the walls, and the crocheted bedspread smelled like Impulse body spray. It was the place where Amy had first kissed her.

Their relationship had been intense and beautiful and heated and tender. But then Amy ended it abruptly, and Jac'd had to get as far away as possible from the worst thing that had ever happened to her.

There had been others after that, but one by one she'd detached them from her life, not staying in touch with any. Not Priya the radiographer with the slight drinking problem, not Noel the skier, not Quinn the gender non-conforming disability worker, not Xavier the event organiser with two kids, and not Jenn the dog lover who was obsessed with every-thing German. It was as if she'd packed them away in a box, like that sleeveless flannelette shirt. She didn't follow them on social media and she stopped visiting places they frequented. But she didn't completely forget about them. Sometimes the good bits would replay in her mind—the way Quinn would hear a phrase, recognise it from a song, and start singing. Or how Jenn would leave funny notes—not something simple and straightforward like *Taken the dog for a walk*, but *Gone to get my arsehole bleached* or *Out cruising the high schools for fresh blood. Will send pics.*

Jac had shielded ninety per cent of these people from her family because, despite all evidence to the contrary, she did want to give these relationships a chance. But there was always *some-thing.* Quinn was a loud breather who refused to take a holiday; Xavier's ex-wife wasn't quite 'ex' enough; and Noel disagreed with her about *everything* (the yellow walls were the tip of the iceberg). Priya would have been a real contender if it hadn't been for her dislike of children. Jenn was close to perfect, but it wasn't Jac's choice to end that one.

After each of these break-ups she'd decide it was easier to be on her own. She could hook up with someone from time to time, but anything more was too complicated. But then she'd see a cute toddler in a pusher or an old couple holding hands at the supermarket and she knew she could never talk herself out of wanting more.

At the Circle Cafe, Jac stood at the counter with Dane, waiting for takeaway coffees. Her eyes swept over the glass cabinet stocked with roasted vegetable frittatas, mixed salads in large white bowls and panini with pink ham and Swiss cheese or silvery corned beef spilling from all sides. 'This is a cool place,' she said over the whir of the coffee machine. The barista, a young woman with pink-streaked hair, heated milk in a silver jug. 'Is the name supposed to be ironic?'

Dane gave her a sideways glance. 'What do you mean?'

'It's called the *Circle* Cafe and it's in a *square*. Calling it the Square Cafe would've made more sense.'

Dane shrugged indifference. 'Never thought about it.'

The barista snapped black lids on the cups and placed them on the counter. 'Here you go, Dane.'

Jac pointed to the individual quiches in the display case. 'Can I get one of those?' she asked. 'The bacon-and-mushroom one. Don't worry about heating it up.'

'Didn't you eat lunch?' he asked.

'This is a snack.'

The girl handed her a takeaway bag and Dane tapped his credit card on the EFTPOS terminal.

'Receipt?'

'No thanks, Mads.'

They passed through the door into the bright day. 'You really are entrenched in Pent, aren't you?' she said.

'Well . . . yeah. 'Course I am. What makes you say that?'

'You call the staff by name. *Nicknames*, no less.'

'I'm there every day. If I did that in the city, the same thing would happen.'

They crossed the one-way road that encased the square and walked under the gums towards a concrete bench facing the curling concrete apple peel.

'I'm not saying it's a bad thing,' she said. 'I kind of like it, actually.' Was modern-day Pent growing on her? 'It must be nice to walk down the street and run into people you know. Make you feel like you're a part of something.'

'Mostly. It has its downsides.' Dane gestured to the bench and they sat.

'Like everyone knowing you're having IVF because you've got weak swimmers?'

'Yeah, like that.'

'And the whole town knowing that the shopping centre project fell over because—'

Dane held up his hand. 'Like all that.'

She grinned, setting her cappuccino on the bench.

'But I kind of like that they know those things,' he said, as though realising it for the first time. 'It eases something, knowing you've got nothing to hide.' He twisted the cap off his coffee and licked frothed milk from its underside. 'But you don't really know them, do you?'

'Who?'

He replaced the cap. 'Anyone. We thought we knew Dad.'

She tore open the paper bag; small discs of grease were seeping through. 'We knew him.' She took a bite. *Didn't we?* 'So what's it like being the boss at work?'

Dane glanced across the square towards the lake opposite the highway. 'Okay.'

'Okay?'

'Not great, to tell you the truth.'

She took another bite of her pastry, licking oil from her lips.

'Have you ever met Leigh?' he asked. 'The commercial guy?'

She shook her head.

'He does the same job as me, except he looks after the commercial projects and I look after residential. Anyway, I can't shake the feeling that he's up to something.' He took a sip of coffee through the little spout. 'There're things he doesn't want me to see.'

'So what are you going to do about it, chief?'

The weather had taken a turn. In the distance, clouds cloaked the sky over the lake. It would rain soon.

'Don't know. He'd say I'm paranoid.'

'Could it be something illegal?'

'No.' His voice was weak. 'He just doesn't like sharing stuff with me. And I can't afford to lose him.'

'Why not?'

'Because then I'd be doing three jobs, two of which I'm not qualified for.'

'So talk to him.'

He snorted. *If only it were that easy.* 'And if he denies it? Things are already tense between us. He and Dad . . .' He shook his head. 'Anyway, rocking the boat wouldn't be my best move right now.'

Jac stretched her legs out, crossing them at the ankles. 'Trust your gut. This is how twenty-million-dollar fraud cases start, you know. Maybe I should check it out?'

'No . . . it's . . .'

'I could make some calls. Discreetly.'

He shook his head. 'I'll keep an eye on it.'

She turned to him. 'You're a people-pleaser, Dane. You let people exploit you.'

He shrugged, as if he accepted this about himself but didn't care, or maybe thought that there were more important things in life.

'Don't let it slide.'

He took a deep breath. 'I need him. And sometimes that's a good enough reason to let sleeping dogs lie.'

She gave him a look.

'It's not a cop-out,' he said. 'You can't let pride or pig-headedness get in the way of making the right decision.'

She made a noise of acknowledgement, not agreeing or disagreeing. 'Hey, what about Josh?' she said. 'As a project manager?'

They held each other's gaze and then both burst out laughing.

'Was he home when you left?' Dane asked.

'Nup.'

'I texted him after his appointment. Panic attack, apparently.'

'Do you think that's really what it is?'

Dane raised his eyebrows as if it hadn't occurred to him that Josh might be hiding something. 'I guess. But maybe he wasn't honest with the doctor. I mean, with everything he's been through in the last few months, how could he not be affected by it? He's always been sensitive.'

Jac nodded. 'I want to believe he's telling the truth about this harassment thing, but part of me . . .' She paused. 'Even if something did happen, he probably genuinely feels he did nothing wrong.'

'We all have to be a bit more honest with ourselves.'

That was probably her cue to say something honest about herself, but she pushed the last of the quiche into her mouth instead and changed the subject. 'What's this memoir Ngaire's writing?'

He gave her a look: *Don't start.*

'I'm not tossing shit. I'm interested.'

He sighed. 'I haven't read any of it—she won't let me—but it's about her struggles with IVF.'

A motorbike screamed past too fast on the main road, the rev of the engine piercing the air.

'Why anyone would want to write down all their innermost thoughts and feelings on paper for all the world to see, I'll never know,' Jac said. 'I prefer the stoic, bottle-it-all-up-inside-until-you-explode approach.'

'Me too.'

She licked a greasy film from her teeth. 'Turns out we're like Dad in that way, you and me. Now, *Ma*—she'd be *more* than happy to bare all in a memoir: *The Adventures of Blaise Vanderbilt.*

Do you remember when she was asked to tour with that eighties revival show? That could have been very embarrassing for all concerned. I mean, could you imagine? Ma, up on stage, bouncing around like she did when she was twenty? She'd probably throw her back out.'

'It would've been good for her—she always missed that life.'

'And don't we know it. She's spent the last forty years running away from it while at the same time talking about it nonstop.'

Her brother frowned. 'Harsh. It must've been hard to give up all that attention, the feeling like you're touching people's lives.'

'So why didn't she do the tour?'

'It would have clashed with Josh's Year 12 exams. She wanted to be around to support him.'

Ma had never shown any interest in their education. She had fronted up to all of Dane's footy games, but that's where the support for her children had ended. 'That sounds unlikely.'

'Well, it's true.'

She stood, brushing flakes of pastry out of her lap.

'Hey, can I ask you something?' Dane said. 'Why are you marrying Gillon?'

She screwed up the empty paper bag. 'Because I want to.'

Dane tried again. 'I mean, I was talking to Josh . . .'

'Let's walk around the lake.'

They joined the path at the point near the rotunda where locals used to perform Christmas carols every year. She wondered if they still did that.

'Are you trying to replace Dad?' Dane asked as they rounded the first bend.

Was that what they thought? That she was marrying her father? It was bad enough having people speculate about her sexuality, which she knew they did, but replacing Dad? That was a new one.

'I feel good when I'm with him. He's so sure about everything.'

'But what's the rush?' He pulled a stupid face. 'Are you knocked up?'

'Charming. No.' At least she didn't think she was. When was her last period?

'So . . .?'

'I do *everything* on my own, Dane. Make *every* decision by myself.'

'That's not a reason to get married.'

'No, but— When I'm sick, I want someone to bring me dry toast and flat lemonade. Or to get me a blanket when I'm cold.'

'You can get your own blanket.'

'I know that . . .'

'Or keep one near the couch, like Ngaire does.'

'Jesus, Dane, it's a metaphor. It's not about the fucking blanket!'

He turned away, looking bruised.

'Anyway. I want to settle down. I want to *be* settled. And Gil is . . . Look, it's not all starbursts and thunderclaps, but I'm actually happy with him. And that's a massive achievement.'

'Define happy.'

The wind picked up, blowing off the lake, and she caught a trace of its earthy smell.

'Serene. He's good for me.'

It was easier to talk when they were side by side, looking straight ahead, not having to eyeball each other, but that part of the conversation was over.

They neared the lakeside cafe; the ping of cutlery and hum of chatter from the outdoor tables carrying towards them on the breeze.

She loosened the lid from her coffee cup and popped it off. 'Forensics are looking over Dad's car.'

'What for?'

'Faulty mechanics.'

'Oh.'

'Or tampering.'

She thought she detected a sigh, but he didn't say anything. She licked the froth from the underside of the lid and tossed it in a bin. 'I found an overdue phone bill on his desk.'

'So?'

'I don't think he had the money to pay it.'

'Jac, what was it? Fifty bucks? I'm sure he could cover it. It probably slipped his mind.'

'There's something else. I found a list of names in his desk drawer at home. They had dollar amounts next to them. Big ones.'

She pulled out her phone with her spare hand and angled the screen towards him, displaying the photo. 'Recognise any of these names?'

Dane shaded the screen with his hand to block the glare. 'I know Damian. He plays golf with Dad. Works at the council. Wayne Harper—Dad went to school with him. Became a firey. Don't know the others.'

'Why would they be on this list together?'

He shook his head. 'Damian, Dad and Wayne are all the same age. School? Footy maybe?'

'The list was in the back of a notebook with press clippings about the church development. Maybe it's a list of his first buyers?'

'I could check, but . . . no, I doubt Damian would be buying one. He works in town planning. He's signing off on the permits. But you could ask him.'

'I thought about it, but what if it's something dodgy? What if Dad owed them this money or they owed him? That would be awkward.'

He shrugged. 'How else are you going to find out?'

'I could ask Ma if she recognises the names?'

'Don't tell her about the money, though.'

She pulled a face. 'I'm not a complete moron, Dane.'

His raised his eyebrows and took a strategically timed slurp of coffee.

'Something else. What was going on with Dad at the council? Gayle mentioned it.'

'You saw Gayle?'

'Yeah. There were disagreements?'

'He was on the outer,' Dane said. 'Maybe for the first time ever. There was a new sheriff in town.'

'I assume you don't mean that literally—about the sheriff.' Did Pent even have a sheriff?

He smiled, indulging her. 'New mayor. Dad was gonna run but didn't have the numbers. The guy who got it . . . let's just say they didn't see eye to eye.'

'And Dad felt pushed out?'

'Not completely. He's still got a lot of mates—*had* a lot of mates there. He never said this to me, but I reckon he felt he was losing his influence.'

'He would've hated that.'

'Tried his best to hide it, though. Angus Chu—that's the new mayor—he and Dad had different ideas. Dad didn't like any change that he wasn't driving himself, but he liked his position on the council. It helped him get things done—that peel sculpture in the square, the new library, the community garden.'

'Nothing illegal, though?'

'No!' Dane shook his head, emphatic at first, but then wavered. 'Problem is, there's invisible boundaries. That's why it's so hard to work out when you've crossed them. Chu's young—our age, maybe—and he's idealistic. He's all about transparency; that's the issue he ran on. And that's fine, but what it implied, without saying it in so many words, was that things at the council weren't transparent already.'

'Were they?'

'Who knows? You can get away with stuff in small organisations that you can't in bigger ones. There was this growing sense in Pent—mostly spurred on by Chu—that the council had to move into the 2020s and start acting like a professional, modern organisation and drop the footy-club, jobs-for-mates mentality. People were ready for change.'

'How did Dad react?'

'A few big decisions didn't go his way, and he wasn't getting the support he felt he deserved.'

'Gayle told me about the overpass thing.'

Dane shook his head in disbelief. 'He was talking about stepping down. Tried to make out it didn't bother him, but it played on his mind. I could tell by the way he went out of his way to let you know it didn't. But his heart wasn't in it anymore. He would've resigned soon. Before the next election, I reckon. But I guess he didn't want people—especially Chu—to think that he'd been forced out.'

They walked in silence, watching the world go by, families of ducks paddling across the lake, birds flying in formation overhead. The sun disappeared behind a cloud, turning the lake from silver to grey.

Dane asked, 'Do you honestly believe Dad would have killed himself because he didn't gel with the new mayor?'

It seemed unlikely, but she wanted to understand every angle. 'Maybe it was a cumulation of things. Are you sure nothing was going on at work?'

Dane shook his head. 'Nothing *that* bad.'

'Maybe he left a note in his office? Or on his computer?'

'Like a suicide note? I don't think so.'

'Can you check?'

He took a swig from his cup. 'Jac, I doubt he—'

'Just check, alright?'

'Fine.'

'What about social media? Did he have any accounts? Maybe he was being bullied.'

'He wasn't a fourteen-year-old girl.'

'We should look. Maybe that mayor or one of his supporters was mounting a hate campaign at the council?'

She could hear the desperation in her own words as she flitted from possibility to possibility, hoping one would stick.

They stopped walking. Dane turned to her, his voice deadpan. 'You think the local mayor was bullying Dad online and that's why he drove into that pylon?'

'Do you have a better— *another* explanation?' She threw her unfinished cup into a bin.

'Maybe there isn't one. Or not *just* one. It was probably a lot of things. Most of us are killing off parts of ourselves bit by bit. I guess he wanted to do it in one swift move.'

'That's bleak.'

'We have to accept it, Jac.'

'Sounds like *you* have.'

'It doesn't mean I don't hate it. You know, the cop I spoke to after the crash said it was the twelfth suicide attempt he'd dealt with this year. Just in Pent. Seven had been successful. That's seven other families going through what we are. There were eight suicides last year, and there'll probably be another eight next year.'

'He's not a statistic, Dane. He was our dad.'

Dane shook his head. 'Goddamn it, Jac. You act like you're the only one in pain. Well, you're not,' he said, his voice breaking.

'I feel so helpless and sad and angry and confused. I mean, *him*. Why him? He seemed so strong. If he couldn't get through it, what hope is there for the rest of us?' He turned and walked away, throwing his cup at the bin but missing, milky coffee splashing over the top of the yellow lid.

Dane was right—she'd been selfish. But she had to admit, it was comforting to know that she wasn't alone.

WEDNESDAY

26

Flowers kept appearing at work as the news of Dad's passing spread. Clients, suppliers, the company that vacuumed the office after hours: they all sent something, and the place had not only started to look like a florist shop but to smell like one too—the mixed perfume of roses and other fragrant flowers, blended with the stink of foliage rotting in still water.

This colour, this radiance around the office, it only highlighted how everything was different. It had become a cartoon version of itself, an imitation of life. Dane had never had to see or hear Dad in the office to know he was there. His presence was an energy field; it gave the air a distinct charge.

In Dad's glass-walled office, Dane lifted the screen on his father's laptop gingerly, as though it might self-destruct. He didn't expect to find anything, but he'd promised Jac.

He scanned the files on his desktop: 'Europe itinerary', 'Letter for Gayle' and 'Certificate of currency'—nothing resembling the words 'suicide note'. He swept through the file folders, locating one called Personal, and clicked it. Resetting the list order to chronological, he found only one new document from within the past two weeks, but it was called 'Background check'. He opened it.

The file was on the letterhead of a company called EP Investigations and the subject was Leigh Alexander Grimwade.

Dad had ordered a background check on Leigh?

Bolded headings ran down the page: *Personal history, Business interests, Financial position, Criminal history, Credit defaults.* Dane focused on the parts someone had highlighted in yellow— Leigh had defaulted on a loan two years ago, owed $600,000 on his house and another $22,000 on his Hilux. His credit cards were maxed out—$15,000 on the Visa and $20,000 on a Mastercard.

Jesus! His house would only be worth about $700,000, Dane thought. The repayments on the loans and the cards must be sucking him dry.

'Dane?'

Gayle stood in the doorway, hands clasped in front of her. He angled the laptop away from her line of sight.

'Sorry to interrupt, but I've got Joel Hutchison in reception. He wants to see you.'

Fuck! Joel was pissed off about the soil report for the restaurant job; that was the obvious conclusion. Or maybe he'd come to warn him that he was taking the matter further? Maybe to the building commission?

'Dane?'

'Sorry. I'll just be a sec.' He shook his head clear. 'By the way, what are we going to do with all these flowers?'

'I bought more vases. Jan said she'd take home some of the ones we haven't put in water yet. Is that okay?'

'Yeah. Take them. Give them away.' He fluttered a hand in the air.

Gayle gave him an uneasy look then turned and headed back towards her desk. He checked that his shirt was still tucked in and followed her from the office, glancing across at Leigh's desk to find it vacant.

Dane had only met Joel Hutchison a few times—passing through the office, at celebratory drinks. Joel had engineered the geotech on dozens of their projects—*all* of Harding's projects over the past few years, as far as he knew.

Now the engineer stood with his back to the reception desk, hulking under a blazer and jeans, looking through the side windows towards Shepparton to the west.

'Joel?'

Joel turned, extended a beefy hand. 'Hello, Dane. A word?'

Dane took his hand back, hoping it wasn't clammy. 'Sure. Come into the conference room. Would you like a coffee or something?' He glanced at Gayle, who stood ready to oblige.

Joel shook his head. 'This won't take long.'

Dane led the way, feeling the bulk of Joel Hutchison hovering behind him. He stopped at the open door to the conference room, noticing how his own breathing had shallowed, and ushered him in.

Dane pulled out a chair at the head of the gleaming glass table and gestured to another for Joel. 'What can I do for you today?'

God, he sounded like a robot. Like a customer service person at a chain clothing store.

Joel clasped his hands together on the tabletop and leaned an inch towards him. 'Dane, I wanted to come in person to offer my condolences about your dad. I was shocked, and so saddened, to hear about his passing.'

Joel's shoulders were hunched, dispelling the air of broad confidence of a few moments ago, and Dane felt his own shoulders relax.

'Thank you.' Dane exhaled. 'Thanks for taking the time.'

'He was a passionate man,' Joel said. 'Dedicated to Pent, to this business, and to his family. This is going to leave a big void.'

Dane nodded.

The silence took on an uncomfortable shape before Joel said, 'Did you know my son took his own life?'

The air in the room stilled and, for a moment, Dane didn't know how to respond. 'No, I didn't. I'm sorry.' He knew nothing about Joel's family. He didn't even know the man'd had a son.

'It was a long time ago—nine years—but I can tell you, time doesn't heal all wounds. We knew he had problems, but we had no clue what to do with him. We tried. We tried really hard to get him help. But there's not enough GPs around here, let alone mental health specialists. Not that he would've gone. The tough-it-out attitude of country people is great when you're facing a drought, but not so great when you've got mental health problems.'

'It can be hard to ask for help,' Dane said, recalling what Josh alluded to about stigma. 'How old was your son?'

'Twenty-seven. Just turned. Had his own farm. But between the financial hardship and the isolation out there . . . He took an overdose of pills and ended up in hospital. I was away. Bette, my wife, begged them to keep him in for another night until she could get there, and they agreed.' Joel glanced away, his eyes hazy. 'But then they discharged him. I don't know why. He rang his mother, told her he loved her, then he killed himself.'

Tears leaked from Dane's eyes and he wiped them away with the heel of his hand.

Joel kept talking. 'Staff in our tiny hospitals—God bless them—don't always know how to deal with this stuff, so people get shunted to emergency departments and then, if they're not *in crisis*'—he put air quotes around the words—'they're sent home because there's nowhere else.'

Dane wiped his face again, his whole body suddenly heavy.

'I'm sorry, mate. I didn't come here to upset you.' Joel reached out a hand and squeezed Dane's shoulder. 'I just wanted to let you know that I understand what you're going through. We were all over the place when we lost Thomas. Like we were the first people it had ever happened to. Friends avoided us. People ran a mile because they didn't know what to say. I didn't want to be that guy.'

'I appreciate that, Joel. I really do.'

Joel stood and they shook hands once more. 'Take care of yourself, Dane. And take care of your family. One thing you learn from experiences like ours is that business should always come second.'

First, second, third . . . It occurred to Dane that there was no order of priorities in his life. Everything seemed urgent; everything had to get done. 'It feels pretty all-consuming right now.'

'I bet.' Joel pushed his chair back under the table. 'You'll work it out. I know we haven't had much to do with each other, but I know that people around here respect you.'

On the way out, Joel mentioned that he'd be lining up on Monday week to sign the paperwork and pay the deposit for his St Augustine's apartment.

'You're buying one?'

Dane had no idea who had signed up—he'd never looked at the buyers list.

'Sure. Got to retire sometime. I've got my eye on one at the back so I can get views of the golf course and lake.'

'Lake *glimpses*,' Dane clarified.

Joel grinned. 'Yeah, glimpses.'

They shook hands.

'If you don't mind me asking,' Joel said, 'did the soil report on the St Augustine's site turn up anything?'

Dane looked at him, puzzled. 'Didn't you do it?'

The engineer shook his head. 'Stephen booked us, but Leigh cancelled at the last minute.'

'I see. Well, Leigh says it's fine.' But something about the tone of Joel's question caught his attention. 'Did you expect problems?'

'Wouldn't have surprised me. There was a cattle and sheep dip site on the river just up the road for years. Closed down before you were born.'

'What river?' There was no river near St Augustine's.

'The Broken River. Used to go right past the church before they diverted it to make the lake. Lot of pesticides used to come down from the dip yard. Arsenic, too. We've seen it show up in sites all around there. Expensive to get rid of. And a real occupational health and safety headache. No one wants to work on a site contaminated with arsenic.'

Not to mention time-consuming, Dane thought. That kind of thing would delay the project, as well as blowing out the budget.

'Wouldn't council be all over that?' he asked.

'Not necessarily. It might not've occurred to them to request the report. Usually all they ask for in soil tests is bearing capacity and reactivity. Plus, they really want this development to go ahead. Sometimes we work with councils that go looking for reasons to reject a development they don't want, but that's not the case here. Things can get overlooked when you're not trying to find faults.'

Dane rubbed the back of his neck. 'When did Leigh cancel on you?'

'Last week. The day before we were due to start. Wednesday.'

Wednesday. Leigh didn't tell him about Joel's issues with the soil at the restaurant site until the following day.

'I remember it clearly,' Joel continued, 'because it was the day after Stephen's crash.'

27

Josh sat in the lounge, one leg flung over the arm of the couch, scrolling through NBA results on his phone, a plastic shaker of Milo empty on the side table. The doorbell rang. Ma was out somewhere and Jac was collecting Gil from the airport.

That morning, he'd shopped. He'd bought most of the gear he was after from one clothing store—Mensland in the square. It had been there forever. Dad shopped there; probably Grandpa before him. Then, on the way home, he'd picked up six cases of wine (three white, three red) and four of beer (two of which were mid-strength) from the bottle shop and collected five boxes of drinking glasses from the golf club. The whole outing had taken less than an hour, but that was long enough. The less time he spent in public, the less chance he had of being stared at. Not only was there the Tabeetha thing to worry about—now he was the guy whose father had killed himself, too.

He transferred the cat to the floor and heaved himself off the couch, brushing fur from his crotch. He hoped it wasn't more flowers (the smell was getting to him) or, worse, another lasagne. He loved lasagne, but they'd been eating it twice a day since Ma had stopped cooking; neither he nor Jac knew their way around a kitchen beyond scrambled eggs and cheese toasties.

He opened the door to find Jordan on the front step, Dot ensconced on her hip. At first her presence there, in Pent, confused him, as if his wife might have gone for a leisurely drive and lost her way. Then the reality of it slapped him around head and he swallowed, overcome by the vision of them.

'Hello,' she said.

There was something distinctly different about her, something disturbingly unfamiliar. She wore a cropped jacket he didn't recognise, her hair was in cornrows, and she was carrying a large nappy bag that must've been new. But it was more than that; it was something in the way she held herself upright, as if standing her ground. Still, there was enough of her there—in the way her body ensnared him and the way her eyes penetrated his insides—to cause his legs to tremble.

'Jordan. What are you doing here?'

Behind her, he could see their family SUV parked at the kerb.

Her eyebrows furrowed. 'You texted me.'

'I know, but I thought . . .'

She kissed him on the cheek, and it was soft, but painful. Then Dot reached for him and he lifted his daughter into his arms. He pressed his lips to her scalp, inhaling the smell of her head, then kissed both plump cheeks. She still had only a fuzz of black hair, but she'd grown since he'd last seen her—what? a month ago?—and now looked disturbingly like Ma; she had the same frown and there was something about the shape of her eyes.

He took a quick mental tally of the situation. Jordan had come to see him; she'd reached out. This must mean . . . she wouldn't have come unless . . . Was she ready to let him come back home?

He opened the door wider. 'Come in.'

She moved through the doorway, bringing the outside world in. He closed his eyes and breathed deep, filling his lungs with her.

When he opened them again she was heading for the lounge room.

'Wow! So many flowers!'

'And they keep coming.'

Having Jordan and Dot in his childhood home shifted something in the air. Ever since Dad died, the house had become closed in and stale, but with Jordan's presence, everything brightened slightly, as if someone had applied a filter over an Instagram post.

'Would you like a drink?' he asked.

'Got any mineral water?'

'The fizzy kind?'

She nodded.

'Doubt it. I'll check the fridge.'

She followed him through the dining room to the bar, Dot tugging at his whiskers. He opened the small fridge under the benchtop.

'I'm so sorry about your dad,' Jordan said. 'Are you alright?'

'Yeah. There's soda water.'

'That'll do.'

Seeing him struggle to manage both baby and drinks, Jordan took Dot from him. 'Anyone else home?' she asked.

'Not right now.'

He reached for a beer but hesitated, settling on a can of Coke instead.

'Are you hungry?' he asked Dot.

'She's okay. She had a bottle on the way.'

Back in the lounge room, he motioned to the easy chair, but Jordan sat on the couch, lowering Dot onto the floor.

'Look, Dot, pussy cat,' he said in his best toddler-dad voice. He pointed to Harry, who was lounging in a square of sunlight on the living room floor. Harry rose, stretched, and approached Dot cautiously, but when Dot clumsily reached out her hand to touch him, he scurried off into the kitchen. Dot tried to follow, speed-crawling across the rug, but Jordan grabbed her. 'No, you don't!' She brought Dot back to the mat and took a set of oversized colourful plastic keys from the nappy bag. She handed them to Dot then perched on the sofa edge, ready to pounce. Josh watched her watching Dot. He wanted to reach out and touch her, to crawl under her shirt and stay there, breathing in her smell.

'Your parents' house is nothing like I pictured,' she said. 'It's so modern.'

He leaned back in the easy chair. 'Ma gets restless. She likes to update. My room's about the only one that hasn't been touched.'

Jordan unscrewed the cap from her soda water and took a long sip. 'It must be like stepping back in time.'

Given his current lifestyle—Ma washing and ironing his clothes, telling him to clean his room and busting his chops about putting coasters under his glasses—it *was* like rewinding ten years. Lying in that same bed a decade ago, he'd spent a lot of time dreaming of a better future. He was doing that again now.

'Did your dad ever regain consciousness after the accident?'

'Nah. And it wasn't an accident.'

Jordan raised her eyebrows in query.

'Apparently he drove himself into a pylon.'

'On purpose?'

He nodded and took a slug of his soft drink. 'They put him into a coma and everything was going okay, and then he just . . . died.'

How casual he must've sounded, talking about his father's death dispassionately, as if describing a sequence they'd shot that day.

'So he *tried* to kill himself?'

'Yep.' A warm tear slid down his cheek. 'Succeeded too.'

'Josh, I'm so sorry.'

She tilted towards him and rested a hand on his thigh. She was still wearing her wedding ring, and the sight of it made his chest loosen.

'The first few days were okay because we were busy letting everyone know and planning the funeral. But now all that's done . . . I don't know. It's so messed up.'

He thought about telling her he was on medication for depression. Maybe it would help her to understand him better. Or maybe it would have the opposite effect—making her want to run a mile. No, he told himself; she wasn't like that.

'Does anyone know why he might have . . .'

'Nope. It's one big mystery. And now we can't ask him.'

He tried to smile but it didn't help. His eyes settled on Dot, sucking on a bright yellow key. He suddenly felt exposed, as if the stitches had broken and a gaping wound that he didn't even realise was there had once again split open. He wiped the tear away with the back of his hand. 'Funeral's tomorrow.'

'I'm glad I'm here then,' she said. 'Are you planning on staying in Pent for a while?' Her eyes wandered the room.

'No idea.'

Dot took the key out of her mouth and rattled the plastic chain. He wondered if she knew he was her dad. Could she sense they were bonded by blood?

They chatted about nothing for a while—one of Jordan's friends had bought a house, the neighbour had a puppy that barked at all hours, and her parents were in Sri Lanka visiting family. She told him about Dot's eight-month check-up (all good) and he shared Jac's engagement news. They were conversing like old workmates who hadn't caught up in a while. Where was the tenderness? Where was the emotional connection?

'How's it being back here with your family?' she asked.

'Good. Weird. Ma's . . . Ma. Dane's boys are cool. But with Dane and Jac, it's like this thing has pulled us together. We have this sadness to share, which sounds kind of depressing, but it's as if we finally have something in common.'

'That's good. Deaths in a family either bring the people left behind closer or they destroy them. What's going to happen with your dad's business?'

There was a question. He supposed he was entitled to a share. Maybe after Ma died. That must've been what Jordan meant by deaths destroying families. It could turn into a fight over money and who got what. 'Dane reckons he'll keep it going.'

Dot had lost interest in the kiddie keys and Jordan gave her the actual car keys. They were louder, rattling together when she shook them. She gasped in delight, jiggling her whole body, making bouncy *ahh* noises.

Josh watched her, scratching his beard self-consciously. He hadn't shaved once since he'd been in Pent, despite Ma planting a canister of Dad's shaving cream on the bench in the upstairs bathroom alongside a bag of disposable razors. Now, under Jordan's gaze, he felt dirty, seeing what she must see. Seeing what they all must see.

'Josh, I don't want to burden you with this now,' Jordan said, 'but I need money. I've been working part-time, but it's not enough, and with Mum and Dad away, I have to pay for child care.'

He wanted to say that she never needed to pay for child care, that he was always available, but there was a difference between 'available' and 'able' that he was only just beginning to fathom. He squeezed his eyes shut. 'I know.'

'Is there *anything* happening?'

'No.'

'How much longer are you going to— I mean, what are you going to do?'

You. What are *you* going to do? There was no 'we' anymore.

He shook his head to indicate that he didn't know. Maybe he could borrow money from Ma or Dane to tide them over for a few months? 'I just need time,' he said. 'The public needs time. These things settle down after a while and I'll be back to work.'

'Really?'

'Yeah. It'll be fine.'

'What does Kelsey say?'

'She's optimistic, I think.'

Was she optimistic? The tone of Kelsey's voice rarely altered from upbeat and shouty.

Jordan stood and walked around the room, lingering on the ornaments on the sideboard and the books stacked at angles on the coffee table—*The World Atlas of Tea, Great Golf Courses of Scotland* and *New York: In Pictures*. She stopped at the fireplace and took in the picture of Ma from the eighties on the mantel-piece. 'Is that Blaise?'

'Yeah. Cool, huh?' he said with a swell of pride.

'Very.' She leaned in for a closer look. 'You've got your dad's body but her face. She was quite a stunner. Still is.' She turned to him. 'What are your plans for tonight?'

He felt the heavy, grey layer of despair that had been smothering him begin to peel away—Jordan was here, Dot was here. They were discussing dinner plans. 'Probably just eating at home. Everyone'll be thinking about tomorrow.' *Stay cool.*

She picked up a framed photo of Dad and Ma, then put it down again. 'I might go find a motel and get settled in. I can come back later.'

Then it occurred to him that she hadn't brought her luggage in. She had no intention of staying in the house. 'You can stay here. In my room.'

She gave him a dubious look. 'With you?'

He nodded. 'And Al Pacino.'

She crinkled her nose, his attempt at levity lying flat on the floor between them. 'I'd better stay in a motel.'

'Ma won't allow it.'

She smiled. 'She's going to have to. I'm not staying here.'

His mind searched frantically for another option—one that would keep Jordan and Dot close by. 'You can sleep in the twins' room. There's two single beds.'

She hesitated for a moment, then shook her head. 'No, I'll stay in a motel. Pent does have a motel, doesn't it?'

'Yeah,' he said, deflated. 'Several.'

'Can I leave Dot with you for a while?'

On the floor, Dot sucked on the car remote.

The lightness in his chest returned. 'Of course, yeah. Please. No problem. Leave her here. We'll just— We'll play or something. Ma will be home soon anyway. She'll be rapt.'

Jordan drained her soda water and left the bottle on the side table. 'I'll be back in a bit.'

She took back the car remote from Dot and pulled her phone and purse from the nappy bag. She turned to him then, placing her hand on his chest. 'Don't read anything into this, okay? I didn't come here so we could get back together.'

His heart shattered into little pieces and showered into his stomach. 'Yeah, 'course. I know.'

She gave him a flat smile and left, taking his fractured heart with her.

The bag Jordan had left behind was bursting with disposable nappies, wet wipes, a change of clothes for Dot and toys. The zip was either broken or she didn't even bother trying to close it anymore. He plunged his hand inside and his fingers found a squeaky bear he'd bought Dot a few months ago and a rubbery truck. He placed them both within reach on the rug.

He watched his daughter playing, a part of his brain committing all the details to memory—the way her little fingers stretched out to grab a toy; the way she wanted to taste everything first; the way she flapped her arms when she was excited. He sensed it was all he'd be left with in the years to come.

No. Stop. Hit pause on the negative thoughts pressing in. It was a good sign that Jordan had come for the funeral. It meant she still wanted to support him. Surely she hadn't meant what she'd said about not getting back together? They'd been so good as a couple; they had a child together. Surely what they had was worth saving.

From what he'd gathered, Jordan had been in good, healthy relationships before meeting him, but it was all new to Josh. He'd met her during a particularly dark period of his life, after his co-star Emalie died. He'd been going out every night, flirting shamelessly and drinking Scotch until the dark clouds in his head dissipated, as if his life was stuck on repeat. He'd started up with a barista named Saskia who worked at the coffee place

near his house. At first it was great—intense and full of excite-
ment. She was older, with jet-black hair, an earring in her nose
and tattoos that ran up and down both arms and one of her legs.
Something vividly sexual pulsated through her.

But whenever he tried to get close to her—properly close—
she'd freeze him out. She'd be loving one minute and standoffish
the next. She'd scream abuse at him and then want hard, rough
sex, refusing to kiss him.

One day he got hold of her phone and discovered that
she was having casual hook-up sex with strangers. His hand
wobbled as he swiped through the countless texts organising
meeting places—motels, bars and apartments. After the breath
returned to his lungs, he realised how deeply ingrained her
issues were.

He tried to talk to her about it, but she shut down. He wanted
to understand her better but his attempts to reach out only
drove her deeper into her hole. Then she disappeared—quit her
job, changed her number, moved house and stopped posting to
Instagram. He worried for a time, trying every now and then
to make contact.

But then he met Jordan. Well, *re*-met Jordan. They had met
once before, briefly, on the set of *Trapped*, the TV movie set in
a cave. Jordan was the make-up artist, and one day, while on a
break, he came across her on the beach, crouched on the sand,
cradling what looked like a baby. When he got closer, he saw
that it wasn't a baby; it was an injured seagull.

'I think it got swooped by an eagle,' she said. 'Here, give me
your jacket.'

The way she'd looked at that helpless bird in need of rescuing
moved him.

They'd met again one chilly night three years later, at an
industry party held at a rooftop bar, city lights twinkling below.

She was as he'd remembered—guarded but friendly, pretty in a natural, effortless way, and super no-nonsense. She wasn't impressed by his public profile (which had grown substantially by then) and had no interest in raising her own. She was self-possessed without being self-absorbed. He didn't know how to be that way himself, but he wished he could.

They saw each other a couple of times a week in that first month, then three or four nights a week in the second. He left for the Gold Coast to shoot season one of *Relationship Rescue*, and soon after he came back, they moved in together.

Life was good. He introduced her to Dad and Ma, and they talked about starting their own family, but neither of them expected it to happen so quickly.

One night, as he lay with his head in her lap watching a rom-com on Netflix, she'd brought up baby names.

'If it's a girl, I want to name her after Nan.'

'Dorothy? Really?'

'Dot. That's cute for a little girl, don't you think?'

'Okay.'

'And if it's a boy, after my dad.'

'Do I get a say in this?'

'It'll have your surname.' She stroked his head. 'Actually, that raises a good question—will it be a Vanderbilt or a Harding?'

Without pausing to think, he said, 'Vanderbilt.'

'But legally . . . You've never officially changed your name, have you?'

'What better time, then?'

The swiftness with which he'd decided this caught him off guard, but it had been building since the first time Dad had passed him over for a better offer—a long lunch with the lads or one of his solo fishing trips. 'Harding was the name of my childhood. I left it behind for a reason.'

She ran her fingers through his hair and then along his jawline, all the while studying him with deep, dark eyes—the way she had looked at that injured seagull on the beach.

Within three weeks they were married. A small, COVID-restricted wedding.

Dot came nine days early, in January. Six weeks later he was back on the Gold Coast shooting season two of *Relationship Rescue*.

They'd hit bumps before but had come through them. And now she was in Pent. This was his best chance to get her back.

His phone rang. Kelsey. 'Hello?'

'I got you a job.'

He wasn't sure he'd heard her correctly.

'Don't get too excited,' she said. 'It's voice work. An audio book.'

'Really?'

'Really. A crime novel. Can you be in Melbourne on Monday week?'

'Yep. Absolutely.'

His body hummed with anticipation, with gratitude, with relief.

'I'll email you the details.'

His mind whizzed forwards, and he pictured himself telling Jordan the news. The fee would be minimal, but it was a start. Maybe this was the start of a side career as a voiceover artist?

'Are you there, Josh?'

'Yes. Thank you, Kelsey. I'm . . . thank you.'

She hung up and he hurled his phone onto the couch.

'Did you hear Daddy's news, Dot?' He extracted the squishy truck from her hands, picked her up and whirled her around the room, planting a hard, wet kiss on her cheek. 'I'm coming back!'

28

D ane stood at the council's town-planning desk reviewing all their submissions for the St Augustine's project.

The soil test, it turned out, had been completed by a company called Solid Rock Geotechnics; the name was vaguely familiar, but Dane had never come across them personally. They'd found no issues with bearing capacity or reactivity on the site. The only issue was a water table they would have to drill below. But there was no testing for contamination, not even of the water. Then he remembered: Solid Rock. That was the invoice Leigh had pulled out of Jan's pile.

'Anything I can help you with?' asked Isaiah, the junior planning officer.

Dane handed him the file, making a mental note to delve further once he was back at the office. 'No, mate. Thanks for indulging me.'

He was on his way out of the council building when he heard
someone call, 'Mr Harding!'

Turning, he saw the mayor, Angus Chu, hurrying towards
him.

'Hello, Mayor Chu.'

It was impossible to guess Angus Chu's age. He could have
been thirty-five or forty-five. He *looked* young, with his swept-
back hair, his muscular chest pushing out a check shirt with
sleeves folded to the elbows.

'Call me Angus.'

'Dane.'

They shook hands.

Standing by the sliding glass doors that led to the forecourt,
Dane could see through the glass a statue dedicated to all the Pent
residents lost in war. Inside, they were surrounded by pictures of
the town through the ages: the original pub (long gone); an old
homestead (now an upmarket restaurant); St Augustine's; and
the lake being created from the waters of the Broken River in
the early seventies.

'I wanted to express my sincere condolences on the loss of
your father,' the mayor said. 'He was an institution around here.'
His eyes scanned the space. 'Very . . . *spirited.*'

'Thank you. Yes, he was.'

Katherine Warren brushed past them on her way in but didn't
look up.

'What a shame he never got to see those apartments come to
fruition,' the mayor said. 'Still, I guess they'll be a long-lasting
monument to his work.'

'Yes, thank you.'

He'd been thanking people a lot over the past few days.

I'm so sorry for your loss.

Thank you.

He was a wonderful man.

Thank you.

'I'm buying one,' the mayor said. 'For my daughters.'

It took Dane a second to realise he was still talking about the St Augustine's apartments.

'My girls are only in primary school, but I hope I can entice them to stay in Pent when they're older.'

He'd seen the mayor's daughters in the local paper: big smiles and braided hair. They were at school with the twins but were a few years older.

The mayor nudged his glasses up his nose with an index finger. 'I was planning on paying your mother a visit, but since you're here now, perhaps I could run it by you instead . . . I wanted to speak about how we, at council, might go about ensuring your father's legacy is kept alive.'

'Okay.'

'I have to say, I was shocked when I looked into the statistics of this terrible disease.'

Dane frowned. What disease? Dad hadn't died from a disease.

'The rate of . . . especially among young men, well, it's worse than the road toll. And in rural settings it's—'

'I'm sorry,' Dane said. 'I don't understand what you're talking about.'

'Depression, Dane.'

Depression. *This terrible disease.*

'We have some funds—significant funds—set aside for well-being programs, but it hasn't been allocated yet, so I thought we could sit down at some point and . . .'

Dane's attention was caught by a commotion at the town planning desk on the far side of the customer service centre. Katherine Warren was there; she appeared to be agitated and was arguing with Isaiah. Meanwhile, the mayor was still talking facts and figures, like a true politician. On hearing Katherine utter the words, 'St Augustine's,' Dane said, 'Excuse me, Angus. I just have to see to this . . .'

He approached the desk, where Isaiah was visibly shrinking under the weight of Katherine's ire.

'What's going on?' he asked, his eyes moving from Katherine to Isaiah. 'You mentioned St Augustine's, Katherine?'

'Dane!' Katherine pushed away strands of grey hair that had caught in the corner of her mouth. 'They've lost my form.'

'*Misplaced,*' Isaiah corrected.

Angus Chu joined them. 'What form?'

'I lodged a form and now they're saying they don't have it.'

'What form?' Angus repeated.

'To request an Aboriginal heritage survey,' Katherine said, as though it were obvious. 'Didn't you know the Taungurong people had corroborees on that site?'

'Haven't we done that already?' Angus asked Isaiah.

'It's not mandatory.'

Katherine placed both palms flat on the benchtop. 'But there could be sacred objects, tools used in ceremonies, ancestral remains. You could be decimating graves!'

'We don't have a record of any form,' Isaiah said.

'Well, I handed it in. Right here.' She tapped the countertop. 'At this desk.'

'Do you have a receipt?' Angus asked.

Katherine's shoulders dropped. 'He didn't give me one.' She turned to Dane. 'And I told your man about it, too. Leigh Grimwade.'

A clutch of fear seized him, the realisation sitting in his stomach like sludge. This must be the application she mentioned when she visited the office waving the *Gazette*.

'I can ask Damian,' Isaiah said. 'But he's in a meeting and

we've already issued the building permit.' He looked to the mayor for guidance.

'Well, *un*issue it,' Katherine demanded. 'Retract it.'

'We can't do that, I'm afraid,' said Angus Chu. 'I know you *say* you submitted it, but if there's no record . . .'

Dane caught Katherine's gaze. 'When did you hand in the form?'

She sighed. 'A week ago.'

'Wednesday?'

'Could've been.'

Wednesday. The same day Leigh cancelled Joel Hutchison's survey of the site and replaced him with Solid Rock. The day after Dad's crash.

'Excuse me,' he said abruptly. 'I have to go.'

Back at the office, Dane had just fired up his father's computer and clicked on the St Augustine's folder when Leigh appeared in the doorway.

'So you moved in,' Leigh said.

'I'm looking for something.' Dane motioned to the chair opposite. 'Have a seat.'

Leigh was wearing a suit and he'd shaved. It looked as if he had an important meeting scheduled.

Ignoring Dane's invitation, Leigh remained standing, looking a question at him.

'Why didn't we use Hutchison for the St Aug's soil survey?' Dane asked. 'You cancelled them and appointed Solid Rock.'

Leigh rubbed his nose. 'So?'

'Why them?'

'Geotech is geotech.'

'Is it?'

'Do you need a tutorial on the—'

'Leigh!'

The project manager stuck his hands in his pockets. 'I thought there might be a conflict of interest—Joel's buying one of the apartments.'

Did that sound reasonable? Dane wasn't sure, so he went on.

'Why didn't you have the soil tested for contaminants?'

'What for?'

'There used to be a dipping station up the road from the site. There could be arsenic in the ground.'

'Really? It wasn't mentioned.'

'Are you sure?'

'Yeah. What have you—'

'I'm ordering another test.'

'Dane, Mike Vincent's a good guy. I'm sure he wouldn't have cut any corners.'

Mike Vincent? Where had he heard that name?

'I hear the historical society tried to lodge another council application,' Dane continued. 'Indigenous significance or something.'

Leigh made a show of squeezing his eyebrows together. 'What is this? Have you been checking up on me?'

'What do you know about the application?'

Leigh shrugged. 'Why would I know anything about it?'

'Are you saying you *didn't* know about it? Katherine Warren tells me it's gone missing.'

'What's that got to do with us?'

'She said she told you she was lodging it.'

He shrugged again. 'It's a council matter, we don't have any—'

Dane slammed his hand on the desk. 'Stop dicking around, Leigh. Did she speak to you about it or not?'

Leigh glanced out the window and then back at him. 'She said something.'

'Fuck! But you went ahead and booked the demolition anyway? When is that scheduled for, by the way?'

'End of next week, I think. Look, that application would've held us up for *months*. And for what? Some rubbish artefacts that probably don't even exist?' His voice took on an edge. 'We have a council permit to build on the site. We have project deadlines. Why wouldn't we start?'

'Why? Because you knew they'd put in another application!'

Leigh rolled his eyes. 'What do you want me to say, Dane? It's business.'

'Not my kind of business. What happened to the application?'

Leigh sniffed the air. 'Sometimes you have to get creative.'

The way he said it, so matter of fact, riled Dane.

'Leigh, there's a big difference between *creative* and *dodgy*.' He exhaled. 'And that's not an answer. Did you deliberately wait until Dad was incapacitated so you could *get creative* with the application?'

'*What?* How could I have known he'd end up in hospital?' Leigh shifted his weight from foot to foot, considering some-thing. 'Katherine Warren told me she was planning to lodge the application two weeks ago. I told Stephen.'

'When?'

'Two weeks ago! Stephen arranged with Damian Davenport to lose the application when it came in.'

No. Leigh was lying to divert the blame away from himself, now that Dad couldn't mount a defence.

Leigh moved closer. 'You really think I've got the clout to pull this off? Who am I mates with at the council?'

Dane suddenly felt disorientated, as if a football had bounced off his head.

'Sorry, Dane. He didn't want you to . . . I didn't want to have to . . .'

Full knowledge flooded in and Dane felt his body lose its frame.

Dad did this. He and Damian Davenport conspired to lose the form to circumvent a potential hold-up. Damian's name was on the list Jac had found in Dad's study. Had Dad paid Damian off? Had he given money to all those guys on the list?

Then there was the bigger question. If Dad had done that, if he had wilfully and knowingly swindled the system to get his way on this job—Dane leaned back into the chair—what else had he been capable of?

29

Josh couldn't take his eyes off Gil. He had known the man was older than Jac, but seeing that white hair and weather-beaten face in the flesh unnerved him. He pictured the two of them in ten, twenty years' time, her driving kids to school in their SUV while he rode around on his mobility scooter. Gil would have been good-looking when he was younger, Josh decided—in a Don Draper kind of way—but even from two metres away, he could smell the woody cologne that belonged to another generation. His sister's fiancé probably watched cosy crime shows on the ABC on Saturday nights and still listened to the Doobie Brothers on CD.

They were all sitting in the lounge room—Ma, Jac, Gil and Josh. Dot was on the floor playing with a multicoloured truck panel—red steering wheel, yellow honking horn and a whirling speedo. Over text, Jordan had agreed to return to the house for dinner.

The coffee table was a chaotic mess of half-eaten platters of cold meats, marinated olives, stuffed vine leaves, crumbed something-or-other, fancy crackers and soft cheeses, all of which Gil had magically produced out of nowhere and had fastidiously assembled in front of them as if preparing for a cookbook photo shoot.

Jac sat beside Gil on the couch, their knees touching. One of his tanned hands clutched a brown bottle of beer and the other rested on Jac's thigh. He was laughing at something she'd said, causing the creases around his eyes to deepen even further. Josh pictured him at the helm of a sailboat in a stylish white sea captain cap, the tiller in one hand and a glass of whisky—an old-fashioned—in the other.

Jac, too, was watching him, a smile on her face that radiated pride, fascination and awe. He was talking about the weekend just gone, when he'd visited his holiday house in Port Stephens.

'So, I got there, been working all week, all I wanted to do was to get inside, have a cold one and put my feet up. And, lo and behold, there's this kid—maybe early twenties—sitting on my couch, hand buried in a bag of veggie chips, drinking my beer!'

'Who was he?' Ma wanted to know.

'*She*. It was a girl.'

Ma's eyes widened.

'I don't know who she was,' Gil said. 'Some kid looking for a place to crash.'

'Well, what did she say? How long had she been there?'

'Just one night, she said. But I could tell by the empty fridge she'd probably been there three or four. Said she had to get away from her abusive boyfriend.' He turned to Josh. 'There wasn't a mark on her.'

'There are all kinds of abuse, Gil,' Jac pointed out.

'Sure. I guess. Anyway, I gave her some money and sent her on her way.'

'You didn't call the police?' Jac asked.

'What would be the point? No harm done. Except for the lock on the back door. She'd broken that.'

His ready smile and easygoing personality were difficult to resist and it was plain to see why Jac had fallen for him—though it was less obvious why he'd fallen for her. Ma, too, was entranced, hanging on his every word like a teenager meeting a pop idol.

Josh, however, had other things on his mind. 'So, this beach house,' he said to Gil. 'It's empty most of the time?'

The doorbell rang.

Knowing it would likely be Jordan, Josh got up.

He went to the door and found his wife on the stoop wearing a yellow pants-and-top combination—or was it all one piece?—and holding a bottle of rosé. Her hair was pinned in some magic, undetectable way at the back of her head, leaving nothing to distract from her immaculate face.

Inside, Jordan kissed everyone hello, including Gil, and held out the bottle of wine to Ma.

'Oh, thank you.' Ma accepted the bottle with a smile, making a point of examining the label. 'Lovely,' she said. 'Thank you, sweetheart.'

'I'm so sorry about Stephen,' Jordan said, looking from Ma to Jac. 'I can't imagine how you all must be feeling.'

Ma nodded in acknowledgement, but no one said anything.

Jordan stepped towards the fireplace. 'I love this picture of you, Blaise. What a looker!'

Ma dipped her head but then straightened up. 'It's from my album cover. Number one for three weeks. Here *and* in New Zealand.' She attempted a smile but it didn't reach her eyes. 'Shall we open some bubbles?'

They discussed TV shows, grazed on Gil's platter and drank the sparkling wine Dane had bought to celebrate Jac's engagement. Everyone was amazingly normal considering they were cremating Dad the next day.

After an hour, with Dot asleep in a portable cot, they moved into the kitchen. From the stove, Gil continued to entertain with stories from his extensive overseas adventures. He fried slabs of haloumi while Jac stood at the bench slicing a lemon into wedges. Ma was quiet, watching Gil and Jac at the stove.

Like a double act, Josh and Jordan dished the dirt on celebrities they'd worked with and, for a moment, the old Jordan was there—the one who'd handed him his daughter, the umbilical cord still attached, and smiled as though no day could ever be better. The Jordan from before he'd fucked everything up. His personality had flattened without her, but now, sitting by her side, he felt himself returning to life.

Gil served the fried cheese, now cut into golden triangles, and Josh held up his empty stubby. 'Anyone else?'

Jordan shook her head. 'I have to drive later.'

'You're not staying?' Ma asked.

Jordan's eyebrows raised in surprise. 'No. I've booked a motel.'

'I know, but . . .' Ma waved a hand in the air. 'Dot's settled now, and there's plenty of room. Have another drink!'

Josh was torn between joining the chorus to coax Jordan to stay, which was what he wanted, and backing up his wife, which was his primary obligation.

'You could sleep in the twins' room,' Jac suggested. 'If you don't mind a single bed.'

Jordan gave Josh a bitter look, as if he'd sold her out. 'It's fine,' she said. 'You don't need to be woken at all hours by a hungry baby. Especially tonight.'

'As if any of us will be sleeping anyway,' Josh said, to end the pain of the conversation.

Jordan leaned in to speak in his ear. 'Can we talk?'

He swallowed. 'Sure.'

'Let's go out the back,' she suggested.

'Won't you be cold?'

'Grab me a blanket. I'll meet you out there.'

Josh ran his hand over the available blankets in Ma's linen press, searching for one that wasn't too scratchy. He could guess what Jordan wanted to talk about—their future. But what would he say? Their relationship already felt so precarious, like it was held together with sticky tape.

What does my character want out of this scene? he asked himself, as if speaking to an imaginary director. The answer was easy. It was the same thing his character always wanted—to get the girl.

He chose the softest blanket he could find—a mint green one with satin edging—and headed out to the back porch.

Jordan was already there, sitting under the light of a half-moon, on one of two timber chairs set on either side of a small table. He passed her the blanket, wishing he'd brought one for himself now that the chill nipped at his nose and ears.

She grabbed a long-barrelled gas lighter that Josh hadn't even noticed was there and lit a candle on the table that separated them.

'I got some work,' he said.

'Really? TV work?'

'Voice work. A book.'

'That's great. Well, it's a start,' she said. 'I have something for you.'

She produced a square parcel wrapped in textured brown paper. 'It's an early Father's Day gift, since we won't be here on Sunday.'

He'd forgotten all about Father's Day. 'Oh. Thank you.' He rolled the parcel over in his hands—hard but not heavy—then tore off the paper to reveal a clear plastic box with what looked bizarrely like a small foot.

'It's a bronze cast of Dot's foot,' she explained. 'Do you like it?'

It *was* a foot. 'Um . . .'

He opened the box and lifted it out, his hand shaking, as if it were his daughter's actual foot, separate from her body, like something taxidermic. On the flat part, where it would have been cut off from the leg, was a tiny inscription that he squinted to read in the candlelight: *To Daddy, Happy 1st Father's Day. Love, Dot.*

His eyes stung, but not from the squinting.

'It's useless, I know,' Jordan said. 'And it's a bit weird—I mean, being a disembodied foot and all—but it's cute.'

He held it in his hands, rubbing the smooth edges, and turned it over a few times. 'I love it. Thanks. I was saving a spot on my top shelf for my first Oscar, but this is . . .' Better? No. A good placeholder? No. 'This is special. Maybe a little morbid.'

'You can rub it and pray for what you want. Think of it like that statue of St Peter in the Vatican.'

He gave a look of mock surprise. 'You want me dead?'

Jordan scrunched her eyebrows together.

'I'm pretty sure they rub the foot because they want St What's-his-name to open the gates of heaven if they die during their pilgrimage.'

'Really? How the hell did you know that?'

He cocked an eyebrow. 'I've been to Rome. I'm cultured.'

'If you say so. Just rub it for good luck then, like a Buddha's belly.'

He had his own Buddha's belly to rub.

He bunched the wrapping paper around the box and set it down on the deck beside him.

'So, this is kind of momentous,' Jordan said. 'Your first Father's Day as a dad and your first one without a dad. How does it feel?'

He hadn't thought of that. The truth was, he'd always felt like a fraud on Father's Day—buying Dad mugs that said *World's Best Dad* and giving cards with pre-printed words that he didn't believe.

'I don't know. I don't really know what it means to be a dad yet, and as for my dad . . .'

'You don't have to be like him.'

He thought about the pills Dr Sampson had prescribed.

'You can be there for Dot.'

He needed to close the wounds of his childhood, when he'd not had the father he wanted and needed. He knew so well what it was like to live without love. So why did he take it for granted now?

'I want to be there for her. If you'll let me.'

'Of course I will.'

He thought better than to point out that she'd been stingy about access to Dot for the past three months. She was probably angry, and fair enough—but maybe now, since being in Pent, she could see he was making progress.

'I'm going home on Friday,' Jordan said.

A band tightened around his chest, his feet suddenly cold. 'So soon?'

She nodded. 'That's why we need to talk—about how we're going to manage things.'

The subject of their future sat in the middle of every room they'd occupied together since the Twitter explosion, but they'd always skirted around it, like a wet patch in the carpet.

'I knew who you were when I married you,' Jordan said, her body angled towards him, 'but I thought you'd changed.'

'I did! I have!'

'And then I thought that once Dot came along . . .'

He cupped his hand over his mouth and exhaled. 'I slept with Holly. I told you that.'

'Only after you got caught.'

He hated talking about the affair with Holly, a producer on *Relationship Rescue*—the affair that didn't get out.

'But she was the only one,' he continued. 'A lapse.'

'A lapse?'

'Nothing happened with Tabeetha. I fucked up with Holly and I apologised. What else can I do?'

She shook her head. 'I don't know. I want us to be a family again, but this feeling I have . . . I'm worried I'll never be enough for you.'

'Of course you're enough. I fucked up *once*.'

'It was only once to you, but to me . . .' She shook her head. 'Josh, this is who you are. You get bored. You get your fill of something and want to move on. You latch onto a thing, go full pelt at it for a while then, when you get it, you lose interest. It's the thrill of the chase, maybe.'

'I didn't lose interest in you. I *haven't* lost interest in you.'

What *was* the reason he'd cheated on Jordan? Why did he feel the need? He'd always assumed it had something to do with the conquest. Achieving. Winning. Perhaps it was boredom, like she said. But he wasn't bored of Jordan. He never had been.

She was silent, waiting for him to answer.

There was something there, a clue trying to present itself to him, but he couldn't grab hold of it. How could he describe the emptiness that had always lived inside him?

'I've always been kind of . . . searching for something,' he tried to explain—to her, to himself. 'I don't know what it is. I thought it was fame. I still think it might be. Everything was better when my career was going well.'

Jordan shook her head as if he were a naive child. 'It's not fame, Josh. It's love. You were looking in the wrong places. And when you found it in the right place, you didn't want it. It's like you're deliberately sabotaging your happiness. Punishing yourself. I don't really understand it. But I can tell you, it's no fun being on the receiving end.' She took his hand. 'I love you,' she said. 'I do. But it's not enough for you.'

'It *is*,' he said. His words came out strong, but something inside felt wrong.

'The distant love of millions is never going to fill that hole you're talking about, I promise you. It's not real.'

How could she say it wasn't real when he felt it so intensely? The way his heart leaped when people would cheer him at shopping centre appearances and when he clicked on YouTube videos fans had cut together of his best scenes from *Common Law*. *That* felt real.

But even when he was on top, self-doubt pecked at his feet.

'It's not just that,' Jordan said, sounding disappointed that she'd just thought of another really good reason why they shouldn't get back together. 'This thing with Tabeetha—whether you did it or not—it brought up all those feelings again. I thought I'd forgiven you, I thought I'd moved on, but it just made me realise that I haven't, and that this is going to keep happening.'

'It won't,' he said, more emphatic now. 'I promise.'

'No, I mean, I'm going to keep feeling this way. And I don't want to live like that. Do you?'

He turned away, taking his hand back. He needed to go inside himself for a minute and he couldn't do that while he was physically connected to her. Everything she'd said about one person never being enough for him, and his tendency to move on to the next shiny thing, was true. But the three months apart, his dad dying . . . he'd felt something shift inside. He wanted more. He wanted to give more. What she'd said about not wanting to live like that, though, suffocating under a blanket of mistrust . . . she was right. He couldn't live like that either, and this knowledge gave him his answer.

He turned back. 'I don't want to live under a cloud of suspicion either. That's not a marriage—you wondering if I'm having an affair every time I come home late or take a phone call in another room. I don't want to spend the rest of our lives like that.' He folded his hand around hers. 'I made a mistake. And I'm sorry about it. I hate that I did it, but I can't change it. All I can do is apologise and promise that it won't happen again. But that has to be it. If we can't move on, if we can't get past it, we'll never be happy.'

She nodded slowly, as though it would help her to decide, or to buy time. 'Okay.'

'Okay, what?'

'Okay, that's something to think on. But I need you to tell me if there are any more *lapses* I should know about. I couldn't handle another surprise.'

'There are no more. I swear.'

She nodded. 'Okay,' she repeated. 'We'll talk again when you come back to Melbourne.'

For the past three months it had been as if, day by day, a weight had been building on his chest to the point where he could no longer breathe. Hearing those words—*We'll talk again*—was enough for now.

'By the way,' he said, 'Kelsey's kicking me out of her flat in, like, three weeks, so if you could, you know, get on to it.'

Jordan smiled. 'If it doesn't work out, you could always live here.'

He tried to picture a life in Pent but nothing would crystallise in his mind. It was unimaginable. 'Then my life really would end.'

30

After they'd finished cleaning the kitchen and set up the lounge and dining area for the wake, Gil went to have a shower and Jac found Ma sitting on a sofa that had been pushed to the edge of the room, a half-full wineglass resting on her thigh.

'I rang his mobile this morning,' Ma said. She was staring at her oversized album cover on the wall.

'Dad's?'

Jac took a seat in the easy chair.

'Don't worry,' Ma said. 'I'm not that far gone. I just wanted to hear his voice.' She gazed into her wineglass. 'I wanted to crawl into the phone just to be closer to him.'

The image of Ma reaching out to Dad squeezed at her.

'I did love him, you know,' Ma continued. 'I didn't always show it. I know that.' She pressed a closed fist to her mouth. 'I hope he knew.'

Seeing Ma like this, her defences worn away, that layer of hardness dissolved, Jac felt a pang of something unrecognisable.

'I miss him,' Ma said.

Jac felt a fleeting urge to cross the room and comfort her mother, but then it was gone.

'I'll find out why,' she said. 'Maybe then we won't all feel so . . . stuck.'

The police had confirmed there was nothing mechanically wrong with Dad's car. But should she ask Ma about the list of names she'd found at the back of Dad's notebook? No, not now. Not the night before the funeral. She wouldn't worry her mother; she would find out what it all meant on her own.

'Jacinta, you need to move on.'

That, she knew, was impossible. She couldn't walk through the next door when the one behind her was still ajar. 'I'm not ready,' she said. 'I want to stay here with—'

'Your grief?' Ma looked at her now, her face daring Jac to disagree.

'I was going to say *you*, and Josh, and Dane. I don't have anything else I can— I can't think about anything else right now.'

Ma's eyes drifted back to the photo. 'That *would* be easier than facing up to this thing with Gil.' Ma looked at her then. 'What are you doing?'

'What do you mean?'

'With *him*?' She angled her chin towards the bathroom.

'You mean the age difference?'

Ma gave her a look—*drop the charade*. 'You're not in love with him.'

It was the last thing Jac had expected her to say. 'What would you know about love?' she snapped.

'Nothing. Not a thing.'

'I'm marrying Gil for the right reasons.'

'Are you?'

'Yes!'

She wanted to get up and walk away. She didn't need this. But something made her stay.

'Would it really be fair?' her mother continued. 'To either of you?'

'I know what I'm doing.'

Ma shook her head. 'I don't understand.'

'You don't have to. It's my life.'

'Yes, it is. And, like always, you'll do exactly as you want. Damn the consequences, damn who you hurt in the process.'

'Ma, I don't want to *hurt* anyone.'

'But it's okay to hurt yourself?'

Jac's jaw clenched. 'Don't pretend you give a shit, Ma. It's really off-brand.'

'What's that supposed to mean?'

'It means that I don't remember you ever—not once— supporting me as a kid. It was only ever criticism: *Change your hair, dress like a girl, stop talking like a wharfie.*'

'The world is cruel, Jacinta. I was arming you for it. What more important job is there for a parent?'

'*You* were cruel.'

Ma took a quick sip of wine, swallowing hard. 'Oh, phooey! You never listened to me anyway. You couldn't see past your father.'

Jac sensed a quake in Ma's voice but disregarded it. 'I *did* listen. And what I heard was that being who I wanted to be was all wrong. *I* was all wrong. No wonder I'm so—'

She had to stop herself. She was a grown woman. Why was she still blaming her mother?

She heard the soft thud of the pipes as the shower shut off. 'Ma,' she said more calmly, 'I want to get married.'

'What for?'

'Isn't that what *you* want me to do?'

Ma's expression loosened. 'I'll admit, there was a time, a long time, when all I wanted was for you to settle down with a decent man and have children. That would have made me happy.'

'Yes, you made that very clear.'

'I thought it would make you happy too. But it won't. Not you. You need to be loved.' She glanced at the photo of herself and Dad on the sideboard. 'Taking the easy road doesn't make anyone happy, in the end.'

Ma was talking about her own life now. But Jac had her own laundry list of times when she, too, had opted for the safer, less heart-rending option. But, as Jac had discovered, no pain is quite as unrelenting as regret.

Gil came into the study in his pyjamas, bringing with him the smell of soap and aftershave lotion, a toiletry bag tucked under his arm and a towel flung over his shoulder. In the light from the desk lamp, she saw the dark hairs on his tanned feet.

He folded the towel, laying it on the desk, and returned the toiletry bag to his case.

In the car from the airport, with Gil talking about what he'd been doing since she'd left Sydney, she'd realised that for the whole week she'd been living in a kind of alternative dimension, as if the outside world didn't exist. While he'd been carrying on with his life, it was as if hers had stopped, suspended in time.

'Have you decided where we're going to live?' he asked now.

She looked at him, standing there in his pyjamas, and tried to smile. She needed space to think.

'Gil, I'm not sure that this is the right time for us to be getting married.'

He sat down on the bed next to her.

'I keep thinking: what's the point if Dad isn't here to see it?'

'What's the point?' he echoed. 'The same point as there was two weeks ago when we decided. And you didn't want your parents to be part of it in the first place.' He kept his voice light.

He was right. She was making excuses.

'Look, I know all this stuff with your dad has been very disorientating. Of course it has. But how can you see anything clearly when your eyes are blurry with tears?' He squeezed her hand and went on. 'I heard it takes a full year—a full turn of the calendar—to get over losing someone close to you. And, no doubt, there'll be plenty of aftershocks along the way.'

It was true—the ground beneath her feet swayed constantly, and she felt the need to grab on to something.

And Gil had arrived at the perfect time. It was only a month before she'd met him that Jenn, the dog owner who wrote the funny notes, had broken up with her.

'I can't date half a person,' Jenn had said one Sunday morning while they watched her German shepherd sniff its way around the off-lead park. 'I want to introduce you to my friends and take you to dinner parties.'

Jac shook her head.

'Fine.' Jenn crossed her arms over her chest. 'Then I don't want to be with you anymore.'

'Okay,' Jac said.

'Okay? *Okay?*' Jenn wound the lead around her hand. 'Is that all you can say?'

She walked back to Jenn's house on her own, packed her overnight bag, and left.

So this is how it feels, she'd thought then. *Being dumped*. She didn't like it. Not one bit. She'd been bitten hard by love, she'd realised. Hard enough this time to draw blood.

It was stupid, really, letting herself fall for Jenn. Riding the train home that day, she'd vowed not to give anyone the power to hurt her again. Four weeks and a mountain of greasy takeaway later, she'd reached a threshold. Then she met Gil.

'Nothing's changed between us, has it?' Gil asked now. 'All the reasons we had for wanting to get married are still there, aren't they?'

'Yeah, but . . .' Something *was* different. *She* was different, but she couldn't pin it down. The person who'd had a father had died along with Dad. And something had dislodged inside her.

But maybe Gil was right. Perhaps her change of heart was temporary. She was too blinded by grief to make any long-term decisions.

She inclined her head. 'Okay.'

He nodded too. 'Listen, one more thing. I know the timing isn't great, but I promised Jacob I'd spend Father's Day with him.'

'Of course.'

'You want me to cancel?'

'No, no. Be with your son. It's important.'

He rubbed the back of her hand with his thumb. 'What are your plans?'

She exhaled; she hadn't thought much beyond tomorrow. 'I'll stay here, I guess.'

'Have you spoken with work?'

'They're fine.'

'Then you should take all the time you need.'

How long would that be? It was impossible to know. But she couldn't leave while everyone and everything around her was so brittle—Ma, Josh, her own internal organs. The air in the house felt wobbly. She couldn't imagine doing anything to upset what was already a fragile situation.

Gil let go of her hand and stood, grabbing his toiletry bag out of the case. 'I forgot to brush my teeth.'

With Gil gone, a sudden fear gripped her. What if Gil died too? The plane back to Sydney could crash. He could be hit by a garbage truck or killed in the crossfire of a convenience store hold-up. He could be the victim of a terrorist attack! Any of these things could happen, because bad things happened around her all the time.

People always left just when she needed them most.

THURSDAY

31

On the morning of the funeral, the rain came down in buckets. Dane hovered in the chapel entranceway as women tiptoed through the puddles on the paved forecourt, clutching onto men holding umbrellas. A squally wind blew, billowing up dresses and gusting hair in all directions.

The funeral people said the family should stand at the entrance to greet everyone as they arrived, but Ma wasn't having it.

'People will probably approach you anyway,' said Carmel Tyler.

'Well, I won't be able to stop them,' Ma said, 'but I won't be greeting them as if it's a birthday party.'

Dane didn't think you would stand at the front greeting your guests at a birthday party either, but he didn't say so. In any case, he felt someone from the family should be there.

Tyler's Funerals had constructed its own grand room for conducting services at the back of the period homestead they had occupied for three generations. It had the appearance of a chapel, with its high, gabled ceiling at one end, but was generic enough for any religious service or, in Dad's case, no religion at all. Flowers emerged from the floor in cone-shaped vases, like ice creams in an assortment of flavours.

At the front of the room stood the coffin. Polished mahogany; that was what they'd chosen from the images Carmel Tyler had presented from her iPad at Ma's kitchen table three days before. The coffin was positioned longways, resting on a steel gurney with concertina legs. Dane imagined Dad inside it, lifeless, his skin deteriorated by now. That was the image that might replace the steel locker Dane had been picturing him in for the past six days.

A framed photo of Dad taken on his sixtieth birthday, the same one they'd used for the funeral book, looked out from the casket, framed by a long bouquet of flowers piled high behind it. What would happen with Dad's body from here, they still hadn't decided—cremation, yes, but his final resting place was uncertain, as if there was still time to stop what they all knew was unstoppable.

People continued swarming through the doors, flicking water from their coats, pausing to collect the order-of-service brochures and sign the condolence book. A fresh, musky smell of rain moistening the earth wafted in each time the doors opened.

Dane shook the men's hands, nodded through their words of sympathy, and accepted the women's kisses. Between greetings, he felt for the speech, A4 and folded in three, in his inside jacket pocket. Jac and Josh had helped him with it, but last night, under the light of his bedside lamp, his laptop resting on his thighs, the words had felt forced, somehow untrue. The stories he'd prepared happened the way he'd written (the details negotiated between his and Jac's inconsistent memories), but the other stuff—the stuff about the type of man Dad was—rang false, knowing the deceitful part he'd played in securing the St Augustine's building permit. Dane had booked Solid Rock for a follow-up soil test but hadn't yet decided what to do about the Aboriginal site survey. He supposed he should organise that too. What if they began excavating and skeletons started turning up? That would be the end of it.

Now, reading out the words he'd prepared about Dad's integrity and community-mindedness . . . well, it didn't seem right. Dad had not proposed the St Augustine's project to fill a need for more housing—to propel Pent into the modern era, as he'd been quoted as saying in the *Gazette*. He'd approached it doggedly, like a personal crusade. Now, as the head of the company, Dane felt covered in something that wouldn't wash off.

So, he'd pushed the speech aside, toggling out of Word and googling 'suicide statistics Australia'. He'd read the horrifying numbers; he'd read about slipshod service coordination and the need, still, to destigmatise depression and suicide. He'd thought about Joel Hutchison's son, Thomas, and the countless sons, daughters, brothers and sisters like him. He'd closed the laptop, set it on the floor by the bed and switched off the light, feeling overwhelmed by the enormity of it all, and his own smallness.

Josh arrived at the chapel then, one hand clutching the handle of a black-and-white golf umbrella, his spare arm wrapped around Jordan and Dot. They hurried through the doors behind Jac's friend from the bar. Amy, was it?

Jordan, in a navy-blue dress, was even more beautiful than Dane remembered. Her hair was set in thin braids woven close to her head. Josh, clean-shaven and wearing a suit, almost resembled his real self—or perhaps his *reel* self: the TV presenter. All he needed was a red rose in his lapel and he could've been back on the set of *Relationship Rescue*.

'Hello, Dane,' Jordan said. 'I'm so sorry about your dad.' She kissed his cheek.

'Thanks, Jordan. And thanks for coming.'

'Of course.'

Jordan held Dot towards Dane. 'This is your uncle Dane,' she told the little girl. Dot raised one hand, moving her fingers like she was trying to catch the air.

Dane planted a kiss on the polka-dotted headband that circled Dot's crown. She'd grown so much since he'd last seen her in Melbourne, just after she was born. She had Jordan's dark skin and hair, but the shape of her eyes and mouth reminded him of Josh as a baby.

Without warning, Josh wrapped his arms around Dane's torso, pressing his cold ear against his brother's cheek. He stayed there a long moment, breathing heavily, before pulling away, sniffing and rubbing his eyes. 'Ma and Jac already inside?' he asked.

'Yeah, front row. I'll be there in a tick.'

Dane clasped Josh's forearm briefly before Josh broke away and placed his hand on the small of Jordan's back, ushering her down the aisle.

Once everyone was inside and the music lowered, Carmel Tyler approached the podium, repositioned the microphone closer to her mouth and announced that they would be starting in a moment. She paused for a count of five, letting the last of the chatter die down. Then, closing her slate-coloured blazer over her waist with one hand, she spent ten minutes summarising Dad's life. Her delivery seemed heartfelt, but Dane knew she'd only met him twice.

When Carmel was finished, a guy from the golf club, Ian Sharp, stood up to speak, sharing stories of Dad's prowess on the golf course and in the bar. 'He always had time for people, Stephen did. Everybody liked him,' he said, while Ma crumpled a tissue between her fingers and Jac squeezed Gil's hand as if she didn't trust herself not to run.

They played a song—K.D. Lang's version of 'Hallelujah'—and then Carmel Tyler called on Dane.

Standing at the podium, looking across the congregation, quiet and expectant, his eyes clocked Gayle, and Olivia, and Dad's sister Susan. Andrea, who owned the Circle Cafe, was there with her husband, as was Sam Donovan, their accountant. Damian Davenport, Dad's mate from the council, sat in the row behind Wayne Harper. Dane wasn't sure that he could ever look at Damian the same way again.

He reached inside his jacket and pulled out the page, unfolded it, and flattened it across the lectern.

'Thank you everyone for coming. Dad loved you all and would have appreciated you being here.'

He looked at the page, the words blurring through the tears pooling in his eyes.

'You've heard a lot about who Dad was from the eulogy and from Ian. You all knew him, so I won't . . .'

He stopped, realising how untrue that statement was. Dane grew up with him, saw him every day, but he didn't really know him: the man behind the facade—the tortured man, the man who acted in ways that Dane never would have predicted. He scanned the room, recognising nearly every face—clients, relatives, school friends. None of them really knew Dad either.

He folded the page back into three and placed it on the flat surface in front of him, clearing his throat. 'Yesterday I was at the council offices.'

Gazing at the centre of the room, he saw Angus Chu's expression change.

'Outside, in the concourse, there's a statue that commemorates all the sons and daughters of Pent we've lost in wars over the years. You all know the one. We walk past it; we probably don't even notice it anymore, let alone stop to think about all the names on it. Because that's all they are now—names. Statistics.'

He took a breath, unsure of where he was heading but knowing that, somehow, he must go there.

'But it's not battles overseas that are taking our men now. We're losing them here in Pent, young *and* old, right out of our homes. We're not doing enough to help them and that's not okay.'

He caught the eye of Joel Hutchison, who gave him an encouraging nod.

'Events like this make us stop and reflect. But for how long? How long until . . . until the memory fades and we go back to our shopping and our bills and our weekend sport, ignoring what's going on right under our noses? Maybe some of us don't stop at all. Maybe we ignore it because it's happening to someone else. Well, I can tell you, it's not happening to someone else. It's happening to me and it'll probably happen to you, if it hasn't already.'

He gripped the sides of the podium and took another deep breath. For a moment, the congregation disappeared and it was like he was talking to himself, trying to knit it all together in his mind, to make sense of the nonsensical.

'We pretend we're okay; family and friends believe we're okay—or turn a blind eye—but too often nothing happens until it's too late.'

He squeezed his eyes closed to stop the tears, but then opened them again. 'We need to talk about this,' he said. 'We have to end the shame and end the silence. We have to change the way we view mental health and mental health problems so that instead of seeing people going through emotional turmoil as being . . . as being fundamentally different from us, we see them as being fundamentally the same.'

Maybe he should shut up and sit down, he thought. Was anybody even listening? Was he making any sense? And who was *he* to be talking about this?

No, he decided, there was more to say.

'My family and I have been touched by the gestures of support from everyone—the flowers, the food left on our doorsteps. Thank you. But why is it only at times like this that we reach out? We never see our neighbours anymore; there are no street parties, and the council banned New Year's Eve celebrations in the square.' He glanced around the room. 'Remember those? Banging pot lids and letting off illegal fireworks?' He detected a handful of nods from the floor. 'And we've just accepted it.'

He thought then of the Pent of his childhood—the one he'd talked to Josh about: a time when everyone knew each other, cared about each other, and banded together.

'We're arguing about pulling down churches or not pulling down churches, and complaining about the . . . about the *hassle* of having to change the route we take to the supermarket because of roadworks. But meanwhile our brothers and sisters, our sons and daughters, our mums and dads are struggling.'

He felt the momentum building, the words coming without thought now, as though planted there by someone else.

'We don't need new apartments; we don't need to build more places to hide ourselves away. We need more spaces to come together—to ask each other, *Are you okay?* We need community hubs; we need crisis centres. Because, make no mistake, this *is* a crisis. And we're smack-bang in the middle of it.'

He blinked back a tear. 'Dad wanted to die alone. Why would someone who was so gregarious and full of life choose to leave us in that way? I guess we'll never know. But what we do know is that something was wrong. Dad loved Pent. And he loved you all. But let's admit it: he wasn't living well here.

How can you live well when you're fighting every day to pass yourself off as someone else? Someone "normal"? Someone not in pain?'

In the front row, Jac wiped her eyes with her forearm.

'We're building these speed humps around town for people in wheelchairs and mobility scooters. We can see, with our own eyes, that they might need some extra help. What are we building for people with mental health issues? Not being able to see that a person is grappling with something doesn't mean that they're not, and it's not good enough to pretend we don't notice because, God forbid, it makes *us* feel uncomfortable.'

He took a breath, casting his eye across the room at the blank faces, looking as daunted as he felt by the hopelessness of it all. Where would they even start?

'I know it can be hard to admit that the time has come for us to face a new problem. But we've faced down new problems before: the global financial crisis, Black Saturday, coronavirus— challenges that seemed, at the time, like they might cripple us. In fact, these things have made us stronger. As individuals, though, being strong also means having the courage to ask for help when we need it.'

He thought back to his reading from the night before. 'We can't push all the responsibility for this on to hospitals or doctors. It's got to start at work, in our schools and in our footy club.' He thought about Dad and about Thomas Hutchison, and about the reluctance of people to call for help. 'Sometimes, in our darkest moments, we just need someone . . . someone to reach out, to take us by the hand and guide us to the light switch. And some- times we need to ask someone else to switch the light on for us.' He moistened his lips and swallowed, only now registering how dry his mouth was. 'There's nothing noble in suffering, and there's nothing shameful in asking for help.'

Just then, a sense of calm descended on him—the sense that he'd said what he'd needed to, even if he couldn't remember a word of it. But there was one more plea he needed to make.

'So the task falls on all of us. Be a good mate, be a good neighbour. Listen to what people say, but, more importantly, hear what they're *not* saying, and reach out.'

He looked at Ma and Jac and Josh, and at the next generation of Hardings—Dylan, Marcus and Dot. 'Dad's life meant something. But let's make his death mean something too.'

32

The air inside Ma's house was heavy with people smells—perfume, aftershave, hairspray—and the buttery aroma of heated pastry, enclosing Dane in the shrunken lounge room. Why had Ma insisted on having the wake at home? The rain meant that everyone had to cram into the house and only a few smokers stood in the backyard under the pergola, plumes of grey smoke curling into the mist.

There must have been eighty or so people in the house, crowding the lounge, the dining room and the kitchen, with their paper plates of sandwiches and mini spring rolls. The previous night, Josh and Gil had pushed all the larger pieces of furniture to the sides of the rooms to make more space, but still the walls seemed too close together and the ceiling had somehow lowered.

He stood at the makeshift bar—a trestle table arrayed with glasses of wine and stubbies of beer. The boys were upstairs playing, and Ngaire was talking to Josh and Jordan by the front windows.

He grabbed a beer, twisted the top, and turned to find Gayle, dressed in a dark grey suit and colourful scarf, standing behind him. She held a glass of white wine, red lipstick smeared on the rim. 'That was quite a speech you gave.'

'Was it? I don't really remember what I said.'

She tilted her head to the side. 'It was inspirational—all that stuff about community and coming together. You're right. We've lost that.'

He cringed, wondering what else he'd said. Funerals weren't the place to climb on a soapbox and preach from on high. It was embarrassing and indulgent, like Oscar recipients who used the stage to sermonise about a political cause. He should apologise to Ma for going off script.

'And something about not needing to build new apartments?' Gayle said.

'Oh, shit, did I?'

What had he said? Something about the community debate over whether or not to demolish it, wasn't it?

'Don't worry,' Gayle said. 'I'm sure it got missed in all the stuff about losing touch with each other.'

'I hope so.'

Gayle sipped her wine. 'You're not overjoyed about the project, are you?' Dane had the sense she was asking out of concern for him rather than the business.

'No,' he admitted. 'And even more so since—' He paused. 'Did Dad use his connections at the council to push jobs through?'

'I'm sure he did,' she said plainly. 'And why not?'

'I don't mean fast-tracking a permit or overlooking a slight bend of the planning code—I know he did that. I mean being blatantly deceitful, maybe even illegal.'

She looked pensive. 'Such as?'

He lowered his voice. 'I've found out the planning process for the St Aug's apartments hasn't been above board. And who knows what else was rammed through?'

'Oh,' Gayle said, looking into her glass. 'Well, he was hellbent on getting those apartments built, I know that much. I think he saw it as his opportunity to really *do* something. I think he would've paid double for that site if he'd needed to.'

'I don't get it. He wasn't like this before.' He shook his head. 'Or maybe he was.'

She touched his arm. 'Don't be angry with him, Dane. Not today.'

'I'm not. I'm just . . . a little confused, I guess.'

'Those apartments are going to be his legacy. And what's done is done. The plans have gone through.'

'But if it ever comes out . . .'

'He was a smart man. I'm sure he covered his tracks.'

But for how long?

Dane lowered his voice again. 'Did you know Dad had hired someone to look into Leigh's . . . affairs?'

She glanced around to see who was close by. 'He was concerned about him,' she said softly. 'Leigh's struggling financially and Stephen was worried that it might . . . cloud his judgement.'

'But why hire an investigator?'

Gayle leaned in. 'Stephen tried to get Leigh to open up but he wouldn't. So he went another way. He wanted to know the extent of Leigh's problems.'

'Did Leigh find out what Dad was up to?'

Gayle blinked in surprise. 'I don't think so. How could he?'

'He had access to Dad's computer.' He could have used it at any time, Dane thought, but he was thinking now of the

Saturday after Dad died, when he'd found Leigh leaving the office and discovered that Dad's computer had been moved.

Frank Fevola, a school mate of Dad's, was suddenly at Dane's side. 'Hello, Dane, Gayle.' He slipped his long-shanked frame between them. 'Compelling speech, Dane. But I hope it doesn't mean you're not going to build my new apartment?'

Dane wouldn't let the question rattle him. 'No, Frank, of course not. I was . . . spit-balling. I wasn't talking about the St Augustine's development specifically.'

Frank nodded. 'Good, because I'll be lining up with my cheque on Monday.'

'Great. That's fantastic. Thank you.'

In a corner of the lounge room, on a two-seater sofa, Ma sipped on a glass of white wine. Angus Chu sat on the couch next to her, talking, but she didn't appear to be listening, her eyes staring blankly across the room.

'Can you excuse me a second?' Dane said.

As he approached, the mayor was asking, 'What is it, Mrs Harding? You don't like the name? It's not final.'

He must have been pitching her the depression program in Dad's name.

'I don't like the idea at all,' she said in a flat voice.

Angus Chu pushed his glasses up his nose. 'Oh, well, we thought it would be . . . We'd make sure that it's very respectful. Dignified. And after what Dane said in his speech about . . .' Angus Chu looked to Dane for backup, but he didn't receive it.

'I'm sorry, Angus,' he said. 'Maybe now's not the time?'

'Of course. Let's revisit it again later. A meeting at my office?'

'Sure.'

Angus Chu moved away.

'Are you okay, Ma?'

'Fine.'

'About the speech . . .'

Leigh tapped his shoulder. 'Can I have a word?'

'Now?'

'Yep.' Leigh was scanning the room with narrowed eyes, as if on the lookout for spies.

'Back in a minute, Ma.'

In the backyard, under the pergola, the rain spilling down around them, Leigh laced his fingers together and hammered them at chest height like in desperate prayer. 'I'm sorry to do this to you today, mate, but I don't think it can wait. What you said at the funeral about Pent not needing apartments . . .'

'Oh, Jesus.' Dane exhaled. 'I didn't mean *our* apartments. Everyone's blowing this way out of proportion.'

'You think? Fiona from the *Gazette* just asked Olivia if there's a story in it.'

'What?'

Beer fumes wafted from Leigh's mouth. 'You need to nip this in the bud before Monday, Dane. We can't afford to have buyers pulling out at the last minute.'

'They won't. I didn't mean . . .'

'You may not have meant it, but you said it. People will interpret it in their own way, and we don't need the whole town thinking we're not a hundred per cent behind this project.'

Dane tried of think of what they called it when you said something you didn't mean, but you kind of did . . . a Freudian slip; that was it. 'They won't,' he repeated. 'And so what? I made a passing comment about apartments. It was general and said at a highly emotional time. I don't think people are going to take it seriously, and even if they do, it's not going to stop them buying into the development. It's not like we're *not* going to build it. And even if a few drop out, we've still got plenty of time to sell them. Once people see the quality—'

'Have you even looked at the numbers? The business will haemorrhage money unless we sell eighty per cent before construction. The bank won't give us the loan to build and, either way, we won't be able to carry the debt.'

He'd looked at the financials but not closely enough. He needed to be more on top of these things. Well, he had a meeting with their accountant lined up for the following day. He'd get his head around it all then. 'It won't come to that. Lots of people are excited about this project.'

Leigh's mouth tightened. 'Dane, despite what you said at the funeral, I think you're underestimating the power of public opinion in this town—and how much people admire you.'

People might like him, Dane thought, but *admire* him? He'd never done anything to earn it.

Leigh persisted. 'When the community decides they want to back something—or, in our case, *not*—you're dead in the water. You going around saying you don't support the project? Even if it doesn't get in the paper, word will spread. By this time tomorrow, the whole town will have heard. I know you're not a fan of this development, but you can't let your biases show. It's bad for business.'

Dane held up both hands in surrender. 'Alright, drop the lecture. I'll speak to Olivia. But I reckon our best move is to stay quiet. Trust me, it'll blow over. The more we talk about it, the longer we keep the story alive. It'll grow into something it's not, and we don't want that.'

Leigh shook his head. 'I can't believe this.'

'What?'

'Can't you see what you're doing? *Again?* You're risking another big project because you're hanging on to some child-hood fantasy of what Pent should be. You're stuck in the past, mate, and that speech you made proves it . . . Banging pot lids in the square. If you care about this town like you say you do, you should want it to be a place that thrives, that moves with the times. Young people are the future, and they don't want to live in a town that's at a standstill. They want to be somewhere with opportunities and modern facilities, not dead churches that no one needs or cares about.'

'It's not about the church, Leigh. I'll admit I don't like seeing our past erased like this, but now it's about the process. It needs to be above reproach, otherwise, when all this comes out—and it will—there's going to be a big black cloud hanging over those apartments and an even bigger one hanging over Harding Construction. Then we really will be dead in the water, if not in prison.'

Leigh kicked a bottle cap, sending it skidding across the decking. 'Oh, for Christ's sake. No one's going to . . . This is why Stephen didn't tell you about the Aboriginal heritage application. He knew you couldn't handle it. He knew—we all do—that you don't have the balls to take this company into the future he'd planned.'

Dane drew a sharp breath. Before then, it had never bothered him that Dad didn't involve him more in the St Augustine's development, even though it was, technically, a residential project, which was his domain. But now he understood why—because Dad thought he was weak-willed and wouldn't have the stomach to do what had to be done to make it happen.

Other things dropped into place then, too—why Dad had never shared a succession plan with him or ever involved him in the business side of the company. He had no intention of handing it down to him, because he didn't trust him to run it.

And that, more than all the dubious dealings at Harding Construction, was what cut the deepest.

33

Throughout the funeral service, and now at the wake, Jac felt laid bare—one tear away from either crumpling to the floor or exploding in a blaze of anger. Both were a real possibility. And that speech Dane made, about fighting every day to pass yourself off as someone else . . . She'd gone out and bought a dress for the funeral, for crying out loud—if that wasn't a sign she was losing herself, she didn't know what was. Still, she held it together, albeit with a single stitch, moving, robot-like, from person to person in Ma's house, introducing Gil, thanking people for their kindness, offering food.

She wasn't at all hungry herself, but at Gil's insistence she relinquished her wineglass and nibbled on a mini quiche while Ma's friend Rosie admired her engagement ring and told her how happy her father would have been with her news.

When Gil disappeared to get more food, Rosie said, 'He's lovely. You're lucky to have found each other.'

269

'I'm the lucky one,' Jac said, repeating yet another version of the line she'd been uttering all day.

It occurred to her that this was precisely what she'd wanted—the smiles on people's faces, the congratulations, the confirmation that she'd made the right decision. So why did she feel so hollow?

Over Rosie's shoulder, she saw Ma on the couch, surrounded by people hovering around her solicitously, pressing drinks into her hand and bringing her plates of food. This was Ma's last chance to be Mrs Stephen Harding and she couldn't face it. Jac had seen her in hostess mode many times growing up—waving platters of appetisers, checking if people's glasses were full and complimenting women on their outfits. She would ask after sick relatives and pretend to marvel at the accomplishments of her guests' children. But now she was inhaling wine and nodding mindlessly through conversations.

'So, when's the big day?' Rosie asked.

Jac blinked, taking a second to realise Rosie was talking about the wedding. 'We haven't decided yet. Next year sometime.'

Near the front window, at Jordan's feet, Dot cooed, sitting up on a crocheted blanket, while the twins entertained her with funny faces. She couldn't work out if this sight—the next genera-tion of Hardings, not yet damaged, not yet beset by the miseries and the unjust horrors of the world—made her joyful or sad.

She excused herself from Rosie and crossed the room, her hands urging to pick up Dot and squeeze that beautiful bundle of flesh to her chest.

'Are you okay, Jac?' Jordan asked.

'Yes.'

'You're crying,' Josh said.

And so she was, with no idea why. It was just that the children were so beautiful.

'She's gorgeous, Josh.'

'Thanks?' her brother said, extracting the wineglass from her hand.

The afternoon pressed on, becoming blurrier as the minutes ticked by. Her head felt spongy, her eyelids heavy. People asked the same questions, delivered the same condolences, until Jac started to wish everyone would just leave. Her hands had become jittery and her patience was stretched thin. It was all so fake, she decided as she plonked another empty glass on the drinks table and picked up a full one: the civility, the platitudes, everyone tiptoeing around the reality of why they were there. Dane had made it plain enough at the funeral—Dad had killed himself without a hint as to why. Was nobody else angry about that?

Beside her, a man she didn't recognise was introducing another. She heard the name Mike Vincent and her ears pricked. Mike Vincent. From the list. She pushed her way into the group. 'Excuse me, are you Mike Vincent?'

'Yes.'

Mike was a short man, about Dad's height, with a full head of brown hair—dyed, she thought. He was clean-shaven and the skin on his face had an even, almost synthetic tone.

'I'm Jac. Stephen's daughter.' Even she could hear the slur in her own words now.

'Oh, hello.' He frowned sympathetically. 'I'm sorry for your—'

She flapped a hand at him. 'Yeah, yeah, yeah. Can I talk to you?'

His brow creased. 'Okay.'

She placed her hand under his elbow and drew him away from the group.

'Why are you on a list of names with big amounts of money next to them?'

'I beg your pardon?'

'Did you owe Dad money? Did he owe *you* money?'

Something flickered in his eyes, but then it was gone. 'I don't know what you mean.'

'Yes, you do. You're on the list. Your name. It's on the list.'

'Jacinta, I—'

'It's Jac!' she said, too loudly, probably, as she sloshed wine on the front of her new black dress.

Then, like an apparition, Amy was by her side, prising the wineglass from her hand. 'Jac, can you show me to the loo?'

Seeing her, it felt like a gust of fresh air had blown through the fug in Ma's house. Like when she'd seen Amy at the train station a week ago. She forgot, for a moment, what she'd been saying. 'Sure. I'll take you.'

Instead of directing her to the bathroom, she led Amy to the study. She wanted her to herself for a moment.

'What was that all about?' Amy asked as Jac shut the door.

'Nothing, nothing.' She kicked off her evil heels, flinging them at the fold-out.

'Is this where you're sleeping?' Amy asked.

Jac rested her bum on the edge of Dad's desk. It was as if she'd just woken up, the events of the day since the funeral a blur. 'Come over here. I need to tell you something.' She beckoned with a hand.

'Are you okay?'

'Sure, sure.'

Amy closed the distance between them.

'Why did you duck away when I tried to kiss you the other night?'

Amy eyed the door. 'Jac, is this really the—'

'I want to know. Why?'

Amy looked at her a moment, tipping her head to one side. 'Because you're engaged.'

Jac's fingers found the top button on Amy's navy shirt and pushed it through the hole, revealing the edge of her flesh-coloured bra. 'What if I wasn't?'

Amy shimmied her shoulders, wiggling away.

Jac grappled with the second button, jamming it loose with her thumb. She just wanted to feel Amy's warmth. To feel something good.

'Jac!'

With both hands, Jac grabbed Amy's shirt by the collar and yanked it down, pinning Amy's arms to her sides.

'Stop it, Jac. You're—'

'What? I'm what? Reckless? Irrational? *Impulsive?*'

Amy stood in front of her, shoulders bare and her bra fully visible now. 'I was going to say sad.'

Jac touched the top of Amy's right shoulder with her fingertips, leaned over and kissed the skin there. She smelled floral, like spring, and faintly of chlorine.

'And maybe a little confused,' Amy said.

Jac turned her head and rested an ear on Amy's shoulder so her mouth was almost touching the fleshy part of her neck.

The voices from the wake suddenly got louder. Amy shifted her shoulder to rouse Jac, who lifted her head. Her eyes cut to the door and she saw Gil, beer in hand, his mouth open. He looked at Jac, then at Amy, standing there half-undressed, then back at Jac, a wounded expression in his eyes.

Then he banged the door closed.

34

After everyone left, Dane stayed behind to clean up. Josh helped him move the furniture in the lounge and dining rooms to its rightful place, while Jac stood over the kitchen sink washing the glasses that wouldn't fit in the dishwasher. Gil was nowhere to be seen.

When Dane was done, he found Ma curled in an armchair upstairs, staring into space. She was still dressed in her funeral outfit, but her make-up had worn away and she wore fluffy, open-toed slippers on her stockinged feet.

'I'm heading off,' he told her.

She glanced at him. 'You look tired.'

He was tired. The kind of tired that felt stored up and made his bones feel heavy.

He tried to swallow but was cotton-mouthed. 'I'm okay, I'm just . . .' His voice broke. His eyes welled and then a single tear dripped down his chin. 'I can't believe he's gone,' he said.

'He was here just last week.'

'I know.'

'His coffee cup's still in the lunchroom at work, for God's sake.' He looked up. 'He still feels alive to me.'

She extended a hand to him and he sat in the armchair next to hers.

This flood of emotion—it was not the Harding way. But everything about his life felt wrong now. The world held his head under water, then yanked it out. He would find he could breathe again, and things were okay—he'd had some wins at work and he was starting to feel more self-assured. Then something would happen to pull him under again—Leigh, the shit with St Augustine's.

'I don't think I can do it, Ma. The business.'

She squeezed his clenched hand. 'Of course you can. It's your birthright!'

Something inside him broke loose. 'Just because I'm the first-born Harding, it doesn't mean I was born somehow *intrinsically* knowing how to run a construction company.'

She snatched her hand back, clutching it to her chest. 'You're great at your job!'

'Yeah, *my* job. Not his. A bathroom renovation, I can manage that—but I can't run an entire company.'

'What's the difference?'

'The difference is financial forecasting, forward planning, marketing, managing staff . . . I don't have those skills. I don't know anything about that stuff.'

'So you'll learn.'

'Yeah, I can learn how to read a profit-and-loss statement, but it's not enough. I'm not him.'

She sat up and straightened her legs out until her feet touched the carpet. 'And no one expects you to be. He certainly didn't.'

Part of him was angry that he would never get to prove himself to Dad, but he had to admit he felt relief too. He no longer had Dad breathing down his neck, regarding everything he did with a critical eye. That had been unbearable. More unbearable than this.

'The way he did things,' he said. 'I don't agree with it.'

Ma pulled back, squaring her shoulders.

'I've found out some stuff recently.'

'You mean the church project?' she said softly, but without emotion.

'You knew?'

'He talked to me about work sometimes.'

'Was he at least *troubled* by it?'

'Not *that* much.' She shook her head. 'I don't know the details. He didn't tell me and I didn't ask. He used his influence and he made it happen.'

There must have been other regulations Dad sidestepped on the St Augustine's project. And what about before that? How many other times had he strong-armed his way into deals?

'That's a generous way of putting it,' he said.

It could have taken years for Dad to grow into that person. For him to become bolder, more hungry, or more desperate for success with each new achievement. Maybe he could never fill the well. Maybe achieving these things made him feel proud at the time but, in the aftermath, empty. Maybe that's why he ploughed his car into the Marshall Road overpass.

'Business was business,' Ma said. 'Or perhaps things weighed on his mind more than I thought. I don't know.'

'He didn't trust me enough to tell me,' Dane said.

'He was protecting you.'

Dane struck the soft arm of the chair with his knuckles. 'I don't want to be protected! It's just more proof that he thought I don't have what it takes to run this company.'

'That's not it.' She rested her fingertips on the back of his hand. 'He didn't want to taint you with this—that's what I think. Or perhaps he didn't want to lose your respect. Believe it or not, he looked up to you; he admired your integrity, your faithful heart.' She tapped his hand to make sure she had his attention. 'Dane, you *are* the man to take this company into the future. But you can't lead the company the way you think Dad would have done it. It has to be your way.'

He shook his head, burying his face in his hands. 'I don't know what my way is.'

'Yes, you do. Trust your instincts.' She patted his arm. 'You'll figure it out.'

By the time he arrived home, Ngaire was already in bed, her laptop charging on the bedside table.

He flicked on the light in the walk-in robe and she made a small noise of protest.

'Sorry,' he said as she rolled over, away from the glare.

He undressed, hung up his suit and deposited his shirt and socks into the laundry basket. He shut the light off and felt his way to the bed, climbing under sheets warmed by the electric blanket.

'I think there's going to be some more stuff in the paper about St Aug's,' he said into the darkness.

'Mmm.'

'The *Gazette*'s asking questions, and I don't know if I have the answers.'

She didn't respond, so he turned to face her. 'Ngaire?'

She sighed. '*Now* you want to talk?'

'Is that okay?'

She opened her eyes, the sheen of them reflecting the dim glow of moonlight leaking under the blinds. 'This is the most you've said about work in a year.'

The statement surprised him. They discussed their lives all the time. 'I talk about work.'

'Yeah, you say it's fine, or okay, or alright.'

'That's because I don't want to . . . I think of them as my problems, I guess.'

'You're more like your dad than you think.'

He didn't believe that. Any traits he shared with Dad were a matter of statistical probability, not genetics.

Ngaire rolled over and propped herself up on one elbow. 'So talk.'

He sighed; it was all too depressing. 'I don't want to.'

She made a sound somewhere between a huff and a laugh. 'Fine. I will. They hate it.'

She was talking about the St Aug's development, he presumed. 'Who?'

'My writing group.'

His eyes had adjusted to the light now, and he could see the disappointment on her face, but he was confused.

'It *fails to connect*,' she murmured. 'That's what Ingrid said.'

Who was Ingrid? he wondered. Had she been at the funeral?

Ngaire was watching him. 'You don't know what I'm talking about, do you?'

He tried to put it together, like the pieces of two different puzzles that didn't quite fit. 'Um . . . your book group?'

'This is the most important thing in my life right now—I'm pouring my heart and soul into it—and you never even ask me about it.'

Understanding dawned. 'Your book?'

'Yes, Dane, my book.'

'I thought you didn't want me to read it.'

She gave him a look. 'That doesn't mean you shouldn't ask about it. It's like you don't care. No, I *know* you don't care.'

The whole concept of writing a book seemed so foreign to him, and there was nothing tangible about it that he could hold on to. He wasn't sure if his lack of interest was because she'd roadblocked his access to the process or because he was too focused on his own concerns.

'I do care—I'm just not that interested,' he admitted.

'Interest is the definition of caring! Anyway, it doesn't matter. I lack emotional honesty, apparently. *I can't translate my feelings to the page.*' She rolled onto her other side, turning away from him, sliding her hands under her cheeks. 'A year's work . . . That brought me back to earth, I can tell you.'

The problem wasn't that they had stopped talking but that they had lost interest in the things the other person was talking about. Despite how busy they were, there was an emptiness to their lives, which felt unspeakable given what they had been through to get the twins and how unthinkable a life without them would be.

Josh had pegged it on his first night in town—*Maybe you'll live through your kids . . . but as for yourself, what are you ever going to have of your own?* That applied as much to Ngaire as it did to him.

They had barred each other from those parts of their lives that cultivated them as individuals—her writing, his dream of opening a bar—and that was the reason they'd veered so much from the path they'd started down together.

'I'm sorry,' he said to her back.

He switched his electric blanket to zero and rolled over to stare at the bedside clock. He didn't want to live like this anymore—hitting the snooze button every morning because there was nothing that felt worth getting up early for.

'That was a good speech you made today,' Ngaire said. She reached back and squeezed his thigh. 'I didn't know you could be so passionate.'

FRIDAY

35

At lunchtime, Jac sat at the breakfast bar snacking on leftover curry puffs. They were soggy and disappointing, the pastry having lost its flakiness, now drooping over the filling like a sodden blanket. She shouldn't have reheated them in the microwave; she should have been more patient and used the oven. She should really do things properly the first time.

Ma came in wearing a long, knitted top over ribbed leggings. Her hair was damp and she smelled of Trésor—the same perfume she'd been wearing daily since the nineties. She opened the fridge and peered inside.

'Do you want some lunch?' Jac asked. 'There's mini quiches.'

'I'm not hungry.' Ma closed the fridge then moved around the kitchen mechanically, checking the water level in the coffee machine, dropping a pod in the top compartment and pressing a button to start it whirring.

'Gil's gone,' Jac said.

'I know. He said goodbye.'

'How was he?'

Ma didn't answer, her eyes fixed on the coffee spurting into her cup.

Gil had returned to the house after they'd folded the trestle tables, vacuumed the floor and moved the furniture back into position. He hadn't stayed long.

'I don't care that she's a woman,' he'd said as he'd layered his silky pyjamas into his suitcase. 'I knew about that part of you. I care that she's another person and that we're engaged, and I worry about what's going to happen when we're married.'

'Gil, it wasn't—'

He paused in his packing, a pair of balled socks in his fist. 'You're so afraid of getting hurt and yet you don't seem to care about . . .' He tossed the socks into the case. 'You can't be both the people you want to be. If you want real love, you've got to give it.'

In the kitchen now, Jac exhaled, long and deep. 'I really messed up,' she told Ma.

'Messed what up?' Ma's eyes still hadn't moved from the coffee maker and she spoke absently, as if she wasn't actually part of the conversation.

'Sorry, I should clarify . . .' She blew out a puff of air. 'There have been so many things.'

Ma took the cup and lifted it to her nose. 'Wait until you get to my age. The list grows.'

Jac pushed her plate aside.

'What are you going to do now?' Ma asked.

'What I do best.'

'When?'

'Monday.'

Ma set the cup on the countertop. 'Jacinta, you have to stop doing this.'

'Messing up?'

'Running every time life gets hard. You've been doing it since the day you left Pent.'

Something inside her flared. 'That's funny. You've been doing it since the day you arrived.' Appalled at herself, Jac put a hand over her mouth, but it was too late.

If Ma was offended, she didn't let it show. 'Yes, I have. Now the place—the man—I was running to is gone. So what's the point in running now?' Ma put down her cup. 'You need to work out what it is you want, Jacinta. You can't treat people like they're expendable and expect them to stick around.'

'Why not? It worked for you.'

She couldn't do this anymore. She was turning into the worst version of herself and creating a trail of destruction in the process. Did she still want to marry Gil? Would he even take her back? She couldn't think clearly about what she wanted under the hot light of Ma's merciless gaze. She couldn't do it in a place that constantly reminded her of Dad and everything else she'd lost. She had to get home to her cave. She stood. 'I need to book a flight.'

36

In the afternoon, Josh sat at the kitchen counter, bent over a bowl of ice cream, listening to an NBA podcast through AirPods jammed into his ears. Jordan breezed in humming a lullaby, and the sight of her was almost too much. He snapped a mental photograph of the moment and then conjured another from two days ago—Jordan on the doorstep, Dot in her arms. These two snapshots bookended three landmark events—a leap forwards in their relationship, him finally landing paid work, and saying goodbye to Dad. No wonder he needed sugar.

'She's finally asleep. What you got there?' She peered into his bowl, holding her hair in a fist at the back of her head. 'Is that Ice Magic?'

He nodded. His mouth was full, but he talked through it. 'It used to be my favourite. Except Ma got the plain chocolate one. I liked the choc mint best.'

He removed the earbuds and pushed them into the pocket of his trackpants, alongside his phone.

'I didn't even know they still made it. Where are the bowls?'

He pointed his spoon at a bank of deep drawers next to the stove.

Jordan helped herself to a bowl and then headed for the freezer.

She'd come over, she'd said, to help them clean up after the wake, but there wasn't much left to do. Still, she'd fluttered around the place, wiping surfaces with a dry rag and plumping cushions.

Something had altered between them since their conversation on the verandah. Thinking about the way Jordan had softened towards him warmed the pit of his stomach. Finally, the road ahead was clearing. There'd be potholes, of course, but at least the car was moving.

She'd said she'd be leaving the day after the funeral but hadn't mentioned it again. Maybe she planned to stay?

Jordan scooped vanilla ice cream into her bowl with a dessert spoon then shook the container of Ice Magic to check it was still runny. She upended the plastic bottle and squeezed the chocolate sauce over the ice cream.

'How long do I leave it?'

'Minute or so.'

She put her elbows on the benchtop and rested her chin in her palm, observing the chocolate as it hardened.

'Fascinating, isn't it?' he said.

'Totally,' Jordan said, captivated. 'When are we going home?'

We? Home? Jordan had obviously been doing some thinking overnight. 'Whenever you're ready. Today?'

She smiled. 'I've already paid for the motel tonight. Tomorrow?'

'Sure.'

'Will your mum be okay?'

The sound of Dot's whimpering cry drifted down the stairs.

'Yeah. Jac's here.'

They paused for a moment, listening, and Dot's cry intensified.

'I'll go,' Josh said.

In the twins' room, Dot was sitting up in the portable cot, her face scrunched as she wailed.

'Hey, hey,' Josh said gently. He lifted her into his arms. 'There's nothing to cry about. We're all going home tomorrow.' He held her to his chest, patted her back and bounced her softly.

In his pocket, his phone emitted two quick beeps—a text message.

He held Dot a minute longer, then lay her back down in the cot and rubbed her back until her eyelids began to flutter closed. With his spare hand, he took out his phone to check the message. It was from Kelsey: *Someone out there still likes you.* He clicked on the attachment, a video.

It was shot from the high corner of a room, like CCTV footage, except it was much clearer, almost broadcast quality. He recognised the room instantly as one from the Gold Coast mansion where they'd all stayed during production for *Relationship Rescue*. And he recognised the people—Tabeetha and himself—and knew exactly what was about to happen. But he was confused: the private rooms weren't supposed to have cameras. There was no audio, but then he realised his phone was still connected to the earbuds in his pocket. He hit pause, retrieved the buds, and sat on one of the single beds. In the cot, Dot slept soundly.

With the earphones in place, he hit play and at once heard their voices, surprisingly clear.

On the screen, he stood in Tabeetha's room in his bathers, a striped beach towel draped over his shoulders, having just come in and passed on Holly's message to get ready for the next segment. Where had this footage come from? he wondered. It didn't matter—finally the truth would come out. People would see Tabeetha's part in what happened between them.

'*Come on,*' he said to Tabeetha in the video. '*You need to get dressed.*'

'*Don't you like me in this?*' She tugged at the belt of her pink bathrobe, smiling.

'*Holly's given us five minutes.*'

He turned to leave.

'*Josh?*'

He looked over his shoulder. Now she was leaning against the dresser, the robe falling open over her bare legs.

'*Yeah?*'

Although his back was to the camera, he remembered how his eyes had flitted to those beautiful, long, bronzed legs. He could see them close up, in colour, right now.

'*What are we doing after this?*' she asked.

'*After the masquerade ball sequence?*'

'*No,*' she said playfully. '*After the show's done.*'

'*Well*'—he grabbed the ends of the towel that hung over his shoulders—'*we go home. In three months' time, you'll all watch yourselves on TV saying things you barely remember and being kind of horrified at all the good stuff you said that didn't make the cut.*'

'*And then?*'

'*And then the phone will start ringing.*'

'*Will it?*'

'*If you play your cards right.*'

'*Which cards?*'

He stepped closer. '*You'll have a small window, Tabeetha. You'll have to catch the wind while it's open.*'

'*My fifteen minutes?*'

'*Exactly. Because the following month there'll be a new season of* The Bachelor *or* Married at First Sight *or* Love Island *and you'll be yesterday's news.*'

'*But you're still going to help me, right?*'

He looked down, smiling. *Everybody uses everybody.*

'*Look, Tabeetha.*' He grabbed the tie of her robe and wrapped it around his hand. '*You're good talent, but there's only so much I can— There's six other women on this show who all want the same thing. Dakota's got her handbags. Ava's got her fitness thing.*'

'*But you don't like them as much as me, though, right?*'

'*Of course not!*' he said with a grin.

She smiled back and held his gaze—one of those lingering looks that can only mean one thing. He leaned in and kissed her. Watching it play out now on his phone, he saw that she'd hesitated at first—he didn't remember that—but then she kissed him back.

The kissing became more passionate as he leaned further into her space, pushing down the shoulders of her robe until the heavy terry-towelling swept away odds and ends from the dresser—a hairbrush, a make-up bag, a perfume bottle—sending them skittering across the bedroom floor.

He pulled at her underpants, but they wouldn't budge. He yanked harder. *Couldn't she give him a hand?* he remembered thinking at the time. At least lift her bum off the dresser to make the passage easier? They eventually came away and he tossed them off to the side, then pulled down his bathers to mid-thigh, just enough to give himself full access.

As he entered her, she let out a small noise and turned her head in the direction of the camera, looking towards what must have been the bedroom door.

It was so strange watching himself from that angle, having sex when he didn't even know he was being filmed—like something from a true-crime documentary. Like he was watching someone else.

Tabeetha bit down on her lower lip as though trying to heighten her pleasure, but there was something in her eyes that pulled at him now. There was confusion there, apprehension. Maybe even a kind of panic. Then she closed them, as though it would close off her thoughts too.

His phone rang. Kelsey.

'Are you the luckiest man alive, or what?' Kelsey said without preamble.

He looked at Dot, still sound asleep, something heavy settling in his stomach. He moved into the hallway.

'Who sent this?'

'Don't know, don't care. But it's pretty clear what really went down—so to speak—in that bedroom. This is going to shut that slapper up real quick.'

'Must have been someone from the show,' he mused aloud.

Reaching his own bedroom, he sat on the edge of the bed.

'Got it anonymously,' Kelsey said. 'A private number.'

Holly. It had to have been. She was Tabeetha's producer— she would have had access to Tabeetha's room and could have easily installed the hidden camera.

'No message with it?' Josh asked.

'Nuh.'

He felt suddenly out of control, like when he saw Tabeetha's initial accusation on Twitter. Once something like that is in the public domain, there's no stopping the speeding train and the Twitter mob aboard it.

'What if it's been sent to a hundred people? Or posted on social media?'

'I've been online and found nothing. I think it's for our eyes only. For now.'

'But what do they want? Why would they—'

'Gift horse, Josh. Stop staring at its mouth. If the sender wanted it out there, it would be by now. And if it was some kind of threat or message, they would have been more explicit.'

But why would Holly hand over the footage now? Maybe the vision of him dancing at the Cherry Tree and the negative press that followed caused a change of heart; maybe she'd let him sweat for long enough.

'Josh,' Kelsey said down the phone.

'What?'

'I said once this gets out, everyone will finally know the truth of what happened.'

He heard a noise and looked up.

Jordan was standing at the door.

'Don't do anything until you hear from me,' Josh told Kelsey down the phone. 'I'll call you back.' He hung up.

'What was that all about?' Jordan moved further into the bedroom. 'Are you okay? You don't look so good.'

'I'm— That was Kelsey. Just an issue with the, um . . .'

'The voice job?'

'Yeah.' He stood, pocketed his phone and earbuds, and rubbed his sweaty hands on the thighs of his trackpants.

'They didn't cancel, did they?'

'No, they didn't cancel. I need to go out.'

'Where?'

'I'll be back.'

He brushed past her in the doorway and descended the stairs, slamming the front door behind him. He trudged down Schofield Street, along Baker to Stanley, his head feeling overloaded, as if nothing more could be crammed in there.

The existence of this video put him in an impossible position. If he allowed the footage to be released—assuming that decision was even in his control—he could get his career back. But in the process, he would lose Jordan for good. He'd promised her only the night before that there had been no other women after Holly. No more *lapses*. He'd lied, and she'd find out. But that wasn't the thing that troubled him most.

He crossed the road at Dundee, angling around the new speed humps, unable to shake the look on Tabeetha's face from his mind.

After the sex was over, he remembered now, she hadn't said anything, just gave him a small smile and reminded him that they had to get ready. They hadn't talked much on the set after that. She was probably feeling guilty, he figured, or didn't want to draw attention to what had happened in case someone picked up something in the way they moved around each other.

He reached the square and, under the glow of fairy lights draped from tree branches, made his way across the concrete path to *The Peel*. Inside, his hand tracing the bumpy surface, he kept seeing Tabeetha's face in that video. He didn't need to watch it again—it was burned into his brain. Her clenched jaw. Her trepidation.

He hadn't seen it on the day because she'd turned her head, but what if he had seen it? Would he have noticed? Would he have cared?

That was what terrified him most.

Extracting himself from the sculpture, he retraced his steps towards home. He would have to tell Jordan the truth.

37

Dane walked to Sam Donovan's office, just on the other side of the square, for his appointment at 3.30 pm. The imprint on the frosted glass leading into Sam's second-floor workspace said he shared it with a mortgage broker called Rhonda Macdonald-McKenzie, but Dane had never met her.

The accountant sat behind an L-shaped faux cherry wood desk, chewing gum. He motioned to a chair on Dane's side of the desk. 'Was gutted to hear about Stephen. Nice funeral, though. Dignified.'

Dane acknowledged this with a nod.

Sam was around fifty, spindly, with a jumble of curly black hair flecked with white at the temples. His goatee, by contrast, was fully grey. Dad had known Sam's family for years; Sam's mum often performed the Welcome to Country at council events.

'Sorry.' Sam pointed to his champing jaw. 'Nicorette. Promised the kids I'd give up by Father's Day and I've got'—he glanced at a watch he wasn't wearing—'less than forty-eight hours to go.' He angled his chair towards Dane, his face fixed in a hopeful expression that reminded Dane of how he might look at his own clients—eager to please. 'So, what's your plan for the business, now that, um . . .'

Dane breathed out. 'Stay afloat. Keep it going as best I can for Dad.'

'Glad to hear it. You'll do fine. How are sales for the St Augustine's development?'

'On track.'

'Good. There's a lot at stake, but I'm sure you know that.'

Dane had studied the company's financials again that morning, stooped over Dad's desk with a takeaway coffee and a chocolate-chip muffin at his elbow. From what he could discern, they were scraping by for the time being. But with each month, the balance sheet was descending deeper towards the red.

'Help me understand the position we're in, Sam.'

Sam rubbed his nose. There was a restlessness about him, but Dane put that down to the nicotine withdrawal. 'Well, the company's taken on a huge financial load with this development.'

'The margins are good.'

'Yeah, on paper. But as you well know, they could diminish pretty quickly if you encounter anything unforeseen. And construction's notorious for it.'

Anything unforeseen. Contaminated soil, buried cultural artefacts . . .

'So, financially speaking, what's the—'

'The skinny?' Sam smiled, pleased with himself.

'Yeah.'

Sam turned to one of the two monitors on his desktop and made a few clicks on a wireless mouse. 'Let's see. You bought the block for one-point-two million and change; repayments are about five and a half a month. Outgoings so far—architects' fees, engineering, risk management plan, rental of the site office, marketing, permits . . . Did you get the building permit?'

'Yep.'

'So you're already in for about one-point-four, give or take, minus the contribution from the angel investors. Obviously, ahead of you there's construction and everything that goes with that—demolition, traffic management, landscaping . . . Sorry, is this the stuff you want to hear or am I telling you how to suck eggs?'

'No, this is good. I need to absorb it all.'

Dane's phone, which was face up on Sam's desk, chirped. He glanced at the screen—Fiona from the *Gazette*. It was her second call that day, no doubt following up on the comments he made about apartments at the funeral. He rejected the call and switched his phone to silent.

'Sorry,' he told Sam.

Sam waved away his apology. 'Between you and me,' the accountant began, lowering his voice, 'Leigh's good on the construction side, but I'm not sure how clued in he is to the budget. I'd keep an eye on that, if I were you. How's your cash flow?'

'Fine. For now.'

He had no idea how long they could sustain the monthly downturns, though the boost they would get from the first round of payments for the apartments on Monday would keep their heads above water until they could secure the construction loan. But there was still a big what-if banging around in his head.

'So, just say,' Dane began, 'hypothetically speaking, we weren't able to build them?'

Sam stopped chewing. 'Weren't able to or decided not to?'

'Either. Say there was an issue with the site. Hypothetically speaking.'

'If you had to pull the pin—for whatever reason—you'd be left with one hell of a debt. You could sell the land, and the plans for the apartments with it, but you wouldn't recoup what you spent.' He leaned over the table. 'I reckon Stephen paid too much. I told him that, but he wouldn't listen.' He sat back. 'And you'll never claw back all the outgoings already incurred—design, the engineering fees, marketing and what-not.'

Okay, so *not* building the apartments wasn't an option. They would just have to shave the construction budget if they needed to. Easier said than done, no doubt. He didn't know what they had specified in their applications for the permits, but maybe there was still time to look at lower-cost materials and applying cheaper building methods. There were ways. But some of those ways came with their own risks, he knew that—he'd heard of shoddy Chinese electrical wiring being recalled and about cheaper cladding from overseas combusting.

Then a thought occurred. What if Dad knew all this? What if Dad knew about, or at least suspected, a soil problem? What if he knew that it would blow the budget and that he would never recover his overheads? What if he knew he was captaining a sinking ship and chose to jump overboard rather than going down with it? His reputation would never have weathered such a loss. As a businessman, and a community leader, he would have been deeply embarrassed. The business would never have bounced back—construction, after all, is an industry that lives and dies on reputation.

And now Dane was left holding the screaming, jaundiced baby. His only option was to push ahead, but then what if . . .?

'Sam, what if we built them and then something went wrong?'

'Like a work health and safety issue?'

'Sure. Or something, like, hypothetically speaking'—God,

he was saying that a lot—'a big flood, or movement on the site that caused cracking or leaking or something.'

'That's what insurance is for.'

'But what if it was something . . . overlooked?'

If Dad and Leigh had cut corners on the soil test and the Aboriginal heritage survey, what other aspects of the process had been conveniently ignored or bypassed with the assistance of Damian Davenport at the council?

'You mean something that Hardings should have known about or done but didn't, and now the buyers are left high and dry?'

'Yeah.'

Sam chewed his gum, contemplating him. 'What's going on, Dane?'

Full disclosure was his wisest move here, but what was the truth? Everything was speculation at this point—at least, that's what he told himself. But it was like when you had a searing pain in your gut that you pretended was only food poisoning.

'Nothing. Nothing. I just want to understand all the risks . . . all the possibilities. I've never been involved in a project of this size and, you know, I'm responsible now.'

'Responsible you are, and would be if anything went wrong—and I mean personally responsible. *Liable*.'

'Meaning?'

'Meaning, as a director in the business, if you yourself caused the company some loss as a result of breaching your duties—say, if it's found you acted illegally or missed something you should have picked up—you may have to compensate the company for the loss.'

Dane stared at him. 'Me personally?'

The accountant nodded. 'If you're knowingly trading insolvently—in other words, you can't meet your debts when they fall due—that amounts to a criminal offence.'

Where would he get the money to bankroll those kinds of losses himself?

'And if I couldn't pay my debts?'

'You could be fined. It's up to two hundred thousand dollars now, I think.'

Dane felt his mouth drop open.

'And you might be looking at jail time.'

'*Jail?*'

'Up to fifteen years. The buyers would be skinned too, after the bank takes their cut—that is to say, *all* of it.'

He felt something crack in his chest. 'What would happen to the company?'

Sam raised one shoulder in a shrug. 'Receivership. Liquidation. And for you personally, it might come at the cost of your own financial future—job prospects, your ability to ever get another loan or to start another business—at least in the short term.'

He couldn't open the bar if he had that kind of black mark against his name. He wouldn't even be able to get a loan to set it up—if he wasn't in jail. Plus, the whole town would hate him for sinking all the buyers' money, so he'd never see a customer.

'You could file for bankruptcy, but then you'd be forced to sell all your assets—your house, any other property you own. Other valuables.'

He swallowed as he imagined having to sell his home, moving the family in with Ma (if Ngaire didn't leave him altogether), getting some minimum-wage job because he wasn't qualified to do anything.

But Sam wasn't done. 'Then there's your mother.'

'What about her?'

'She's a director too. She would lose everything she owns as well.'

★

Ma was in her bathrobe filling out the tiny squares of a crossword puzzle at the head of the kitchen table when Dane stuck his head through the doorway after work. 'Where is everyone?'

She peered over the rim of her glasses. 'Hello, sweetheart.' The glasses came off, and she let them dangle between her thumb and forefinger. 'They're around. I'm not sure where.' She gave him a disapproving look. 'Have you been at work today?'

'Stuff that can't wait.'

Ma put her glasses and magazine on the side table. 'You seem preoccupied.'

He shook his head, not knowing what to say, but aware that if he opened his mouth—if he gave voice to his impossible predicament—the floodgates would open.

No doubt recognising something in his face, Ma rose and joined him in the kitchen doorway, wrapping her arms around his waist. He nestled his head into the soft space between her shoulder and neck. Funny how they were hugging each other more than ever now.

After his meeting with Sam, he'd wandered along Main Street, beyond the lake, along the shopping strip, past the old State Savings Bank building and circled back to the office. The day had turned grey. It wasn't dark yet, but the road signs and the traffic lights had begun to lose their edges. So had he.

He was in a no-win situation. If he aborted the apartment development, the company would never recover, and he'd be fucked. If he went ahead, with the very likely possibility of an insurmountable budget blowout, he'd be fucked. If something went wrong, he would lose everything—no home, no bar, no future. Fucked. And he'd drag Ma down with him. By the end of the walk, he still had no answers.

'Shhh,' Ma whispered, patting his back. It came out more like an instruction than comfort. 'Come sit.' She led him to the table

and sat at the head, while he took the seat to her left. He placed
his keys and phone on the tabletop and rubbed at his eyes with
the tips of his fingers.

He was so angry with Dad. The position he'd left Dane in—
not to mention Ma—was unforgivable. The anger, which had
risen in a hot, rapid wave as the implications of Sam's warning
sank in, was still boiling away inside him. He was trapped.

Ma placed her hand over his and squeezed it.

How much should he tell her? Should he warn her about
what could be coming? The business was her only source of
income now that Dad was gone, and she could never live well
on the age pension alone.

She looked at him. Waiting.

Nothing. That was the answer. He would tell her nothing.
This wasn't the time—not so soon after Dad's funeral. And he
didn't know the nature of the damage yet, only that it would be
colossal.

'Jordan's gone.' Her words pulled him back. 'Josh . . . he had
an affair, apparently.' She shifted in her seat. 'I don't understand.
This is not *him*, Dane,' she said, a pleading note in her voice, as
if she wanted him to explain it—to make it okay. 'He's affec-
tionate, that's all.'

'Oh, please, Ma, it's not affection. That's a foreign word to us.'

Ma looked at him strangely, as if trying to work out his
meaning. 'Oh, no. You kids— Don't blame this on me and your
father.' She shook a finger at him and her face hardened. 'You
were raised just fine. Who drove you to every football practice,
every game, every . . . *place*?' Her voice lost its momentum.

'No, Ma. Dad was not okay. The three of us kids, we're not
okay.' It felt harsh, unfair even, but he was sick of lies, sick of
people ignoring the truth until it exploded in their faces.

'Of course you are!' Ma said. 'I mean, everyone has *problems* . . .'

He'd hit on something; an exposed nerve. 'No, Ma. Jac was going to marry someone because she was sick of being alone. Josh is out there—'

She held up a shuddering hand to silence him. *No.* 'Don't speak about your brother like that. You wouldn't understand. You don't know about showbusiness.'

Josh. All she cared about was Josh.

'Yeah, okay,' he said, but she didn't seem to catch the sarcasm.

'These girls, *they're* the predators. They just want . . .' She shook her head, frustrated. 'He's not an *indecent* person. He was always such a sweet boy.' Ma considered this, as though lost in a memory. 'He wants to believe that people like him. That's what we all want. He's so used to that. Everybody wanting him. You get accustomed to it, you know?' Her voice was quiet now, almost unrecognisable. 'And then it's gone.'

They'd all grown up feeling the ache of Ma's lost music career. *I was number one for three straight weeks, did I ever tell you that?* She always said it flippantly, pretending it had only just that moment occurred to her, except when she was drunk, when it came out in a jumbled, wistful mess.

'Oh, Dane. I'm so tired.' The bones holding Ma's face together seemed to sag, drawing the sides of her mouth downwards.

'Go to bed.'

She shook her head. 'Sleep won't help.'

He knew what she meant—and she was right. Sleep wasn't the answer. We go to bed, dream that maybe tomorrow everything will be okay. But it won't.

'Ma, it's time to really wake up to how things are.'

38

Outside, on the verandah, Josh watched the stars twinkle: diamonds lying on a black felt tray of sky. The light would have left these stars years ago, he thought—they were the illusion of something that hadn't been there for a long time.

Jac was next to him, where Jordan had sat the previous night, and he could hear the faint voices of Dane and Ma inside.

He'd lost her. For good this time. He'd carried around the hope of a reconciliation in his pocket, touching it every now and then, just to make sure it was still there. But now it had disintegrated, like a tissue that had gone through the wash.

He was aware of being miscalibrated in some way, his emotional meter out of whack. The deep well never seemed to fill—the barista, Holly, Tabeetha. He turned on the tap, and even when the water was gushing, it was draining just as fast down a hole somewhere.

He wasn't equipped for it. For all these losses—Jordan, his dad, Josh Vanderbilt. It was as if there wasn't enough adult in him to know how to deal with it.

He felt, too, as if there was a layer of skin missing, leaving him extra vulnerable. He'd had it for a while, but now it had driven away in the family SUV.

'Is it really over?' Jac asked.

She was talking about Jordan but could have meant more than that.

'Would *you* have me back?'

'I'm the wrong person to ask about fidelity.'

He tipped his head, resting it on the timber frame of the chair. 'What's wrong with me?'

Jac paused before answering. 'How honest do you want me to be?'

He exhaled. He hadn't told her about the video or what he now knew about himself. 'I did it, Jac. What Tabeetha said. I took advantage of the situation.'

She looked at him then, but it was hard to read her expression. Was she keeping her face neutral for his benefit or did she already know?

'The worst part is, I didn't even realise.' He rubbed the back of his neck. 'There's a big difference between consenting to and wanting to.'

She nodded. 'What are you going to do?'

He closed his eyes. He didn't want the video getting out—it wouldn't be good for Jordan, or Tabeetha, or himself. People would talk about it endlessly, analyse it, discuss it on talk shows, get body language experts in to debate who led on whom. There would be different interpretations, but either way, Tabeetha would be trolled, he would be trolled, and Jordan and Dot would be dragged into the shit with them.

Jac looked at him, waiting for an answer.

'I'm going to end it.'

39

Jac followed Josh back into the kitchen, where Dane and Ma were sitting at the table. Dane looked wrung out, all sloping shoulders and droopy-faced.

'I wondered where you two got to,' Ma said. She didn't look much better than Dane. Everyone was spent, ground down by the events of the past week. 'Something to drink?' she asked.

Jac shook her head.

'I will,' Josh said. 'I'll get it.'

'There's cake.' Ma motioned to the centre of the table, where squares of store-bought fruitcake left over from the funeral crumbled on a dinner plate.

Jac shook her head again.

Josh returned from the fridge with a stubby of beer in his hand. 'Now that you're all here, you should know that I'm bringing Dad home on Monday and then I'm leaving Pent.'

Jac wasn't sure which part of Josh's declaration to deal with first. That he was leaving, or that he'd suddenly, without consulting anyone, decided to collect Dad's ashes.

'You're taking him with you?' Ma asked, looking bewildered.

'Of course not. But I'm not leaving him alone in that place while you all make up your minds about what to do.'

'So, you're leaving him *here*?' Ma asked.

'Yeah.'

Jac spoke up. 'Let's just do the niche in the mausoleum.'

'No,' Ma said. 'The rose garden. He liked roses.'

'I told you, Ma,' Dane said. 'There's no rose gardens left. If you want that, he'll have to go to Wangaratta.'

'He's not going to Wangaratta.' Ma shook her head. 'We shouldn't have cremated him.'

'That was your idea, Ma,' Jac pointed out.

'No, it wasn't. I would never have said that.'

'You did,' Josh said.

'No, it was Dane!'

'You agreed!' said Dane.

'Oh, how would any of you know what he wanted?' Ma snapped. 'You never visited him anyway—you're too busy having affairs and cooking up weddings in secret.'

Jac, feeling a stab to the chest, wanted only to stab back. 'And you were so observant. You lived in the same house, for God's sake. Why didn't you notice anything, Ma?'

Ma slapped both palms flat on the table. 'I don't know, Jacinta! I don't know! You want to blame me? Will that make all this easier for you? So do it. Blame me. There's your answer. I was a terrible wife and a terrible mother. I never deserved your father and I never appreciated what I had. I'm sorry I didn't see this coming. I'm sorry *every* fucking hour of *every* fucking day, but there's nothing I can do about it now. Nothing.'

Dane stood. 'Don't blame Ma.'

'Then who should I blame? You? You worked side by side with him five days a week. Why didn't you see it? Why didn't you help him?'

Josh held up his palms. 'Stop this, Jac. It's nobody's fault. No one could have helped him.'

'Bullshit, Josh. That's a cop-out. You were too busy being *Josh Vanderbilt* to care about Dad.'

Josh faltered, but only for a second. 'Yeah, I left. Like you did. But you had him. That whole time—for your whole childhood *and after*, you had him. You and Dane . . . you don't even know what you had.'

'Oh, come on, Josh,' Dane said. 'You could have tried harder.'

'We were supposed to have time.' Josh's voice split at the midpoint. 'So much more time.'

'Don't talk to me about wasted time,' Dane said. 'I'm the one who got stuck with all the responsibility—the Harding name, the Harding business, the Harding *crap* . . . I had to carry it all. Ma, I don't care what you do with him.'

'No, Dane,' Jac said. 'You don't mean that. We owe it to him.'

'For what?'

'For failing him,' Jac said.

'Rubbish. He made his choices.'

Jac slumped into a chair, shaking her head. 'I have to know,' she said. 'I have to know why.'

'Let it go,' Dane said.

Ma was the calmest of the four of them now, staring into her teacup. 'It doesn't matter anymore.'

'It matters to me,' Jac said. 'It's the only thing that matters.' She looked up. 'Because then I'll know there was nothing I could have done.'

She squeezed her eyes shut. Only then did she realise why

she'd been pushing so hard; only then did the well of guilt spill over and pour from her eyes. She'd pretended she didn't notice anything wrong; she'd blocked out conversations with Dad in which something seemed off, telling herself she must have misheard or misinterpreted his tone of voice, read too much into a gesture or turn of phrase. The phone conversation they'd had when she'd joined the fraud unit six months ago came back to her.

'Why don't you come to Sydney this weekend?' she'd suggested. 'We could go to a show. Or just drink beers in a seedy pub somewhere . . . You could break out that new shirt I sent you. Have you worn it yet?'

'It's a bit big on me.'

He was losing weight.

'Is it? You should have said something.'

'I would have if you'd given it to me in person. Anyway, your mother's helping out with the Pent Fair this weekend.'

'Perfect. She'll be out, and you'll have nothing to do.'

'I was looking forward to the quiet.'

Not going out anymore . . .

'Come on . . .'

'Things are complicated at work. I was planning on cracking a shiraz and catching up on some of my shows that your mother hates, falling asleep on the couch . . .'

Drinking alone, withdrawing from family and friends . . .

'All weekend? Aren't you golfing?'

'Not this week—I've got a dicky shoulder.'

Muscle pains . . . or maybe just an excuse not to play—not doing activities they usually enjoy . . .

It was all there, right in front of her, but she hadn't seen it, though it had been niggling at her since the crash. She'd sensed something was wrong back then, she had to admit it, but discovering that her dad was mortal, and struggling, was too unsettling when her own life was dangling off a ledge. Thinking that someone else had caused this was more bearable.

It was time to face what she'd known subconsciously all along: she was as much to blame as anyone.

Jac drove around in the teeming rain until she found herself opposite Amy's house. She sat by the roadside, in the car, with the ignition off, watching droplets streak the windscreen.

Then she got out, shielding her face with her hand and crossed the street, shiny with rainfall.

She rang the doorbell. To her left, wisteria snaked around the pillars that fortified the porch, giving off a vanilla fragrance. She heard light footsteps padding down the hallway.

Amy opened the door wearing blue jeans with rips in the knees and an argyle jumper in greys and white. She opened her arms and Jac fell into them. 'It's going to be okay,' Amy whispered into Jac's neck. The feel of Amy's lips on her skin, especially there, made her tingle. She pulled away.

Inside, the front part of the house was dark. Further in, as she followed Amy to the rear of the house, golden lamplight lit the way.

Jac thought of her previous visit—her hands flat across Amy's back, the foiled kiss—and how she felt now: like a felon revisiting a crime scene.

'How are you?' Amy asked. 'After yesterday.' She stepped behind the kitchen bench, stark under a convoy of downlights. The faint smell of dishwashing liquid floated through the air.

'Not my finest moment. What's the protocol after making a drunken pass at someone and having them reject you?'

Amy held up a small, Japanese-looking teapot. 'Tea.' She smiled. 'You want?'

Jac nodded, placing her keys and phone on the benchtop where she'd eaten pasta bake a week before.

'Funerals stir up all kinds of emotions,' Amy said, filling a retro stainless-steel kettle with water. 'It doesn't help that people have no idea how to talk to someone who's grieving. We avoid talking about death, as if it's a taboo subject.' She placed the kettle on its base and flicked the switch.

Jac concurred with a nod, but Amy was being too generous, dancing around Jac's diabolical behaviour in the study.

Amy leaned against the bench and crossed her arms over her chest. 'When Penny died, people would literally ignore me in the supermarket or cross the street to avoid me. I hated them for it at the time, but now I realise they just had no clue how to be around me.'

Penny. That was her girlfriend from the photo on the bureau. Jac wanted to turn around to look at it again, to remind herself what Penny looked like, but she didn't.

'What happened to her? Penny?' Saying her name sounded strange, as if she'd known her.

'We were in Thailand. Three years ago. She cut her arm on a piece of coral while we were snorkelling and contracted a flesh-eating disease. It was awful. Her organs started to shut down almost immediately. She only lasted four days.'

'Fuck.'

Amy's chin quivered. 'I felt so helpless.' She moistened her lips. 'I was angry about it for a long time. I wanted to sue the snorkelling company, sue the resort that'd recommended them, sue the hospital, sue the country. I was out of control. Lucky I didn't own a flamethrower at the time. Dad had to fly over and bring me back before I got myself arrested.'

The kettle boiled, steam billowing into the air, but Amy kept talking. 'It went on for months. I tried to rail against it, blocking it out with booze and fighting with anyone who tried to help me.' She took in a deep breath. 'But then I realised I had to let myself feel it all, rather than trying to fight it. It helped. It's not the pain that destroys us; it's all those things we do to avoid the pain.'

Feel it all? That sounded like a shitty option.

Amy turned and went to the fridge.

'Gil left,' she said to Amy's back.

Amy returned holding a small floral tin, presumably the tea, and placed it on the counter next to the teapot. 'I'm sorry.'

Jac shrugged, then looked down, straightening a rug she'd disturbed with her foot.

'Are you alright?'

She watched in silence as Amy spooned loose-leaf tea into the pot and topped it up with boiled water. 'No.' She went to straighten the rug again but it was perfectly square. 'I feel like I've been dropped off in some derelict neighbourhood and abandoned. I'm no longer Dad's daughter, no longer some- one's fiancée. Two weeks ago, I thought I had it all figured out.'

'No one's got it figured out, Jac. I thought I'd be with Penny forever.' Amy twirled the pot. 'I haven't been able to date since. Staying home every weekend, cursing Netflix for only airing a thousand shows rather than two thousand because now there's nothing left to watch.'

Jac pictured herself leaving Pent, going back home to her own television, alone, everything unresolved. 'I'm just so *angry*,' she said. 'I don't know what to do with it. It's like Dad was murdered and I'm furious at his killer, only he was the victim *and* the perpetrator. Finding out why . . . I can't imagine ever doing anything again until I know.'

'But you already know. He was depressed.'

'Yeah, but what tipped the scales? Why that day? If only I could go back. Talk to him.'

'I get it. What if we'd never gone to Thailand? Or hadn't snorkelled? The snorkelling was my idea. I insisted! *Let's go. It'll be fun.*' She cast a quick glance towards the bureau. '*That's* the part I couldn't get over. It was *my* idea.' Amy squeezed her lips together briefly. 'It's maddening thinking this way, but you're helpless against it.'

Jac nodded. 'I know I can't change what happened,' she said. 'But that doesn't stop me trying to somehow will it with my mind. To bargain with—I don't know—*God*. I don't even believe in God!'

Jac watched as Amy poured the tea. She couldn't go back to Sydney in this state of flux. She had to resolve at least *some* things. 'Why did you break up with me?'

'What?' Amy's eyebrows lifted. 'When?'

'What do you mean, when? Twenty years ago.'

She placed the pot on the counter. 'I didn't break up with you. You left.'

'Because you broke up with me.'

Her eyes narrowed. 'Jac, all I said was that I needed some space.'

'And I gave it to you.'

'By moving to Sydney?'

Her mind turned to a missing person's case she'd worked on years ago. Twenty-nine-year-old Julia Cudwell was reported missing after leaving her home in Castle Hill one Tuesday night. Her husband, Finn, had filed the report, but it turned out he was the one person who knew where she was—he'd buried her at the east end of the Cumberland State Forest.

Finn had found out she'd been meeting up with a guy called Ben Coughlan, every Tuesday afternoon for five weeks.

What she hadn't had time to tell him, before he smashed her over the head with a ceramic flowerpot, was that Ben was a relationship counsellor and that she was only seeing him in the desperate hope of saving her marriage.

Finn killed Julia because of a misunderstanding. He was so enraged by what he perceived as her betrayal, that he hadn't thought to ask any questions. Jac thought at the time and again now about how sad and wasteful that was, of how this one moment had rippled out. Julia was dead, and Finn sent to prison for eighteen years. Jac, too, had been incarcerated, in a way, since walking away from Amy.

Your prison is walking through this world all alone.

'I thought you hated me,' Amy said now. 'I thought you wanted nothing to do with me.'

For a moment, Jac got a glimpse into what her life might have been. Maybe living in this house, Amy making tea, chatting over crumpets with honey in the mornings and sinking into that great big club lounge with a glass of whisky at night.

'No,' Jac said. 'I didn't hate you.'

Amy held out one of the teacups and directed her to the sitting room, where they reclined in those oddly comfortable chairs in silence. Jac used the time to examine the photo of Penny. She was standing alongside Amy, dressed up on a bright day, with their faces pressed together.

'How did you . . . move on?'

Amy shook her head. 'You don't move *on*, you move *forwards*. It takes time.' Amy placed her cup on the floor beside her. 'And, unfortunately, you can't do anything but live through it. Grief has its own itinerary. It comes when it comes—when I'm standing in the shower, or over a sink full of dishes, or in front of a room of fourteen-year-old boys. You get *some* warning. But when it comes it forces itself on you and there's no point resisting. You just have to let it have its way with you.'

Was that what she had to do? Let the grief pass through her unopposed? She had said goodbye to two people within a week of each other—three, if she counted herself. No, that wasn't right. She'd lost herself right after her distorted conversation with Amy all those years ago.

'Losing Penny almost killed me,' Amy said, 'but I wouldn't erase that time for anything. The joy was worth the pain.'

But exactly how much pain was it worth?

Jac tipped her head back until it hit the chair. She exhaled. 'I've fucked things up so many times.'

Amy leaned forwards. 'Gil's not going to wait for an apology forever. You need to decide what you want.'

After leaving Amy's, Jac drove down Marshall Road and came to a stop under a gum tree twenty metres from the overpass. On top of the bridge, which she'd never seen up close, moonlight shone through the leaf-shaped punctures in the steel panels, the kind that form a rusted coating almost immediately, as if they'd been weathering the elements for decades. The pylons holding the bridge aloft were light-grey concrete and she could see the scars from where Dad had collided with it at speed.

The person she loved most in the world was gone. The person who loved her the most was also gone. Continuing to fight it meant she would only be experiencing the loss over and over again.

A few hundred metres along the track, a Pent-bound train curled its way through the field of green. It was quiet for now, but soon it would be upon her, thunderous and unstoppable, like her grief, but then it would be gone again.

The train rattled towards the bridge, louder now, stirring up a gust of wind. Pink blossom from a roadside plum tree puffed into the air, showering the windscreen with confetti.

She pulled out her phone and found Gil's number. *I'm sorry,* she texted. *Can we please talk?*

SATURDAY

40

Jac pushed open the door to Hideaway, a bar on the fringes of Wangaratta, far enough out of Pent that she was unlikely to run into anyone she knew. The name had changed but it still had the same feel—Nashville honky-tonk meets upscale New Orleans Creole bar—with its decorative ironwork, French-inspired chandeliers and blue-clothed pool tables.

There was something about that meshing of styles that had never seemed to work before, but now it felt bolder, more confident in its own skin.

Jac breathed in the air. Bars always smell different in the afternoon, she thought, before patrons have saturated them with the odour of beer and perfume and pheromones.

Only a few of the small, round tables were occupied. Two women dressed in biker jackets leaned their elbows on the bar. Tracy Chapman echoed through speakers somewhere.

In a back corner, under the light of a stained-glass lampshade,

Gil sat alone in a booth, two schooners of beer on the table before him.

She crossed the hardwood floor, past the imitation Wurlitzer, kissed him briefly on the mouth and slid onto the upholstered bench opposite. 'Thought you would've gone back to Sydney.'

'Decided to wait till the weekend. We both needed time to think. I'm flying back tonight.'

She nodded.

'Want some food?' he asked. 'They've got jambalaya.'

'Beer's fine for now.'

His skin was pale, even under the warm light of the lampshade, and he wore a knitted jumper that she hadn't seen before, something that a twinkly-eyed father in a Country Road catalogue might wear.

'Why'd you pick this place?' he asked, eyeing the postcards advertising line-dancing classes and rockabilly nights pinned to the wall beside them.

'I used to work here a long time ago. It was called Tink's then.'

'Here?' He scanned the room. 'Where are all the men?'

She smiled, humouring him. 'That's the point.' She took a sip of beer. It was an IPA and a little warm; he must've been sitting there a while. 'I met Amy here—the woman from the study. She was my first real relationship.'

'I see.' He lifted one shoulder and lowered it again. 'First loves can be hard to forget.'

'It wasn't the love I couldn't forget,' she said. 'That was the first thing to go. It was the heartache. I know now that I never got over it. And it's contaminated every relationship since.'

'The walls. I understand.'

'But I didn't learn, did I? I let myself fall for someone else. Jenn was her name. Six months ago. But she dumped me too, and it hurt. Too much. Then I met you.' Jac twirled the engagement ring around her finger. 'You were right. I push people away before they can get close.' She shook her head. 'Before *I* can get too close.'

Gil exhaled, his shoulders softening.

'I'm so sorry for the way I behaved,' she said. 'I was . . . I didn't mean to . . .'

He reached across the table and placed his hand over hers. 'You were in pain.'

'Can you forgive me?'

'Of course.'

She took another sip of beer, a long one this time, then replaced the glass on the coaster. She slid the engagement ring from her finger and set it on the table between them. It came off easier than she'd expected.

He stared at it, his eyes twitching, then at her, as if trying to work out what it all meant.

'I'm sorry,' she said.

The muscles in his jaw knotted. 'You're leaving me?'

She pushed the ring across the table. 'I'm letting you off the hook.'

He pushed it back. 'There's no hook.'

She didn't deserve him, and the timing wasn't right. She had too much to sort out. Something had shifted inside her when Amy said that she'd never wanted to break up. Some long-held belief about herself, about love, had disintegrated.

She did love Gil; he was never the problem. None of them—not Noel or Xavier or Jenn—were ever the problem. She had cordoned herself off, intent on safeguarding her heart, and in the process closed the door on any hope of real happiness. She'd held on to the hurt from her break-up with Amy all those years ago, like a muscle she couldn't unclench.

'Is this what you really want?'

'No,' she said.

He took a breath. 'Then get out of your own way and let's get married!'

She couldn't trust herself. She would keep hurting him. 'What if I get cold feet again?' she said.

He reached across the table and grabbed her hands with his. 'Then I'll bring you a blanket.'

MONDAY

41

Dane woke at seven-thirty with what felt like a hangover but couldn't possibly have been because he'd only had a few drinks at Father's Day lunch with Ngaire's family the day before. His alarm hadn't gone off, but he realised what had woken him: his phone beeping with a text. Ngaire was asleep beside him—she was taking a week off writing to be with the twins—and he could hear the faint sound of the TV downstairs.

He rubbed his eyes, a vice squeezing his brain at the temples. He'd hardly slept, reliving the argument at Ma's that had ended in everyone abruptly going their separate ways. But what had become clear was that they were all struggling to breathe under the weight of the guilt they carried over Dad's death—for not reaching out to him.

He snatched up his phone from the bedside table, yanking out the charging cord. The message was from Katherine Warren: *The bulldozers are here! You have to stop them!*

Suddenly, he was wide awake. He threw off the sheet and sprang out of bed. He didn't eat or shower, just squeezed into yesterday's pants and a striped polo—a Father's Day gift from the boys—and climbed into his Ranger. He roared through the quiet streets of Pent, the sun streaming through the windscreen. As he rounded the corner on Pakington Street, he could see a single bulldozer inside the perimeter of the St Augustine's site. Two tip trucks stood by, ready to haul the rubble away. There was no sign of Katherine Warren.

He screeched to a halt behind them, got out of the car and ran towards the bulldozer.

'Hey!' he screamed, waving his arms at the driver. 'Hey!'

The driver wore earmuffs and apparently didn't have the peripheral vision to see him.

'Hey!' he shouted again, running in front of the bulldozer. Only a few metres separated the bulldozer and the side of the church building. 'Stop!'

The driver caught sight of him and hit the brakes, leaning out of the cabin. 'What the hell are you doing? Get out of the way!'

By then, the two tip-truck drivers had made their way over.

'You need to stop!' Dane called out.

The bulldozer operator killed the engine and Dane moved to the side.

'Who are you?' the driver asked. 'What the fuck are you doing?'

'Dane Harding. I'm from the company developing this site.'

The driver dismissed him with a meaty paw. 'Sorry, mate. I've got my work order. We're demolishing these two buildings today.'

'No, wait. There's been a mistake.'

'That's not what my paperwork says.' He started the engine.

'No!' Dane lifted both hands again. 'This isn't supposed to happen. Turn it off.'

'Listen,' the driver shouted over the hum of the engine. 'Not my problem and you're holding us up.' He pointed to the road. 'Step off the site for your own safety.'

The men from the tip trucks grabbed him by each arm.

'Stop!' Dane yelled. 'I just need an hour to sort this out. You'll still be paid for the whole job, I promise.'

Nobody moved.

'Come on!' he continued. 'You've got nothing to lose and potentially an extra day's work to gain. Please stop.'

The driver pulled off his hard hat and rubbed his beard. Then he killed the engine.

42

Jac folded all her absurd new clothes and packed them as neatly as she could manage into her case so she wouldn't have to rush in the morning. She would probably bin most of them when she got back to Sydney, anyway. The white linen shirt was okay, and maybe she'd wear the capri pants again (Gil was always being invited to barbecues; he had, it seemed, an endless circle of friends), but the rest could go. Maybe Ma would wear the poncho?

Ma had been on her mind all morning—how she had justified her criticisms of her daughter as preparing her for the harsh world. But it meant that, ever since, she'd felt her mother was constantly judging her, whether Ma intended to or not.

In the corner of the room, the box of her old belongings from the garage sat quietly, and she imagined it asking a question: Hang on to the past, or let it go?

She picked up the dust-covered box and carried it out through the laundry door to the wheelie bin, remembering only when she arrived at an empty space that it was rubbish day, and the bins would be waiting for collection by the kerb.

She walked up the sideway, across the lawn—emerald green from the recent rain—and flipped the lid on the bin.

She upended the box, and all the remnants of her old life spilled out. On top of the pile was the flannelette shirt, because she'd pushed it to the bottom of the box. She looked at it, wondering what it represented to her now.

Nothing. That girl was gone. She closed the lid and crushed the box, dropping it in the recycling bin.

She headed for the front door, feeling lighter, but halted at the sight of a pearl-white envelope on the doormat, her name written on the front in blue pen.

She picked it up and turned it over, looking for the sender, but the flap was blank. She tore it open.

She unfolded the page inside and saw what appeared to be a black-and-white photocopy, with a handwritten note, torn from a small notebook, stapled to the front.

Jacinta,

I'm sorry I lied to you at the wake. I do know about the list. I hope this explains things. Damian, your father and I never came forward.

Regards,

Mike Vincent

She flipped over to the attached page. It was a printout of a *Gazette* article downloaded from the internet; she recognised it from Dad's St Augustine's scrapbook.

SEXUAL ABUSE IN LOCAL CHURCH 'SWEPT UNDER THE CARPET'

She didn't have to read too far into the article before two names leaped off the page.

Two local men, Wayne Harper, 62, and Peter Harman, 63, last week filed charges against the Catholic Diocese of Shepparton pertaining to historical abuse they claimed the Diocese 'swept under the carpet' in the 1970s. The charges named Father Robert Gene West, a former priest at St Augustine's Catholic Church in Pent, as the abuser, although Fr West is believed to have passed away in 2006.

She finished the article and returned the pages to the envelope, holding it to her chest. She leaned against the front door and exhaled.

43

Dane stood at the window of his new office overlooking the square. Down below, a line of people amassed at the door of the St Augustine's sales office, ready to pay their deposits when it opened at nine. He didn't know whether to laugh or cry—whether to be relieved that his funeral speech hadn't deterred them or to dread delivering the news that there would be an indefinite delay to construction. Legally, he had no idea where he stood. Who knew how long the Aboriginal heritage survey would take? And, depending on what it revealed, whether the project would go ahead at all. But he had to act this time.

The alternative, after all, was worse. He couldn't stomach the idea of driving past a six-storey apartment block every Saturday morning on the way to Auskick, knowing that a hundred-and-fifty-year-old piece of Pent history had been forever obliterated because he'd buried his head in the sand.

Not to mention potentially destroying millennia-old Aboriginal artefacts.

Gayle's voice broke into his thoughts. 'You had an exciting morning,' she said.

'Exciting' wasn't the word he would have used.

'Fiona from the *Gazette*'s been calling,' she said.

Of course she has. 'She'll really be out for blood once she finds out about this,' Dane said.

Gayle crossed the office to join him at the window and he caught a trace of her perfume. It wasn't the one she usually wore. She peered out the window. 'That's quite a crowd down there.'

'Yeah.'

She turned to him. 'How did it feel?' A smile flickered at the edges of her lips.

'Finding out about a premature demolition that my own company organised?'

She smiled fully. 'No—putting a stop to it.'

'Oh, that.' He fought his own smile but couldn't repress it. 'That felt pretty good.'

She went to leave, but he called her back. With everything going on, he had neglected his staff at the worst time—more confirmation of his lack of leadership. He would have to work on that.

'I'm sorry that I haven't . . . Are you okay?' he asked Gayle. 'I mean, I know you and Dad were close, and I thought you might need some time to . . .'

She shook her head. 'Thank you, but I'd rather come to work and be useful than sit around at home.'

'Maybe you could take a holiday?'

'Now?' She smiled, knowing that that was the last thing he'd want.

He thought about where he'd be without her. 'Ah . . .'

'I'll get you some coffee.'

He pivoted back to the window. In the square, Olivia was fighting her way through the crowd to unlock the door to the sales office. Only thirty-five people had put down a deposit; there must have been new buyers lining up too.

'Well, that was fucking stupid,' said Leigh's voice from behind him.

Dane turned. 'Good morning, Leigh.'

The project manager stood in the doorway, a hand on either side of the glass panels, smudging them. 'I feel like I've just been fucked with my clothes on. Do you know how much your little stunt is going to cost us?'

Dane felt himself straighten, grow taller. 'One, it wasn't a stunt, and two, I'm more concerned about our reputation in this town, where we have to live and maintain a business, than a short delay.'

Leigh let his hands drop to his sides. 'Are you serious? We've already sunk more than a million dollars into this project. The future of this company is on the line, and you can't say how long this crap is going to hold us up.'

'By crap, do you mean due process?'

'Whatever. Stephen had a vision. He didn't want us surviving off shitty little renovations and laundry upgrades forever. He wanted us to be in the big league. He understood that these big development jobs were our future. Man, he'd be turning—' Leigh stopped, as if realising he was on the verge of going too far.

'I understand all that, but . . .' Dane, too, stopped. What was the point in arguing about it? They had different ideas; that had been clear for a long time, and going back and forth wasn't going to solve anything. They had to get on the same page if they were going to continue to work together, but that conversation would have to wait. Leigh was too focused on his promised commission.

'Leigh, I know you need money. I know all about it. But it's affecting your judgement. We can't storm ahead with this project, overlooking everything that's off, just so you get your payday. Why didn't you tell me about the demolition?' Dane asked.

Leigh ran his fingers through his hair, jittery, like he'd overdosed on caffeine.

'We gave the order—you knew that—but I didn't know they were doing it today.'

Dane turned and looked through the window. Down below, people were moving through the doors of the sales office.

'Dane, this is *not* what your dad wanted. This is not the way to honour his memory.'

Dane took a breath. 'His memory? What about mine? I'm not going to be the guy who conned his way into pulling down a historic building just to make a buck.'

His phone chimed on the desk and he glanced at it. There was a message from Jac: *Read this. Mike Vincent gave it to me. It explains about the list. Can I be there with a sledgehammer when they demolish that fucking church?*

She'd attached a photo of a newspaper article and he zoomed in to read the first two paragraphs. It was familiar to him now. He'd read it, a year ago maybe, but hadn't linked the names in the story to the list.

'Dane,' said Leigh impatiently.

Dane held up a hand and turned back to the window, all fight suddenly seeping out of him. What had Dad suffered?

He covered his face with both hands, thinking of his own boys, of all the boys whose innocence was taken against their will over the years.

So that explained the list, and why Dad wanted the church gone, but what about the money?

He rubbed his eyes and turned back to Leigh.

'What's wrong?' Leigh asked.

Dane shook his head. He couldn't explain now. 'Sam Donovan mentioned some angel investors for St Aug's. Do you know who they are?'

Leigh shook his head.

'Do you know how much they invested?'

'A hundred and ten grand,' Leigh said. 'They pretty much provided the deposit.'

The sum total of Dad's list. They all wanted to see the back of that church and had committed generous amounts from their own coffers to see it happen.

Just then, Gayle tapped on the door. 'I'm sorry, Dane, but Olivia needs you down at the sales office. There's been a— Well, you'd better go down.'

In the square, people still spilled from the doors of the sales office, many milling around on the footpath. Among them was Katherine Warren, presumably trying to convince people to change their minds at the last minute and boycott the project.

He made his way through the crowd, Leigh and Gayle close behind. He passed Angus Chu, Joel Hutchison, the Doheneys, the Comerfords and the Hudsons, all standing around, papers in hand, talking, as if waiting for something to happen—an announcement, perhaps.

Had they already heard about the stalled demolition?

Standing behind a glass table, a huge artist's impression of the finished apartments on the wall behind her, Olivia had her fingertips pressed to her temples as if she had a headache.

'What is it, Olivia? What's the problem?'

'I don't know what to do.'

'About what?'

She removed her fingers, placing them on an assemblage of papers on the table. 'Some people are asking for their deposits back.'

'Fuck!' Leigh said from behind him. 'I told you!'

'Okay,' Dane said to Olivia, 'so give it to them. That's what we agreed.'

'What about everyone else?' she asked. 'The ones who don't want it back?'

'What?' He looked at Gayle to enlighten him.

'They want to donate it,' Gayle said.

'Donate it? To what?'

'Your crisis centre,' she said.

He glanced around. A hush had fallen over the crowd.

Brent Doheney spoke first. 'We want you to convert the church into a community hub—into a place of healing, like you said at the funeral.'

Dane blinked. 'But I didn't . . .'

'We all agree,' said Andrea Comerford, the cafe owner. 'Well, most us of us, anyway.' She glared at a young guy in a suit whom Dane didn't recognise.

They'd been discussing this? For how long? It didn't matter. What they were suggesting was impossible.

Dane held up his hands. 'That's all very . . . I mean, I appreciate the— But we can't *really* do that.'

Joel Hutchison stepped forwards. 'Why not?'

Dane remembered the desolate look on Joel's face when he'd said, less than a week ago, what it might have meant for his son to have had somewhere to go, to talk to health professionals who knew how to deal with people on the brink of taking their lives.

But Dane's mind jumped to practicalities. 'Well, because . . . the money, for one. How would we pay for it? How could we afford to run it?'

'Don't worry about that,' Angus Chu said.

'Don't worry?'

'You've already got at least sixty thousand dollars committed from this room,' Angus pointed out. 'And there'll be a hundred grand every year from the council—not that I'm making any promises, you understand.'

'Thank you, Angus, but—'

Joel broke in. 'I'll partner with you. Between my contacts and yours . . . we can call in some favours.'

Just then, Katherine Warren elbowed her way to the front. 'And you know how persistent I can be. We'll fundraise.'

Dane glanced again at the artist's impression of the completed apartments behind Olivia, thinking about the money they had already sunk into the project, the plans they had in place. No. He couldn't do it. This project was Dad's dream, and now that Dane understood why his father and those other men had wanted to see the church torn down, how could he let it stand?

Joel Hutchison rested his hand on Dane's shoulder. 'Let us be the change, Dane.'

Dane realised then that he had an opportunity to do something. He couldn't erase the church's ugly history, but he could change its story. He could keep the building but alter what it meant to people—rather than pulling it down and trying to pretend nothing bad had ever happened there, he could turn it into a place of recovery and healing.

Maybe there was a way. It was a big parcel of land—maybe they could subdivide, sell off parts of it. They could keep the drawings for another project, on another site, or flog them too. He would have to reimburse the angel investors. Or would they be prepared to contribute to a project like this?

He glanced around the tiny office, crammed with people. 'But we still have buyers. People still want their apartments.'

Joel pulled out a chair from behind the desk, planted a leather boot on the seat and heaved himself up. He was already a tall man, and standing on the chair he was an imposing figure. 'There will be other sites,' he announced. 'Other apartments. But we have a chance to do something really good here. For Pent. For all of us. Right now. Who still wants their apartment?'

Leigh closed in. 'You can't put them on the spot like this,' he told Joel.

'No,' Dane agreed. 'That's not fair.'

One guy, receipt in hand, turned around and walked out. Another followed.

Andrea Comerford, small and birdlike, motioned for Joel to step down, then took his place. She held up a hand to command attention. 'I know it's a hard decision to give up your apartment, but it shouldn't be. This is not the worst thing that can happen. You want to know about the worst thing? Ask Dane, ask Joel. Ask anyone who's lost someone to suicide. Because a person who takes their own life dies once, but those of us who are left behind die a thousand times over.'

Voices murmured, paper shuffled, but no one spoke. Andrea placed a hand on her chest. 'Most of us, me included, never do anything great. But we all have a chance here, each of us, to do something small. And if we all do something small, together we can create something big.'

Silence fell, the only noise coming from the air conditioner blowing a warm breeze into the space.

But then there was the sound of paper being torn. It was the young guy in the suit who had wanted his deposit back. 'Take it,' he said, launching the scraps of his receipt into the air.

'Me too,' said Frank Fevola, tearing his own receipt in four and flinging it to the ceiling.

And suddenly all around the room, pages were being ripped.

'Make that seventy thousand right here in this room,' the mayor said.

Dane's hands began to tingle, then shake, and his head swelled with what felt strangely like belief.

'So,' Joel said. 'What do you say?'

Dane scanned the room. Half of Pent, it seemed, was packed into that tiny office, the other half leaking out into the square. They trusted him. They were prepared to give over their money so he could make a difference, so they could do it together. *This* was the Pent he'd longed for.

'Yes,' Dane said, his voice strong. 'I say *yes*.'

44

Jac opened the double doors to the back verandah and saw the sun glistening off the dew-soaked grass. 'Good morning,' she said.

Ma was sitting on one of the outdoor chairs in her fluffy bathrobe, facing the backyard, steam rising from a mug of tea cupped between her hands. On the table beside her was a plate with a portion of fruitcake left over from the wake.

'Morning,' Ma answered without turning her head.

She would tell Ma what she'd found out about Dad's past, but not just yet. She had something else to say first.

Jac lowered herself into the vacant chair. 'I'm sorry about the tour,' she said.

Ma looked at her. 'What tour?'

'The revival shows when Josh was in high school.'

'Oh, that,' Ma said, waving it away with a sweep of her hand. But then her voice softened. 'I wanted to go.'

'I know.'

'But I was scared.'

Something clicked into place then—like a DNA profile that sits in a police database for years before finally hitting on a match.

'It's agonising,' Jac said, 'to let yourself be happy for a minute when you know it's not going to last.'

'That's true, but that wasn't it.'

'No?'

'No.'

Jac readied herself for an excuse—maybe Ma would say she didn't want to be around her former bandmates or that she couldn't bare bussing across the country with a bunch of yesterday's pop stars.

'I should've said yes,' Ma said. 'I gave up my last chance to feel that way again.'

'What way?'

'Wanted.'

Jac felt a pang of recognition. 'You were wanted here.'

Ma smiled. 'It's kind of you to lie.'

'What you do for Dane, looking after his kids all the time . . .'

'It's penance.' She took another sip of her tea. 'I didn't agree to the tour because I was too worried about it never getting off the ground or slow ticket sales or cancellations. Then there'd be no doubt about my . . .' She held her mug to her chest. 'I preferred to hold on to the fantasy.'

Few drugs must be as addictive as fame, Jac thought. Or as destructive. But then again, it could be like an elevator—one of the ways for women to gain power and a voice in a patriarchal world.

Maybe she'd misjudged Ma. And Tabeetha.

Ma continued to stare across the backyard. 'Maybe saying yes would have tied it up for me,' she said. 'I could have finally let go.' In a tree overhanging the verandah, a magpie collected twigs for a nest. 'I thought it was all worth it—that I gave up music for a good reason. Your father. You kids. But I stuffed that up too.'

Jac closed her eyes then opened them again. 'It's a big ask to live up to someone's expectations.' *The attentive mother, the idealised daughter, the father with no frailties.* 'But none of that matters now,' she said. 'What's important is what we do next.'

Ma collected her plate and mug and stood, looking at her a moment, deciding something. 'I'm glad you're marrying Gil. I like him. I hope you'll make each other happy.'

That possibility felt much less like a hope now and more of a matter of course. She was no longer settling for a payout but taking home the whole prize pool.

As her mother headed towards the door, Jac said, 'Ma?'

Her mother paused, turned.

'There's a revival of *Cat on a Hot Tin Roof* opening in Sydney next month,' Jac said. 'Want to go?'

Ma smiled. 'I'd like that.'

45

After lunch, Josh sat at the kitchen bench with a cup of coffee, Ma's laptop open in front of him, his duffel bag at his feet and a canister containing Dad's ashes beside him.

He'd already said goodbye to Ma, and she'd left for the cemetery to look at options for Dad's final resting place.

Jac entered the kitchen in a zipped hoodie over jeans, no sign of the patterned clothes she'd been wearing for the past week or so. 'All set?' she asked.

'Yep.' He closed the laptop.

'Hey, I'm sure Dad's got a waterproof jacket if you need something for the trip home.'

He gave her a confused look.

'In case it starts raining chocolate milk again.'

'Ha!'

Jac's eyes snagged on the canister. She looked away, crossing to the sink to fill a glass with tap water. She took a sip, then moved to the bench and placed a hand on the canister. 'Are you ready to go back? I mean, mentally?'

He thought about Dane's funeral speech—about ending the silence. 'Sampson put me on pills for depression.'

She nodded. 'How long do you think you've . . .?'

'A month, a year, ten years. In one form or another.'

Josh knew his depression was more than a chemical imbalance. It stemmed from life experiences—and the meaning he extracted from those experiences, rightly or wrongly.

Drugs might save him for the moment, but they could only do so much. He had to stop blaming his life on what came before—what Dad said or Ma didn't say.

Jac's thumb stroked the top of the canister, considering something. 'Come to Sydney, if you need a place to crash. Gil would love to have you. There's always the phone, too, I guess. I've heard mine does more than just text and hook me up to the internet.'

'You mean use the phone to *talk*? What are we, Neanderthals?'

'I'm sure I could reacquaint myself with Zoom or whatever, if I have to.'

She finished her water and turned to the sink to rinse the glass.

Josh opened the laptop and spun it around so the screen was facing her. 'Read this. Tell me what you think.'

For the past half-hour he'd been composing a letter to Tabeetha, acknowledging, apologising.

When she was finished reading, Jac folded the screen down. 'She's going to publish this somewhere, you know—Twitter, Instagram. It could put you on shaky ground, legally speaking.'

He shrugged. It was Tabeetha's turn to make the rules.

He rotated his coffee mug so he could read the inscription. It was one of Dad's; a long-ago Father's Day gift that had faded over countless cycles in the dishwasher, although he could still make out the words: *Ain't no hood like fatherhood*. He'd bought it because he'd thought it sounded cool—like something Will Smith would say in *The Fresh Prince of Bel-Air*—and not too mushy.

He drained the rest of the coffee, flipped off the cap he was wearing and wrapped it around the mug for protection.

'You taking that?' Jac asked.

'Yeah, I thought I would.' He opened his duffel bag and tucked it inside. 'In case I ever need reminding.'

Jac waited with him on the platform at Pent station, the mid-afternoon sun glinting off the tracks.

They stood in silence, Josh aware of the overpass to their right, the city to the left and Pent behind them. With the tip of his sneaker he rubbed at a piece of chewing gum that had become embedded in the asphalt surface.

'I'm bowing out of the industry,' he said. 'No matter what happens with that letter, I'm getting out.'

Jac turned back to him. 'But you love it.'

He nodded. He did love it, but maybe he'd been looking for something in it that he'd never find. 'I don't function well in that world—plus, I might not have much say in it. I'm tainted.' He glanced at the ring on his finger. 'It just doesn't seem that important anymore, anyway.'

'What will you do?'

He shrugged. 'Something. Anything. I don't know. I have to move out of Kelsey's apartment; I know that.'

'Melbourne's got plenty of bridges.'

He gave her questioning a look. 'To drive my car into?'

She smiled. 'To sleep under. Summer's coming. It won't be so bad. All I ask is that you clean yourself up for my wedding.'

He heard the train trundle towards him, clacking over joins in the track in the distance.

Moments from the past ten days flashed through his mind: singing 'Desperado' at the Cherry Tree; Dane grabbing him in a headlock; sitting on a park bench with Jac, watching the twins play.

The train came to a stop in front of them and the doors parted.

'Say bye to Dane for me, would you?'

'Call him yourself.'

He nodded. 'Yeah, I will.' He leaned over and gave her a kiss on the forehead, and she didn't even seemed surprised.

46

With Josh gone, Jac made her way down the ramp back to street level, pulling out her phone as she walked. She dialled Gil.

'Hey,' she said. 'Do you like dogs?'

'Sure, I like dogs.'

She could hear street noise in the background. He must be out at lunch somewhere.

'Let's get one. A *big* one. Like a lab or a golden retriever.'

'Okay . . . Does this mean we're not moving into your apartment?'

'Yeah.' She hadn't thought about that, but it seemed decided. 'Maybe we could get a house? Something with grass out the back?' *Somewhere for the kids to play.*

'Alright. Hey, I've got to go. Can I call you later?'

'Sure,' she said. 'I'll be here.'

And she meant it.

Author's note

I didn't set out to write a book so threaded with the subject of grief. In fact, when I realised where the story was taking me, I tried to change course. But, like grief, stories can sometimes have their own momentum and we are powerless to stop them.

Once I'd accepted where the story was headed, I stopped writing and did some research. I read a handful of books about grief because I wanted to understand the process better. What I learned is that people experience grief in myriad ways and that it swells and wanes according to its own timetable. It rarely resolves quickly and without some work on the part of the grieving person. Grief can take months or years to work through. Sometimes people never get over the death of someone close to them.

If the content of this book has raised issues for you, I hope you'll pull someone aside and talk to them about it. It doesn't have to be a counsellor—it can be a family member or a trusted friend. You can always call Lifeline on 13 11 14 (Australia) or 0800 54 33 54 (New Zealand). If you think someone in your life is struggling—a friend, a work colleague, a classmate, someone in your book group—please reach out to them.

At the time of writing this book, Beyond Blue had a series of videos on its website (www.beyondblue.org.au) for people feeling suicidal, worried about someone else being suicidal, who have attempted suicide or who are grieving a suicide death. I found these especially helpful in my research. Maybe you or someone you know will too.

Acknowledgements

My heartfelt thanks to the team at Pan Macmillan Australia who supported me so gently and completely through every step of turning my scrappy manuscript into the beautiful book you hold in your hands today. Thanks particularly to publisher Alex Lloyd, editor Rebecca Lay, copyeditor Ali Lavau and cover designer Christa Moffitt.

My thanks to Phil Watt, building surveyor, for taking time to answer all my detailed questions about soil contamination and the building process. I am also grateful to Don Henley and the estate of Glenn Frey for permission to reproduce lyrics from 'Desperado'. Listen to it sometime—it's such a stirring song and encapsulates Jac's story so perfectly. Once you do, it won't leave you.

Thank you also to the readers who gave me feedback along the way: Chris Bell, Adam Fleet, Angela Meyer, Nadine Davidoff, Robyn Parker, Carmen Kelly, Gina Ezard, Jem Tyley-Miller,

Bianca Simpson and my parents, Gayle and Ian Davies. Your suggestions, advice and encouragement were invaluable in bringing the Hardings' story to life.